中文详注剑桥莎士比亚精选

威尼斯商人

原版创始主编：[英] 瑞克斯·吉布森（Rex Gibson）
原版主编：[英] 瑞查德·安褚斯（Richard Andrews）
　　　　　[英] 维姬·维南德（Vicki Wienand）
原版编注：[英] 罗布·史密斯（Rob Smith）
总主编：陈国华
分册主编：谢世坚

社图号 20124

Cambridge School Shakespeare: The Merchant of Venice [Third edition] [978-1-107-61539-7] was first published by Cambridge University Press in 2014. All rights reserved.

This Simplified Chinese edition for the People's Republic of China is published by arrangement with the Press Syndicate of the University of Cambridge, Cambridge, United Kingdom.

© Cambridge University Press & Beijing Language and Culture University Press 2020.

This book is in copyright. No reproduction of any part may take place without the written permission of Cambridge University Press or Beijing Language and Culture University Press.

本书版权由剑桥大学出版社和北京语言大学出版社共同所有。本书任何部分之文字及图片，如未获得出版者书面同意，不得用任何方式抄袭、节录或翻印。

This edition is for sale in the People's Republic of China (excluding Hong Kong SAR, Macao SAR and Taiwan Province) only. 此版本仅限在中华人民共和国境内销售。

北京市版权局著作权合同登记批字：01-2020-4100 号

图书在版编目（CIP）数据

中文详注剑桥莎士比亚精选．威尼斯商人：英文 / 陈国华总主编；谢世坚分册主编．-- 北京：北京语言大学出版社，2020.9

书名原文：Cambridge School Shakespeare：The Merchant of Venice

ISBN 978-7-5619-5731-8

Ⅰ.①中… Ⅱ.①陈… ②谢… Ⅲ.①喜剧-剧本-英国-中世纪-英文 Ⅳ.① I561.33

中国版本图书馆 CIP 数据核字（2020）第 152209 号

中文详注剑桥莎士比亚精选：威尼斯商人
ZHONGWEN XIANG ZHU JIANQIAO SHASHIBIYA JINGXUAN: Weinisi Shangren

项目策划：李 亮	责任编辑：孙冠群
封面设计：乔 剑	排版制作：北京创艺涵文化发展有限公司
责任印制：武晓东	

出版发行 北京语言大学出版社

社　　址：北京市海淀区学院路 15 号，100083
网　　址：www.blcup.com
电子信箱：service@blcup.com
电　　话：编辑部 8610-82301019/0178
　　　　　发行部 8610-82303650/3591/3648
　　　　　北语书店 8610-82303653
　　　　　网购咨询 8610-82303908
印　　刷：北京博海升彩色印刷有限公司

版　　次：2020 年 9 月第 1 版　　印　　次：2020 年 9 月第 1 次印刷
开　　本：787 毫米 × 1092 毫米 1/16　　印　　张：13.75
字　　数：432 千字
定　　价：69.00 元

PRINTED IN CHINA

序

由于观察角度不同，评判标准不同，关于哪个国家哪位诗人或小说家的成就最大，世人可能难以达成一致；可是说到剧作家，大家的共识是，莎士比亚不仅是英语国家有史以来最伟大的剧作家，也是全世界最伟大的剧作家，在知名度、影响力和传世作品的数量上，没有任何一位剧作家可以与之比肩。正是由于其公认的文学成就和人文精神，在过去400多年里，莎士比亚戏剧的演出在英语国家和许多非英语国家经久不衰，莎剧的阅读和鉴赏已成为这些国家英文教学的必选内容。

莎剧进入中国，已经有100多年历史，莎士比亚全集已经有了四个中文译本。不懂英文的人可以通过译本来欣赏莎士比亚剧作。然而文学作品的语言，尤其是诗歌的语言，具有相当程度的不可译性，而几乎所有莎剧的大部分台词都是素体诗（blank verse）。例如《哈慕雷》（Hamlet）里主人翁的名言"To be, or not to be, that is the question"，不论怎样译，都难以完全再现原文的深刻内涵和形式特点。要想真正欣赏莎士比亚的语言和戏剧艺术，还得阅读其英文原作。最早由剑桥大学出版社出版的这套莎剧精选，收录了最受读者和观众喜爱的14部剧目，涵盖莎剧的各个类别，以其独具匠心的设计和编排，成为所有英文原版莎剧中最适合英语学习者阅读、最适合戏剧爱好者排演的莎剧选集。

本选集的创始主编瑞克斯·吉布森（Rex Gibson）在本书引言（Introduction）里指出："不论做什么，都要记住，莎士比亚写下他的剧本是为了演出、观看和享受的。"秉承这一宗旨，这一新版莎剧选集有四个鲜明的区别性特点：

一、书的开本和页面的宽高比例特别适合学校的老师和学生以及剧团的导演和演员在排练莎剧时把书打开，拿在手里，随时参阅，而且左边页面上有许多有关排演活动的建议。

二、书中配有大量世界各国莎剧演出的彩色剧照，为莎剧爱好者和剧团排演莎剧提供了灵感。

三、书的正文部分打开后，右页是未经删减、原汁原味的剧本原文，左页是多种不同栏目，包括导演技巧（Stagecraft）、剧中语言（Language in the play）、人物分析（Characters）、主题分析（Themes）、写作练习（Write about it）及词语注释等。每幕之间（本幕回顾）和最后一幕后（本剧回顾）有与剧情相关的各种思考题。

四、在剧本之后有各种针对全剧的专题论述，以《哈慕雷》为例，包括视角与主题（Perspectives and themes）、人物分析（Characters）、《哈慕雷》的语言（The language of Hamlet）、《哈慕雷》的演出（Hamlet in performance）、笔论莎士比亚（Writing about Shakespeare）、笔论《哈慕雷》（Writing about Hamlet），还有一份莎翁年表（William Shakespeare 1564–1616）。

左页上的栏目对于解读和排演莎剧特别有帮助，剧本后面的专题论述对于撰写有关莎士比亚的文章特别有帮助，而参加莎剧排演，背诵台词，撰写论文，又是提高英语水平的极好途径。

为了方便更多的中国读者阅读、欣赏、排演莎士比亚原作，北京语言大学出版社携手剑桥大学出版社，将这套莎剧精选引入中国。我有幸应邀担任这套书的中文版总主编，组织起一个团队，对原版进行一定程度的改编和汉化，以适应中国读者的需求。我们不仅将原版提供的关键注释基本译成了中文，而且针对中国英语学习者和莎剧爱好者阅读理解上的难点，主要做了以下四件事：

一、参考 The Oxford Dictionary of Original Shakespearean Pronunciation (David Crystal 2016)、Oxford Dictionary of Pronunciation for Current English (Clive Upton 2003) 和 Shakespeare's Names: A Pronouncing Dictionary (Helge Kökeritz 1950)，给每个剧本前面人物表里的人名加上了国际音标。为了便于读者识别，我们将第一本发音词典里一般中国读者不认识的个别音标替换成了大家熟悉的近似音标。

二、为左页顶端的剧情简介添加中文译文。

三、左页中以及剧本后面论文部分里有一些具有挑战性的词和术语（如tableau），我们为其中的大部分添加了相应的中文释义。

四、适当增加了原版里没有的词语注释。

给剧中人物的名字加了国际音标之后，我们发现，现有莎剧中文译本里一些人名的中文译名与原文的读音差别较大且互不相同。根据定名不苟、译音循本、音义兼顾、音系对应的原则，我们给出了新译名。根据前两个原则，我们将剧本 Julius Caesar /ˈdʒuːlɪəs ˈsiːzə(r)/ 译成《儒略·恺撒》，而没有采用《尤利/力乌斯·恺撒》《裘利/力斯·凯撒》《居里厄斯·恺撒》等现成译名中的任何一个，因为从公元前1世纪到公元16世纪西方使用的儒略历（Julian calendar）就是以这位 Julius Caesar（拉丁文读音是 /ˈjuːlɪ.ʊs ˈkae̯sar/）命名的。根据音义兼顾的原则，我们将剧本 Hamlet /ˈ(h)amlət/ 译成《哈慕雷》而不是《哈姆莱特》或《哈姆雷特》，因为"慕雷"比"姆莱"或"姆雷"更适合用来给男子起名，结尾的辅音 /t/ 在实际说话中往往不发音。根据音系对应的原则，我们借鉴了曹禺的译法，将剧本 Romeo and Juliet 译成《柔密欧与茱丽叶》，没有将 Romeo 译成更常见的"罗密欧"，因为"柔 /rou/"比"罗 /luo/"更接近原名 Romeo /ˈroːmɪoː/ 的读音；同时我们将 Juliet /ˈdʒuːlɪət/ 译成"茱丽叶"而不是"朱丽叶"，因为这样做不容易让人误以为这个女孩姓"朱"。

这套经过改编并且带中文注释的《中文详注剑桥莎士比亚精选》不仅可以用作中国高中和大学的英文教材，而且适合中国所有具有较高英语能力的莎剧爱好者阅读和欣赏，将戏剧从书中提升到自己心中，将剧本从课堂搬演到戏台。

相信《中文详注剑桥莎士比亚精选》会带给中国广大英语爱好者一个惊喜。

陈国华

北京外国语大学

2020年5月于英国剑桥家中

Contents 目录

Introduction 引言	iv
Photo gallery 剧照精选	v

The Merchant of Venice 《威尼斯商人》

List of characters 人物表	1
Act 1 第1幕	3
Act 2 第2幕	33
Act 3 第3幕	75
Act 4 第4幕	115
Act 5 第5幕	145
Perspectives and themes 视角与主题	166
Characters 人物分析	171
The language of *The Merchant of Venice* 《威尼斯商人》的语言	180
History and the Jews 历史和犹太人	186
The Merchant of Venice in performance 《威尼斯商人》的演出	189
Writing about Shakespeare 笔论莎士比亚	198
Writing about *The Merchant of Venice* 笔论《威尼斯商人》	200
William Shakespeare 1564–1616 莎翁年表	202
Acknowledgements 鸣谢	203

Introduction 引言

This *The Merchant of Venice* is part of the **Cambridge School Shakespeare** series. Like every other play in the series, it has been specially prepared to help all students in schools and colleges.

The **Cambridge School Shakespeare** *The Merchant of Venice* aims to be different. It invites you to lift the words from the page and to bring the play to life in your classroom, hall or drama studio. Through enjoyable and focused activities, you will increase your understanding of the play. Actors have created their different interpretations of the play over the centuries. Similarly, you are invited to make up your own mind about *The Merchant of Venice*, rather than having someone else's interpretation handed down to you.

Cambridge School Shakespeare does not offer you a cut-down or simplified version of the play. This is Shakespeare's language, filled with imaginative possibilities. You will find on every left-hand page: a summary of the action, an explanation of unfamiliar words, and a choice of activities on Shakespeare's stagecraft, characters, themes and language.

Between each act and in the pages at the end of the play, you will find notes, illustrations and activities. These will help to encourage reflection after every act, and give you insights into the background and context of the play as a whole.

This edition will be of value to you whether you are studying for an examination, reading for pleasure or thinking of putting on the play to entertain others. You can work on the activities on your own or in groups. Many of the activities suggest a particular group size, but don't be afraid to make up larger or smaller groups to suit your own purposes. Please don't think you have to do every activity: choose those that will help you most.

Although you are invited to treat *The Merchant of Venice* as a play, you don't need special dramatic or theatrical skills to do the activities. By choosing your activities, and by exploring and experimenting, you can make your own interpretations of Shakespeare's language, characters and stories.

Whatever you do, remember that Shakespeare wrote his plays to be acted, watched and enjoyed.

Rex Gibson
Founding editor

This new edition contains more photographs, more diversity and more supporting material than previous editions, whilst remaining true to Rex's original vision. Specifically, it contains more activities and commentary on stagecraft and writing about Shakespeare, to reflect contemporary interest. The glossary has been enlarged too. Finally, this edition aims to reflect the best teaching and learning possible, and to represent not only Shakespeare through the ages, but also the relevance and excitement of Shakespeare today.

Richard Andrews and Vicki Wienand
Series editors

This edition of *The Merchant of Venice* uses the text of the play established by Elizabeth Story Donno in **The New Cambridge Shakespeare**.

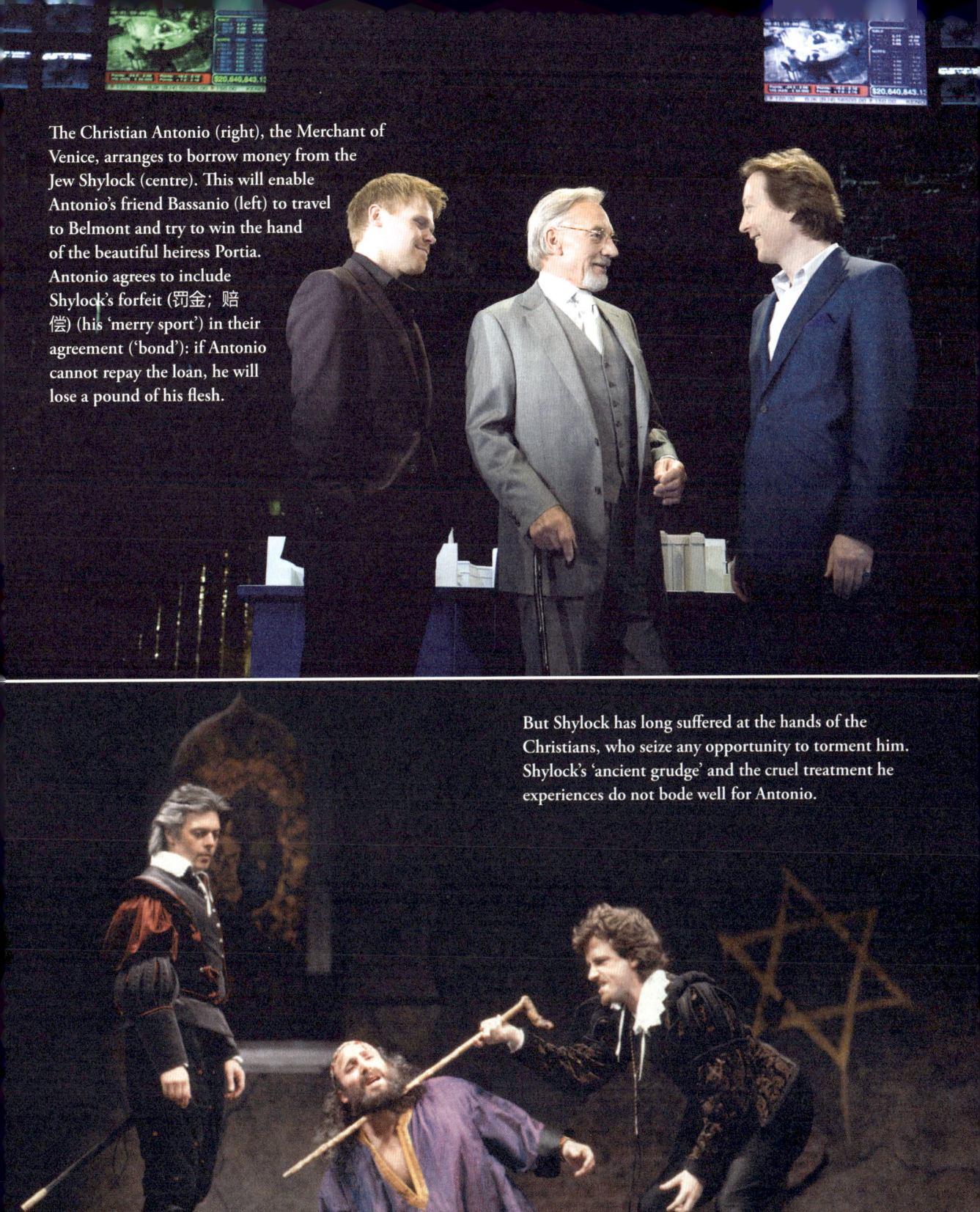

The Christian Antonio (right), the Merchant of Venice, arranges to borrow money from the Jew Shylock (centre). This will enable Antonio's friend Bassanio (left) to travel to Belmont and try to win the hand of the beautiful heiress Portia. Antonio agrees to include Shylock's forfeit (罚金；赔偿) (his 'merry sport') in their agreement ('bond'): if Antonio cannot repay the loan, he will lose a pound of his flesh.

But Shylock has long suffered at the hands of the Christians, who seize any opportunity to torment him. Shylock's 'ancient grudge' and the cruel treatment he experiences do not bode well for Antonio.

Portia (left), the wealthy mistress of Belmont, explains to her maid, Nerissa, the restrictions placed upon her by her dead father's will – 'the will of a living daughter curbed by the will of a dead father'. (Note his portrait on the wall in the background.) She can only marry the man who solves the riddle set by her father about three caskets (匣子), each one made of gold, silver or lead.

Two of Portia's suitors (the Prince of Morocco, top, and the Prince of Arragon, below) attempt to solve the riddle. Whoever opens the casket containing Portia's portrait will win her as his wife. Morocco chooses gold; Arragon chooses silver. Much to Portia's relief, they both fail.

'Our house is hell'. Jessica is Shylock's only child and she finds life at home with her father very difficult. (Shakespeare does not show or tell what has happened to her mother.) Jessica has fallen in love with a Christian, Lorenzo, and plans to elope (私奔) with him. She is relieved to escape from her home but her betrayal of her father, and her stealing of some of his wealth, send him into a grief-stricken rage.

'Hath not a Jew eyes?' Shylock, bitter over the loss of his daughter and his hostile treatment by the Christians, tries to rationalise his feelings. He stresses the common humanity of all men, but then pledges to follow a course of action taught to him by the Christians – revenge! Antonio's fragile finances put him within Shylock's reach as he decides to enforce his 'bond', and pursue his 'pound of flesh'.

◀ Bassanio has travelled to Belmont. Wary of the deceptive appearance of gold and silver, he correctly chooses the lead casket and claims his reward – Portia: 'Myself, and what is mine, to you and yours / Is now converted.' The couple are happy and look forward to their wedding.

Shylock resolves to take the financially stricken Antonio to court to pursue the full terms of the contract. Since Antonio cannot repay the loan, the court assembles to judge if Shylock can cut the pound of flesh from Antonio. Portia (centre), disguised as the male legal expert Balthazar, appears at the trial to act for Antonio.

Portia (right, in this distinctive all-male production) pleads for Shylock to show mercy: 'The quality of mercy is not strained …'

▲ 'You must prepare your bosom for his knife.' Shylock is triumphant (洋洋得意), anticipating the shedding of Antonio's blood and the gaining of his much-desired revenge.

◀ 'Tarry a little ...' At the last moment, Portia reveals a loophole (漏洞) in the contract that releases Antonio from the threat of death. In addition, Shylock has half his wealth confiscated (充公) and must convert to Christianity or forfeit his life. He leaves the court a broken man.

▼ The final act moves back to Belmont to focus on reconciliation (和解) and harmony. Lorenzo and Jessica (right) are joined by Bassanio and Portia (centre), and Nerissa and her recently acquired husband, Gratiano (left). Antonio (foreground), alone and isolated, reflects on the events of the play.

List of characters 人物表

Venice 威尼斯

Christians 基督教徒
THE DUKE OF VENICE （威尼斯公爵）
BASSANIO /bəˈsɑːnɪoː/ （博萨纽） a lord
ANTONIO /anˈtoːnɪoː/ （安托纽） a merchant
SOLANIO /səˈlɑnɪoː/ （塞拉纽）
SALARINO /saləˈriːnoː/ （萨勒瑞诺）
GRATIANO /ˌgratsɪˈɑːnoː/ （格拉奇阿诺） } Friends of Antonio and Bassanio
SALERIO /səˈliːrɪoː/ （塞理瑞欧）
LORENZO /lɒˈrenzoː/ （劳仁佐）
LANCELOT GOBBO /ˈlɔːnslət ˈgɒbɒ/ （朗斯勒·高博） servant first to Shylock, then to Bassanio
GOBBO /ˈgɒbə/ （高博） his father
STEPHANO /steˈfɑːnoː/ （斯迪法诺） a messenger
JAILER （狱卒）
LEONARDO /lɪəˈnɑː(r)doː/ （列纳窦） servant of Bassanio
SERVINGMAN （下人） employed by Antonio
MAGNIFICOES OF VENICE （威尼斯众贵族）
COURT OFFICIALS （众法官）

Jews 犹太人
SHYLOCK /ˈʃɑɪlɒk/ （夏洛克） a rich money-lender
JESSICA /ˈdʒesɪkə/ （婕丝柯） his daughter
TUBAL /ˈtjuːbɑl/ （图巴尔） his friend

Belmont 贝尔蒙

Portia's household 鲍霞家中的人
PORTIA /ˈpɔː(r)sɪə/ （鲍霞） a rich heiress
NERISSA /nəˈrɪsə/ （讷瑞莎） her lady-in-waiting （侍女）
BALTHAZAR /ˈbɑltəˌzɑː(r)/ （巴尔特扎） her servant
SERVINGMAN （下人）
MESSENGER （信使）

Portia's suitors 鲍霞的求婚者
THE PRINCE OF MOROCCO /məˈrɒkoː/ （摩洛哥亲王）
THE PRINCE OF ARRAGON /ˈarəgɒn/ （阿若岗亲王）

The action of the play takes place in Venice and Belmont.

Antonio says he does not know what causes his sadness. Salarino and Solanio suggest that he is worried about the safety of his ships, in which he has invested so much money.

剧情简介：安托纽说他不知道自己为何悲伤。萨勒瑞诺和塞拉纽暗示他是在为自己的船队担心，因为他在这些船上投了大笔的钱。

Characters 人物分析

Focus on Antonio – why is he so sad?

The opening line of the play quickly establishes that Antonio, the Merchant of Venice, is in a melancholy (忧郁) mood. He goes on to explain how weary it makes him and how he is losing sight of who he really is. But he is also puzzled by why he is sad.

- As the first scene unfolds, compile a list of possible reasons for his sadness. At the end of the scene, the whole class pools its ideas. Start a Character file on Antonio and write down what you feel are the most interesting possibilities; amend and qualify them as the play unfolds. Link the points you make to quotations and other evidence from the script.

Stagecraft 导演技巧

Where do they meet? Set the scene (in pairs)

At the beginning of each scene a location is given (here it is simply 'Venice'). But in Shakespeare's theatre the action took place on a bare stage, with little or no scenery (see the illustration on p. 189). Since Shakespeare's day, each director of a stage production has had to make decisions about whether they will indicate precise locations.

- Try your hand at scene-setting. Decide on a suitable place in Venice for the three friends' meeting. Perhaps they meet in a house or an office, or in a public place such as a bar, a café or the Venetian Stock Exchange. Select your favourite suggestions.
- Then imagine that you are preparing to direct a performance of *The Merchant of Venice*. Start your own Director's Journal and write down your ideas under the heading 'Scene-setting'. Use your journal to record further ideas about stagecraft as you go through the play.

1 In sooth 老实说
2 to learn 一无所知
3 want-wit 没脑子的人
4 ado 困难
5 And … myself 忧郁使我变成了糊涂虫，我都有点儿不明白自己了
6 tossing 起起伏伏
7 argosies 海船（希腊神话里有一位名叫阿尔戈斯[Argus]的船匠，在女神雅典娜[Athena]的指导下，为英雄伊阿宋[Jason]周游世界寻找金羊毛[the Golden Fleece]建造了一艘海船，这艘船被命名为阿尔戈号[Argo]；后来大型海船便称为argosy)
8 portly 盛大；富丽堂皇
9 signors 绅士
10 burghers 市民
11 flood 海
12 pageants 庆典；盛会
13 Do overpeer the petty traffickers 蔑视小商船
14 curtsey 致意
15 do them reverence 俯首称臣；鞠躬作揖
16 venture forth 有这种风险在外
17 The … affections 我最关心的
18 still 一直，无休止
19 Plucking … wind 拔一把草扔出去以辨别风向
20 Piring in 凝视
21 roads 锚地，停泊处

The Merchant of Venice

Act 1 Scene 1
Venice

Enter ANTONIO, SALARINO, *and* SOLANIO

ANTONIO	In sooth[1] I know not why I am so sad.		
	It wearies me, you say it wearies you;		
	But how I caught it, found it, or came by it,		
	What stuff 'tis made of, whereof it is born,		
	I am to learn[2].	5	
	And such a want-wit[3] sadness makes of me,		
	That I have much ado[4] to know myself[5].		
SALARINO	Your mind is tossing[6] on the ocean,		
	There where your argosies[7] with portly[8] sail		
	Like signors[9] and rich burghers[10] on the flood[11],	10	
	Or as it were the pageants[12] of the sea,		
	Do overpeer the petty traffickers[13]		
	That curtsey[14] to them, do them reverence[15],		
	As they fly by them with their woven wings.		
SOLANIO	Believe me, sir, had I such venture forth[16],	15	
	The better part of my affections[17] would		
	Be with my hopes abroad. I should be still[18]		
	Plucking the grass to know where sits the wind[19],		
	Piring in[20] maps for ports, and piers, and roads[21];		
	And every object that might make me fear	20	
	Misfortune to my ventures, out of doubt		
	Would make me sad.		

Antonio says he is not worried about business matters. He has invested his money in several ships. That is much safer than relying on only one. He's not in love either!

 剧情简介：安托纽表示他并不是为生意上的事而忧虑。他已将钱分散投资于多艘船只，这比仅投在一条船上安全得多。他也并非因为爱情而忧伤！

Write about it 写作练习

Disasters at sea

Salarino says that if he were in Antonio's situation, everything he did or saw would constantly remind him of all the disasters that might happen to his ships as they transported their valuable cargoes across the ocean.

- Blowing his soup to cool it would make him think of the dangers of violent tempests (lines 22–4).
- Watching the sand pass through an hourglass would remind him of a beached ship (lines 25–8).
- Gazing at the stone walls of a church would make him imagine them as rocks on which the vessel might founder (沉没) (lines 29–36).

Take each of these sections of the script in turn. Write advice for an actor about how to deliver the lines and about what gestures (or 'stage business' [戏台动作]) to add as he speaks his words. Add this advice to a new section in your Director's Journal.

1 wind 吹出的气
2 broth 羹汤
3 blow me to an ague 让我打冷战
4 hourglass 沙漏
5 wealthy Andrew 满载货物的大船（"圣安德鲁号"，一艘价值连城的西班牙船只，1596年被英国缴获）
6 Vailing her high top 低下船的主桅杆
7 ribs 船肋；龙骨
8 holy edifice of stone 石头砌成的圣殿
9 bethink 想起
10 Enrobe … silks 汹涌的波涛上漂满我的绸缎
11 but even now 方才
12 bechanced 发生
13 bottom 船
14 Janus 雅努斯（罗马神话中的门神，头部前后各有一张脸）
15 framed 造就
16 peep through their eyes 眯着眼（笑眯了眼）
17 laugh … bagpiper 不合时宜地笑（鹦鹉听到悲伤的音乐会发笑）
18 vinegar aspèct 板着脸
19 Nestor 涅斯托（古希腊国王，以严肃著称）

1 I'm not in love (by yourself)

When Solanio implies that Antonio's sadness is caused by being in love (line 46), Antonio is quick to deny it ('Fie, fie!' [呸，呸！]).

- Experiment with different ways of delivering these two words in order to bring out exactly how you think Antonio feels. For example, what might the brevity of his response suggest about his attitude to love – and to women? Show your favourite version to others in your class.

2 Janus: facing two ways (in pairs)

The play contains many references to figures from classical mythology. Here, Solanio alludes (暗指) to Janus, a Roman god who faced in two opposite directions at the same time. Solanio uses this reference to demonstrate his belief that all humans have the capacity to be happy and sad simultaneously.

a First, have a go at drawing an image of Janus. Then talk together about what your drawing suggests about the world of Venetian males that Shakespeare creates at the start of the play.

b Summarise your thinking in one written sentence, ready to share with other pairs.

SALARINO	My wind[1] cooling my broth[2]

        Would blow me to an ague[3] when I thought
        What harm a wind too great might do at sea.
        I should not see the sandy hourglass[4] run   25
        But I should think of shallows and of flats,
        And see my wealthy Andrew[5] docked in sand,
        Vailing her high top[6] lower than her ribs[7]
        To kiss her burial. Should I go to church
        And see the holy edifice of stone[8]   30
        And not bethink[9] me straight of dangerous rocks,
        Which touching but my gentle vessel's side
        Would scatter all her spices on the stream,
        Enrobe the roaring waters with my silks[10],
        And (in a word) but even now[11] worth this,   35
        And now worth nothing? Shall I have the thought
        To think on this, and shall I lack the thought
        That such a thing bechanced[12] would make me sad?
        But tell not me: I know Antonio
        Is sad to think upon his merchandise.   40

ANTONIO   Believe me, no. I thank my fortune for it,
        My ventures are not in one bottom[13] trusted,
        Nor to one place; nor is my whole estate
        Upon the fortune of this present year:
        Therefore my merchandise makes me not sad.   45

SOLANIO   Why then, you are in love.

ANTONIO   Fie, fie!

SOLANIO   Not in love neither? Then let us say you are sad
        Because you are not merry; and 'twere as easy
        For you to laugh and leap, and say you are merry
        Because you are not sad. Now by two-headed Janus[14],   50
        Nature hath framed[15] strange fellows in her time:
        Some that will evermore peep through their eyes[16],
        And laugh like parrots at a bagpiper[17];
        And other of such vinegar aspèct[18],
        That they'll not show their teeth in way of smile   55
        Though Nestor[19] swear the jest be laughable.

More friends arrive. One of them, Gratiano, comments on how careworn Antonio has become. He recommends laughter over misery and warns against false seriousness.

剧情简介：又有朋友加入，其中的格拉奇阿诺看到安托纽忧心忡忡，建议他笑对苦难，不必总摆出一本正经的样子。

1 True friends? (in fours)

The entrance of Bassanio and two friends, Lorenzo and Gratiano, can be used to change the mood of the scene. There are now six men on stage, but Salarino and Solanio quickly decide to leave when the others arrive. What prompts their departure? Are there tensions between these two groups of friends? Or do you think their departure is entirely natural?

- Take parts and read aloud lines 57–68. First, make the words friendly and polite; then play them in a manner that suggests some unpleasantness and mistrust. Decide which version you think is more effective and show it to the other groups in the class for comment.

Write about it 写作练习
Thoughts about Antonio (in pairs)

What have Solanio and Salarino made of Antonio's behaviour in the first part of the scene? Write their thoughts on taking their leave of him as a scripted conversation between the two men. Use modern English.

Themes 主题分析
Appearance and reality: all the world's a stage

Antonio's lines 77–9 echo well-known words from Act 2 Scene 7 of Shakespeare's *As You Like It*:

> All the world's a stage
> And all the men and women merely players:
> They have their exits and their entrances
> And one man in his time plays many parts

Although Antonio views the part he currently has to play as 'a sad one', Gratiano makes it clear that he wants to 'play the Fool' (line 79). Both men acknowledge that they live in a world where false actions and feelings are prominent. Gratiano's long speech satirises (makes fun of) the ways in which many Elizabethan men pretend to be what they are not.

- Read lines 88–99 and write an explanation for a younger student of exactly what Gratiano is saying. Add a paragraph discussing what the lines suggest about Gratiano's character, his attitudes and his values.

1 prevented me 抢我风头
2 Your ... regard 您是我的挚友
3 embrace th'occasion 借此机会
4 morrow 早晨（古语）
5 laugh 欢聚
6 strange 冷淡，关系疏远
7 We'll ... yours 等您有空，我们一定奉陪
8 You ... world 您对世事过于认真了
9 They ... care 人若对生活太过认真，便会失去生活的乐趣
10 marvellously 极大地，不可思议地
11 And ... groans 宁可饮酒来温暖肠胃，也不让痛苦的呻吟冰冷我的心
12 Sit ... alabaster 正襟危坐，如同墓地中祖先的雪花石膏塑像
13 creep into the jaundice 得了黄疸病
14 visages 面孔
15 Do cream and mantle 泛起一层黏稠的泡沫（面色苍黄）
16 like a standing pond 像一潭死水
17 dressed in 得到
18 do ... wisdom 故作沉静，以显示自己睿智
19 Oracle 无所不知的人，圣贤
20 when ... bark 只要我开口，低贱的人就闭嘴吧（ope = open）

THE MERCHANT OF VENICE ACT 1 SCENE 1

威尼斯商人

Enter BASSANIO, LORENZO, *and* GRATIANO

	Here comes Bassanio, your most noble kinsman,
	Gratiano, and Lorenzo. Fare ye well;
	We leave you now with better company.
SALARINO	I would have stayed till I had made you merry,
	If worthier friends had not prevented me[1].
ANTONIO	Your worth is very dear in my regard[2].
	I take it your own business calls on you,
	And you embrace th'occasion[3] to depart.
SALARINO	Good morrow[4], my good lords.
BASSANIO	Good signors both, when shall we laugh[5]? Say, when?
	You grow exceeding strange[6]; must it be so?
SALARINO	We'll make our leisures to attend on yours[7].

Exeunt Salarino and Solanio

LORENZO   My Lord Bassanio, since you have found Antonio
            We two will leave you, but at dinner time
            I pray you have in mind where we must meet.

BASSANIO   I will not fail you.

GRATIANO   You look not well, Signor Antonio.
            You have too much respect upon the world[8]:
            They lose it that do buy it with much care[9].
            Believe me, you are marvellously[10] changed.

ANTONIO   I hold the world but as the world, Gratiano:
            A stage where every man must play a part,
            And mine a sad one.

GRATIANO   Let me play the Fool.
            With mirth and laughter let old wrinkles come,
            And let my liver rather heat with wine
            Than my heart cool with mortifying groans[11].
            Why should a man whose blood is warm within
            Sit like his grandsire cut in alabaster[12]?
            Sleep when he wakes? And creep into the jaundice[13]
            By being peevish? I tell thee what, Antonio –
            I love thee, and it is my love that speaks –
            There are a sort of men whose visages[14]
            Do cream and mantle[15] like a standing pond[16],
            And do a wilful stillness entertain,
            With purpose to be dressed in[17] an opinion
            Of wisdom[18], gravity, profound conceit,
            As who should say, 'I am Sir Oracle[19],
            And when I ope my lips, let no dog bark[20]!'

Gratiano advises Antonio against using sadness to gain a reputation for wisdom. Antonio asks Bassanio whom he loves. Bassanio begins by explaining his plans to pay off his debts.

剧情简介：格拉奇阿诺建议安托纽不要用悲伤来博取智慧的名声。安托纽问博萨纽谁是他钟情的人。博萨纽开始细说他偿还债务的计划。

▲ Gratiano, Bassanio and Antonio pictured together in the opening scene. Identify each of the three characters and justify your decision by linking it to evidence from the script. What do you make of the relationship between the three Christians that is presented in this image? Write a couple of sentences in response.

1 That ... nothing 因一言不发而博得智慧的名声
2 damn ... fools 听见他们说话的人都会说他们傻
3 fish ... opinion 不要用悲伤做诱饵，来钓取"名誉"这条蠢鱼
4 exhortation 劝诫
5 moe = more
6 this gear 建议（或事情）
7 neat's tongue dried 干牛舌（还有另外一层意思："性无能的老头儿"）
8 vendible 能卖出去的（指引起性欲的）
9 speaks ... nothing 废话连篇
10 reasons 想法
11 bushels 蒲式耳（1蒲式耳约合36升）
12 ere = before
13 secret pilgrimage 秘密朝圣（指爱情之旅）
14 disabled mine estate 透支了我的财产
15 By ... continuance 因为要维持我负担不起的光鲜生活
16 Nor ... rate 不因要缩减花销而抱怨
17 come fairly off 还清
18 prodigal 浪费，挥霍
19 gaged 欠债
20 from ... purposes 您待我极好，我可以放心告诉您

Characters 人物分析

First impressions of Bassanio (in small groups)

a Bassanio's first words in the play are a mocking put-down of his 'friend' Gratiano. Talk together about whether you think Gratiano deserves Bassanio's scornful judgement. Why, or why not?

b When he is invited by Antonio to speak about the 'lady' he's in love with, Bassanio answers by talking extensively about his debts. He has spent all his money and owes a great deal. One person reads aloud lines 121–33. The others echo every word that is connected with money or financial transactions. Afterwards, talk together about:

• what the 'echoing' activity and the lines suggest about Bassanio's attitude to wealth
• your response to Bassanio's lines suggesting that his 'secret pilgrimage' is simply a ploy to 'get clear of all the debts I owe'.

c On your own, write a few sentences giving your initial assessment of Bassanio's character. Display your evaluation of Bassanio on a large sheet of paper and add to it as you read on.

8

	O my Antonio, I do know of these	95
	That therefore only are reputed wise	
	For saying nothing[1]; when I am very sure	
	If they should speak, would almost damn those ears	
	Which, hearing them, would call their brothers fools[2].	
	I'll tell thee more of this another time.	100
	But fish not with this melancholy bait	
	For this fool gudgeon, this opinion[3].	
	Come, good Lorenzo. Fare ye well awhile;	
	I'll end my exhortation[4] after dinner.	
LORENZO	Well, we will leave you then till dinner time.	105
	I must be one of these same dumb wise men,	
	For Gratiano never lets me speak.	
GRATIANO	Well, keep me company but two years moe[5],	
	Thou shalt not know the sound of thine own tongue.	
ANTONIO	Farewell; I'll grow a talker for this gear[6].	110
GRATIANO	Thanks, i'faith, for silence is only commendable	
	In a neat's tongue dried[7], and a maid not vendible[8].	

Exeunt [Gratiano and Lorenzo]

ANTONIO　It is that anything now.

BASSANIO　Gratiano speaks an infinite deal of nothing[9], more than any man in all Venice. His reasons[10] are as two grains of wheat hid in two bushels[11] of chaff: you shall seek all day ere[12] you find them, and when you have them they are not worth the search.　　115

	Well, tell me now what lady is the same	
ANTONIO	To whom you swore a secret pilgrimage[13]	
	That you today promised to tell me of.	120
BASSANIO	'Tis not unknown to you, Antonio,	
	How much I have disabled mine estate[14]	
	By something showing a more swelling port	
	Than my faint means would grant continuance[15].	
	Nor do I now make moan to be abridged	125
	From such a noble rate[16], but my chief care	
	Is to come fairly off[17] from the great debts	
	Wherein my time, something too prodigal[18],	
	Hath left me gaged[19]. To you, Antonio,	
	I owe the most in money and in love,	130
	And from your love I have a warranty	
	To unburden all my plots and purposes[20]	
	How to get clear of all the debts I owe.	

Antonio is ready to help Bassanio, whatever the circumstances. Bassanio explains that he wishes to marry Portia, a wealthy heiress. Rich and famous men from all over the world come to woo her.

 剧情简介：无论如何，安托纽都乐于帮助博萨纽。博萨纽说他要向富家嗣女鲍霞求婚。世界各地的有钱有名的人都来向她求婚。

1 Antonio: reckless devotion? (in pairs)

In lines 134–8, Antonio offers to do everything in his power to help his friend Bassanio.

a Take it in turns to read the lines aloud. Then discuss whether Antonio is being foolish in offering to bail out his friend again, after the way Bassanio has wasted Antonio's money before. Does Bassanio's honest admission that he has behaved like a 'wilful youth' really excuse his previous mistakes?

b One of you is Antonio, the other a friend he goes to for advice. Improvise (即兴表演) a conversation in which you discuss Bassanio's situation and his requests for further credit.

Characters 人物分析

First impressions of Portia (in small groups, then by yourself)

In lines 160–71, the audience first hears of Portia. Bassanio uses stories of ancient Greece and Rome to praise her. He compares her (line 165) to Portia, the daughter of Cato, a famous Roman politician, and the wife of Brutus, the 'honourable man' who was one of Julius Caesar's assassins (行刺者). Bassanio also sees her as a rich prize (see 'Characters', p. 177, on the position of women in Elizabethan society), like the Golden Fleece the Greek hero Jason sought in Colchis (see 'The language of *The Merchant of Venice*', p. 181). These references suggest that Bassanio is an educated man and that Portia is a lady of high social status.

a Read aloud lines 160–71. Each person reads up to a punctuation mark, then hands on to the next. Emphasise all the words and phrases Bassanio uses to praise Portia.

b Working on your own:
- Use Bassanio's description to write a paragraph giving your own impressions of Portia. Include a comment about the impact of Bassanio's use of classical references in describing her.
- Suggest at least two possible reasons why Shakespeare chose to have Bassanio begin the description of Portia by explaining that she is 'a lady richly left'.
- Finally, write a sentence explaining why you think Shakespeare has Bassanio describe Portia at this point, even though she is not introduced into the play until the following scene.

1 **And ... honour** 如果您的计划与您一贯的立身行事一样光明正大
2 **My ... occasions** 我的全部钱财都任君取用
3 **shaft** 箭
4 **his ... flight** 向同一方向射出一支相同的箭
5 **advisèd** 细心
6 **oft** = often
7 **urge** 执意提出
8 **proof** 经历
9 **like ... lost** 像一个任性的孩子把借来的钱挥霍一空
10 **hazard** 冒险
11 **rest** 仍旧做
12 **To ... circumstance** 拐弯抹角地试探我对您的情谊
13 **In ... uttermost** 怀疑我不肯尽力帮忙
14 **prest unto** 尽力办到
15 **a lady richly left** 一位富家嗣女
16 **Sometimes** 有一次，以前
17 **undervalued** 逊色
18 **Renownèd suitors** 有名望的求婚者

ANTONIO	I pray you, good Bassanio, let me know it,	
	And if it stand as you yourself still do	135
	Within the eye of honour[1], be assured	
	My purse, my person, my extremest means	
	Lie all unlocked to your occasions[2].	
BASSANIO	In my schooldays, when I had lost one shaft[3],	
	I shot his fellow of the selfsame flight[4]	140
	The selfsame way, with more advisèd[5] watch	
	To find the other forth; and by adventuring both	
	I oft[6] found both. I urge[7] this childhood proof[8]	
	Because what follows is pure innocence.	
	I owe you much, and like a wilful youth	145
	That which I owe is lost[9]; but if you please	
	To shoot another arrow that self way	
	Which you did shoot the first, I do not doubt,	
	As I will watch the aim, or to find both	
	Or bring your latter hazard[10] back again	150
	And thankfully rest[11] debtor for the first.	
ANTONIO	You know me well, and herein spend but time	
	To wind about my love with circumstance[12];	
	And out of doubt you do me now more wrong	
	In making question of my uttermost[13]	155
	Than if you had made waste of all I have.	
	Then do but say to me what I should do	
	That in your knowledge may by me be done,	
	And I am prest unto[14] it: therefore speak.	
BASSANIO	In Belmont is a lady richly left[15],	160
	And she is fair, and – fairer than that word –	
	Of wondrous virtues. Sometimes[16] from her eyes	
	I did receive fair speechless messages.	
	Her name is Portia, nothing undervalued[17]	
	To Cato's daughter, Brutus' Portia.	165
	Nor is the wide world ignorant of her worth;	
	For the four winds blow in from every coast	
	Renownèd suitors[18], and her sunny locks	
	Hang on her temples like a golden fleece,	
	Which makes her seat of Belmont Colchos' strand,	170
	And many Jasons come in quest of her.	

Antonio's cash is tied up in his ships, but he allows Bassanio to borrow money on his behalf. In Belmont, Portia complains that her dead father's will prevents her from choosing her own husband.

剧情简介：安托纽的钱都投在了商船上，不过他愿意以自己的信用为担保，让博萨纽去借钱。在贝尔蒙，鲍霞抱怨父亲的遗嘱使得她无法按自己的心意来选择丈夫。

Themes 主题分析
The conflict of love and money

The opening scene contains many references to a major theme of the play: the clash between the pursuit of love and the desire for wealth. In Bassanio's pursuit of Portia, the two come together.

- Find quotations in Scene 1 that highlight the importance of love or money. In each case, explain what the quotation suggests about the speaker's attitude to either love or money. Then write a paragraph exploring the conflicting viewpoints presented.

Stagecraft 导演技巧
Belmont: Portia's home

The action of the play must move swiftly from the financial, all-male world of the public places of Venice to the female world of Belmont (literally 'fair mountain'), which is Portia's home.

a Using the illustration of Shakespeare's stage on page 189, suggest a few simple ways to convey to an Elizabethan audience that this next scene takes place in 'the garden of Portia's house'.

b Think about how you might evoke the wealth and splendour of Portia's home in a modern production. Study the images on pages vi, 90, 165 and 183, then write up or sketch your design ideas in your Director's Journal.

c As you read on, look out for the way Shakespeare alternates scenes that are played out in public areas in Venice, and those that have intimate domestic locations. Can you think of any reasons why the play might unfold like this?

1 I have … thrift 我预感我一定会大获成功
2 at sea 投资于海上（商船）
3 commodity 货物
4 racked even to the uttermost 竭尽全力
5 furnish thee 为你提供资金
6 presently 立即
7 To have … sake 用我的信用做担保，凭借我与对方的交情
8 Exeunt （剧本中的说明，两个以上演员）退场，下场
9 troth 信念，信仰
10 aught = anything （任何事）
11 surfeit 饮食过度
12 seated in the mean 位于中间（不多不少）
13 superfluity … longer 奢侈的生活会使人加速衰老，小康生活可以延年
14 divine 牧师
15 The brain … decree 理智为情感立法，但头脑发热会做出违反冰冷法律的事
16 meshes 篱笆网
17 But … husband 这番议论并不能帮助我找到一位夫君

1 Portia's weariness – like Antonio's sadness?
(in pairs)

Portia's opening words in Scene 2 echo Antonio's at the start of Scene 1.

- Share a quick reading of Scene 2 and identify possible reasons for Portia's comment that she is 'aweary of this great world'. (For example, Nerissa tells Portia that riches don't bring happiness: people can be made sick by having too much.) Compare your conclusions about Portia's state of mind with your observations about Antonio's sadness in the first scene.

The Merchant of Venice Act 1 Scene 2
威尼斯商人

	O my Antonio, had I but the means
	To hold a rival place with one of them,
	I have a mind presages me such thrift[1]
	That I should questionless be fortunate. 175
ANTONIO	Thou know'st that all my fortunes are at sea[2];
	Neither have I money nor commodity[3]
	To raise a present sum; therefore go forth,
	Try what my credit can in Venice do,
	That shall be racked even to the uttermost[4] 180
	To furnish thee[5] to Belmont to fair Portia.
	Go presently[6] enquire, and so will I,
	Where money is, and I no question make
	To have it of my trust or for my sake[7].

Exeunt[8]

Act 1 Scene 2
Belmont   The garden of Portia's house

Enter PORTIA *and* NERISSA

PORTIA	By my troth[9], Nerissa, my little body is aweary of this great world.
NERISSA	You would be, sweet madam, if your miseries were in the same abundance as your good fortunes are; and yet for aught[10] I see, they are as sick that surfeit[11] with too much as they that starve with nothing. It is no mean happiness, therefore, to be seated in the mean[12] – superfluity comes sooner by white hairs, but competency lives longer[13].
PORTIA	Good sentences, and well pronounced.
NERISSA	They would be better if well followed.
PORTIA	If to do were as easy as to know what were good to do, chapels had been churches, and poor men's cottages princes' palaces. It is a good divine[14] that follows his own instructions; I can easier teach twenty what were good to be done, than be one of the twenty to follow mine own teaching. The brain may devise laws for the blood, but a hot temper leaps o'er a cold decree[15] – such a hare is madness the youth, to skip o'er the meshes[16] of good counsel the cripple. But this reasoning is not in the fashion to choose me a husband[17]. O me, the word 'choose'! I may neither choose who I would, nor refuse who I dislike, so is the will of a living daughter curbed by the will of a dead father. Is it not hard, Nerissa, that I cannot choose one, nor refuse none?

Nerissa recaps the will: potential husbands (suitors) must choose between three caskets of gold, silver and lead. Whoever chooses correctly wins Portia! Nerissa begins describing Portia's suitors.

剧情简介：讷瑞莎概括遗嘱的大意：若想成为鲍霞的丈夫，求婚者必须在金、银和铅三个匣子中挑选一个。选对了匣子就能赢得鲍霞！讷瑞莎开始描述鲍霞的求婚者。

Write about it 写作练习

Portia's world: always controlled by men?

Although she is mistress of Belmont's immense wealth, Portia's freedom is strictly limited by the conditions imposed on her by her dead father's will. It seems that she will be given a husband in an extreme form of an arranged marriage: whoever is to gain her as his wife must solve the 'lottery that he [her father] hath devised in these three chests of gold, silver and lead'.

a Read Portia's lines 19–22 carefully several times and work out how she feels about her father's attitude and behaviour. Remember that these lines are spoken publicly to Nerissa (her lady-in-waiting).

b Write an entry in Portia's secret diary, in which she elaborates (详细阐述) upon her predicament (窘况，困境). What does she privately think about her father and about the ways her life is not her own?

c Write a further short piece, in role as a modern woman, in which you explore honestly what you think about this type of parental control and how you might react to such restrictions.

1 Six suitors: a mini-pageant (小型选美比赛) (in sixes)

Lines 30–81 describe Portia's six suitors:
- The Neapolitan prince (lines 33–7) is a 'colt', obsessed with horses.
- The County (伯爵) Palatine (lines 38–44) is too sad and melancholy.
- The Frenchman (lines 45–53) merely copies people and has no personality: 'he is every man in no man'.
- The Englishman (lines 54–62) is uneducated, and dresses and behaves badly.
- The Scotsman (lines 63–7) is a man who likes violence and fighting.
- The German (lines 68–81) is a drunkard.

Each person in your group steps into role as a different suitor:

a Experiment with ways of portraying your suitor, according to the description Portia gives.

b Present your work to the rest of the class in mini-pageant form: the grand entry of your suitors to Belmont.

c Afterwards, comment on each other's presentations and try to identify which suitors were which.

---

1 his meaning 他的用意（他看中的那只匣子）
2 rightly 正确
3 over-name 把名单说一遍
4 level at 猜测
5 colt 毛头小伙子（原义为"雄马驹"）
6 and … himself 他会自己钉马掌，就以为是天大的本事
7 played false 私通
8 smith 铁匠
9 as who would say 好像在说
10 unmannerly 粗鲁
11 pass for 勉强算是
12 he … man 别人的特点他都有，可就是没有自己的个性
13 throstle 画眉鸟
14 he falls straight a-capering 他开始手舞足蹈
15 fence 与……比剑
16 requite him 对他以爱相报

NERISSA	Your father was ever virtuous; and holy men at their death have good inspirations. Therefore the lottery that he hath devised in these three chests of gold, silver, and lead, whereof who chooses his meaning[1] chooses you, will no doubt never be chosen by any rightly[2] but one who you shall rightly love. But what warmth is there in your affection towards any of these princely suitors that are already come?	25
PORTIA	I pray thee over-name[3] them, and as thou namest them I will describe them – and according to my description, level at[4] my affection.	30
NERISSA	First, there is the Neapolitan prince.	
PORTIA	Ay, that's a colt[5] indeed, for he doth nothing but talk of his horse; and he makes it a great appropriation to his own good parts that he can shoe him himself[6]. I am much afeared my lady his mother played false[7] with a smith[8].	35
NERISSA	Then is there the County Palatine.	
PORTIA	He doth nothing but frown, as who should say[9], 'And you will not have me, choose.' He hears merry tales and smiles not; I fear he will prove the weeping philosopher when he grows old, being so full of unmannerly[10] sadness in his youth. I had rather be married to a death's head with a bone in his mouth than to either of these. God defend me from these two!	40
NERISSA	How say you by the French lord, Monsieur Le Bon?	45
PORTIA	God made him, and therefore let him pass for[11] a man. In truth I know it is a sin to be a mocker, but he! – why, he hath a horse better than the Neapolitan's, a better bad habit of frowning than the Count Palatine: he is every man in no man[12]. If a throstle[13] sing, he falls straight a-capering[14]; he will fence[15] with his own shadow. If I should marry him, I should marry twenty husbands. If he would despise me, I would forgive him; for if he love me to madness, I shall never requite him[16].	50
NERISSA	What say you then to Falconbridge, the young baron of England?	55

The two women end their mocking of Portia's suitors. Nerissa reports the men's intention to return home immediately. She reminds Portia of her past meeting with Bassanio.

剧情简介：两个女人结束了对求婚者的嘲讽。讷瑞莎说这些人打算即刻打道回府。她提醒鲍霞与博萨纽曾经的会面。

Language in the play 剧中语言
Portia's intolerance? (in pairs)

In Shakespeare's time the suitors were recognised as national stereotypes (刻板印象), and Portia's descriptions probably provoked laughter from the audience. But stereotyping is unfair and inaccurate, and Portia's words contain a scornful and racist edge.

a Take it in turns to read aloud Portia's descriptions of her six suitors, starting with the 'Neapolitan prince' at line 34 and ending with the German at line 81.

b After each description, identify words or phrases that a modern audience might find distasteful or unpleasant. Write them down in a Language file, and explain in each instance exactly which elements of Portia's language might be problematic.

Characters 人物分析
How to present Portia – actor and director (in pairs)

This is the first scene in which Portia appears. She has been described glowingly by Bassanio (see Act 1 Scene 1, lines 160–71), using references that praise her virtue and link her to classical figures. Yet now she can appear openly racist, intolerant and dismissive. That attitude is compounded in lines 105–8 when she makes a remark about not wanting to marry the soon-to-arrive Prince of Morocco because he has 'the complexion of a devil'. Elizabethans believed that devils were black.

a One of you takes on the role of the actor playing Portia in a modern production, the other is the director. Before you start, think carefully about the initial impressions you want to create of Portia, and the kind of relationship you want her to strike up with the audience.

b Working independently, review Portia's role in the scene and write down specific queries you might have about how to perform the part.

c Stage the meeting between actor and director and work through all the queries until you arrive at what you think is the most appropriate and effective interpretation. Write up your key ideas in your Director's Journal.

1 have … English 几乎不会说英语
2 a proper man's picture 英俊小伙的画像
3 dumbshow 哑剧
4 doublet 小双衣（流行于伊丽莎白时代的男士紧身上衣，有的带短裙）
5 round hose 圆鼓紧腿裤
6 borrowed … of 挨了一记耳光
7 became … another 也挨了那位英国人的打，发誓要报复他（法国人做了苏格兰人的担保人，保证他能复仇）
8 make shift 设法
9 set 放置
10 contrary 错误的
11 without 在外边
12 sponge 酒鬼（吸水的海绵）
13 the having 嫁给
14 determinations 计划
15 suit 求婚
16 sort 方法
17 imposition 强加的方式
18 Sibylla （这是拉丁文，英文通常写作Sibyl）悉碧菈（希腊神话中的女预言家，她能活的年数跟握在她手里的沙粒一样多）
19 Diana 荻阿娜（贞洁 [处女] 守护神与月亮女神）
20 hither = here

The Merchant of Venice Act 1 Scene 2
威尼斯商人

PORTIA   You know I say nothing to him, for he understands not me, nor I him: he hath neither Latin, French, nor Italian, and you will come into the court and swear that I have a poor penny-worth in the English[1]. He is a proper man's picture[2], but alas who can converse with a dumbshow[3]? How oddly he is suited! I think he bought his doublet[4] in Italy, his round hose[5] in France, his bonnet in Germany, and his behaviour everywhere.

NERISSA   What think you of the Scottish lord his neighbour?

PORTIA   That he hath a neighbourly charity in him, for he borrowed a box of the ear of[6] the Englishman and swore he would pay him again when he was able. I think the Frenchman became his surety and sealed under for another[7].

NERISSA   How like you the young German, the Duke of Saxony's nephew?

PORTIA   Very vilely in the morning when he is sober, and most vilely in the afternoon when he is drunk. When he is best he is a little worse than a man, and when he is worst he is little better than a beast. And the worst fall that ever fell, I hope I shall make shift[8] to go without him.

NERISSA   If he should offer to choose, and choose the right casket, you should refuse to perform your father's will if you should refuse to accept him.

PORTIA   Therefore, for fear of the worst, I pray thee set[9] a deep glass of Rhenish wine on the contrary[10] casket, for if the devil be within, and that temptation without[11], I know he will choose it. I will do anything, Nerissa, ere I will be married to a sponge[12].

NERISSA   You need not fear, lady, the having[13] any of these lords. They have acquainted me with their determinations[14], which is indeed to return to their home, and to trouble you with no more suit[15] unless you may be won by some other sort[16] than your father's imposition[17], depending on the caskets.

PORTIA   If I live to be as old as Sibylla[18], I will die as chaste as Diana[19] unless I be obtained by the manner of my father's will. I am glad this parcel of wooers are so reasonable, for there is not one among them but I dote on his very absence; and I pray God grant them a fair departure.

NERISSA   Do you not remember, lady, in your father's time, a Venetian, a scholar and a soldier, that came hither[20] in company of the Marquis of Montferrat?

A servant announces that the suitors are about to leave, and that another, the Prince of Morocco, will soon arrive. In Venice, Bassanio tries to borrow money from Shylock.

剧情简介：仆人禀报，众求婚人即将离开，又一位求婚者摩洛哥亲王将很快抵达。在威尼斯，博萨纽在跟夏洛克谈借钱。

1 Hints of love? (in pairs)

In performance, most actors playing Portia use the few words she speaks about Bassanio to show that she is already deeply attracted to him, but tries not to show it.

- Take it in turns to speak lines 95 and 98–9 in ways that bring out this impression. Afterwards, talk together about whether you think this makes Portia more interesting and/or sympathetic to the audience, and the impression it creates after her tart (尖刻) dismissal of the other suitors.

◀ Compare your impressions of the Portia pictured here with what you think of the way Shakespeare presents her in Scene 2.

1	the best deserving	最配得上
2	take their leave	告辞
3	forerunner	先行官，传令官
4	condition	德行
5	complexion	肤色，面色
6	I … me	与其让他做我的丈夫，还不如让他做神父听我忏悔
7	sirrah	伙计（对下人的称呼）
8	ducats	达克（威尼斯的一种金币）
9	shall be bound	将必须偿还
10	stead	帮助
11	pleasure	使如愿
12	good	（夏洛克的意思是"财力可靠"）
13	Have … contrary?	（难道）您听过不同的说法？

2 Shylock doing business with Bassanio (in pairs)

Shylock's very first words are about money: he is talking to Bassanio about the terms of a loan that Bassanio is seeking. Often the lines are played in a 'cat and mouse' (猫戏老鼠) fashion, as Shylock (a Jew) and Bassanio (a Christian) are uneasy companions and both try to assert their importance and superiority.

- Take parts and read lines 1–12. Notice that words are repeated and echoed ('three', 'well', 'bound'). Experiment with different ways of sparring verbally in these lines. Who do you think controls this exchange and how does that come across in your performances? Explain your thinking to other pairs.

PORTIA	Yes, yes, it was Bassanio! – as I think so was he called.	95
NERISSA	True, madam; he of all the men that ever my foolish eyes looked upon was the best deserving[1] a fair lady.	
PORTIA	I remember him well, and I remember him worthy of thy praise.	

Enter a SERVINGMAN

How now, what news? 100

SERVINGMAN The four strangers seek for you, madam, to take their leave[2]; and there is a forerunner[3] come from a fifth, the Prince of Morocco, who brings word the prince his master will be here tonight.

PORTIA If I could bid the fifth welcome with so good heart as I can bid 105 the other four farewell, I should be glad of his approach. If he have the condition[4] of a saint, and the complexion[5] of a devil, I had rather he should shrive me than wive me[6].

Come, Nerissa; sirrah[7], go before:
Whiles we shut the gate upon one wooer, another knocks at 110
the door.

Exeunt

Act 1 Scene 3
Venice

Enter BASSANIO *with* SHYLOCK *the Jew*

SHYLOCK	Three thousand ducats[8], well.	
BASSANIO	Ay, sir, for three months.	
SHYLOCK	For three months, well.	
BASSANIO	For the which, as I told you, Antonio shall be bound[9].	
SHYLOCK	Antonio shall become bound, well.	5
BASSANIO	May you stead[10] me? Will you pleasure[11] me? Shall I know your answer?	
SHYLOCK	Three thousand ducats for three months, and Antonio bound.	
BASSANIO	Your answer to that?	10
SHYLOCK	Antonio is a good[12] man –	
BASSANIO	Have you heard any imputation to the contrary?[13]	

Shylock doubts the security of Antonio's ships, but seems willing to lend the money. He tells the audience that he hates Antonio for a variety of reasons, and intends to harm him if he can.

 剧情简介：尽管夏洛克怀疑安托纽的商船有风险，但似乎愿意借钱给他。他对观众说，由于种种原因，他恨安托纽，打算有机会的话就报复他。

Characters 人物分析
Focus on Shylock – joking or sincere? (in pairs)

a Look carefully at lines 18–21. Shylock plays on the words 'rats' and 'pirates'. Is he making a joke of it? Take it in turns to read the lines aloud – first seriously, and then jokingly. Which version has the greater dramatic impact?

b How should Shylock speak lines 27–31? On stage they are often performed as sincere and serious, but is he still being playful and joking with Bassanio? Try them out together, then talk about how you think they should be delivered. After your experiments, write brief notes for an actor playing Shylock about how to deliver these lines. Add them to your Director's Journal.

1 Shylock's hatred of Antonio (in pairs)

An aside (旁白) is a remark made by a character to the audience, which is not heard by the other characters on stage.

a One of you reads aloud Shylock's aside in lines 33–44, pausing at each punctuation mark. The other uses the pause to paraphrase in modern English exactly what Shylock is saying. (Use the glossary to clarify the meaning of obscure words and phrases.)

b Work together to write a summary of the reasons behind Shylock's hatred of Antonio. (You will find help on the religious context of the play in 'History and the Jews', pp. 186–8.)

c Take turns to perform Shylock's aside, giving each key idea its full emotional weight. Show your performances to other pairs for comment.

Write about it 写作练习
Now it's Antonio's turn!

What if Shakespeare had also written an aside for Antonio to voice his feelings about Shylock? Look at lines 40–3, where Shylock describes Antonio's view of him and his race. (The 2004 film of the play opened with a sequence in which Antonio was seen spitting on Shylock, an idea that has also been used in stage versions of the play.)

- Write Antonio's aside in the same style and rhythm (节奏) as Shylock's. (See also 'The language of *The Merchant of Venice*', pp. 182–3.)

1 good　（此处指有还债能力）
2 is sufficient　有足够现款
3 in supposition　悬而未定（指安托纽的财产都不在威尼斯）
4 Rialto　威尼斯牲畜交易所
5 squandered　分散
6 bethink me　再三考虑这件事
7 pork　猪肉（犹太人因宗教原因不吃猪肉）
8 to smell … into　去闻猪肉味儿，吃猪的肉，它的身体里住着魔鬼，那是你们拿撒勒人的先知驱赶进去的（参见《新约·马太福音》）
9 publican　收税官
10 low simplicity　愚不可及
11 gratis　不收利息
12 rate of usance　高利贷的利率
13 catch … hip　有朝一日抓住他的软肋
14 feed fat the ancient grudge　痛痛快快地报复过去的冤仇（此处将怨恨比作可以养肥的牲口）
15 rails　斥责
16 I … store　我正在计算手中有多少现金
17 gross　总额

THE MERCHANT OF VENICE ACT 1 SCENE 3

威尼斯商人

SHYLOCK Ho no, no, no, no: my meaning in saying he is a good[1] man is to have you understand me that he is sufficient[2]. Yet his means are in supposition[3]: he hath an argosy bound to Tripolis, another to the Indies; I understand moreover upon the Rialto[4] he hath a third at Mexico, a fourth for England, and other ventures he hath squandered[5] abroad. But ships are but boards, sailors but men; there be land rats, and water rats, water thieves and land thieves – I mean pirates – and then there is the peril of waters, winds and rocks. The man is notwithstanding sufficient. Three thousand ducats: I think I may take his bond.

BASSANIO Be assured you may.

SHYLOCK I will be assured I may; and that I may be assured, I will bethink me[6] – may I speak with Antonio?

BASSANIO If it please you to dine with us –

SHYLOCK Yes, to smell pork[7], to eat of the habitation which your prophet the Nazarite conjured the devil into[8]. I will buy with you, sell with you, talk with you, walk with you, and so following; but I will not eat with you, drink with you, nor pray with you. What news on the Rialto? Who is he comes here?

Enter ANTONIO

BASSANIO This is Signor Antonio.

SHYLOCK [*Aside*] How like a fawning publican[9] he looks!
I hate him for he is a Christian;
But more, for that in low simplicity[10]
He lends out money gratis[11], and brings down
The rate of usance[12] here with us in Venice.
If I can catch him once upon the hip[13],
I will feed fat the ancient grudge[14] I bear him.
He hates our sacred nation, and he rails[15]
Even there where merchants most do congregate
On me, my bargains, and my well-won thrift
Which he calls interest. Cursed be my tribe
If I forgive him!

BASSANIO Shylock, do you hear?

SHYLOCK I am debating of my present store[16],
And by the near guess of my memory
I cannot instantly raise up the gross[17]
Of full three thousand ducats. What of that?

Shylock gently taunts Antonio for his past opposition to charging interest. He tells a story from the Bible to show the benefits of profiting by lending.

剧情简介：夏洛克温和地嘲讽安托纽以前反对放贷取利。他用《圣经》中的一个故事，讲述借贷获利的好处。

1 Thinly veiled contempt? (in pairs)

This is the first exchange between Antonio and Shylock in the play. Antonio dislikes both Jews and money-lending, but he has to ask Shylock for a loan. Actors like to use these lines to show how the two characters are at odds with each other. Enmity and loathing are usually barely under control on both sides, even though they are conducting a 'civilised' public conversation.

a Choose parts and read aloud lines 56–62. Pause after each sentence to voice the secret thoughts of your character. (This is like speaking the thought bubbles in a comic strip.)

b Read the lines again, this time without pauses but instead adding appropriate gestures and expressions to enhance the impact of your character's words.

2 Jacob and his sheep

Shylock uses a Bible story (Genesis 30) to justify his way of doing business. Jacob, a descendant of Abraham, agreed to look after his Uncle Laban's sheep. In return, he could keep any new-born lambs that were streaked or multicoloured. During the mating season he made a fence of branches ('wands') partly stripped ('pilled') of their bark, so that the ewes would see the fence when they conceived. (It was believed that offspring resemble what the mother sees at the moment of conception.) As a result of Jacob's ingenuity, a large number of streaked lambs were born, which he could keep for himself. Shylock's insistence that 'thrift is blessing' makes a clear connection between religion and profit.

a Why do you think this point is important at this stage in the play?

b Find a copy of the Bible and read the original story there of Jacob and his sheep. How closely does Shylock's version of the tale follow the original?

c Bassanio listens silently to Shylock's Bible story; Antonio interrupts only once (line 67). How might a director have the two characters act or react as Shylock's tale unfolds? Give a few suggestions about the kind of reactions that might make for powerful drama, then jot down your ideas in your Director's Journal.

1 furnish me 为我提供资金
2 soft 等一下
3 in our mouths 我们正谈到
4 albeit 尽管，虽然
5 I … excess 我贷出或者借入，从来不收取也不支付高利 (excess: 高利，非一般利息)
6 ripe wants 燃眉之急
7 Is … would? 他知道您需要多少钱吗？
8 Upon advantage 为了利润
9 compromised 同意
10 eanlings 刚出生的羊羔
11 pied 杂色的
12 hire 工钱
13 rank 发情
14 work of generation 交配
15 me （赘词，无实义）
16 And … kind 正在交配
17 fulsome ewes 发情的母羊
18 conceiving 怀胎
19 eaning 产羊羔

	Tubal, a wealthy Hebrew of my tribe,	
	Will furnish me¹. But soft², how many months	50
	Do you desire? [*To Antonio*] Rest you fair, good signor!	
	Your worship was the last man in our mouths³.	
ANTONIO	Shylock, albeit⁴ I neither lend nor borrow	
	By taking nor by giving of excess⁵,	
	Yet to supply the ripe wants⁶ of my friend	55
	I'll break a custom. [*To Bassanio*] Is he yet possessed	
	How much ye would?⁷	
SHYLOCK	Ay, ay, three thousand ducats.	
ANTONIO	And for three months.	
SHYLOCK	I had forgot, three months; [*To Bassanio*] you told me so.	
	Well then, your bond; and let me see – but hear you,	60
	Methoughts you said you neither lend nor borrow	
	Upon advantage⁸.	
ANTONIO	I do never use it.	
SHYLOCK	When Jacob grazed his uncle Laban's sheep –	
	This Jacob from our holy Abram was	
	(As his wise mother wrought in his behalf)	65
	The third possessor; ay, he was the third –	
ANTONIO	And what of him, did he take interest?	
SHYLOCK	No, not take interest, not as you would say	
	Directly interest. Mark what Jacob did:	
	When Laban and himself were compromised⁹	70
	That all the eanlings¹⁰ which were streaked and pied¹¹	
	Should fall as Jacob's hire¹², the ewes being rank¹³	
	In end of autumn turnèd to the rams,	
	And when the work of generation¹⁴ was	
	Between these woolly breeders in the act,	75
	The skilful shepherd pilled me¹⁵ certain wands	
	And in the doing of the deed of kind¹⁶	
	He stuck them up before the fulsome ewes¹⁷,	
	Who then conceiving¹⁸, did in eaning¹⁹ time	
	Fall parti-coloured lambs, and those were Jacob's.	80
	This was a way to thrive, and he was blest;	
	And thrift is blessing if men steal it not.	

Antonio is not convinced by Shylock's argument. He warns Bassanio not to be deceived by the Jew's use of the Bible. Shylock reminds Antonio of the contemptuous way he has been treated in the past.

 剧情简介：安托纽并不听夏洛克那一套。他告诫博萨纽不要被犹太人利用《圣经》蒙骗。夏洛克提醒安托纽别忘了过去对他的侮辱。

Stagecraft 导演技巧

Antonio's scorn

Antonio dismisses Shylock's parable (《圣经》中的寓言), ignores his joke in line 88, and interrupts him to warn Bassanio against Bible-quoting villains.

- In some productions, Shylock overhears Antonio's lines 89–94. In others he does not. Which of these alternative stagings do you think would have greater dramatic effect? Why? Write your thoughts in your Director's Journal.

Themes 主题分析

Appearance and reality (in small groups)

Antonio's lines 90–4 contain several images of falsehood, exploring the difference between how things appear on the surface and what they are really like underneath. He seems to refer to Shylock, for example, as 'a villain with a smiling cheek'.

a Turn this image into a tableau (亮相；舞台造型 [演员全部静止不动]) for other students to look at. Then make tableaux of all the other images related to this theme that you can find in Act 1. (Your first might be Janus.)

b On the basis of your reading of the scene up to this point, how far do you think Antonio has justifiable (有道理，讲得通) cause to beware of Shylock's 'false' appearance? Explain your thinking in one or two sentences.

1 Shylock versus Antonio (in pairs)

Although Shylock has just been accused of being deceitful, he now makes a very open and public attack on Antonio, taking the opportunity to air some of his grievances (抱怨) about how the Christians have treated him.

a Read the section on 'History and the Jews' on pages 186–8. Then take turns to speak and perform Shylock's lines 98–121 to each other.

b Experiment with different tones of voice, gestures and the positioning of the two enemies. In one production, Shylock stood face to face with Antonio. In another, he lay relaxed on cushions and spoke in a half-amused tone. In another, he sneered at Antonio as he circled him, whining in mockery of his reply. Work through several possibilities and then show your final version to other students. Ask them to respond to your presentation of Shylock and Antonio. What do they make of the way you depict them?

---

1 This … heaven （意思是雅各的幸运是上帝赐予的）
2 inserted 提及
3 note me 听我说
4 holy witness 《圣经》里的证据
5 beholding 感激
6 oft = often
7 rated 辱骂
8 usances 放贷
9 suff'rance = sufferance (忍耐)
10 badge 标记（威尼斯的犹太人必须在衣服上佩戴一圈黄色带子）
11 dog （特别针对犹太人的侮辱）
12 gaberdine （中世纪犹太人穿的）粗布长外套
13 void your rheum 吐口水
14 foot 踢
15 stranger cur 丧家犬
16 bondman's key 奴才的腔调
17 bated breath 低声下气

THE MERCHANT OF VENICE ACT 1 SCENE 3
威尼斯商人

ANTONIO	This was a venture, sir, that Jacob served for,
	A thing not in his power to bring to pass,
	But swayed and fashioned by the hand of heaven[1].	85
	Was this inserted[2] to make interest good?
	Or is your gold and silver ewes and rams?
SHYLOCK	I cannot tell, I make it breed as fast.
	But note me[3], signor –
ANTONIO	Mark you this, Bassanio,
	The devil can cite Scripture for his purpose.	90
	An evil soul producing holy witness[4]
	Is like a villain with a smiling cheek,
	A goodly apple rotten at the heart.
	O what a goodly outside falsehood hath!
SHYLOCK	Three thousand ducats, 'tis a good round sum.	95
	Three months from twelve, then let me see, the rate –
ANTONIO	Well, Shylock, shall we be beholding[5] to you?
SHYLOCK	Signor Antonio, many a time and oft[6]
	In the Rialto you have rated[7] me
	About my monies and my usances[8].	100
	Still have I borne it with a patient shrug
	For suff'rance[9] is the badge[10] of all our tribe.
	You call me misbeliever, cut-throat dog[11],
	And spit upon my Jewish gaberdine[12],
	And all for use of that which is mine own.	105
	Well then, it now appears you need my help.
	Go to, then, you come to me, and you say,
	'Shylock, we would have monies' – you say so,
	You that did void your rheum[13] upon my beard,
	And foot[14] me as you spurn a stranger cur[15]	110
	Over your threshold: monies is your suit.
	What should I say to you? Should I not say
	'Hath a dog money? Is it possible
	A cur can lend three thousand ducats?' Or
	Shall I bend low, and in a bondman's key[16],	115
	With bated breath[17] and whisp'ring humbleness,
	Say this:
	'Fair sir, you spat on me on Wednesday last,
	You spurned me such a day, another time
	You called me dog: and for these courtesies	120
	I'll lend you thus much monies.'

Antonio remains contemptuous, but Shylock claims to want his friendship, offering not to charge interest on the loan. Instead, if Antonio fails to pay, Shylock will take a pound of his flesh.

 剧情简介：安托纽仍然鄙视夏洛克。但夏洛克声称，为赢得安托纽的友情，他可以不收取利息。不过如果安托纽不能按时还钱，他将割下安托纽的一磅肉（抵债）。

1 Anger management? (in pairs)

Imagine you are actors rehearsing the parts of Antonio and Shylock. You want to clarify questions about the script between lines 122 and 135:

- 'Antonio' wants to explore just how angry he should be (lines 122–9).
- 'Shylock' wants to understand why he seems to back down, and whether to play his expressions of friendship as genuine or contrived.

Stage the actors' meeting, work through the issues to your mutual satisfaction, then write up your notes for your director. Finally, perform this scene in the way you have discussed.

2 Friends don't profit from each other
(in small groups)

Antonio's reply to Shylock's taunting (lines 122–9) reveals his deep prejudice against Shylock and his money-lending business. He says that friends should not take advantage of each other by charging interest ('A breed for barren metal') and making money from money.

- Research what Elizabethans thought about the business of money-lending (see 'Perspectives and themes', p. 169). Then talk together about what you think are the rights and wrongs of charging interest.
- Prepare a mini-presentation for your class that deals with both Elizabethan and modern perspectives.

3 Should Shylock lend the money? Should Antonio sign up to the bond?

Antonio wants to borrow the three thousand ducats from Shylock, but will not see him as his friend. He still describes Shylock as the 'enemy' and threatens to 'spit on' and humiliate him in the future, even if he lends the money. Shylock proposes 'a merry sport': if Antonio cannot repay the loan, he must forfeit a pound of his flesh.

There has been argument for centuries about whether or not Shylock thinks up 'the pound of flesh' on the spur of the moment (一时冲动，心血来潮), or whether he had it in mind earlier. There is also argument over whether, at this moment, he intends it seriously or just as 'a merry sport'. What do you think?

- Put each character in the hot-seat*. Ask Shylock exactly what's in his mind. Then fire questions at Antonio. If he mistrusts Shylock so much, why does he call the bond a 'kindness' and agree to sign it?

---

1 barren metal 无生殖力的金属
2 take ... friend 以借钱给朋友让钱生钱
3 break 破产
4 no doit / Of usance 不计一分利息
5 notary 公证人
6 single bond 无附加条件的契约
7 in a merry sport 开个玩笑
8 condition 条款
9 nominated 注明
10 equal 不多不少，精准
11 dwell in 忍受
12 I'll ... necessity 我宁愿继续受穷
13 forfeit 丧失
14 break his day 到期爽约
15 exaction of the forfeiture 索求处罚物（一磅肉）

* hot-seat 热座位，一种课堂游戏，玩法是请一位同学坐到讲台上的一把椅子上，其他同学轮番给他/她出难题，哪个问题他/她回答不出就算输。

ANTONIO	I am as like to call thee so again,	
	To spit on thee again, to spurn thee too.	
	If thou wilt lend this money, lend it not	
	As to thy friends, for when did friendship take	125
	A breed for barren metal[1] of his friend[2]?	
	But lend it rather to thine enemy,	
	Who if he break[3], thou mayst with better face	
	Exact the penalty.	
SHYLOCK	Why look you how you storm!	130
	I would be friends with you, and have your love,	
	Forget the shames that you have stained me with,	
	Supply your present wants, and take no doit	
	Of usance[4] for my monies, and you'll not hear me.	
	This is kind I offer.	
BASSANIO	This were kindness.	135
SHYLOCK	This kindness will I show.	
	Go with me to a notary[5], seal me there	
	Your single bond[6], and, in a merry sport[7],	
	If you repay me not on such a day,	
	In such a place, such sum or sums as are	140
	Expressed in the condition[8], let the forfeit	
	Be nominated[9] for an equal[10] pound	
	Of your fair flesh, to be cut off and taken	
	In what part of your body pleaseth me.	
ANTONIO	Content, in faith! I'll seal to such a bond,	145
	And say there is much kindness in the Jew.	
BASSANIO	You shall not seal to such a bond for me;	
	I'll rather dwell in[11] my necessity[12].	
ANTONIO	Why, fear not, man, I will not forfeit[13] it.	
	Within these two months, that's a month before	150
	This bond expires, I do expect return	
	Of thrice three times the value of this bond.	
SHYLOCK	O father Abram, what these Christians are,	
	Whose own hard dealings teaches them suspect	
	The thoughts of others! Pray you tell me this:	155
	If he should break his day[14] what should I gain	
	By the exaction of the forfeiture[15]?

Shylock insists that he can gain nothing from the deal except Antonio's friendship. Antonio agrees to the terms, and Shylock leaves to fetch the money. Bassanio is still uneasy about the contract.

剧情简介：夏洛克强调，他此举只是想得到安托纽的友谊，此外别无所得。安托纽同意借契条款，夏洛克离开去取钱。但博萨纽对这个契约感到不安。

Write about it 写作练习
Bassanio's anxieties

Antonio smugly (自鸣得意) agrees to the terms of the bond, confident that his trading ships will return to Venice with a handsome profit for him long before the deadline for the repayment. Bassanio ('I like not fair terms and a villain's mind') is not taken in by Shylock's apparent generosity in forfeiting any interest in return for the 'merry sport' of the bond.

- In character as Bassanio, recount your worries in a letter to another friend. Explain how the whole thing has come about, and elaborate on your views about Shylock and your friend Antonio.

Language in the play 剧中语言
Insults and accusations

Shylock's trouble with the Christians dates back to well before the start of the play. He speaks of an 'ancient grudge' when he first appears (line 39), and later gives a vivid account of Antonio's racist bullying (lines 98–121). In turn, Antonio condemns the practice of charging interest on loans (lines 53–4) and clearly mistrusts Shylock's benign appearance and behaviour.

- Head up two columns on a sheet of paper: 'Christian' and 'Jew'. Fill each column with examples of the kind of language that each religious group uses to talk about the other.
- Add a comment of your own to each example, in which you explore the particular impact of the language.

1	estimable	有价值
2	muttons, beefs	羊、牛
3	favour	好感
4	adieu	再会
5	love	好意
6	wrong	冤枉
7	forthwith	立刻
8	direction	指示
9	straight	立刻，马上
10	fearful guard	让人担心（靠不住）的看管
11	unthrifty knave	粗心的仆人
12	Hie	赶紧
13	gentle	（双关，安托纽话语中使人联想到Gentile [非犹太人]）

▼ What does this image suggest about the relationship between Shylock and Bassanio?

	A pound of man's flesh, taken from a man,	
	Is not so estimable[1], profitable neither,	
	As flesh of muttons, beefs[2], or goats. I say	160
	To buy his favour[3], I extend this friendship.	
	If he will take it, so; if not, adieu[4],	
	And for my love[5], I pray you wrong[6] me not.	
ANTONIO	Yes, Shylock, I will seal unto this bond.	
SHYLOCK	Then meet me forthwith[7] at the notary's.	165
	Give him direction[8] for this merry bond,	
	And I will go and purse the ducats straight[9],	
	See to my house left in the fearful guard[10]	
	Of an unthrifty knave[11], and presently	
	I'll be with you.	*Exit*
ANTONIO	Hie[12] thee, gentle[13] Jew.	170
	The Hebrew will turn Christian, he grows kind.	
BASSANIO	I like not fair terms and a villain's mind.	
ANTONIO	Come on, in this there can be no dismay,	
	My ships come home a month before the day.	
		Exeunt

The Merchant of Venice 威尼斯商人

Looking back at Act 1 第1幕回顾
Activities for groups or individuals

1 Venice and Belmont

Act 1 establishes two seemingly very different worlds. Venice is portrayed as a patriarchal world of money and commerce. In contrast, Belmont seems a feminine world of romance, trading in love.

- Write down your impressions of what life is like in Venice and in Belmont. Think about such matters as religion, class, occupations, attitudes to race, and gender roles. Find at least one quotation from the play about each of these aspects.
- Use your ideas to design two settings that could be used in a modern film version to show the difference between the two worlds of the play.

2 Conflict

Act 1 portrays many conflicts, some evident, and some hidden. The clearest sign of conflict to come is the ominous bond that Shylock describes as 'a merry sport'.

- List all the conflicts you can detect in Act 1, linking each one to evidence from the script. Add to your list as you read on.

3 Antonio: a case study

What do you make of Antonio? He is obviously popular and has a close relationship with Bassanio, but he has been cruel to Shylock. He is also depressed, though there is no clear explanation for his sadness.

- Imagine you are a psychiatrist. Using the Character file that you started on page 2, write a case study of Antonio, based on his language and behaviour as well as what others say about him in Act 1.

4 Nerissa

Explore Nerissa's contribution to Scene 2 and write a couple of paragraphs about how you view her role. Use the photograph opposite (below) as a basis for a class discussion of Nerissa's relationship with Portia.

5 Continuing conversations

At the start of all three scenes in Act 1, the characters are already deep in conversation when they enter.

- Choose one scene and script the characters' conversation before the scene begins. Try to use the kind of language and rhythm that Shakespeare employs (see 'The language of *The Merchant of Venice*', pp. 182–3).

6 Shylock's asides

No one knows for certain which lines Shakespeare intended to be spoken directly to the audience as asides. Over the centuries, directors, actors and editors of the play have made their own judgements.

- Imagine you are playing Shylock. Look through Scene 3 and decide which of his lines you would speak as asides. Give reasons for your choices in your Director's Journal.

7 Bassanio and Antonio

In modern productions, the relationship between Bassanio and Antonio is often presented as homoerotic (同性恋) (see photo opposite, above).

- Would you choose to follow this interpretation if you were directing a new stage version? Review the evidence of Act 1 and decide. Present reasons for your decision to your classmates.

8 Arranged marriages

Marriages in which partners are chosen by the parents are a feature of some modern societies. Portia is in a similar predicament to a modern young woman who is about to undergo an arranged marriage.

- Talk with a partner about the advantages and disadvantages of arranged marriages in general and in relation to Portia's situation. Then write a discursive essay that formalises your thoughts.

The Prince of Morocco arrives to try to win Portia's hand in marriage. Portia stresses that she must obey her dead father's will and marry the man who solves the riddle of the caskets.

 剧情简介：摩洛哥亲王抵达，想要赢得鲍霞的芳心，缔结婚姻。鲍霞强调，她必须遵循先父遗愿，只与解开匣子谜题的人结婚。

1 A grand entry? (in large groups)

The Prince of Morocco has come to Belmont to seek Portia's hand in marriage. What kind of impression do you think he wants to create as he prepares to meet Portia?

- Read quickly through this scene, taking a line or two each, then passing on to another reader.
- Study the stage direction at the beginning of the scene, then act out the entrance of the two groups of characters in different ways to test out Morocco's possible intentions. How should Portia and her attendants respond? Try adding music to match your chosen mood.
- When you have settled on your best version, show it to other groups.

Write about it 写作练习

Morocco and Portia (in pairs)

This is a short scene, preparing for Morocco's choice of casket, and his words are intended to make an instant impression on Portia.

a Share a reading of Morocco's two speeches (lines 1–12 and lines 22–38), then work together to rewrite them in simple, modern English prose. Afterwards, place your new script alongside Morocco's original. Now write a few paragraphs about the differences between the two versions and what Morocco's language suggests about him as a character.

b Morocco is described in the stage direction as a '*tawny Moor*'. He asks Portia not to dislike him for the colour of his skin (lines 1–2). Her reply is polite, but is she being ironic when she calls him 'fair'? She also seems critical of her dead father, referring to the way in which he 'scanted' (restricted) and 'hedged' (limited) her actions. Write a diary entry in modern English in which Portia reveals her true feelings about Morocco and her father.

1 *cornets* 喇叭奏花腔（表示重要人物登场）
2 *Moor* 摩尔人（来自非洲或中东，肤色暗黑）
3 *train* 随从
4 *shadowed livery* 深色制服
5 *burnished* 打磨光亮
6 *near bred* 近亲
7 *Phoebus* 福玻斯（希腊神话中太阳神Apollo的别称）
8 *icicles* 冰柱
9 *make incision* 割破皮肤
10 *aspèct* 仪表；行为
11 *feared* 让人畏惧
12 *best-regarded* 最受仰慕的
13 *clime* 国土
14 *hue* 肤色
15 *nice* 挑剔
16 *scanted* 限制
17 *hedged* 约束
18 *yield ... who* 把我嫁给
19 *scimitar* 弯刀
20 *Sophy* 波斯王
21 *fields* 战役
22 *Outbrave* 以勇气压倒
23 *a* = he

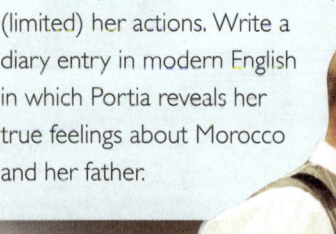

Act 2 Scene 1
Belmont   A room in Portia's house

A flourish of cornets[1]. *Enter the Prince of* MOROCCO, *a tawny Moor*[2] *all in white, and three or four followers accordingly; with* PORTIA, NERISSA, *and their train*[3]

MOROCCO Mislike me not for my complexion,
The shadowed livery[4] of the burnished[5] sun,
To whom I am a neighbour and near bred[6].
Bring me the fairest creature northward born,
Where Phoebus'[7] fire scarce thaws the icicles[8],   5
And let us make incision[9] for your love
To prove whose blood is reddest, his or mine.
I tell thee, lady, this aspèct[10] of mine
Hath feared[11] the valiant; by my love I swear
The best-regarded[12] virgins of our clime[13]   10
Have loved it too. I would not change this hue[14],
Except to steal your thoughts, my gentle queen.

PORTIA In terms of choice I am not solely led
By nice[15] direction of a maiden's eyes.
Besides, the lottery of my destiny   15
Bars me the right of voluntary choosing.
But if my father had not scanted[16] me,
And hedged[17] me by his wit to yield myself
His wife who[18] wins me by that means I told you,
Yourself, renownèd prince, then stood as fair   20
As any comer I have looked on yet
For my affection.

MOROCCO   Even for that I thank you.
Therefore I pray you lead me to the caskets
To try my fortune. By this scimitar[19],
That slew the Sophy[20] and a Persian prince   25
That won three fields[21] of Sultan Solyman,
I would o'er-stare the sternest eyes that look,
Outbrave[22] the heart most daring on the earth,
Pluck the young sucking cubs from the she-bear,
Yea, mock the lion when a[23] roars for prey,   30

Portia reminds Morocco that he must swear an oath and, after dinner, is to make his choice of casket. Scene 2 introduces Lancelot Gobbo, Shylock's servant, who is considering deserting his master.

 剧情简介：鲍霞提醒摩洛哥亲王，他必须发誓遵守诺言，晚饭后再选择匣子。第二场夏洛克的仆人朗斯勒·高博出场，他在纠结是否要背弃他的主人。

Themes 主题分析

Public versus private

This is the second scene to feature Portia. She appeared before in Act 1 Scene 2, describing her suitors to Nerissa.

a List the differences between Portia's manner of speaking privately to her lady-in-waiting, and publicly in this courtship with Morocco.

b Write a paragraph about Portia. Is she simply behaving as a dutiful daughter, sincere in her respect for her dead father's wishes? Or is she more manipulative (操纵力强) and cunning than that? Explain your thinking and support it with evidence from the script.

Write about it 写作练习

'Forward to the temple' – Morocco's thoughts

At 'the temple' (Belmont's church), Morocco must swear an oath never to marry if he chooses the wrong casket. The consequences of failure are high, and success rests on luck.

a **By yourself** Write a short interior monologue (独白) for Morocco, capturing the tension and anxiety of his predicament and his true thoughts about Portia.

b **In pairs** Read aloud your monologue, then listen to your partner reading Portia's diary entry from the previous page. How do Portia and Morocco's thoughts differ?

1 Hercules and Lichas 赫丘力与利哈斯（希腊神话中的英雄和他的仆人）
2 Alcides 阿尔赛迪斯（赫丘力的别称）
3 blind Fortune 盲目的命运女神（希腊神话中的命运女神一手拿天平，一手执剑，双眼紧闭或被蒙住，转动命运之轮）
4 hazard 冒险
5 cursèd'st 最倒霉
6 will serve me 会允许我
7 fiend 魔鬼
8 aforesaid 像方才所说
9 courageous 鼓舞人的
10 pack 离开
11 rouse up 振奋
12 brave 有勇气
13 did something smack 做了某种"嘣"的一声的事（指亲嘴时发出的声响，暗指其父喜欢与妻子之外的女人厮混乱搞；smack、grow to和taste均含有粗俗淫秽之意）
14 something grow to 某种贴近的事
15 had a kind of taste 有某种口味

1 Lancelot, 'conscience', 'fiend' (in threes)

Lines 1–24 of Scene 2 are a **soliloquy** (独白) (a speech delivered by one character alone on stage, see 'The language of *The Merchant of Venice*', p. 182). Lancelot is debating whether to leave his master, but he never uses Shylock's name – referring to him as 'the Jew' and confusing his words so that 'incarnate' comically becomes 'incarnation'.

- Read Lancelot's speech aloud. One person plays Lancelot Gobbo, another speaks and acts as his 'conscience' and the third as 'the fiend'. Add actions and gestures in order to emphasise Lancelot's confusion and uncertainty.

- What advice would you give an actor performing this speech? Does it work best to play it as humorous, or edgy (急躁) and serious?

THE MERCHANT OF VENICE ACT 2 SCENE 2
威尼斯商人

        To win thee, lady. But alas the while,
        If Hercules and Lichas[1] play at dice
        Which is the better man, the greater throw
        May turn by fortune from the weaker hand.
        So is Alcides[2] beaten by his rage,   35
        And so may I, blind Fortune[3] leading me,
        Miss that which one unworthier may attain,
        And die with grieving.
PORTIA   You must take your chance,
        And either not attempt to choose at all
        Or swear before you choose, if you choose wrong,   40
        Never to speak to lady afterward
        In way of marriage: therefore be advised.
MOROCCO   Nor will not. Come, bring me unto my chance.
PORTIA   First forward to the temple; after dinner
        Your hazard[4] shall be made.
MOROCCO   Good fortune then,   45
        To make me blest – or cursèd'st[5] among men!

Cornets. Exeunt

Act 2 Scene 2
Venice   Near Shylock's house

Enter LANCELOT GOBBO, *the Clown, alone*

LANCELOT   Certainly, my conscience will serve me[6] to run from this Jew my master. The fiend[7] is at mine elbow and tempts me, saying to me 'Gobbo, Lancelot Gobbo, good Lancelot', or 'Good Gobbo', or 'Good Lancelot Gobbo, use your legs, take the start, run away.' My conscience says 'No: take heed, honest Lancelot, take heed, honest Gobbo' – or (as aforesaid[8]) – 'honest Lancelot Gobbo; do not run, scorn running with thy heels.' Well, the most courageous[9] fiend bids me pack[10]. 'Fia!' says the fiend, 'Away!' says the fiend. ''Fore the heavens, rouse up[11] a brave[12] mind', says the fiend, 'and run.' Well, my conscience, hanging about the neck of my heart, says very wisely to me, 'My honest friend Lancelot, being an honest man's son, or rather an honest woman's son' (for indeed my father did something smack[13], something grow to[14]; he had a kind of taste[15]): well, my conscience says 'Lancelot, budge not!' 'Budge!'
        5
        10

剧情简介: 朗斯勒·高博决意不再做夏洛克的仆人。他父亲来找他，但因为眼睛几乎失明没有认出自己的儿子。朗斯勒决定捉弄一下老父亲。

1 Tricking a blind man (in pairs)

Focus on the exchange between Lancelot and his father (lines 25–92). In a long section of dialogue, Lancelot decides to play a series of tricks on his virtually blind father who arrives looking for his son but does not recognise him. Sometimes audiences find this section tedious and difficult to follow, or even distasteful and offensive.

a Take parts and read lines 25–92, thinking about how Lancelot uses his voice and other techniques to deceive Gobbo. Experiment with different ways of reading Lancelot's asides to the audience (for example, try them as showing affection for his father, then as a little more barbed [讽刺的] and intolerant). Afterwards, talk together about whether you feel the episode is humorous or merely cruel.

b Write up your thoughts in your Director's Journal. Make it clear whether you would keep, cut down, or completely remove this section in performance. Explain your thinking by referring to the dramatic impact of whatever decisions you take.

▼ Write a paragraph about the kind of relationship this photograph suggests between Lancelot (right) and his father.

1 **saving your reverence** 请原谅
2 **incarnation** 化身（朗斯勒把 incarnate 说成了 incarnation）
3 **Master young-man** 少爷
4 **true-begotten** 亲生的（此为戏语，实际上是父亲生 [beget] 小孩）
5 **sand-blind** 半瞎
6 **high gravel-blind** 几乎全瞎（gravel [砾石] 比 sand [沙子] 大，故 gravel-blind 程度甚于 sand-blind）
7 **try confusion with him** 和他捣捣乱
8 **Marry** 向圣母马利亚起誓（从 Virgin Mary 演化而来，是一句语气温和的誓言）
9 **Be God's sonties** 向上帝的圣人们起誓
10 **raise the waters** 使他流泪
11 **well to live** 活得好好的
12 **a will** = he will（随他意愿）
13 **ergo** 因此（拉丁语）
14 **beseech** 恳求
15 **father** 老爹（此处朗斯勒并没有使用该词的字面意思）
16 **the sisters three** 命运三女神
17 **branches of learning** 各门学问

says the fiend. 'Budge not!' says my conscience. 'Conscience', say I, 'you counsel well.' 'Fiend', say I, 'you counsel well.' To be ruled by my conscience, I should stay with the Jew my master who – God bless the mark! – is a kind of devil; and to run away from the Jew, I should be ruled by the fiend who – saving your reverence[1] – is the devil himself. Certainly the Jew is the very devil incarnation[2], and, in my conscience, my conscience is but a kind of hard conscience to offer to counsel me to stay with the Jew. The fiend gives the more friendly counsel: I will run, fiend, my heels are at your commandment, I will run.

Enter OLD GOBBO *with a basket*

GOBBO Master young-man[3], you, I pray you, which is the way to Master Jew's?

LANCELOT [*Aside*] O heavens! This is my true-begotten[4] father who being more than sand-blind[5], high gravel-blind[6], knows me not. I will try confusions with him[7].

GOBBO Master young-gentleman, I pray you, which is the way to Master Jew's?

LANCELOT Turn upon your right hand at the next turning, but at the next turning of all on your left. Marry[8], at the very next turning turn of no hand but turn down indirectly to the Jew's house.

GOBBO Be God's sonties[9], 'twill be a hard way to hit! Can you tell me whether one Lancelot that dwells with him, dwell with him or no?

LANCELOT Talk you of young Master Lancelot? [*Aside*] Mark me now, now will I raise the waters[10]. Talk you of young Master Lancelot?

GOBBO No 'master', sir, but a poor man's son. His father, though I say't, is an honest, exceeding poor man and, God be thanked, well to live[11].

LANCELOT Well, let his father be what a will[12], we talk of young Master Lancelot.

GOBBO Your worship's friend and Lancelot, sir.

LANCELOT But I pray you, *ergo*[13] old man, *ergo* I beseech[14] you, talk you of young Master Lancelot?

GOBBO Of Lancelot, an't please your mastership.

LANCELOT *Ergo* Master Lancelot. Talk not of Master Lancelot, father[15], for the young gentleman, according to fates and destinies, and such odd sayings, the sisters three[16], and such branches of learning[17], is indeed deceased, or as you would say in plain terms, gone to heaven.

After several attempts, Lancelot convinces his father that he is indeed talking to his own son. Lancelot plans to enter Bassanio's service.

剧情简介：几番努力后，朗斯勒终于说服父亲：他的确是在跟自己的儿子说话。朗斯勒打算去给博萨纽做仆人。

1 Stage 'business' (戏台动作) (in pairs)

Actors often invent stage 'business' to help modern audiences understand language and jokes that are no longer clear. A modern audience may need some help with a few of the expressions used in the script opposite. Work out what 'business' could be added to the following to bring out their humour:

- 'Do I look like a cudgel (短棒) or a hovel-post, a staff or a prop (支柱)?' (line 56)
- 'Thou has got more hair on thy chin than Dobbin my fill-horse has on his tail' (lines 77–8)
- 'I have brought him a present' (line 83; see line 111)
- 'Give him a halter!' (line 86)
- 'you may tell every finger I have with my ribs' (lines 87–8).

Show your ideas to the rest of the class and ask them to guess which is which!

Characters 人物分析

Lancelot, Shylock's servant

Lancelot dominates the first part of Scene 2. He begins with a dramatic soliloquy, then bamboozles (愚弄) his nearly blind father with some striking horseplay (恶作剧). Most productions use his flamboyance (浮夸) and comic energy to counterbalance (抵消) the more sombre elements of the play. In one production, he was played as a swaggering Elvis Presley (猫王，美国著名摇滚歌手) lookalike who frequently punctuated (打断) his lines with snatches (片段) of song and music.

However, there are darker elements to Lancelot's character. In his soliloquy he will not mention Shylock's (his master's) name. Instead he uses the label 'Jew' four times and calls him 'devil' twice. Here, in lines 84–92 he again berates (斥责) his master. 'Give him a halter! I am famished in his service'.

a Imagine you are Lancelot sending news home to your father just after entering Shylock's service. Write a letter to him, describing your experiences as Shylock's servant. You'll need to decide whether to give your father full and frank information or leave out some of the details. Write in a style that you feel reflects Lancelot's manic character.

b Begin a Character file on Lancelot, noting down details of the key characteristics he displays in this scene (he exits at line 140). Link all your comments to evidence from the script.

1 **staff of my age** 我晚年的拐杖
2 **hovel-post** 茅棚的立柱
3 **it … child** 聪明的父亲才识得自己的孩子（有句谚语是 it is a wise child that knows his own father [聪明的孩子才识得自己的父亲]，朗斯勒特有意反着说）
4 **fill-horse** 辕马
5 **grows backward** 倒着长，越长越抽抽
6 **'gree = agree**（合得来）
7 **set up my rest** 下定决心
8 **halter** 上吊用的绳套
9 **famished** 挨饿
10 **in his service** 给他当差
11 **liveries** 仆从的制服
12 **run … ground** 跑到地球的尽头（能跑多远就跑多远）

THE MERCHANT OF VENICE ACT 2 SCENE 2
威尼斯商人

GOBBO   Marry, God forbid! The boy was the very staff of my age[1], my very prop.

LANCELOT   Do I look like a cudgel or a hovel-post[2], a staff or a prop? Do you know me, father?

GOBBO   Alack the day, I know you not, young gentleman, but I pray you tell me, is my boy – God rest his soul! – alive or dead?

LANCELOT   Do you not know me, father?

GOBBO   Alack, sir, I am sand-blind, I know you not.

LANCELOT   Nay indeed, if you had your eyes you might fail of the knowing me: it is a wise father that knows his own child[3]. Well, old man, I will tell you news of your son. [*Kneels*] Give me your blessing; truth will come to light, murder cannot be hid long, a man's son may, but in the end truth will out.

GOBBO   Pray you, sir, stand up; I am sure you are not Lancelot my boy.

LANCELOT   Pray you, let's have no more fooling about it, but give me your blessing; I am Lancelot your boy that was, your son that is, your child that shall be.

GOBBO   I cannot think you are my son.

LANCELOT   I know not what I shall think of that; but I am Lancelot the Jew's man, and I am sure Margery your wife is my mother.

GOBBO   Her name is Margery indeed. I'll be sworn if thou be Lancelot thou art mine own flesh and blood. Lord worshipped might he be, what a beard hast thou got! Thou has got more hair on thy chin than Dobbin my fill-horse[4] has on his tail.

LANCELOT   It should seem then that Dobbin's tail grows backward[5]. I am sure he had more hair of his tail than I have of my face when I last saw him.

GOBBO   Lord, how art thou changed! How dost thou and thy master agree? I have brought him a present. How 'gree[6] you now?

LANCELOT   Well, well; but for mine own part, as I have set up my rest[7] to run away, so I will not rest till I have run some ground. My master's a very Jew. Give him a present? Give him a halter[8]! I am famished[9] in his service[10]; you may tell every finger I have with my ribs. Father, I am glad you are come; give me your present to one Master Bassanio, who indeed gives rare new liveries[11]: if I serve not him, I will run as far as God has any ground[12]. O rare fortune, here comes the man! To him, father, for I am a Jew if I serve the Jew any longer.

Bassanio sends a servant to fetch Gratiano. Lancelot and his father try to persuade Bassanio to employ Lancelot. Bassanio says that Shylock has already recommended Lancelot to him.

 剧情简介：博萨纽派仆人找来格拉奇阿诺。朗斯勒父子试图说服博萨纽雇用朗斯勒。博萨纽称夏洛克已向他推荐朗斯勒。

1 Two people trying to tell the same story – more comic confusion? (in pairs)

Take parts and read aloud Lancelot and Gobbo's lines 97–115 so that each speech follows on quickly from the other. Stress the comedy and confusion that arise when two characters compete to tell the same story, trying to speak at the same time, and when one of them is almost blind and cannot see the other's actions … and reactions!

Language in the play 剧中语言

a **Malapropisms (搞笑误听)** A malapropism is a comical confusion of words, when a person chooses the wrong word instead of another one that sounds similar. Lancelot and Gobbo use several between lines 103 and 118. Find them and use the glossary opposite to help you write down the words they really meant to use. Make up some sentences of your own that include malapropisms. They are named after Mrs Malaprop, who muddled up her language in Sheridan's play *The Rivals* (1775). Shakespeare would have known malapropisms as 'cacozelia' (蹩脚的模仿，装模作样).

b **Prose (散文；散体) and verse (韵文；诗体)** You will probably have already noticed that the language of the play quite often changes between verse and prose. Opposite, Bassanio shifts from speaking prose to verse (lines 119–23). Turn to page 182 to read about Shakespeare's use of verse and prose, and then suggest two or three possible reasons why he makes the change here.

c **Racist language?** Lancelot thanks Bassanio for employing him by delivering another criticism of Shylock (lines 124–6). He suggests that Christians have 'the grace of God', whereas Shylock has 'enough' (wealth). Most people see this racist proverb as another example of (the Christian) Lancelot's prejudice against his Jewish master in Venice. Add this detail, and others spoken by Lancelot about Shylock, to the Language file you began on page 28. Follow up by commenting on the dramatic impact of this almost casual use of racist expressions at this point in the play. (See 'History and the Jews', pp. 186–8, for more on racist attitudes towards Jews over the centuries.)

1 at the farthest 最迟
2 anon 立刻
3 Gramercy 感谢上帝；多谢
4 specify 细说
5 infection （老高博用错了词，把 infection [感染] 错当 affection [想法，愿望] 用）
6 the short and the long 长话短说
7 scarce cater-cousins 不算是好朋友
8 frutify （朗斯勒可能是想说 fructify [使富有成效]）
9 dish of doves （在伊丽莎白时代的英国，鸽子是可食用的）
10 impertinent （是 pertinent [与……有关] 的误用）
11 defect （是 effect [意图；打算] 的误用）
12 preferred 推荐
13 preferment 晋升
14 The old proverb 古老的箴言（指 the grace of God is enough [上帝的恩佑就是最大的财富]）
15 parted 分配
16 enough （财富）足够了

Enter BASSANIO *with* [LEONARDO *and*] *a follower or two*

BASSANIO You may do so, but let it be so hasted that supper be ready at the farthest¹ by five of the clock. See these letters delivered, put the liveries to making, and desire Gratiano to come anon² to my lodging.

[*Exit one of his men*]

LANCELOT To him, father.

GOBBO God bless your worship!

BASSANIO Gramercy³; wouldst thou aught with me?

GOBBO Here's my son, sir, a poor boy –

LANCELOT Not a poor boy, sir, but the rich Jew's man that would, sir, as my father shall specify⁴ –

GOBBO He hath a great infection⁵, sir, as one would say, to serve –

LANCELOT Indeed, the short and the long⁶ is, I serve the Jew, and have a desire, as my father shall specify –

GOBBO His master and he, saving your worship's reverence, are scarce cater-cousins⁷ –

LANCELOT To be brief, the very truth is that the Jew having done me wrong doth cause me – as my father being I hope an old man shall frutify⁸ unto you –

GOBBO I have here a dish of doves⁹ that I would bestow upon your worship, and my suit is –

LANCELOT In very brief, the suit is impertinent¹⁰ to myself, as your worship shall know by this honest old man, and though I say it, though old man, yet poor man, my father –

BASSANIO One speak for both. What would you?

LANCELOT Serve you, sir.

GOBBO That is the very defect¹¹ of the matter, sir.

BASSANIO I know thee well, thou hast obtained thy suit.
Shylock thy master spoke with me this day,
And hath preferred¹² thee, if it be preferment¹³
To leave a rich Jew's service to become
The follower of so poor a gentleman.

LANCELOT The old proverb¹⁴ is very well parted¹⁵ between my master Shylock and you, sir: you have the grace of God, sir, and he hath enough¹⁶.

Lancelot welcomes the prospect of serving Bassanio, who plans to entertain Antonio that night. Gratiano wishes to travel with Bassanio to Belmont. Bassanio advises him to improve his rough manners.

剧情简介：朗斯勒如愿服侍博萨纽。博萨纽计划当晚宴请安托纽。格拉奇阿诺希望能与博萨纽一同前往贝尔蒙。博萨纽要他改掉粗鲁的言谈举止。

1 Lancelot the fortune-teller (占卜师) (in pairs)

Lancelot fancies himself as a fortune-teller as he reads his own palm.

a Speak his lines 132–9 to discover what he predicts for himself. Have a go together at drawing or doodling (涂抹，乱画) a version of the fortune Lancelot sees for himself. You'll notice that it's typically excessive!

b If Lancelot could read the palms of some of the other characters, what might he foretell? One person plays Lancelot; the other chooses to be Shylock, Antonio, Bassanio or Portia. Take turns to be Lancelot and the person having their fortune told. Base your predictions on what you know of the play so far. Note them down and see if they come true.

Write about it 写作练习

Bassanio's baggage: an inventory (货物清单) (by yourself)

Bassanio is preparing for the trip to Belmont to court the wealthy Portia. He orders Leonardo to buy certain items and then pack them: 'These things being bought and orderly bestowed' (line 142).

- If you were Bassanio, what would you take with you on the ship? Think carefully about why you are going to Belmont; then write your list, explaining in detail exactly what things you require and how you plan to use them.
- Compare your list with those of other students, and discuss similarities and differences.

Characters 人物分析

Gratiano – provoking Bassanio's fears (in pairs)

Bassanio expresses concern that Gratiano's wild behaviour, although acceptable in the male-dominated Venetian world, will spoil his courtship of Portia. Yet their friendship is so strong that Bassanio cannot deny Gratiano's request to accompany him.

a Read Bassanio's lines 151–60 to each other. Emphasise key words, then improvise one example of Gratiano's behaviour ('too wild, too rude, and bold of voice') that has prompted Bassanio's concern. Freeze your improvisation at a key moment and give it a caption, using the words from the quotation.

b Add Bassanio's observations about his friend to a Character file on Gratiano.

---

1 **guarded** 带花边；精致
2 **in** 进去吧 (指下场)
3 **ne'er** = never
4 **fairer table** 更加幸运的掌纹
5 **simple** 简单 (带有讽刺意味)
6 **coming-in** 开端 (指为数不多)
7 **'scape** = escape
8 **peril … featherbed** (朗斯勒言下之意是婚姻会带来危险)
9 **'scapes** 冒险
10 **gear** 事情
11 **twinkling** 一眨眼工夫
12 **orderly bestowed** 整齐装船放好
13 **best esteemed acquaintance** 最好的朋友
14 **herein** 于此
15 **suit** 请求
16 **rude** 嗓门大
17 **parts** 个性
18 **liberal** 肆意
19 **allay** 考验
20 **skipping** 溢出来
21 **misconstered** 误解

THE MERCHANT OF VENICE ACT 2 SCENE 2
威尼斯商人

BASSANIO   Thou speak'st it well; go, father, with thy son;
           Take leave of thy old master, and enquire
           My lodging out. [*To a follower*] Give him a livery
           More guarded¹ than his fellows'; see it done.   130

LANCELOT   Father, in². I cannot get a service, no, I have ne'er³ a tongue
           in my head! [*Looks at palm of his hand*] Well, if any man in Italy
           have a fairer table⁴ which doth offer to swear upon a book! – I shall
           have good fortune. Go to, here's a simple⁵ line of life, here's a
           small trifle of wives: alas, fifteen wives is nothing, eleven widows 135
           and nine maids is a simple coming-in⁶ for one man. And then to
           'scape⁷ drowning thrice, and to be in peril of my life with the edge
           of a featherbed⁸: here are simple 'scapes⁹. Well, if Fortune be a
           woman, she's a good wench for this gear¹⁰. Father, come, I'll take my
           leave of the Jew in the twinkling¹¹.   140

                              Exeunt Lancelot [and Gobbo]

BASSANIO   I pray thee, good Leonardo, think on this.
           These things being bought and orderly bestowed¹²,
           Return in haste, for I do feast tonight
           My best esteemed acquaintance¹³. Hie thee, go.
LEONARDO   My best endeavours shall be done herein¹⁴.   145

                              Enter GRATIANO

GRATIANO   Where's your master?
LEONARDO   Yonder, sir, he walks.   *Exit*
GRATIANO   Signor Bassanio!
BASSANIO   Gratiano?
GRATIANO   I have a suit¹⁵ to you.
BASSANIO   You have obtained it.
GRATIANO   You must not deny me, I must go with you to Belmont.   150
BASSANIO   Why then, you must. But hear thee, Gratiano:
           Thou art too wild, too rude¹⁶, and bold of voice –
           Parts¹⁷ that become thee happily enough,
           And in such eyes as ours appear not faults;
           But where thou art not known, why there they show   155
           Something too liberal¹⁸. Pray thee take pain
           To allay¹⁹ with some cold drops of modesty
           Thy skipping²⁰ spirit, lest through thy wild behaviour
           I be misconstered²¹ in the place I go to,
           And lose my hopes.

43

Gratiano promises to behave respectably in Belmont – but not tonight! In Scene 3, Jessica laments Lancelot's imminent departure. She hands him a letter to give secretly to Lorenzo.

 剧情简介：格拉奇阿诺答应到了贝尔蒙一定彬彬有礼，但今晚照旧！在第三场，婕丝柯为朗斯勒即将离去而忧伤。她交给朗斯勒一封信，让他偷偷交给劳仁佐。

Themes 主题分析

Appearance versus reality (in pairs)

Once again, Gratiano talks about playing a part: in lines 160–8, he promises to behave himself. Remember he has already offered to 'play the Fool' for Antonio (Act 1 Scene 1, line 79). But in lines 172–4, Bassanio urges Gratiano not to change his behaviour until they have left Venice for Belmont.

a Choose one of Gratiano's examples of polite behaviour and mime (演哑剧) it. Then replay the example of Gratiano's genuine (wild and loud) behaviour that you improvised in the 'Characters' activity on page 42. Get other students to comment on just how different the two extremes are.

b Are Bassiano and Gratiano being hypocritical (虚伪) in agreeing that Gratiano puts on an act in Belmont but is his usual raucous (粗声喧闹) self in Venice? One argues for, and the other against, this view.

1	a sober habit	稳重的样子
2	demurely	装作正经
3	hood	遮住
4	civility	礼貌；端庄
5	studied	老练
6	ostent	伪装
7	grandam	祖母
8	bearing	举止
9	bar	除……之外
10	gauge	评价
11	entreat	乞求
12	suit of mirth	心情愉快
13	purpose merriment	打算尽情欢乐
14	exhibit (inhibit [抑制，阻碍] 的误用)	
15	pagan	异教徒
16	deceived	弄错了
17	drops	眼泪

Stagecraft 导演技巧

Jessica and Shylock's home

a The scene needs to change quickly from the street outside Shylock's home to a room inside for this short exchange between Jessica and Lancelot. How would you make this change in a production to be performed in your school? What props or set design would you use to reflect the mood that Jessica speaks of in lines 2–3? Sketch and annotate your ideas, then add them to your Director's Journal.

b Think about how you would costume Jessica. Study the photograph below, and evaluate how successfully Jessica's appearance and demeanour (举止) match the mood created by the script opposite.

GRATIANO	Signor Bassanio, hear me:	160
	If I do not put on a sober habit[1],	
	Talk with respect, and swear but now and then,	
	Wear prayer books in my pocket, look demurely[2],	
	Nay more, while grace is saying, hood[3] mine eyes	
	Thus with my hat, and sigh and say 'amen',	165
	Use all the observance of civility[4]	
	Like one well studied[5] in a sad ostent[6]	
	To please his grandam[7], never trust me more.	
BASSANIO	Well, we shall see your bearing[8].	
GRATIANO	Nay, but I bar[9] tonight, you shall not gauge[10] me	170
	By what we do tonight.	
BASSANIO	No, that were pity.	
	I would entreat[11] you rather to put on	
	Your boldest suit of mirth[12], for we have friends	
	That purpose merriment[13]. But fare you well,	
	I have some business.	175
GRATIANO	And I must to Lorenzo and the rest;	
	But we will visit you at supper time.	

Exeunt

Act 2 Scene 3
Venice

Enter JESSICA *and* LANCELOT *the Clown*

JESSICA	I am sorry thou wilt leave my father so.	
	Our house is hell, and thou a merry devil	
	Didst rob it of some taste of tediousness.	
	But fare thee well: there is a ducat for thee.	
	And, Lancelot, soon at supper shalt thou see	5
	Lorenzo, who is thy new master's guest;	
	Give him this letter, do it secretly.	
	And so farewell: I would not have my father	
	See me in talk with thee.	
LANCELOT	Adieu; tears exhibit[14] my tongue. Most beautiful pagan[15],	10
	most sweet Jew, if a Christian do not play the knave and get thee,	
	I am much deceived[16]. But adieu; these foolish drops[17] do something	
	drown my manly spirit. Adieu! [*Exit*]	

Jessica, ashamed to be Shylock's daughter, plans to marry Lorenzo and become a Christian. In Scene 4, arrangements for a masque are made. Lancelot delivers Jessica's letter.

剧情简介：婕丝柯耻于做夏洛克的女儿，打算与劳仁佐结婚并皈依基督教。在第四场，假面舞会准备就绪。朗斯勒送来婕丝柯的信。

1 Jessica's home life (in pairs)

Scene 3 is very short but it clearly reveals Jessica's unhappiness at home. Read Jessica's sixteen lines, then carry out the following activities.

a Devise a series of three tableaux that you think capture some of the possible reasons for Jessica's unhappiness. Ask other pairs to guess what aspects of Jessica's life you are exploring.

b As Jessica, each write a letter to the problem page of a teen magazine. Describe the problems you have at home, and ask if you are right to desert your father for Lorenzo and convert to Christianity. Pass the letters at random to other members of your class, who should read them and make up suitable replies.

1	heinous	可怕；不可饶恕
2	strife	内心的纠结（孝顺与爱情）
3	torchbearers	拿火把的人
4	quaintly ordered	妥善安排
5	break up	拆开
6	it shall seem to signify	说不定您就知道怎么回事
7	hand	笔迹
8	leave	允许，许可
9	Whither	= To what place; To which place; To whatever place

Characters 人物分析

Jessica and Portia – points of comparison

- Draw up two columns, one headed 'Jessica' and the other 'Portia'. Write in each column what you have so far discovered about them. What similarities and differences can you identify?
- Display your findings for other students to comment on.

Stagecraft 导演技巧

Director's notes (in pairs)

a You have now read the whole of Scene 3. Think in particular about Jessica's state of mind as she says lines 14–20. Work together to discover a dramatically convincing way for her to leave the stage, concentrating on the exact impression you wish to create for an audience. Show the version you like best to other groups.

b In Scene 4, the four men plan to attend a masque (an entertainment with music, torches, dancing and elaborate masks). They must all wear disguises, as was the custom. The disguise might be a mask, a costume, or both. As co-directors, plan the kind of disguise you want each character to adopt in order to highlight a key aspect of their character. Draw your ideas.

c Join up with another pair and read quickly through Scene 4. Then plan and write director's notes for how you want this scene to be played. Remember that it is a scene of intrigue (阴谋诡计), deception and trickery – with Shylock as the ultimate victim!

THE MERCHANT OF VENICE ACT 2 SCENE 4
威尼斯商人

JESSICA	Farewell, good Lancelot.		
	Alack, what heinous¹ sin is it in me		15
	To be ashamed to be my father's child!		
	But though I am a daughter to his blood		
	I am not to his manners. O Lorenzo,		
	If thou keep promise, I shall end this strife²,		
	Become a Christian and thy loving wife.	*Exit*	20

Act 2 Scene 4
Venice

Enter GRATIANO, LORENZO, SALARINO, *and* SOLANIO

LORENZO   Nay, we will slink away in supper time,
               Disguise us at my lodging, and return
               All in an hour.
GRATIANO   We have not made good preparation.
SALARINO   We have not spoke us yet of torchbearers³.   5
SOLANIO   'Tis vile unless it may be quaintly ordered⁴,
               And better in my mind not undertook.
LORENZO   'Tis now but four of clock; we have two hours
               To furnish us.

Enter LANCELOT [*with a letter*]

               Friend Lancelot! What's the news?
LANCELOT   And it shall please you to break up⁵ this, it shall seem to   10
               signify⁶.
LORENZO   I know the hand⁷; in faith, 'tis a fair hand,
               And whiter than the paper it writ on
               Is the fair hand that writ.
GRATIANO   Love news, in faith!
LANCELOT   By your leave⁸, sir.   15
LORENZO   Whither⁹ goest thou?
LANCELOT   Marry, sir, to bid my old master the Jew to sup tonight
               with my new master the Christian.
LORENZO   Hold here, take this. Tell gentle Jessica
               I will not fail her; speak it privately.   20
                                                    Exit Lancelot

Lorenzo tells Gratiano that Jessica plans to disguise herself as a boy and flee from Shylock, taking some of his gold and jewels. Scene 5 begins with Shylock talking of his generosity to Lancelot.

剧情简介：劳仁佐告诉格拉奇阿诺，婕丝柯打算女扮男装，带上一些金银珠宝逃离夏洛克。第五场伊始，夏洛克大谈他对朗斯勒多么慷慨。

Characters 人物分析

Lorenzo – making an impact (in pairs)

a   Read Lorenzo's lines 29–39 aloud to each other. Then explain Jessica's plan to elope with Lorenzo and his reaction to it.

b   One person steps into role as Jessica, and tells in their own words the details of the elopement plan. After hearing that, the other person (as Lorenzo) gives his thoughts on the plan, including the attraction of the 'gold and jewels' that Jessica plans to take with her, and his attitude towards Shylock and his Jewish faith.

c   Lorenzo is going to play a significant part in bringing pain to Shylock but, prior to this scene, he has spoken only three lines in the entire play – and those were to acknowledge how Gratiano talks over him! What do you think are his main characteristics and how would you create a strong impression of Lorenzo in this, his first major scene? Write a paragraph outlining your ideas.

1   masque   化装舞会
2   some hour hence   大概一个小时之后
3   page   年轻男仆，侍童
4   foot   小路
5   under = with （用）
6   issue   孩子
7   faithless   缺乏基督教信仰的
8   of = between （比较）
9   gourmandise   贪吃
10 rend apparel out   糟蹋衣服
11 was wont to tell   经常告诉

▼ What does this photograph suggest about the relationship between Jessica and her father? Justify your comments with evidence from the script.

THE MERCHANT OF VENICE ACT 2 SCENE 5
威尼斯商人

	Go, gentlemen:	
	Will you prepare you for this masque¹ tonight?	
	I am provided of a torchbearer.	
SALARINO	Ay marry, I'll be gone about it straight.	
SOLANIO	And so will I.	
LORENZO	Meet me and Gratiano	25
	At Gratiano's lodging some hour hence².	
SALARINO	'Tis good we do so.	

Exeunt [Salarino and Solanio]

GRATIANO	Was not that letter from fair Jessica?	
LORENZO	I must needs tell thee all. She hath directed	
	How I shall take her from her father's house,	30
	What gold and jewels she is furnished with,	
	What page's³ suit she hath in readiness.	
	If e'er the Jew her father come to heaven,	
	It will be for his gentle daughter's sake;	
	And never dare misfortune cross her foot⁴,	35
	Unless she do it under⁵ this excuse	
	That she is issue⁶ to a faithless⁷ Jew.	
	Come, go with me; peruse this as thou goest.	
	Fair Jessica shall be my torchbearer.	

Exeunt

Act 2 Scene 5
Venice   Shylock's house

Enter SHYLOCK *and* LANCELOT

SHYLOCK	Well, thou shalt see, thy eyes shall be thy judge,	
	The difference of⁸ old Shylock and Bassanio –	
	What, Jessica! – Thou shalt not gourmandise⁹	
	As thou hast done with me – What, Jessica! –	
	And sleep, and snore, and rend apparel out¹⁰.	5
	Why, Jessica, I say!	
LANCELOT	Why, Jessica!	
SHYLOCK	Who bids thee call? I do not bid thee call.	
LANCELOT	Your worship was wont to tell¹¹ me I could do nothing without bidding.	

Shylock intends to dine with Bassanio, even though he is uneasy because of ominous dreams. He leaves Jessica to protect the house, warning her not to watch the masque. Lancelot tells her of Lorenzo's impending visit.

剧情简介：夏洛克虽因不祥之梦感到不安，但仍决定接受博萨纽的宴请。他嘱咐婕丝柯要看好家，并警告她不要去看化装舞会。朗斯勒告诉婕丝柯劳仁佐即将造访。

Characters 人物分析
Judging Shylock's attitude to the Christians (in threes, then by yourself)

This is an important scene featuring Shylock. It's the first time we see him in his home and with his daughter Jessica and his servant Lancelot. Shylock is reluctant to dine with Bassanio. He assumes that the Christians invite him only to 'flatter' him, and is nervous about leaving his house while the 'shallow foppery' of the masque goes on outside. Read the whole scene together, then try the following activities.

a One person reads Shylock's two speeches (lines 11–18 and 27–38). The other two echo any words that reflect Shylock's nervous excitement. Which words seem particularly important in creating his agitated mood?

b Shylock, mistrusting Bassanio, says he will go to dinner with him 'in hate, to feed upon / The prodigal Christian'. Talk about your response to Shylock's attitude at this point. Shylock also angrily describes how he expects the Christians to behave during the masque (lines 27–38). Suggest reasons why he is so opposed to such behaviour. Pick out other examples from these two speeches of Shylock's disapproval of the Christians' attitudes and practices.

c Is Shylock a spoilsport (扫兴之人)? Discuss whether you think Shakespeare is deliberately or unfairly trying to make the audience dislike him.

d In Shakespeare's time, Shylock's 'dream of money bags' represented a vision of loss, not profit. But it causes problems for a modern audience because it seems to define Shylock as a money-obsessed stereotype. Line 18 is often cut in modern productions. Would you cut it? Why, or why not? Write all your responses in your Character file.

1 bid forth 应邀到外边
2 wherefore = why
3 loath 不情愿
4 ill a-brewing 正在发酵的不幸
5 tonight 昨晚
6 reproach 责难（为approach [到来] 的误用）
7 conspired 商量
8 nose fell a-bleeding （鼻子摔流血是厄运的征兆）
9 Ash Wednesday 圣灰日（时间是复活节前七周）
10 vile squealing 尖利刺耳的声音
11 wry-necked fife 歪着脖子吹的横笛
12 casements 窗子
13 with varnished faces 花脸，面具
14 shallow foppery 空洞浅薄的废话
15 worth a Jewès eye （习惯表达法worth a Jew's eye [很有价值] 的戏语）
16 Hagar's offspring 夏甲的后裔（指以实玛利；夏甲为《旧约》中亚伯拉罕 [Abraham] 之妻撒拉 [Sarah] 的婢女，她与亚伯拉罕生有一子，名为以实玛利 [Ishmael]，后来母子二人同遭驱逐）

Write about it 写作练习
Lancelot's thoughts about Jessica

Lancelot dislikes Shylock intensely, yet is very close to Jessica. (He is trusted with all the details of her planned elopement with Lorenzo.)

• In role as Lancelot, write about your feelings for, and attitude to, Jessica in a series of short diary entries. What makes her different from her father? What do you think about her plans?

Enter JESSICA

JESSICA	Call you? What is your will?	10
SHYLOCK	I am bid forth[1] to supper, Jessica.	
	There are my keys. But wherefore[2] should I go?	
	I am not bid for love, they flatter me;	
	But yet I'll go in hate, to feed upon	
	The prodigal Christian. Jessica my girl,	15
	Look to my house. I am right loath[3] to go;	
	There is some ill a-brewing[4] towards my rest,	
	For I did dream of money bags tonight[5].	
LANCELOT	I beseech you, sir, go; my young master doth expect your reproach[6].	20
SHYLOCK	So do I his.	
LANCELOT	And they have conspired[7] together – I will not say you shall see a masque; but if you do, then it was not for nothing that my nose fell a-bleeding[8] on Black Monday last, at six a clock i'the morning, falling out that year on Ash Wednesday[9] was four year in th'afternoon.	25
SHYLOCK	What, are there masques? Hear you me, Jessica,	
	Lock up my doors, and when you hear the drum	
	And the vile squealing[10] of the wry-necked fife[11],	
	Clamber not you up to the casements[12] then	30
	Nor thrust your head into the public street	
	To gaze on Christian fools with varnished faces[13];	
	But stop my house's ears – I mean my casements –	
	Let not the sound of shallow foppery[14] enter	
	My sober house. By Jacob's staff I swear	35
	I have no mind of feasting forth tonight:	
	But I will go. Go you before me, sirrah;	
	Say I will come.	
LANCELOT	I will go before, sir.	
	[*Aside to Jessica*] Mistress, look out at window for all this:	
	There will come a Christian by	40
	Will be worth a Jewès eye[15]. [*Exit*]	
SHYLOCK	What says that fool of Hagar's offspring[16], ha?	
JESSICA	His words were 'Farewell, mistress', nothing else.	

Shylock is glad to be rid of Lancelot, whom he sees as a lazy wastrel. Jessica relishes the prospect of escaping from her father. In Scene 6, Gratiano and Salarino await Lorenzo: he is late.

剧情简介：夏洛克很高兴终于把朗斯勒当个懒惰的废物打发了。婕丝柯憧憬着摆脱父亲后的生活。第六场，格拉奇阿诺与萨勒瑞诺在等待姗姗来迟的劳仁佐。

1 Impressions of home life (in threes)

a Take parts as Shylock, Jessica and Lancelot and quickly read Scene 5 again. Jessica and Lancelot should then re-read Scene 3.

b Work together to produce a wall chart on which you record the various impressions created of Shylock, Jessica and Lancelot. Link each of your ideas to evidence from the script.

c On a separate sheet, gather all your impressions of Shylock's home and what it might be like to live with him. Remember to use quotations to support your investigations.

2 Jessica's farewell – gain or loss? (in small groups)

Jessica is going to leave her father and elope with Lorenzo.

a Work out a tableau to illustrate the final line of Scene 5.

b Talk together about what Jessica will gain and what she will lose from her elopement with Lorenzo. List your key points. What about Lorenzo? How far does he gain or lose from this plan? Again, make a list of the most important points.

3 Is the pleasure in the chase? (in small groups)

Like Salarino in lines 6–8, Gratiano (lines 9–20) talks of there being greater pleasure in the first anticipation of love than when it actually arrives. Notice how he gives different examples to illustrate this theme.

- Read Gratiano's speech, changing reader at each punctuation mark. As you read, stress all the words linked with physical enjoyment.
- Talk about the effect you have achieved. Do you agree with what Salarino and Gratiano are saying?
- What do you think of their attitude towards women?

---

1 patch 傻小子，蠢货
2 wildcat 夜猫子
3 Drones hive not 不干活儿的蜂休想生活
4 crossed 受阻
5 penthouse 屋顶房
6 make stand 等候
7 lovers … clock 恋人总是跑在时间的前面
8 O, ten … unforfeited! 是啊！维纳斯的鸽子飞去缔结新欢的盟约，比之履行旧日的诺言，总是要快上十倍！
9 ever holds 总是正确的
10 untread 折回
11 measures 步子
12 unbated 不减的
13 younger 年轻绅士
14 scarfèd 挂着旗帜
15 bark 帆船
16 strumpet 水性杨花，善变
17 overweathered ribs 饱受风浪的船身
18 Lean, rent, and beggared 瘦骨嶙峋，破烂不堪，穷困潦倒（昔日风光的航船被摧残得支离破碎）

SHYLOCK The patch[1] is kind enough, but a huge feeder,
Snail-slow in profit, and he sleeps by day   45
More than the wildcat[2]. Drones hive not[3] with me,
Therefore I part with him, and part with him
To one that I would have him help to waste
His borrowed purse. Well, Jessica, go in;
Perhaps I will return immediately.   50
Do as I bid you, shut doors after you.
Fast bind, fast find:
A proverb never stale in thrifty mind.   *Exit*

JESSICA Farewell, and if my fortune be not crossed[4],
I have a father, you a daughter, lost.   *Exit*   55

Act 2 Scene 6
Venice   Outside Shylock's house

Enter the masquers, GRATIANO *and* SALARINO

GRATIANO This is the penthouse[5] under which Lorenzo
Desired us to make stand[6].

SALARINO His hour is almost past.

GRATIANO And it is marvel he outdwells his hour,
For lovers ever run before the clock[7].   5

SALARINO O, ten times faster Venus' pigeons fly
To seal love's bonds new made than they are wont
To keep obligèd faith unforfeited![8]

GRATIANO That ever holds[9]: who riseth from a feast
With that keen appetite that he sits down?   10
Where is the horse that doth untread[10] again
His tedious measures[11] with the unbated[12] fire
That he did pace them first? All things that are
Are with more spirit chasèd than enjoyed.
How like a younger[13] or a prodigal   15
The scarfèd[14] bark[15] puts from her native bay,
Hugged and embracèd by the strumpet[16] wind!
How like the prodigal doth she return
With overweathered ribs[17] and ragged sails,
Lean, rent, and beggared[18] by the strumpet wind!   20

Lorenzo meets his friends outside Shylock's house. Jessica, although embarrassed by her disguise as a boy, is ready to elope with him, having already plundered her father's gold and jewels.

 剧情简介：劳仁佐与朋友在夏洛克宅前碰头。婕丝柯已乔装成男孩模样，虽有些难为情，但已卷好父亲的金银珠宝，做好了和爱人私奔的准备。

Write about it 写作练习

What has Lorenzo been up to?

'My affairs have made you wait.' Lorenzo's late arrival contradicts (反驳) all Gratiano has just said about lovers. Think about why Shakespeare makes Lorenzo late, and what he might have been doing while the others have been waiting.

- In role as Lorenzo, write a short story, or a brief soliloquy in modern English, in which you explain the delay. Just what are the 'affairs' that have held you up? (Bearing in mind what you have so far seen of Lorenzo, they may not be entirely innocent!)

Stagecraft 导演技巧

Barriers to love (in pairs)

Jessica, at an upstairs window in her father's house, talks to Lorenzo, who is in the street below.

a Take parts and read lines 27–51, but make sure that you are at some distance from each other, and if possible at different heights. You could also place some kind of barrier or obstacle between you. First, read the lines as tenderly and romantically as possible. Then try reading them to stress the physical awkwardness of the situation and the difficulties of communicating. Which version did you prefer?

b Use your experiments to help write guidance for two actors playing Jessica and Lorenzo, advising them on how to make this episode dramatically compelling. Then add notes to your Director's Journal.

1 Jessica: a woman in a man's world

a List all Jessica's comments about herself and her assumed disguise as a boy in lines 34–51. Alongside each, write what they tell you of her character and what they suggest about the role of women in Venice.

b Jessica declares her love for Lorenzo, but she also steals her own dowry (嫁妆) (line 34) and goes back to plunder even more of her father's wealth before she elopes (lines 50–1). Write a paragraph on what this suggests about Jessica and about Venetian values.

---

1 long abode 长时间的延迟
2 father （夏洛克是他未来的岳父，劳仁佐话里含有讽刺意味）
3 tongue 声音
4 exchange 变装
5 follies 傻事，蠢事
6 light 明显；轻浮
7 office of discovery 暴露的行为
8 garnish 衣装，服饰
9 close 漆黑；隐秘
10 doth play the runaway 很快就消逝
11 stayed for 等待
12 make fast 关好
13 gild 披金戴银
14 by my hood （表示强调的表达，没有实际意义）
15 gentle 有教养的（暗指Gentile [非犹太人]；剧中多处这种用法）

Enter LORENZO

SALARINO	Here comes Lorenzo; more of this hereafter.
LORENZO	Sweet friends, your patience for my long abode[1].
	Not I but my affairs have made you wait.
	When you shall please to play the thieves for wives,
	I'll watch as long for you then. Approach – 25
	Here dwells my father[2] Jew. Ho! Who's within?

[*Enter*] JESSICA *above*[, *in boy's clothes*]

JESSICA	Who are you? Tell me, for more certainty,
	Albeit I'll swear that I do know your tongue[3].
LORENZO	Lorenzo, and thy love.
JESSICA	Lorenzo certain, and my love indeed, 30
	For who love I so much? And now who knows
	But you, Lorenzo, whether I am yours?
LORENZO	Heaven and thy thoughts are witness that thou art.
JESSICA	Here, catch this casket, it is worth the pains.
	I am glad 'tis night, you do not look on me, 35
	For I am much ashamed of my exchange[4].
	But love is blind, and lovers cannot see
	The pretty follies[5] that themselves commit;
	For if they could, Cupid himself would blush
	To see me thus transformèd to a boy. 40
LORENZO	Descend, for you must be my torchbearer.
JESSICA	What, must I hold a candle to my shames?
	They in themselves, good sooth, are too too light[6].
	Why, 'tis an office of discovery[7], love,
	And I should be obscured.
LORENZO	So are you, sweet, 45
	Even in the lovely garnish[8] of a boy.
	But come at once,
	For the close[9] night doth play the runaway[10],
	And we are stayed for[11] at Bassanio's feast.
JESSICA	I will make fast[12] the doors, and gild[13] myself 50
	With some moe ducats, and be with you straight.

[*Exit Jessica above*]

GRATIANO	Now by my hood[14], a gentle[15] and no Jew!

Lorenzo talks of his love for Jessica, then elopes with her. Antonio informs Gratiano that Bassanio's ship is about to leave. In Scene 7, the Prince of Morocco considers which casket to choose.

剧情简介：劳仁佐向婕丝柯表明爱意，和她私奔了。安托纽通知格拉奇阿诺，说博萨纽的船就要启航了。第七场，摩洛哥亲王在考虑选择哪一个匣子。

Themes 主题分析

Appearance and reality – and dramatic irony (戏剧反讽)

This scene is full of deception and betrayal. Gratiano and Lorenzo applaud Jessica's treachery (背叛) against her father. Lorenzo's lines 53–8 seem honest in their admiration of his prospective wife but his words are full of **dramatic irony** (a deeper level of meaning than he may intend to convey). For example, his use of the word 'if' might suggest he still harbours (隐藏) some doubts about Jessica.

- Find all the examples you can in this scene of things not being what they seem. List them and explain why each appears false.

1	Beshrew me	我真该死（温和的诅咒）
2	is come about	转向
3	discover	揭示；展现
4	several	不同
5	inscription	铭文
6	deserves	应得

Stagecraft 导演技巧

The first casket scene (in small groups)

This is the first of the casket scenes and in it we see Morocco make his choice. The three caskets (gold, silver and lead) vary in size in productions, but are always dramatically striking and their disclosure is often performed with elaborate dignity and ceremony.

a Talk about how you think the opening three lines of Scene 7 should be staged. How do Morocco, Portia and all their attendants (their 'trains') enter? Should Portia and Morocco enter separately or together? Where do they position themselves to await the unveiling of the caskets?

b Act out the entrance and unveiling in several different ways. Choose the one you felt worked best to show to other groups.

LORENZO	Beshrew me[1] but I love her heartily.	
	For she is wise, if I can judge of her,	
	And fair she is, if that mine eyes be true,	55
	And true she is, as she hath proved herself:	
	And therefore like herself, wise, fair, and true,	
	Shall she be placèd in my constant soul.	

Enter JESSICA

What, art thou come? On, gentleman, away!
Our masquing mates by this time for us stay. 60

Exit [with Jessica]

Enter ANTONIO

ANTONIO	Who's there?
GRATIANO	Signor Antonio?
ANTONIO	Fie, fie, Gratiano, where are all the rest?
	'Tis nine a clock, our friends all stay for you.
	No masque tonight: the wind is come about[2], 65
	Bassanio presently will go aboard.
	I have sent twenty out to seek for you.
GRATIANO	I am glad on't; I desire no more delight
	Than to be under sail and gone tonight.

Exeunt

Act 2 Scene 7
Belmont   A room in Portia's house

Enter PORTIA *with the Prince of* MOROCCO *and both their trains*

PORTIA	Go, draw aside the curtains and discover[3]	
	The several[4] caskets to this noble prince.	
	Now make your choice.	
MOROCCO	This first of gold, who this inscription[5] bears,	
	'Who chooseth me, shall gain what many men desire.'	5
	The second silver, which this promise carries,	
	'Who chooseth me, shall get as much as he deserves[6].'	
	This third dull lead, with warning all as blunt,	
	'Who chooseth me, must give and hazard all he hath.'	
	How shall I know if I do choose the right?	10

Portia reminds Morocco that he can win her hand by choosing the correct casket. Morocco deliberates over the three choices: lead, silver and gold.

剧情简介：鲍霞提醒摩洛哥亲王，如果他选对了匣子就能得到她。摩洛哥亲王仔细琢磨三个选项：铅匣子、银匣子和金匣子。

Write about it 写作练习

Portia: saying very little, thinking very deeply?

Portia's first two speeches (lines 1–3 and lines 11–12) are simple and direct, recognising the formality of the situation. She speaks in basic commands ('draw', 'discover', 'make') and her words reveal little of her feelings. But surely she must recognise the enormity (严重性) of the situation when she says to Morocco: 'If you choose that [the casket with my picture inside], then I am yours'?

- Imagine that Portia could voice her private thoughts (an interior monologue) at line 3 and again at line 12. Write exactly what's in her mind as if it were delivered as an aside to the audience.

Language in the play 剧中语言

Morocco: full of self-importance? (in small groups)

Morocco delivers a long and swaggering speech as he deliberates on his choice of casket. Many productions present him as full of bombast (浮夸言辞) and arrogance, but occasionally he can be portrayed as more noble and dignified. How do you think he should appear?

- First, try a group reading of Morocco's lines 13–60. Each person reads as far as a punctuation mark, then hands on.
- Read the speech again, echoing all the references that Morocco makes to himself. Each time he makes such a reference, the reader should point theatrically at himself. What kind of dramatic effects does this create?
- Work through the speech again and write down any words and phrases Morocco uses that you think are examples of **hyperbole** (夸张) (exaggerated, extravagant or over-the-top). Look particularly at lines 39–48, in which he talks about the extremes to which men go to woo Portia.
- After identifying your language extracts, write them down as a spider diagram and explain how they are used. For example, Morocco describes Portia in line 40 as 'this mortal breathing saint' and the sea as 'The watery kingdom' in line 44.
- What do your chosen snippets (片段) of language suggest about Morocco and his attitude to Portia? Write a paragraph answering this question.

1 withal 也
2 survey 细看
3 golden 尊贵
4 stoops 屈尊
5 dross 无用之物
6 even 公正
7 be'st rated = should be rated （假如被评价）
8 estimation 价值
9 disabling 贬值
10 strayed 漂泊；徘徊
11 graved 雕刻
12 mortal breathing 活着的
13 Hyrcanian deserts 赫肯涅沙漠（位于亚洲的里海 [the Caspian Sea] 之南）
14 throughfares 通衢大道
15 watery kingdom 大海
16 spirits 有勇气的人

The Merchant of Venice Act 2 Scene 7
威尼斯商人

PORTIA The one of them contains my picture, prince.
If you choose that, then I am yours withal[1].

MOROCCO Some god direct my judgement! Let me see:
I will survey[2] th'inscriptions back again.
What says this leaden casket? 15
'Who chooseth me, must give and hazard all he hath.'
Must give – for what? For lead? Hazard for lead!
This casket threatens: men that hazard all
Do it in hope of fair advantages.
A golden[3] mind stoops[4] not to shows of dross[5]; 20
I'll then nor give nor hazard aught for lead.
What says the silver with her virgin hue?
'Who chooseth me, shall get as much as he deserves.'
As much as he deserves – pause there, Morocco,
And weigh thy value with an even[6] hand. 25
If thou be'st rated[7] by thy estimation[8]
Thou dost deserve enough; and yet enough
May not extend so far as to the lady;
And yet to be afeared of my deserving
Were but a weak disabling[9] of myself. 30
As much as I deserve: why, that's the lady.
I do in birth deserve her, and in fortunes,
In graces, and in qualities of breeding:
But more than these, in love I do deserve.
What if I strayed[10] no farther, but chose here? 35
Let's see once more this saying graved[11] in gold:
'Who chooseth me, shall gain what many men desire.'
Why, that's the lady; all the world desires her.
From the four corners of the earth they come
To kiss this shrine, this mortal breathing[12] saint. 40
The Hyrcanian deserts[13] and the vasty wilds
Of wide Arabia are as throughfares[14] now
For princes to come view fair Portia.
The watery kingdom[15], whose ambitious head
Spits in the face of heaven, is no bar 45
To stop the foreign spirits[16], but they come
As o'er a brook to see fair Portia.
One of these three contains her heavenly picture.

> **剧情简介**：摩洛哥亲王决定打开金匣子，希望从中看到鲍霞的肖像。然而，他看到的是一个骷髅头和一张令他沮丧的纸条。摩洛哥亲王告辞回国，鲍霞放心了。

1 What's inside the casket? (in pairs)

After all his confident declamations (激昂的演说) about why he must choose the gold casket, Morocco opens it to find a human skull inside. He removes a scroll, with a message on it, from inside one of the eye sockets (窝，洞). But why a skull?

a Discuss the possible reasons why Shakespeare chose to include this detail. Share your favourite reason with the rest of the class.

b Make a drawing of the casket's contents.

1	like	很可能
2	rib	装进
3	cerecloth	裹尸布
4	òbscure	黑暗
5	immured	禁闭，封闭
6	tried	纯化
7	insculped	刻印
8	thrive	繁荣
9	form	肖像，相片
10	carrion death	骷髅
11	scroll	纸卷
12	glisters = glitters	(闪闪发光)
13	old	有经验
14	inscrolled	写下
15	tedious	冗长
16	riddance	摆脱；打发

Themes 主题分析

Appearance and reality (by yourself)

'All that glisters is not gold'. Line 65 is one of the best-known lines in the play, and is often used as a proverb today.

a Try writing a poem or a short story with this line as the title.

b Was it inevitable that Morocco would choose the gold casket? Give reasons for your answer.

Language in the play 剧中语言

'Let all of his complexion choose me so' (in small groups)

Portia's final line could well offend an audience, as it clearly refers to the colour of Morocco's skin and appears to be racist. If you were directing the play, would you include it or leave it out?

• Discuss this issue, then give reasons for your choice, and say what the line adds to your impression of Portia. Add notes to your Director's Journal.

THE MERCHANT OF VENICE ACT 2 SCENE 7
威尼斯商人

Is't like[1] that lead contains her? 'Twere damnation
To think so base a thought; it were too gross 50
To rib[2] her cerecloth[3] in the òbscure[4] grave.
Or shall I think in silver she's immured[5],
Being ten times undervalued to tried[6] gold?
O sinful thought! Never so rich a gem
Was set in worse than gold. They have in England 55
A coin that bears the figure of an angel
Stampèd in gold; but that's insculped[7] upon:
But here an angel in a golden bed
Lies all within. Deliver me the key:
Here do I choose, and thrive[8] I as I may. 60

PORTIA There take it, prince, and if my form[9] lie there,
Then I am yours.
                    [*Morocco unlocks the gold casket*]

MOROCCO   O hell! What have we here?
A carrion death[10], within whose empty eye
There is a written scroll[11]. I'll read the writing.
     'All that glisters[12] is not gold; 65
     Often have you heard that told.
     Many a man his life hath sold
     But my outside to behold.
     Gilded tombs do worms infold.
     Had you been as wise as bold, 70
     Young in limbs, in judgement old[13],
     Your answer had not been inscrolled[14].
     Fare you well, your suit is cold.'
Cold indeed, and labour lost;
Then farewell heat, and welcome frost. 75
Portia, adieu; I have too grieved a heart
To take a tedious[15] leave: thus losers part.
                    Exit [*Morocco with his train*]

PORTIA A gentle riddance[16]! Draw the curtains, go.
Let all of his complexion choose me so.
                    Exeunt [*A flourish of cornets*]

61

Bassanio and Gratiano have sailed for Belmont. Jessica, having taken money and jewels, has eloped with Lorenzo. Solanio tells of Shylock's intense anguish at his loss, and suggests that he will seek revenge.

剧情简介：博萨纽和格拉奇阿诺乘船前往贝尔蒙。婕丝柯拿走了家里的金银珠宝，与劳仁佐私奔了。塞拉纽说夏洛克为自己的损失叫苦不迭，定会寻求机会报复。

Write about it 写作练习
Considering structure

The previous scene ended with a loser, and Shakespeare now includes a scene that dramatises reports of two other losers. Salarino and Solanio tell of Shylock's grief at the loss of his daughter, hint at a lost ship, then describe Antonio's sadness at parting from Bassanio.

- Read quickly through Scene 8, then write a few paragraphs about how Salarino and Solanio's dramatic news is used to increase the tension and the pace as we near the end of Act 2.

1 Shylock visits the Duke (in pairs)

Shylock wakes the Duke of Venice to complain about the loss of his daughter and his possessions. He seeks help and support from the laws of Venice. Shylock manages to persuade the Duke to go with him, intending to search Bassanio's ship. Think about why Shylock is aggrieved and his state of mind. How might the Duke (a Christian) receive him? Notice that Solanio, like Lancelot earlier in the act, will not name Shylock and uses insulting, racist language. Do you think the Duke would endorse (认可，赞同) and echo this kind of casual racism or would he be fair-minded?

- Script the meeting between Shylock and the Duke, take parts and record it. Then play it back to other pairs for comment and evaluation.

2 Sympathy for Shylock? (in groups of five or six)

a Solanio and Salarino report what has happened to Shylock (lines 12–24). One student volunteers to be Shylock, and uses as many of his own words as possible. The others follow Shylock round the room, mocking him by ridiculing his words and actions.

b Film this episode, then follow up by interviewing Shylock, in role. The other group members should ask Shylock about his behaviour and his feelings. For example, neither Salarino nor Solanio has any sympathy for Shylock. Solanio does not mention his name but instead calls him 'The villain Jew' and 'the dog Jew'. They mock his response to his losses. How does Shylock feel about them?

c You could then edit and play back your film as a news report for Venice TV. Remember to make your feature objective and unbiased.

1 raised 吵醒
2 gondola 贡多拉（威尼斯特有的一种狭长尖头平底船）
3 amorous 情意绵绵
4 certified 证明
5 passion 情感的爆发
6 confused 混杂
7 Justice 正义，公理
8 stones （他们可能在说夏洛克的宝石，或在开一个粗鲁的玩笑 [俚语中stones指睾丸]；莎士比亚可能有意表达这层冒犯的意思）
9 keep his day 履行合约
10 reasoned 闲谈
11 Narrow Seas 英吉利海峡
12 part 分离
13 miscarrièd 失事
14 fraught 满载

Act 2 Scene 8
Venice

Enter SALARINO *and* SOLANIO

SALARINO	Why, man, I saw Bassanio under sail,	
	With him is Gratiano gone along;	
	And in their ship I am sure Lorenzo is not.	
SOLANIO	The villain Jew with outcries raised[1] the Duke,	
	Who went with him to search Bassanio's ship.	5
SALARINO	He came too late, the ship was under sail.	
	But there the Duke was given to understand	
	That in a gondola[2] were seen together	
	Lorenzo and his amorous[3] Jessica.	
	Besides, Antonio certified[4] the Duke	10
	They were not with Bassanio in his ship.	
SOLANIO	I never heard a passion[5] so confused[6],	
	So strange, outrageous, and so variable,	
	As the dog Jew did utter in the streets:	
	'My daughter! O my ducats! O my daughter!	15
	Fled with a Christian! O my Christian ducats!	
	Justice[7]! The law! My ducats and my daughter!	
	A sealèd bag, two sealèd bags of ducats,	
	Of double ducats, stolen from me by my daughter!	
	And jewels – two stones[8], two rich and precious stones,	20
	Stolen by my daughter! Justice! Find the girl!	
	She hath the stones upon her and the ducats!'	
SALARINO	Why, all the boys in Venice follow him,	
	Crying his stones, his daughter, and his ducats.	
SOLANIO	Let good Antonio look he keep his day[9],	25
	Or he shall pay for this.	
SALARINO	Marry, well remembered:	
	I reasoned[10] with a Frenchman yesterday	
	Who told me, in the Narrow Seas[11] that part[12]	
	The French and English, there miscarrièd[13]	30
	A vessel of our country richly fraught[14].	

Salarino hopes that the shipwrecked galleon was not one of Antonio's. He describes the selfless and loving friendship Antonio has for Bassanio. Scene 9 prepares for the Prince of Arragon's choice of casket.

剧情简介：萨勒瑞诺希望遭遇海难的商船不是安托纽的。他描述了安托纽对博萨纽无私和忠诚的友情。第九场，阿若岗亲王准备挑选匣子。

Write about it 写作练习
The 'amorous Jessica'

In a scene of reported action (rather than action that happens on stage), we learn from Salarino that Jessica and Lorenzo are not aboard Bassanio's ship on its way to Belmont. Instead, Lorenzo and 'his amorous Jessica' have been spied 'in a gondola'. Note that Salarino is implying that Jessica *belongs* to his male Christian friend.

Jessica has made some monumental (重大) decisions and there is no going back. Shylock knows (line 16) that she has 'fled with a Christian' and that she has taken with her bags of his gold coins and precious jewels.

- Imagine that Jessica writes her thoughts in her diary, as Lorenzo pilots the gondola through the Venetian canals. Salarino clearly thinks she's full of feelings of love and desire ('amorous') and such thoughts might dominate her mind. But she might also reflect on the enormity and the consequences of her actions.

1 **'I saw Bassanio and Antonio part'** (in threes)

As one person reads lines 37–50, the other two enact the parting of Bassanio and Antonio, showing all the details described. Can you work out different ways of presenting line 48?

Characters 人物分析
Shylock versus Antonio

Scene 8 gives a dramatic impression of the differences between Shylock and Antonio, especially in terms of how they handle the 'loss' of what is dear to them.

- Head up two columns 'Shylock' and 'Antonio', and produce a list of all the contrasting details you can find. Include as much of Shakespeare's language as possible.
- Review your list in the light of the fact that all the information comes from two Christians who are friends of Antonio and detest Shylock. How does that affect your interpretation of the differences between Shylock and Antonio? Give evidence from the script.

1 grieve 使难过
2 make … return 尽快回来
3 Slubber 匆忙处理
4 the very … time 时机完全成熟
5 employ 投入
6 ostents 展示
7 conveniently become you 适合您
8 affection wondrous sensible 非常强烈的感情
9 wrung 紧握
10 he … him 他完全为了他 [博萨纽] 而活
11 quicken 宽解
12 embracèd heaviness 内心的悲伤
13 tane = taken
14 election 选择

	I thought upon Antonio when he told me,
	And wished in silence that it were not his.
SOLANIO	You were best to tell Antonio what you hear.
	Yet do not suddenly, for it may grieve[1] him.
SALARINO	A kinder gentleman treads not the earth.
	I saw Bassanio and Antonio part:
	Bassanio told him he would make some speed
	Of his return[2]: he answered, 'Do not so.
	Slubber[3] not business for my sake, Bassanio,
	But stay the very riping of the time[4];
	And for the Jew's bond which he hath of me,
	Let it not enter in your mind of love.
	Be merry, and employ[5] your chiefest thoughts
	To courtship, and such fair ostents[6] of love
	As shall conveniently become you[7] there.'
	And even there, his eye being big with tears,
	Turning his face, he put his hand behind him,
	And with affection wondrous sensible[8]
	He wrung[9] Bassanio's hand, and so they parted.
SOLANIO	I think he only loves the world for him[10].
	I pray thee let us go and find him out
	And quicken[11] his embracèd heaviness[12]
	With some delight or other.
SALARINO	Do we so.

Exeunt

Act 2 Scene 9
Belmont   A room in Portia's house

Enter NERISSA *and a Servitor*

NERISSA	Quick, quick, I pray thee, draw the curtain straight.
	The Prince of Arragon hath tane[13] his oath,
	And comes to his election[14] presently.

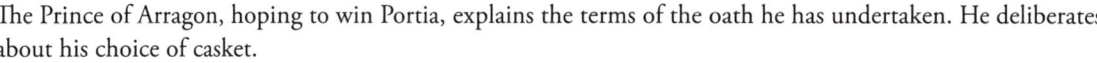

The Prince of Arragon, hoping to win Portia, explains the terms of the oath he has undertaken. He deliberates about his choice of casket.

剧情简介：阿若岗亲王希望赢得鲍霞的芳心，解释了发誓遵守的三项条件，然后盘算选哪个匣子。

Stagecraft 导演技巧

Portia: here we go again (in small groups)

Morocco's choosing of the caskets was prefaced by a grand entrance of the prince and his followers (Act 2 Scene 1), which was matched by Portia and her train. Now she enters alone, even though Arragon is also accompanied by a procession of his companions.

- Consider how you would stage Portia's entrance in this scene and write up your ideas.
- Add a paragraph comparing the dramatic effect created at the start of this scene with that in Act 2 Scene 1. Do you think, for example, that Shakespeare is suggesting that Portia is becoming increasingly bored by the procession of suitors?

1	that wherein I am contained 装有我肖像的那个
2	nuptial rites 结婚仪式
3	solemnised 隆重举行
4	enjoined 宣誓
5	unfold 透露
6	injunctions 条件
7	worthless 卑微
8	addressed 准备
9	fool multitude 许多愚蠢的人
10	fond 愚妄
11	pries not to th'interior 不去窥察内部
12	the martlet 燕子
13	in the weather 暴露在风雨中
14	force and road of casualty 毁灭的威力和通往不幸的道路
15	jump 与……同流
16	rank 把……归类
17	cozen 欺骗
18	stamp of merit 优点的徽章
19	presume 擅自

1 What are the women thinking? (in pairs)

a Take it in turns to read aloud Arragon's long speech in lines 18–51, pausing at the end of each sentence. As one person reads, the other acts Portia's reaction to each sentence. Use these questions to help you:
- Does Portia already know in which casket her portrait is locked?
- How does she feel about the prospect of being married to Arragon?

b Nerissa is silent after the first three lines of the scene, but she observes all that goes on, and she knows Portia intimately (密切). Together, write her developing thoughts as the choosing ceremony unfolds.

Write about it 写作练习

Newspaper report: draft, edit, final version (in pairs)

- You are a news reporter with the *Belmont Gazette*. You have been instructed by your editor to cover Arragon's public courtship (求爱) of Portia. You have a maximum of 200 words plus headline space. Summarise the main points made by Arragon in lines 18–51 as he considers which casket to choose. Comment on your impressions of him as a potential husband to Portia, the mistress of Belmont. Remain as true as you can to his actual words.
- Swap your draft with your partner's for comment and sub-editing. Then rewrite your final version.

[A flourish of cornets.] Enter [the Prince of] ARRAGON, his train, and PORTIA

PORTIA Behold, there stand the caskets, noble prince.
If you choose that wherein I am contained¹,
Straight shall our nuptial rites² be solemnised³;
But if you fail, without more speech, my lord,
You must be gone from hence immediately.

ARRAGON I am enjoined⁴ by oath to observe three things:
First, never to unfold⁵ to anyone
Which casket 'twas I chose; next, if I fail
Of the right casket, never in my life
To woo a maid in way of marriage; lastly,
If I do fail in fortune of my choice,
Immediately to leave you and be gone.

PORTIA To these injunctions⁶ everyone doth swear
That comes to hazard for my worthless⁷ self.

ARRAGON And so have I addressed⁸ me. Fortune now
To my heart's hope! Gold, silver, and base lead.
'Who chooseth me, must give and hazard all he hath.'
You shall look fairer ere I give or hazard.
What says the golden chest? Ha, let me see:
'Who chooseth me, shall gain what many men desire.'
What many men desire: that 'many' may be meant
By the fool multitude⁹ that choose by show,
Not learning more than the fond¹⁰ eye doth teach,
Which pries not to th'interior¹¹, but like the martlet¹²
Builds in the weather¹³ on the outward wall,
Even in the force and road of casualty¹⁴.
I will not choose what many men desire,
Because I will not jump¹⁵ with common spirits,
And rank¹⁶ me with the barbarous multitudes.
Why then, to thee, thou silver treasure house:
Tell me once more what title thou dost bear.
'Who chooseth me, shall get as much as he deserves.'
And well said too, for who shall go about
To cozen¹⁷ Fortune and be honourable
Without the stamp of merit¹⁸? Let none presume¹⁹
To wear an undeservèd dignity.

Arragon, guided by what he feels he deserves, chooses the silver casket. He finds the portrait of a 'blinking idiot' instead of Portia's picture. Disappointed, he takes his leave.

 剧情简介：阿若岗亲王认为银匣子与他相称，于是选择了银匣子。他在匣子里看到的是"眨眼睛的傻瓜"的画像，而不是鲍霞的肖像。失望之下他只好离去。

1 'Too long a pause' (in pairs)

- Read line 52 to each other in as many different ways as possible to convey Portia's thoughts and feelings.
- Make a note of what might be going through her mind. For example, does she already know that the silver casket is not the winning one?
- Decide which of your spoken versions is the most appropriate and effective, and show it to the class.

1 estates, degrees, and offices 地位、阶级和官职
2 purchased 赢得
3 cover 戴帽（显贵的标志）
4 that stand bare 脱下帽子，光着脑袋侍立一旁
5 gleaned 剔除；抛光上色
6 varnished 修饰
7 desert 权利
8 blinking 眯着眼
9 schedule 字条
10 distinct offices 不同的职能部门（完全不是一回事）
11 amiss 错误地
12 shadow's 幻觉里
13 iwis 无疑
14 I ... head 您将永远是个傻瓜
15 you are sped 您没戏了；您速速离开
16 linger 逗留
17 wroth 愤怒和悲伤

▼ Nerissa (left) and Portia (back) look on as Arragon opens the silver casket. What do their expressions suggest about Arragon's choice of the wrong casket?

Characters 人物分析

Arragon – just deserts (应得的报应)?

Arragon, for all his pretentious (自命不凡) self-importance, admits that he will go away not with one 'fool's head' but two, and that he will 'Patiently' bear his punishment. Does this redeem him in your eyes?

- Look carefully at the way he speaks in his 'choosing' speech and at how he is presented in the picture above. Then write a paragraph on what you think of him, and how he compares with Morocco (who is pictured with the gold casket in a photograph from the same production on p. 60).

O, that estates, degrees, and offices[1]   40
Were not derived corruptly, and that clear honour
Were purchased[2] by the merit of the wearer!
How many then should cover[3] that stand bare[4]!
How many be commanded that command!
How much low peasantry would then be gleaned[5]   45
From the true seed of honour, and how much honour
Picked from the chaff and ruin of the times
To be new varnished[6]! Well, but to my choice.
'Who chooseth me, shall get as much as he deserves.'
I will assume desert[7]. Give me a key for this,   50
And instantly unlock my fortunes here.

[Arragon unlocks the silver casket]

PORTIA   Too long a pause for that which you find there.
ARRAGON   What's here? The portrait of a blinking[8] idiot
          Presenting me a schedule[9]! I will read it.
          How much unlike art thou to Portia!   55
          How much unlike my hopes and my deservings.
          'Who chooseth me, shall have as much as he deserves.'
          Did I deserve no more than a fool's head?
          Is that my prize? Are my deserts no better?

PORTIA   To offend and judge are distinct offices[10],   60
          And of opposèd natures.

ARRAGON   What is here?

[He reads]

          'The fire seven times tried this;
          Seven times tried that judgement is
          That did never choose amiss[11].
          Some there be that shadows kiss;   65
          Such have but a shadow's[12] bliss.
          There be fools alive iwis[13]
          Silvered o'er, and so was this.
          Take what wife you will to bed,
          I will ever be your head[14].   70
          So be gone, you are sped[15].'
          Still more fool I shall appear
          By the time I linger[16] here.
          With one fool's head I came to woo,
          But I go away with two.   75
          Sweet, adieu; I'll keep my oath,
          Patiently to bear my wroth[17].

                    [Exit Arragon with his train]

Portia is relieved that Arragon has chosen wrongly. A Messenger informs her that a new suitor has arrived from Venice. Nerissa, for Portia's sake, hopes that it is Bassanio.

 剧情简介： 阿若岗亲王没有选对匣子，鲍霞松了一口气。信差报告一位从威尼斯来的求婚者已经抵达。讷瑞莎心里为鲍霞着想，希望来者是博萨纽。

Characters 人物分析

Another jibe (嘲讽) from Portia (in pairs)

Once more, when her suitor has left, Portia expresses her true feelings. She mocks Arragon as an insect (line 78) and perhaps arrogantly suggests that she is the 'candle' that 'singed' (scorched) him. Furthermore, she claims that Arragon is just another of the 'fools' who resort to excessive reasoning in pursuit of the answer to the casket riddle.

- Talk about what this adds to your impressions of Portia, then make notes in the Character file you are keeping on her.

1 News of Bassanio – a delayed ending (in pairs)

The scene could have ended with Nerissa drawing the curtain across the caskets, but it doesn't. Instead, a Messenger tells of the arrival of another lord wishing to seek Portia's hand in marriage. It seems this lord may be Bassanio.

a Talk together about the reasons why this 'delayed ending' is dramatically effective, and choose your most interesting idea to pool with other students' responses.

b One person reads the Messenger's lines 85–94. The other echoes all the words that create a promising and positive picture of the new arrival. Copy out all the positive and complimentary terms associated with Bassanio. Then alongside, in two different colours, write the words Portia has used when judging Morocco and Arragon.

c The Messenger tells of gifts ('sensible regreets', line 88) for Portia on behalf of a Venetian lord. Nerissa and Portia both hope that it is Bassanio about to arrive at Belmont. What would be appropriate gifts for him to offer? Your ideas should reflect the characters of Bassanio and Portia, as well as the type of society depicted in the play. Remember that you were asked to compile a list of items for Bassanio's voyage on page 42.

2 Finale (最后一场) to Act 2

Use the final two lines of Act 2 to create a tableau that you think provides a suitable ending to the act and also highlights Portia and Nerissa's surging excitement.

1 singed 烧焦
2 deliberate 理智；深思熟虑
3 They … lose 他们自作聪明误了前程
4 alighted 到达
5 signify 通报
6 sensible regreets 摸得着的问候（即礼物）
7 To wit 那就是说
8 commends 赞美
9 breath 话语
10 likely 有前途
11 ambassador 使者
12 costly 华丽，辉煌
13 forespurrer 前驱，先行者
14 kin 亲属
15 highday wit 一大套好话
16 post 信使
17 so mannerly 风度翩翩

THE MERCHANT OF VENICE ACT 2 SCENE 9
威尼斯商人

| PORTIA | Thus hath the candle singed[1] the moth. |
| | O, these deliberate[2] fools! When they do choose |
| | They have the wisdom by their wit to lose[3]. | 80
NERISSA	The ancient saying is no heresy:
	'Hanging and wiving goes by destiny.'
PORTIA	Come draw the curtain, Nerissa.

Enter a MESSENGER

| MESSENGER | Where is my lady? |
| PORTIA | Here. What would my lord? |
| MESSENGER | Madam, there is alighted[4] at your gate | 85
	A young Venetian, one that comes before
	To signify[5] th'approaching of his lord,
	From whom he bringeth sensible regreets[6]:
	To wit[7], besides commends[8] and courteous breath[9],
	Gifts of rich value. Yet I have not seen	90
	So likely[10] an ambassador[11] of love.
	A day in April never came so sweet
	To show how costly[12] summer was at hand
	As this forespurrer[13] comes before his lord.
PORTIA	No more I pray thee, I am half afeared	95
	Thou wilt say anon he is some kin[14] to thee,
	Thou spend'st such highday wit[15] in praising him.
	Come, come, Nerissa, for I long to see
	Quick Cupid's post[16] that comes so mannerly[17].
NERISSA	Bassanio, Lord Love, if thy will it be!	100

Exeunt

THE MERCHANT OF VENICE
威尼斯商人

Looking back at Act 2 第2幕回顾
Activities for groups or individuals

1 Appearances can be deceptive

Act 2 is full of instances when the truth is either hidden or disguised.

- Use the 'Themes' boxes that discuss appearance versus reality on pages 44, 56 and 60 as a starting point for identifying as many examples as you can where appearance does not match reality (there are at least ten).
- When you have compiled your list, use it to write an essay entitled 'How the theme of appearance versus reality is dramatised in Act 2'.

2 Love and hate

Shakespeare uses much of Act 2 to highlight the conflicts of love and hate. Love is clearly a major theme of the play, but it manifests itself in different ways. Hate is more overt – specifically in terms of Portia's racism and the anti-Semitic (反犹太人) treatment of Shylock.

- For each of the nine scenes in this act, find evidence of how you think it explores 'love' or 'hate' (or both). Display your findings visually as a poster to put up on the wall of your classroom.

3 Fathers and daughters

Conflict between fathers and daughters occurs in many of Shakespeare's plays. *The Merchant of Venice* is no exception. In Act 2, both Portia and Jessica try to come to terms with the demands made on them by their fathers (see the photographs of Shylock and Jessica opposite).

- Explore this father–daughter conflict through a modern medium. Imagine you are producing a daytime TV chat show on fathers and daughters. Interview Portia and Jessica as your special guests. You will need three people to do this; the rest of the class can be the studio audience. Encourage them to ask questions, too!

4 Design the caskets

Shakespeare never tells us what the caskets are actually like. He leaves it to our imagination. In one production, they were over six feet tall!

- Draw or make your own version of the gold, silver and lead caskets. Think carefully about their shape, size and design. On pages vii, 60, 86 and 88 are examples of caskets used in various productions of the play.

5 Restructuring the play

In many productions, Act 2 Scene 1 and Act 2 Scene 7 are put together and played as one continuous scene.

- What do you think are the dramatic advantages and disadvantages of playing the Morocco scenes in this way? Discuss this in pairs.

6 An extra scene

Shylock appears in only five scenes, but some directors give him a sixth, which is not in the original script. This is a scene where Shylock returns from supper with the Christians to find that his daughter has deserted him and taken his valuables.

- In small groups, talk about the advantages of adding such a scene, then have a go at writing this extra scene for yourselves. Make sure you give Shylock some lines to speak (a soliloquy?) and add an extra challenge by writing in Shakespeare's style.

7 Salarino and Solanio

These two minor characters tend to be indistinguishable (不易分辨) in productions. (With their other friend Salerio, they are sometimes known as 'the three salads' by professionals!)

- Think about ways to highlight each character's individuality. Review what each of them says and does in Act 2, and look for ways in which you might develop them as distinct personalities. Add your ideas to your Director's Journal.

73

Solanio and Salarino talk of the rumours sweeping the Rialto about Antonio's ship wrecked on the Goodwin Sands. They taunt Shylock about Jessica's elopement. He suspects that they were part of the conspiracy.

 剧情简介：塞拉纽和萨勒瑞诺谈论交易所风传的谣言，据说安托纽的商船在古德温浅滩失事。他们拿婕丝柯私奔的事嘲讽夏洛克。夏洛克怀疑他们也是合谋害他的人。

1 Dramatic structure (in pairs)

Act 3 begins in a relatively low-key manner, with Solanio and Salarino reporting more 'news' (just as they did in Act 2 Scene 8).

- Read what they have to say between lines 1 and 16, then suggest three possible reasons why Shakespeare opens the act in this way. Pick your best reason to share with your classmates.

Stagecraft 导演技巧
Shylock's entrance (in pairs)

a In one production of the play, Shylock entered with Jessica's discarded dress in his arms. Talk about the effect this might have on the audience.

b Think up your own ideas for Shylock's entrance to give the audience an understanding of how he feels about Jessica's betrayal. How does he move? What about his facial expressions and physical appearance? What other meaningful object could he carry on stage? Talk through your ideas for making Shylock's entrance dramatically powerful. On page 113, you will see how two productions showed the impact of his losses on Shylock.

Language in the play 剧中语言
Names and other insults (in threes)

Solanio (lines 10–11) gives a warm and glowing tribute (颂词) to 'the good Antonio, the honest Antonio'. On the other hand, Shylock (lines 17–18) is 'the devil … in the likeness of a Jew'.

a First look back together to Activity 2 on page 62; then share your thoughts about why you think Shakespeare denies Shylock his name again in the opening to this scene.

b Take parts and act out lines 19–30. Try alternatives (for example, with Shylock angry, then hurt, then accusing). Experiment with different tones and attitudes for the two Christians before settling on the version you think is most dramatically powerful.

c Freeze your acted out episode at line 30, showing exactly how Shylock is expressing his anguish at the loss of his daughter and how the Christians are reacting to him. Ask another group to comment on the power of your frozen moment.

---

1 **it lives there unchecked** 不断有传闻说
2 **of rich lading** 载有贵重货物
3 **wrecked** 遇险了
4 **flat** 浅滩；沙洲
5 **carcases** 残骸
6 **knapped ginger** 大吃生姜（伊丽莎白时代的戏剧常提及老人吃姜，或许当时人们以为姜能活血，助消化）
7 **slips of prolixity** 啰唆，长篇大论
8 **crossing … talk** 太多细枝末节的闲话
9 **O … company!** 我希望我的名声和他的一样好！
10 **Come, the full stop** 好了，就此打住
11 **betimes** 及早
12 **cross** 搅了，糟蹋
13 **wings** （指婕丝柯的伪装）
14 **fledged** 羽翼丰满（注意他是怎样继续开玩笑说婕丝柯从她父亲那儿"飞走"的）
15 **complexion** 天性
16 **dam** 母鸟
17 **old carrion** 老不死的

Act 3 Scene 1
Venice   A public place

Enter SOLANIO *and* SALARINO

SOLANIO   Now, what news on the Rialto?

SALARINO   Why, yet it lives there unchecked[1] that Antonio hath a ship of rich lading[2] wrecked[3] on the Narrow Seas; the Goodwins I think they call the place – a very dangerous flat[4], and fatal, where the carcases[5] of many a tall ship lie buried, as they say, if my gossip Report be an honest woman of her word.

SOLANIO   I would she were as lying a gossip in that as ever knapped ginger[6] or made her neighbours believe she wept for the death of a third husband. But it is true, without any slips of prolixity[7], or crossing the plain highway of talk[8], that the good Antonio, the honest Antonio – O that I had a title good enough to keep his name company![9] –

SALARINO   Come, the full stop[10].

SOLANIO   Ha, what sayest thou? Why, the end is, he hath lost a ship.

SALARINO   I would it might prove the end of his losses.

SOLANIO   Let me say 'amen' betimes[11], lest the devil cross[12] my prayer, for here he comes in the likeness of a Jew.

Enter SHYLOCK

How now, Shylock, what news among the merchants?

SHYLOCK   You knew, none so well, none so well as you, of my daughter's flight.

SALARINO   That's certain; I for my part knew the tailor that made the wings[13] she flew withal.

SOLANIO   And Shylock for his own part knew the bird was fledged[14], and then it is the complexion[15] of them all to leave the dam[16].

SHYLOCK   She is damned for it.

SALARINO   That's certain – if the devil may be her judge.

SHYLOCK   My own flesh and blood to rebel!

SOLANIO   Out upon it, old carrion[17]! Rebels it at these years?

SHYLOCK   I say my daughter is my flesh and my blood.

Shylock speaks menacingly of Antonio and the bond between them. He stresses the common humanity of both Jews and Christians, and says he will learn from Christian example and seek revenge.

 剧情简介：夏洛克恶狠狠地谈起他和安托纽立下的借约，强调犹太人和基督徒同样是人，并说他会照着基督徒的做法寻求报复。

1 'I'm the same as you!' (in small groups)

Lines 42–57 are among the most famous Shakespeare ever wrote.

a Stand in a circle and read around the group, changing over at the end of each sentence. Make your first reading angry and vengeful. Then read it again quietly and with dignity, as a plea for understanding and common humanity. Record the two versions and play them back to compare the different effects created. Write a paragraph on your own about which version you prefer and why.

b Two of you are Solanio and Salarino and stand at the opposite end of the room from the rest of the group. The others begin reading the speech in unison, moving towards the two Christians as they speak. Increase the volume, the nearer you get to them. Experiment with gesture and tone of voice. Try your best to share and feel Shylock's angry demand for understanding. You'll end up face to face with your opponents, but keep your concentration! Repeat the exercise to give the first Solanio and Salarino a chance to read.

c Repeat Activity b, but this time Solanio and Salarino can reply. They should intercut (交换，切换) the speech with insults to Shylock taken from this scene or other parts of the script (see the list in 'History and the Jews', p. 188).

d The speech contains ten **rhetorical questions** (exclamations phrased as questions to create dramatic effect, rather than to seek an answer). Identify them and talk together about the effect they create. Write down the three rhetorical questions you think are the most powerful and emotive, and explain why you've chosen them.

1. jet 黑玉
2. Rhenish 白葡萄酒
3. prodigal 挥霍者；败家子（夏洛克为安托纽贴上了这样的标签，因为他为了帮助朋友愚蠢地危及了自己的财产）
4. upon the mart 进入市场
5. He was wont 他习惯于
6. usurer 放高利贷的（基督徒视这个词语为一种轻蔑的称呼）
7. for a Christian courtesy 出于基督徒的客气
8. forfeit 违约
9. hindered me 阻挠我的生意
10. thwarted 使泡汤
11. cooled 使态度冷淡；离间
12. dimensions 身体各个部位
13. what is his humility 他的谦卑是什么
14. sufferance 忍受
15. execute 实施
16. it shall go hard but 定会

Characters 人物分析

Shylock and revenge

'The villainy (恶行) you teach me I will execute' (line 56). Many critics believe this is the moment when Shylock decides on his revenge.

a Write down all that has happened to him since Act 2 Scene 5. (Note that most of it is reported to us, rather than witnessed directly.) Then rank order the experiences that you think would contribute most powerfully to his desire for revenge.

b As you read to the end of the scene, look for other moments when you could reasonably say the script suggests that he has made his mind up to take revenge on Antonio. Note them down to use later in a discussion of Shylock's motivation for revenge.

SALARINO There is more difference between thy flesh and hers than between jet[1] and ivory; more between your bloods than there is between red wine and Rhenish[2]. But tell us, do you hear whether Antonio have had any loss at sea or no?

SHYLOCK There I have another bad match: a bankrupt, a prodigal[3], who dare scarce show his head on the Rialto, a beggar that was used to come so smug upon the mart[4]. Let him look to his bond. He was wont[5] to call me usurer[6]; let him look to his bond. He was wont to lend money for a Christian courtesy[7]; let him look to his bond.

SALARINO Why, I am sure if he forfeit[8] thou wilt not take his flesh. What's that good for?

SHYLOCK To bait fish withal; if it will feed nothing else, it will feed my revenge. He hath disgraced me, and hindered me[9] half a million, laughed at my losses, mocked at my gains, scorned my nation, thwarted[10] my bargains, cooled[11] my friends, heated mine enemies – and what's his reason? I am a Jew. Hath not a Jew eyes? Hath not a Jew hands, organs, dimensions[12], senses, affections, passions? Fed with the same food, hurt with the same weapons, subject to the same diseases, healed by the same means, warmed and cooled by the same winter and summer as a Christian is? If you prick us, do we not bleed? If you tickle us, do we not laugh? If you poison us, do we not die? And if you wrong us, shall we not revenge? If we are like you in the rest, we will resemble you in that. If a Jew wrong a Christian, what is his humility[13]? Revenge. If a Christian wrong a Jew, what should his sufferance[14] be by Christian example? Why, revenge! The villainy you teach me I will execute[15], and it shall go hard but[16] I will better the instruction.

Enter a [SERVING] MAN *from Antonio*

SERVINGMAN Gentlemen, my master Antonio is at his house, and desires to speak with you both.

SALARINO We have been up and down to seek him.

Enter TUBAL

SOLANIO Here comes another of the tribe; a third cannot be matched, unless the devil himself turn Jew.

Exeunt [*Salarino and Solanio with the Servingman*]

SHYLOCK How now, Tubal, what news from Genoa? Hast thou found my daughter?

Shylock rages about the money and jewels Jessica has taken. He wishes her dead. Tubal reports the loss of another of Antonio's ships. Shylock tells him to hire an officer to arrest Antonio.

剧情简介：夏洛克因婕丝柯卷走金银珠宝大发雷霆，恨不得女儿死去。图巴尔向他报告安托纽又有一艘船失事。夏洛克叫他去花钱雇警察逮捕安托纽。

▲ What does this image suggest about the relationship between Tubal (left) and Shylock? Explain your thinking.

1	hearsed	装进棺材
2	lights	落在
3	cast away	翻了船
4	four score	八十
5	at a sitting	一口气
6	divers	许多
7	turquoise	绿松石指环
8	Leah	丽娥（可能是夏洛克的妻子，婕丝柯的母亲）
9	a wilderness of	无数
10	undone	完蛋
11	fee me an officer	帮我雇一名警察（去逮捕安托纽）
12	bespeak	雇请
13	make what merchandise	达成任何买卖
14	synagogue	（犹太人的）礼拜堂，会堂

1 Tubal: write the sub-text (in pairs)

Tubal is important because he can give the audience an idea of how Shylock is regarded in the Jewish community. Is he sympathetic, or does he enjoy Shylock's discomfort?

- Look at lines 77–98. At the end of each speech, decide together what Tubal might be secretly thinking about while giving his news and Shylock's differing reactions to it. Write down your ideas as a 'sub-text' for Tubal.

2 See-sawing (摇摆不定) emotions (in pairs)

a Focus on all Shylock's lines in the script opposite. One person reads them aloud, the other says either 'pleasure' or 'pain' at the end of each sentence to indicate Shylock's feelings at that moment.

b On a second reading, experiment with speaking the 'pleasure' or 'pain' word loudly if you feel the emotion is acute, whispering if you think it is more muted (低声). Afterwards, talk together about the changes in his mood as reflected in your experiment.

c From the evidence in the script, discuss whether you think the loss of his wealth is more troubling to Shylock than the loss of his daughter. One of you argues it is his wealth, the other his daughter.

THE MERCHANT OF VENICE ACT 3 SCENE 1
威尼斯商人

TUBAL   I often came where I did hear of her, but cannot find her.
SHYLOCK   Why there, there, there, there! A diamond gone cost me two thousand ducats in Frankfurt! The curse never fell upon our nation till now, I never felt it till now. Two thousand ducats in that, and other precious, precious jewels! I would my daughter were dead at my foot, and the jewels in her ear: would she were hearsed¹ at my foot, and the ducats in her coffin. No news of them, why so? And I know not what's spent in the search. Why thou loss upon loss – the thief gone with so much, and so much to find the thief, and no satisfaction, no revenge, nor no ill luck stirring but what lights² o'my shoulders, no sighs but o'my breathing, no tears but o'my shedding!
TUBAL   Yes, other men have ill luck too. Antonio as I heard in Genoa –
SHYLOCK   What, what, what? Ill luck, ill luck?
TUBAL   – hath an argosy cast away³ coming from Tripolis.
SHYLOCK   I thank God, I thank God. Is it true, is it true?
TUBAL   I spoke with some of the sailors that escaped the wreck.
SHYLOCK   I thank thee, good Tubal: good news, good news! Ha, ha, heard in Genoa!
TUBAL   Your daughter spent in Genoa, as I heard, one night four score⁴ ducats.
SHYLOCK   Thou stick'st a dagger in me; I shall never see my gold again. Four score ducats at a sitting⁵! Four score ducats!
TUBAL   There came divers⁶ of Antonio's creditors in my company to Venice that swear he cannot choose but break.
SHYLOCK   I am very glad of it. I'll plague him, I'll torture him. I am glad of it.
TUBAL   One of them showed me a ring that he had of your daughter for a monkey.
SHYLOCK   Out upon her! Thou torturest me, Tubal: it was my turquoise⁷, I had it of Leah⁸ when I was a bachelor. I would not have given it for a wilderness of⁹ monkeys.
TUBAL   But Antonio is certainly undone¹⁰.
SHYLOCK   Nay, that's true, that's very true. Go, Tubal, fee me an officer¹¹, bespeak¹² him a fortnight before. I will have the heart of him if he forfeit, for were he out of Venice I can make what merchandise¹³ I will. Go, Tubal, and meet me at our synagogue¹⁴, go, good Tubal, at our synagogue, Tubal.

Exeunt

79

Portia urges Bassanio to delay before choosing. She could tell him how to choose correctly, but she must not break her oath of secrecy.

 剧情简介：鲍霞劝博萨纽要慎重选择，勿操之过急。她本可以告诉他如何正确选择，但她必须遵守誓言，保守秘密。

Stagecraft 导演技巧

The great hall

Portia's earlier suitors were entertained in 'A room' at Belmont as they made their casket choice. Here, Portia greets Bassanio in 'The great hall'.

- Sketch and label a few set designs for a modern production that you feel convey an appropriate mood and atmosphere. Pass your favourite to another student for comment.

Characters 人物分析

Portia – the first sign of nerves? (in pairs)

The third casket scene shows how differently Portia treats Bassanio from her other suitors. Until this scene, Portia has appeared as a composed (沉着), confident, even arrogant young woman, but her speech to Bassanio in lines 1–24 lacks her usual assurance and self-control.

a Read the lines aloud, taking turns to share them between you in any way you feel appropriate. Then talk about how an actor might bring out Portia's feelings for Bassanio in this speech. Is Portia's hesitant and ambiguous (模棱两可) style the way someone in love speaks?

b List the differences between the way Portia thinks about and treats Bassanio and her attitude towards Morocco and Arragon.

c On the basis of all your investigations here, write advice individually for the actor playing Portia about how to make any developments in this character dramatically convincing. Write up your comments in your Director's Journal.

1 Should women keep quiet? (in small groups)

In line 8, Portia seems to be saying that a woman should keep her feelings of love to herself. She's allowed to think them, but not express them, perhaps leaving the man to take the initiative.

a Talk about what this remark adds to your understanding of how women are expected to behave in Venice and Belmont (see pp. 176–7). In your discussion, also consider whether opinions like this are still expressed today, and how important it is that women have a 'voice'. How do you feel about such views?

b Assemble your collective thoughts for a mini-presentation to your class.

1 tarry 等待
2 forbear 有耐心
3 but it is not love 我不是说我爱您
4 I would not lose you 我不想失去您
5 Hate … quality 憎恶不会让您有那种感觉
6 And … thought 女孩子总是把心思埋在心底
7 detain 挽留
8 venture 冒险
9 I am forsworn 我违背了誓言
10 Beshrew 诅咒（开玩笑地）
11 o'erlooked 迷惑
12 naughty 糟糕，恶劣（在莎士比亚时代该词含有更加强烈的意思）
13 bars 障碍
14 peize 耽搁，拖延
15 eche 增加
16 stay you from election 阻止您选择

Act 3 Scene 2
Belmont   The great hall of Portia's house

Enter BASSANIO, PORTIA, GRATIANO, NERISSA, *and all their trains*

PORTIA I pray you tarry[1], pause a day or two
Before you hazard, for in choosing wrong
I lose your company; therefore forbear[2] a while.
There's something tells me, but it is not love[3],
I would not lose you[4]; and you know yourself   5
Hate counsels not in such a quality[5].
But lest you should not understand me well –
And yet a maiden hath no tongue but thought[6] –
I would detain[7] you here some month or two
Before you venture[8] for me. I could teach you   10
How to choose right, but then I am forsworn[9].
So will I never be. So may you miss me;
But if you do, you'll make me wish a sin,
That I had been forsworn. Beshrew[10] your eyes!
They have o'erlooked[11] me and divided me: 15
One half of me is yours, the other half yours –
Mine own, I would say: but if mine then yours,
And so all yours. O these naughty[12] times
Puts bars[13] between the owners and their rights!
And so though yours, not yours. Prove it so,   20
Let Fortune go to hell for it, not I.
I speak too long, but 'tis to peize[14] the time,
To eche[15] it, and to draw it out in length,
To stay you from election[16].

Bassanio is impatient to choose. He and Portia talk playfully of the treachery of love. He insists on choosing without delay. Portia, calling for music, compares him to a dying swan if defeated, and to Hercules should he succeed.

剧情简介：博萨纽迫不及待要选匣子。他和鲍霞戏谑地谈到爱情中的背叛。他坚持做出选择，不再耽搁。鲍霞叫人奏乐，说要是他选错了就如同一只垂死的天鹅，选对了就是大力神赫丘力。

Characters 人物分析

Bassanio feels uncomfortable

Bassanio's lines 24–5 show him growing typically impatient to get on with choosing. To him, the waiting is like being tortured 'upon the rack'. (The rack was a torture instrument that stretched its victims' limbs; it was often used to extract 'confessions' [招供].) Portia continues to use the image of the rack through lines 26–38. Some critics think that Portia's use of the image, and words like 'confess' and 'treason', show that she still has doubts about Bassanio's motives and true feelings.

a What do you think about Bassanio? Read his lines 24–39. Do you think they are sincere and heartfelt, or just another example of appearance masking the true reality underneath?

b Write a paragraph giving your judgement of Bassanio at this point in the play, incorporating evidence from this scene.

Language in the play 剧中语言

Words to describe music and mood

Portia calls for music to accompany Bassanio's choice (line 43). She also speaks in elaborate musical images (lines 45–53). For example, Bassanio's failure would be 'a swan-like end, / Fading in music' and his success a 'flourish' (of trumpets) for a 'new-crowned monarch'.

a Identify words and phrases from lines 40–62 that set the mood for Bassanio's big decision. Then add explanations of how the images or comparisons work, and the kind of mood that Portia's language creates.

b As an extension activity, write about why you think Shakespeare decided to fill Portia's speech (and the whole scene) with such exceptionally rich imagery.

1 Portia as victim? (in pairs)

Portia recalls the story of how Alcides (Hercules) rescued the city of Troy from a sea monster, which demanded that young girls be sacrificed to it (lines 54–62). She compares herself with these unfortunate young women, as if she were some sort of helpless victim.

- Talk together about whether or not you agree with Portia's view of herself. Is she serious or is she joking? What else might be going on?

1 rack 拷刑架（指能强行拉伸犯人肢体直至关节断裂的刑具）
2 mistrust 焦虑
3 fear 担心
4 amity 友谊
5 sum 要旨
6 torment 折磨
7 deliverance 获释
8 all aloof 避开
9 my … stream 我会泪流成河
10 flourish 花腔；号角齐鸣
11 dulcet 美妙
12 howling 号哭
13 Dardanian wives 达达尼亚的妇人们（Dardania是巴尔干半岛的一个古国，邻国是伊利里亚和色雷斯）
14 blearèd visages 泪流满面
15 The issue of th'exploit 大力神争斗的结果
16 fray 冲突，战斗

THE MERCHANT OF VENICE ACT 3 SCENE 2

威尼斯商人

BASSANIO   Let me choose,
For as I am, I live upon the rack¹.   25

PORTIA   Upon the rack, Bassanio? Then confess
What treason there is mingled with your love.

BASSANIO None but that ugly treason of mistrust²
Which makes me fear³ th'enjoying of my love.
There may as well be amity⁴ and life   30
'Tween snow and fire, as treason and my love.

PORTIA   Ay, but I fear you speak upon the rack
Where men enforcèd do speak anything.

BASSANIO Promise me life and I'll confess the truth.

PORTIA   Well then, confess and live.

BASSANIO   'Confess and love'   35
Had been the very sum⁵ of my confession.
O happy torment⁶, when my torturer
Doth teach me answers for deliverance⁷!
But let me to my fortune and the caskets.

PORTIA   Away then! I am locked in one of them: 40
If you do love me, you will find me out.
Nerissa and the rest, stand all aloof⁸.
Let music sound while he doth make his choice;
Then if he lose he makes a swan-like end,
Fading in music. That the comparison   45
May stand more proper, my eye shall be the stream⁹
And watery deathbed for him. He may win,
And what is music then? Then music is
Even as the flourish¹⁰ when true subjects bow
To a new-crownèd monarch. Such it is   50
As are those dulcet¹¹ sounds in break of day,
That creep into the dreaming bridegroom's ear
And summon him to marriage. Now he goes
With no less presence, but with much more love,
Than young Alcides when he did redeem   55
The virgin tribute paid by howling¹² Troy
To the sea-monster. I stand for sacrifice.
The rest aloof are the Dardanian wives¹³,
With blearèd visages¹⁴ come forth to view
The issue of th'exploit¹⁵. Go, Hercules!   60
Live thou, I live. With much much more dismay
I view the fight than thou that mak'st the fray¹⁶.

As music plays, Bassanio begins making his choice from the caskets. He considers false appearances in law, religion, war and beauty. In each case, vice can be concealed beneath a mask of virtue.

 剧情简介：音乐响起，博萨纽开始挑选匣子。他从法律、宗教、战争和美貌的角度一一描述外表给人的假象。不管哪一方面，丑恶都可能藏在美德的面具之下。

Stagecraft 导演技巧

The casket song (in small groups)

Bassanio's choosing is presented differently from the previous suitors'. A song (lines 63–72) accompanies his initial deliberations (盘算).

- Talk about how you would stage this event. Who does the singing and what kind of music would you select? Research different musical accompaniments to create a variety of moods. Afterwards, write up your ideas individually in your Director's Journal.

Themes 主题分析

Private versus public, appearance versus reality

The stage direction in the script opposite says: '*Bassanio comments on the caskets to himself*'.

a Write his thoughts as an aside. (Does it make a difference that Portia isn't meant to hear them?) Use modern English prose and emphasise the frankness of his thinking, which contrasts notably with his flowery way of speaking publicly at line 73.

Lines 73–101 again express a major theme of the play: that the way things and people appear often does not match what they are really like. Bassanio gives examples of this from a wide range of experience.

b Work through the lines, pausing after each example to allow your partner to explain clearly in modern English exactly how Bassanio is illustrating his overall point. Make a list of the examples.

c When you have completed your list, choose your favourite, and illustrate it as a blazon (an inscription or motto) for a coat of arms.

1 fancy 表面的爱
2 Or … or … 是……还是……
3 begot 发生；创造
4 engend'red 产生
5 ornament 装饰
6 seasoned 加调料（使之动听诱人）
7 damnèd error 亵渎神明
8 sober brow 严肃的面容
9 text （从《圣经》）引经据典
10 stayers 台阶
11 inward searched 从里面打开
12 valour's excrement 勇者的外在表现（指胡子）
13 redoubted 恐惧
14 crispèd 卷曲
15 wanton 不正经，淫荡
16 supposèd fairness 伪装的美丽
17 sepulchre 坟墓

THE MERCHANT OF VENICE ACT 3 SCENE 2
威尼斯商人

[*Here music.*] *A song the whilst Bassanio comments on the caskets to himself*

    Tell me where is fancy[1] bred,
    Or in the heart, or[2] in the head?
    How begot[3], how nourishèd?
        Reply, reply.
    It is engend'red[4] in the eye,
    With gazing fed, and fancy dies
    In the cradle where it lies.
    Let us all ring fancy's knell.
    I'll begin it – Ding, dong, bell.

ALL   Ding, dong, bell.

BASSANIO So may the outward shows be least themselves:
The world is still deceived with ornament[5].
In law, what plea so tainted and corrupt
But, being seasoned[6] with a gracious voice,
Obscures the show of evil? In religion,
What damnèd error[7] but some sober brow[8]
Will bless it and approve it with a text[9],
Hiding the grossness with fair ornament?
There is no vice so simple but assumes
Some mark of virtue on his outward parts.
How many cowards whose hearts are all as false
As stayers[10] of sand, wear yet upon their chins
The beards of Hercules and frowning Mars,
Who inward searched[11] have livers white as milk,
And these assume but valour's excrement[12]
To render them redoubted[13]. Look on beauty,
And you shall see 'tis purchased by the weight,
Which therein works a miracle in nature,
Making them lightest that wear most of it.
So are those crispèd[14] snaky golden locks
Which maketh such wanton[15] gambols with the wind
Upon supposèd fairness[16], often known
To be the dowry of a second head,
The skull that bred them in the sepulchre[17].

Bassanio rejects the gold and silver caskets because he fears that their fine appearance might be misleading. To Portia's delight, he chooses the lead casket. Inside he finds her portrait and a scroll.

剧情简介：博萨纽没有选择金匣子和银匣子，因为他不想被它们漂亮的外表误导。他选对了铅匣子，这令鲍霞高兴不已。博萨纽在匣子里找到了鲍霞的肖像和一个纸卷。

Characters 人物分析

Bassanio's chooses the lead casket (in small groups)

Some people argue that Bassanio behaves out of character in choosing the lead casket, because of his shady past and his motives for marrying Portia (see Act 1 Scene 1). Someone like that would be more likely to go for gold or silver!

- Half the group argues that his choice is believable, and that it shows he is a genuine and sincere lover. The other half argues that he is simply hypocritical, an opportunist and a fortune-hunter. Ask another group to judge which side makes the stronger case.

Write a thought bubble for Bassanio at this precise moment. Add it to a whole-group display.

Language in the play 剧中语言

Portia and Bassanio: hyperbole (by yourself)

Portia (lines 108–14) and Bassanio (lines 114–29) both suggest they are overwhelmed with passion and joy. They each use a great deal of exaggerated, high-flown language, or **hyperbole** (see 'The language of *The Merchant of Venice*', p. 180). Portia speaks in an aside, which implies that her feelings are genuine. But what about Bassanio? Is he using elaborate language to mask his true feelings?

- Identify all the examples of hyperbole opposite and write a brief explanation of what each exaggeration actually describes.
- Why do you think Shakespeare gives the two lovers so many hyperboles at this point?

1 guilèd 阴险
2 entrap 坑骗
3 Hard food for Midas 迈达斯的坚硬食物（迈达斯是传说中的弗里几亚 [Phrygia] 国王，酒神狄俄尼索斯 [Dionysus] 曾赐予他点石成金的本领，结果所触之物均立刻变为纯金，连吃饭都成了问题）
4 common drudge 下贱的仆人
5 meagre 不吸引人，朴实无华
6 eloquence 姣好的面容
7 fleet to air 烟消云散
8 allay 减少；克制
9 rain 倾洒
10 scant 适当控制
11 counterfeit 肖像
12 demi-god 半神，本领超凡的人
13 sunder 分开
14 Methinks 我想
15 unfurnished 没有同伴（还缺另一只眼）
16 substance 含义
17 underprizing 贬低
18 continent 内容

Thus ornament is but the guilèd[1] shore
To a most dangerous sea; the beauteous scarf
Veiling an Indian beauty; in a word,
The seeming truth which cunning times put on
To entrap[2] the wisest. Therefore thou gaudy gold,
Hard food for Midas[3], I will none of thee,
Nor none of thee, thou pale and common drudge[4]
'Tween man and man. But thou, thou meagre[5] lead
Which rather threaten'st than dost promise aught,
Thy paleness moves me more than eloquence[6]:
And here choose I. Joy be the consequence!

PORTIA [*Aside*] How all the other passions fleet to air[7]:
As doubtful thoughts, and rash-embraced despair,
And shudd'ring fear, and green-eyed jealousy!
O love, be moderate, allay[8] thy ecstasy,
In measure rain[9] thy joy, scant[10] this excess!
I feel too much thy blessing: make it less
For fear I surfeit.

[*Bassanio opens the leaden casket*]

BASSANIO What find I here?
Fair Portia's counterfeit[11]! What demi-god[12]
Hath come so near creation? Move these eyes?
Or whether riding on the balls of mine
Seem they in motion? Here are severed lips
Parted with sugar breath; so sweet a bar
Should sunder[13] such sweet friends. Here in her hairs
The painter plays the spider, and hath woven
A golden mesh t'entrap the hearts of men
Faster than gnats in cobwebs. But her eyes –
How could he see to do them? Having made one,
Methinks[14] it should have power to steal both his
And leave itself unfurnished[15]. Yet look how far
The substance[16] of my praise doth wrong this shadow
In underprizing[17] it, so far this shadow
Doth limp behind the substance. Here's the scroll,
The continent[18] and summary of my fortune.

The scroll confirms that Bassanio has won Portia. He asks her to approve the casket's truth. She wishes for his sake that she were a better and wealthier woman.

剧情简介：纸卷上的内容证实了博萨纽从此拥有鲍霞。他要鲍霞确认这是真的。为了博萨纽，鲍霞多么希望自己是一个更优秀、更富有的女子。

▲ Find a suitable line from Act 3 Scene 2 to use as a caption for this image.

1	view	外表
2	by note	按照指示
3	prize	比赛，竞争
4	peals	巨大的声音
5	thrice	非常
6	ratified	批准
7	livings	财产
8	in gross	总体
9	unlessoned	没教养
10	unschooled	没读过书
11	unpractised	没经验

1 Bassanio and Portia: love or business? (in small groups, then by yourself)

Bassanio will not believe his good fortune until he has settled his engagement to Portia. His line 148, with its echoes of legal practice, marks a change of tone from what has gone before: their exchange now involves serious business. Portia's lines 149–59 ('You see me … unpractised') also express a mood change. She begins by giving a very modest impression of herself, but increasingly includes words connected with wealth and value.

a Read her speech as a group, taking one line each. Draw attention to any 'commercial' or 'value' words, by repeating them. Then compare the lovers' words here with their hyperbolic language on page 87.

b Working individually, make notes on how this short episode alters your understanding of Portia and Bassanio's relationship.

2 Question Portia – then advise her (whole class)

In lines 160–5, Portia's commitment to Bassanio is absolute. Bassanio will be 'her lord, her governor, her king' (line 165). Then she quite literally gives herself to him (lines 166–7). What is your reaction to this?

a Each person makes a list of questions to ask Portia about her relationship with Bassanio. One takes the role of Portia and is questioned ('hot-seated') by the class. If Portia finds a question too difficult, she should say 'Time out'. Possible answers can then be discussed by everyone.

b Work in groups to draw up a list of 'do's' and 'don'ts' for Portia at this vital time in her life.

THE MERCHANT OF VENICE ACT 3 SCENE 2
威尼斯商人

                [*He reads*]
        'You that choose not by the view[1]
        Chance as fair, and choose as true.
        Since this fortune falls to you,
        Be content and seek no new.
        If you be well pleased with this,   135
        And hold your fortune for your bliss,
        Turn you where your lady is,
        And claim her with a loving kiss.'
A gentle scroll! Fair lady, by your leave,
I come by note[2] to give, and to receive.   140
Like one of two contending in a prize[3]
That thinks he hath done well in people's eyes,
Hearing applause and universal shout,
Giddy in spirit, still gazing in a doubt
Whether those peals[4] of praise be his or no –   145
So, thrice[5]-fair lady, stand I even so,
As doubtful whether what I see be true,
Until confirmed, signed, ratified[6] by you.

PORTIA   You see me, Lord Bassanio, where I stand,
Such as I am. Though for myself alone   150
I would not be ambitious in my wish
To wish myself much better, yet for you
I would be trebled twenty times myself,
A thousand times more fair, ten thousand times
More rich, that only to stand high in your account   155
I might in virtues, beauties, livings[7], friends,
Exceed account. But the full sum of me
Is sum of something: which to term in gross[8]
Is an unlessoned[9] girl, unschooled[10], unpractised[11];
Happy in this, she is not yet so old   160
But she may learn; happier than this,
She is not bred so dull but she can learn;
Happiest of all, is that her gentle spirit
Commits itself to yours to be directed
As from her lord, her governor, her king.   165

Portia gives herself and all her wealth to Bassanio. She hands him a ring, saying its loss will mark the end of his love. Bassanio swears to wear it until his dying day. Gratiano asks for permission to marry Nerissa.

剧情简介：鲍霞把自己连同所有财产都托付给了博萨纽。她给了他一枚戒指，说要是戒指丢了，那他的爱也将随之消失。博萨纽发誓他至死都会戴着这枚戒指。格拉奇阿诺请求准许他娶讷瑞莎为妻。

Characters 人物分析

Gratiano – a question of consistency? (in pairs)

Gratiano has certainly kept to his bargain with Bassanio. The normally loud and brash young man behaves himself and does not say a word in this scene until line 189, and then it's to announce that he has fallen quickly in love and wishes to be married – to Nerissa!

a Look back at the Character file you started for Gratiano on page 42 and review his part in the play so far. On one side of a piece of paper, list his earlier characteristics; on the other, the ones he displays between lines 189 and 208.

b What advice would you give to an actor playing Gratiano about how he could make Gratiano's impetuous (冲动的) falling in love psychologically consistent and convincing?

c Sometimes a playwright will emphasise a character's dramatic role and function rather than making their behaviour realistic. Suggest three advantages there might be in Shakespeare's choosing to follow Bassanio and Portia's betrothal (订婚) with that of Gratiano and Nerissa. For example, what effect does this have on the mood of the scene at this point?

1 presage 预示
2 vantage to exclaim on you 大骂您的机会
3 bereft 剥夺
4 powers 思想，精神
5 oration 言辞，演讲
6 buzzing 兴奋，喜悦
7 blent 混合
8 wild of nothing 大声喧闹
9 our wishes prosper 我们的梦想成真
10 For … me 你们抢不去我的快乐
11 solemnise … faith （指结婚）
12 so … get 如果你自己找到了
13 for … you 我和您同时找到了一个妻子
14 stood 依赖
15 as the matter falls 偶然

▼ As was Elizabethan custom, Portia gives Bassanio a ring (line 171) as a sign of her submission to him. But she also warns him that if he loses it, it will lead to trouble – and the audience can guess that this is very likely to happen! This technique is called foreshadowing (伏笔). As you work through to the end of the play, track the ring and its influence.

THE MERCHANT OF VENICE ACT 3 SCENE 2
威尼斯商人

	Myself, and what is mine, to you and yours	
	Is now converted. But now I was the lord	
	Of this fair mansion, master of my servants,	
	Queen o'er myself; and even now, but now,	
	This house, these servants, and this same myself	170
	Are yours, my lord's. I give them with this ring,	
	Which when you part from, lose, or give away,	
	Let it presage¹ the ruin of your love,	
	And be my vantage to exclaim on you².	
BASSANIO	Madam, you have bereft³ me of all words.	175
	Only my blood speaks to you in my veins,	
	And there is such confusion in my powers⁴	
	As after some oration⁵ fairly spoke	
	By a belovèd prince there doth appear	
	Among the buzzing⁶, pleasèd multitude,	180
	Where every something being blent⁷ together	
	Turns to a wild of nothing⁸, save of joy	
	Expressed, and not expressed. But when this ring	
	Parts from this finger, then parts life from hence:	
	O then be bold to say Bassanio's dead!	185
NERISSA	My lord and lady, it is now our time,	
	That have stood by and seen our wishes prosper⁹,	
	To cry 'good joy'. Good joy, my lord and lady!	
GRATIANO	My lord Bassanio, and my gentle lady,	
	I wish you all the joy that you can wish;	190
	For I am sure you can wish none from me¹⁰.	
	And when your honours mean to solemnise	
	The bargain of your faith¹¹, I do beseech you	
	Even at that time I may be married too.	
BASSANIO	With all my heart, so thou canst get¹² a wife.	195
GRATIANO	I thank your lordship, you have got me one.	
	My eyes, my lord, can look as swift as yours:	
	You saw the mistress, I beheld the maid.	
	You loved, I loved; for intermission	
	No more pertains to me, my lord, than you¹³.	200
	Your fortune stood¹⁴ upon the caskets there,	
	And so did mine too as the matter falls¹⁵.	

Gratiano gives an account of wooing Nerissa. Lorenzo, Jessica and Salerio arrive, having met on the way to Belmont.

 剧情简介：格拉奇阿诺叙述追求讷瑞莎的经过。劳仁佐、婕丝柯和塞理瑞欧到达，他们在来贝尔蒙的路上相遇。

Write about it 写作练习
Nerissa's news

It seems that Gratiano had a hard time courting Nerissa (lines 203–8). However, it is only he who gives details of the engagement; Nerissa is hardly given a chance to speak! What would she say about the affair?

a Write her post on a social networking site for her friends.

b Write the conversation when she phones a close friend to share her true feelings about Gratiano, and explain how she was won over by him. Remember that we've so far seen Nerissa as full of common sense and worldly wisdom, so why exactly has she fallen for Gratiano? And how did she feel during the choosing ceremony, knowing that her wedding plans depended on Bassanio picking the right casket?

Language in the play 剧中语言
Male attitudes to sex (in pairs)

Gratiano may be joking about his proposed bet with Bassanio and Portia (lines 213–14), concerning which couple will produce the first son, but he clearly values sons more than daughters. Also typical of male attitudes at the time is the rude **pun** (双关) (joke based on wordplay) he makes in line 216, twisting Nerissa's innocent 'stake down' (meaning 'lay a bet') into its sexual interpretation ('with a limp penis').

- Discuss why Gratiano might value sons more than daughters, and why Shakespeare might include these details at this point in the scene. Be ready to offer your ideas in a class discussion.

1 Jessica is un-named – and unwelcome?
(in small groups)

Line 217 is the only 'welcome' to Jessica. She knows she must convert to Christianity, yet she is greeted as Lorenzo's 'infidel'. Like her father, she is denied the respect of a name – even though Bassanio welcomes Lorenzo and Salerio personally. In some productions, Jessica is coldly shunned (避开), not just ignored.

- Write down your ideas for how to stage her arrival at Belmont to maximise its dramatic impact and reinforce the key issues you wish to highlight.

1 my very roof 我的上腭
2 We'll … ducats 我们敢拿一千块钱跟他们打赌，我们会先生下儿子
3 stake down 下赌注（又可指生殖器下垂）
4 infidel 异教徒（不信基督教的人，这里指婕丝柯）
5 If … welcome 如果刚成为这里的主人的我有权向你们表示欢迎
6 very 最尊贵
7 countrymen 同乡
8 Commends him to you 向您问好
9 ope = open
10 estate 处境

THE MERCHANT OF VENICE ACT 3 SCENE 2
威尼斯商人

                For wooing here until I sweat again,
                And swearing till my very roof¹ was dry
                With oaths of love, at last – if promise last –   205
                I got a promise of this fair one here
                To have her love, provided that your fortune
                Achieved her mistress.
PORTIA   Is this true, Nerissa?
NERISSA   Madam, it is, so you stand pleased withal.
BASSANIO   And do you, Gratiano, mean good faith?   210
GRATIANO   Yes 'faith, my lord.
BASSANIO   Our feast shall be much honoured in your marriage.
GRATIANO   We'll play with them the first boy for a thousand ducats².
NERISSA   What, and stake down³?   215
GRATIANO   No, we shall ne'er win at that sport and stake down.
                But who comes here? Lorenzo and his infidel⁴!
                What, and my old Venetian friend Salerio!

                Enter LORENZO, JESSICA, *and* SALERIO, *a messenger from Venice*

BASSANIO   Lorenzo and Salerio, welcome hither –
                If that the youth of my new interest here   220
                Have power to bid you welcome⁵. By your leave
                I bid my very⁶ friends and countrymen⁷,
                Sweet Portia, welcome.
PORTIA   So do I, my lord.
                They are entirely welcome.
LORENZO   I thank your honour. For my part, my lord,   225
                My purpose was not to have seen you here,
                But meeting with Salerio by the way
                He did entreat me past all saying nay
                To come with him along.
SALERIO   I did, my lord,
                And I have reason for it. [*Giving letter*] Signor Antonio   230
                Commends him to you⁸.
BASSANIO   Ere I ope⁹ his letter,
                I pray you tell me how my good friend doth.
SALERIO   Not sick, my lord, unless it be in mind,
                Nor well, unless in mind: his letter there
                Will show you his estate¹⁰.   235

Bassanio reads Antonio's letter, turning pale as he learns the bad news. He tells Portia of the debt he owes to Antonio, and asks Salerio to confirm the news of Antonio's shipwrecked vessels.

 剧情简介：博萨纽阅读安托纽的来信，得知他遭遇不幸，脸色瞬间惨白。他告诉鲍霞安托纽为他借债的事，并要塞理瑞欧证实安托纽商船倾覆的消息是真是假。

Write about it 写作练习
Jessica: the 'stranger' in Belmont

Activity 1 on page 92 invited you to consider Portia's and Bassanio's apparent indifference to Jessica. Now Nerissa is instructed brusquely (唐突) by Gratiano to welcome Jessica. Not even Lorenzo speaks to her.

- What might Jessica make of her first experiences of her new life at Belmont? Write a diary entry for her that expresses her thoughts and feelings about the cold reception she receives.
- Place this diary entry alongside the one you wrote for Jessica on page 64. Then write a commentary (评论) on any key differences you notice in tone or mood between the two diary entries.

Stagecraft 导演技巧
'What, worse and worse?' (in groups of three or four)

There is a change of mood as Bassanio opens Antonio's letter and reads its sobering contents. The previous atmosphere of joy, triumph, celebration and humour gives way to one of tension and concern.

a Take small sections at a time of all the lines opposite and on a copy of the script make notes on exactly how the mood changes. For example, Gratiano's typically bragging 'We are the Jasons, we have won the fleece' is immediately followed by a line in which Salerio speaks of what Antonio has 'lost'.

b As individual directors, work out how you would show these changes of mood to the audience. As you work through the lines, remember that you can rely on more than the language of the play. Think about the use of lighting and music and how you might 'block' (arrange on stage) Gratiano, Salerio, Portia and Bassanio. What actions and gestures can they use to show their responses as the bad tidings from Venice sink in? Add all your notes to your Director's Journal.

1 cheer yond stranger 招呼一下那位外乡人
2 Jasons 伊阿宋（见第10页）
3 would 希望
4 shrewd 令人不快，不好
5 Could … man 能够让任何如此沉稳的人失魂落魄
6 blotted 玷污
7 impart 吐露，表达
8 Rating 估价
9 braggart 吹牛皮的人
10 engaged 抵押（借钱）；承诺
11 mere enemy 死对头
12 as 和……一样
13 Issuing 流出
14 hit 成功
15 merchant-marring 让商人遭殃

1 Bassanio opens up: how does Portia respond?

Now that he's 'won' Portia, Bassanio tells her the truth: that he 'was worse than nothing'; that is, he was actually in debt and has put his friend's life in danger in order to further his own ends.

- Portia says nothing immediate in reply, but what is she thinking? Write her spontaneous thoughts (no more than two sentences) at line 262.

THE MERCHANT OF VENICE ACT 3 SCENE 2
威尼斯商人

[Bassanio] opens the letter

GRATIANO   Nerissa, cheer yond stranger¹, bid her welcome.
            Your hand, Salerio; what's the news from Venice?
            How doth that royal merchant, good Antonio?
            I know he will be glad of our success;
            We are the Jasons², we have won the fleece.   240

SALERIO   I would³ you had won the fleece that he hath lost.

PORTIA   There are some shrewd⁴ contents in yond same paper
            That steals the colour from Bassanio's cheek:
            Some dear friend dead, else nothing in the world
            Could turn so much the constitution   245
            Of any constant man⁵. What, worse and worse?
            With leave, Bassanio, I am half yourself
            And I must freely have the half of anything
            That this same paper brings you.

BASSANIO   O sweet Portia,
            Here are a few of the unpleasant'st words   250
            That ever blotted⁶ paper. Gentle lady,
            When I did first impart⁷ my love to you,
            I freely told you all the wealth I had
            Ran in my veins: I was a gentleman.
            And then I told you true; and yet, dear lady,   255
            Rating⁸ myself at nothing, you shall see
            How much I was a braggart⁹. When I told you
            My state was nothing, I should then have told you
            That I was worse than nothing; for indeed
            I have engaged¹⁰ myself to a dear friend,   260
            Engaged my friend to his mere enemy¹¹,
            To feed my means. Here is a letter, lady,
            The paper as¹² the body of my friend,
            And every word in it a gaping wound
            Issuing¹³ lifeblood. But is it true, Salerio?   265
            Hath all his ventures failed? What, not one hit¹⁴?
            From Tripolis, from Mexico, and England,
            From Lisbon, Barbary, and India,
            And not one vessel 'scape the dreadful touch
            Of merchant-marring¹⁵ rocks?

95

Salerio confirms that all Antonio's ships are wrecked. He and Jessica tell of Shylock's burning desire to pursue the case against Antonio. Portia offers to cancel Antonio's debt and pay generous interest to Shylock.

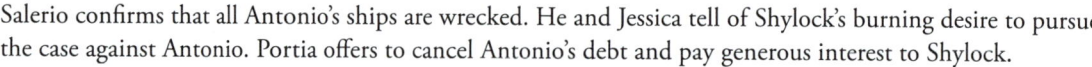剧情简介：塞里瑞欧证实安托纽的船已全部失事。他和婕丝柯都说到夏洛克迫切想要与安托纽对簿公堂。鲍霞提出愿意偿还安托纽欠夏洛克的债，并付给夏洛克高额利息。

1 Changing Shylock's mind (whole class)

Salerio explains that many people have tried to persuade Shylock to release Antonio from his bond, including merchants, high-ranking citizens ('magnificoes') and the Duke himself.

- In small groups, discuss the questions and points these important people would raise with Shylock.
- Then, as a whole class, put Shylock in the hot-seat. Invent names for your character as merchant or magnifico. Your task is to persuade Shylock to cancel Antonio's bond.

Characters 人物分析

Weak or strong women? (in pairs)

a Jessica speaks only once (lines 283–9). She talks about her father and Antonio, confirming Salerio's typically Christian view that Shylock is inhuman, greedily pursuing Antonio's destruction.

- Write advice for the actress playing Jessica about how she should deliver this speech, which is deeply damaging to her father's reputation. Does she speak reluctantly, pressurised by the Christian characters around her into saying what they expect to hear? Or does she use this moment as a way of trying to get into their good books and align herself with the Christians?

b Portia's speech (lines 297–313) consists of eleven sentences. Seven of them are 'orders' and the others are emphatic statements. Her final line (320) contains two further imperatives.

- Read the lines to each other – first in a 'bossy' way, then in a different way. Talk about whether they reveal new aspects of Portia's character, or simply reinforce the characteristics you saw in Act 1 Scene 2 and Act 2 Scenes 1, 7 and 9.

2 Keeping Antonio in mind

The audience does not see Antonio, but other characters give us a vivid impression of him and his nature.

- Focus on lines 236–324, and write down all the references to Antonio (the first mention is 'that royal merchant, good Antonio'). Then explain what impression is created by the Christians' specific choice of words.
- Use your analysis to write a paragraph expressing what the Christians think of Antonio. Write another paragraph saying why the friendship between Antonio and Bassanio is so special.

1	discharge	偿还
2	confound	毁灭
3	plies	缠着
4	impeach	质疑
5	magnificoes / Of greatest port	最显要的市民
6	persuaded	劝谏
7	drive	打消
8	envious	狠毒
9	forfeiture	赔偿金，罚金
10	best conditioned	心肠最好
11	courtesies	仁举
12	deface	取消

| SALERIO | Not one, my lord. | 270 |

Besides, it should appear that if he had
The present money to discharge[1] the Jew,
He would not take it. Never did I know
A creature that did bear the shape of man
So keen and greedy to confound[2] a man. 275
He plies[3] the Duke at morning and at night,
And doth impeach[4] the freedom of the state
If they deny him justice. Twenty merchants,
The Duke himself, and the magnificoes
Of greatest port[5] have all persuaded[6] with him, 280
But none can drive[7] him from the envious[8] plea
Of forfeiture[9], of justice, and his bond.

JESSICA When I was with him, I have heard him swear
To Tubal and to Chus, his countrymen,
That he would rather have Antonio's flesh 285
Than twenty times the value of the sum
That he did owe him; and I know, my lord,
If law, authority, and power deny not
It will go hard with poor Antonio.

PORTIA Is it your dear friend that is thus in trouble? 290

BASSANIO The dearest friend to me, the kindest man,
The best conditioned[10] and unwearied spirit
In doing courtesies[11]; and one in whom
The ancient Roman honour more appears
Than any that draws breath in Italy. 295

PORTIA What sums owes he the Jew?

BASSANIO For me, three thousand ducats.

PORTIA What, no more?
Pay him six thousand, and deface[12] the bond.
Double six thousand, and then treble that,
Before a friend of this description 300
Shall lose a hair through Bassanio's fault.
First go with me to church, and call me wife,
And then away to Venice to your friend!
For never shall you lie by Portia's side
With an unquiet soul. You shall have gold 305
To pay the petty debt twenty times over.

Portia orders Bassanio to Venice to help Antonio. Bassanio reads Antonio's letter explaining his dreadful predicament. In Scene 3, Shylock orders the Jailer to guard Antonio closely.

剧情简介：鲍霞让博萨纽去威尼斯帮助安托纽。博萨纽读了安托纽的信，信中说明了他的危险处境。第三场，夏洛克让狱卒看紧安托纽。

Themes 主题分析

Money versus love: 'I will love you dear' (in pairs)

In line 312, Portia puns on the word 'dear'. This highlights one of the main tensions in this scene (and the whole play): how far can money and love live comfortably together? The theme is exemplified in the relationship between Portia and Bassanio. Do they really love each other? Or does Bassanio still see Portia as a 'lady richly left'?

- Draw an image representing money and an image representing love at the centre of a spider diagram. One of you works through the scene collecting all references to money; your partner does the same with love. Put them all on branches on your diagram.
- Show each other your finished work. Then discuss the ratio of love references to money references in Act 3 Scene 2.

1　hence　离开
2　cheer　脸
3　use your pleasure　您酌情处理吧
4　Dispatch　安排好
5　Nor ... twain　要等到我们再次见面我才敢安睡
6　naughty　糊涂；没用
7　fond　愚蠢

Write about it 写作练习

Bassanio's reply

After reading Antonio's letter (lines 314–19), take on the role of Bassanio and write a reply that you will send ahead of you, to reach Antonio immediately. Think carefully about how you will begin, and how you will respond to each point that Antonio makes in his letter. How exactly will you inform him that you have just won Portia's hand in marriage?

This photograph shows Antonio (left) and Shylock (right). Can you match it with a line from the script opposite?

THE MERCHANT OF VENICE ACT 3 SCENE 3

When it is paid, bring your true friend along.
My maid Nerissa and myself meantime
Will live as maids and widows. Come away,
For you shall hence¹ upon your wedding day. 310
Bid your friends welcome, show a merry cheer²;
Since you are dear bought, I will love you dear.
But let me hear the letter of your friend.

BASSANIO [*Reads*] 'Sweet Bassanio, my ships have all miscarried, my creditors grow cruel, my estate is very low; my bond to the Jew is 315 forfeit, and since in paying it, it is impossible I should live, all debts are cleared between you and I if I might but see you at my death. Notwithstanding, use your pleasure³; if your love do not persuade you to come, let not my letter.'

PORTIA O love! Dispatch⁴ all business and be gone. 320
BASSANIO Since I have your good leave to go away,
I will make haste. But till I come again
No bed shall e'er be guilty of my stay
Nor rest be interposer 'twixt us twain⁵.

Exeunt

Act 3 Scene 3
Venice   A street

Enter SHYLOCK, SOLANIO, ANTONIO, *and the Jailer*

SHYLOCK Jailer, look to him. Tell not me of mercy.
This is the fool that lent out money gratis.
Jailer, look to him.
ANTONIO   Hear me yet, good Shylock –
SHYLOCK I'll have my bond, speak not against my bond;
I have sworn an oath that I will have my bond. 5
Thou call'dst me dog before thou hadst a cause,
But since I am a dog, beware my fangs.
The Duke shall grant me justice. I do wonder,
Thou naughty⁶ jailer, that thou art so fond⁷
To come abroad with him at his request. 10
ANTONIO I pray thee hear me speak –

Antonio suspects that Shylock wants him dead because he has paid the debts of many of Shylock's clients. He feels that the Duke must uphold the law of Venice, and so is resigned to death.

 剧情简介：安托纽怀疑夏洛克想要他的命是因为他帮夏洛克的很多客户还清了债务。他相信公爵一定会依照威尼斯的法律行事，所以他愿听从发落，不惜一死。

1 Shylock: in no mood to back down (in pairs)

In the short time he is on stage, Shylock dominates the dialogue and Antonio struggles to get a word in.

- Read the exchange aloud (lines 1–17). Shylock should circle around Antonio, delivering each short sentence from a different angle to increase its power.
- Try it again, this time with Shylock jabbing (指，戳) his finger sharply towards Antonio as he speaks. Work out how to bring out the menace of 'beware my fangs (尖牙)' and the insistent repetition of 'I'll have my bond'.
- Explore different ways of conveying Shylock's uncompromising, dominant mood. Show your preferred version to the class.

1	dull-eyed	目光呆滞
2	intercessors	调解人
3	kept with	活在……中间
4	bootless	无希望，无用
5	made moan	抱怨
6	commodity	交易
7	impeach	败坏……的名誉
8	Consisteth of	依靠
9	bated	使瘦弱
10	hardly	几乎不能，很难

Write about it 写作练习

Thoughts from prison

Imagine that you are Antonio, in your prison cell, the night before your trial. Shylock has the weight of the law on his side and you know that he wants to destroy you because you have bailed (保释) out many of the men who owed him money – and threatened Shylock's business in the process. You must feel your death is inevitable. You have been so troubled by all your 'griefs and losses' that you have lost a lot of weight through stress. You can only hope that Bassanio will arrive in time 'to see [you] pay his debt'.

- Write down your thoughts in what you fear will be the last entry you will ever make in your diary.

2 Where do your sympathies lie? (in small groups)

Scene 3 gives a very brief glimpse of events in Venice before returning to Belmont for the final two scenes in Act 3. Shakespeare briefly shows us the two adversaries who will later do battle in court as Shylock pursues his 'bond'.

a Together, review the way in which Shakespeare presents Shylock and Antonio in this scene. Explore what they say, how they behave and how other characters react to them.

b Prepare a short group presentation on how you think Shakespeare influences the audience's attitude to the two men.

SHYLOCK	I'll have my bond; I will not hear thee speak;	
	I'll have my bond, and therefore speak no more.	
	I'll not be made a soft and dull-eyed[1] fool,	
	To shake the head, relent, and sigh, and yield	15
	To Christian intercessors[2]. Follow not!	
	I'll have no speaking, I will have my bond. *Exit*	
SOLANIO	It is the most impenetrable cur	
	That ever kept with[3] men.	
ANTONIO	Let him alone.	
	I'll follow him no more with bootless[4] prayers.	20
	He seeks my life, his reason well I know:	
	I oft delivered from his forfeitures	
	Many that have at times made moan[5] to me;	
	Therefore he hates me.	
SOLANIO	I am sure the Duke	
	Will never grant this forfeiture to hold.	25
ANTONIO	The Duke cannot deny the course of law;	
	For the commodity[6] that strangers have	
	With us in Venice, if it be denied,	
	Will much impeach[7] the justice of the state,	
	Since that the trade and profit of the city	30
	Consisteth of[8] all nations. Therefore go.	
	These griefs and losses have so bated[9] me	
	That I shall hardly[10] spare a pound of flesh	
	Tomorrow to my bloody creditor.	
	Well, jailer, on. Pray God Bassanio come	35
	To see me pay his debt, and then I care not.	
	Exeunt	

Lorenzo and Portia talk of the close friendship between Antonio and Bassanio. Portia says she plans to stay in a convent during Bassanio's absence. She appoints Lorenzo master of her household until her return.

剧情简介：劳仁佐和鲍霞谈论安托纽和博萨纽的亲密友谊。鲍霞说在博萨纽不在家的这段时间她打算待在修道院，她聘任劳仁佐做她的管家，直到她回来。

1 Who's who? (in fours)

Stand in a circle. One person slowly reads Lorenzo's speech (lines 1–9). The others take the roles of Portia, Bassanio and Antonio. The whole group points at everyone mentioned on *every* mention; for example, there are three 'points' in line 1. (This pointing is called **deixis** [指示，指示语]. It sounds complicated, but is quickly mastered and will help your understanding of other passages in the play.)

> ### Language in the play 剧中语言
> #### More hyperbole (in pairs)
> Lorenzo's opening lines (1–4) praise Portia extravagantly. Like Bassanio in Act 3 Scene 3, his language veers (猛然转向) towards hyperbole.
> - Talk together about the possible reasons why he is so excessive in his praise of Portia's qualities. Do you think he is being sincere, or is he overdoing the praise? And what do you think are Shakespeare's intentions here?
> - Present your strongest ideas in a whole-class pooling of responses.

2 Friends resemble each other (in pairs)

The language of both characters in lines 1–21 is very formal and polite.

a Take parts and speak the lines. Don't worry if there are lines or phrases you don't understand. (Many people find that the formality of the exchange creates difficulties.) The general sense of the lines is: Lorenzo explains that if Portia knew what Antonio was truly like, she would be even prouder of her action in helping him. Portia replies (lines 11–18) that because close friends are always alike, Antonio must be like Bassanio in appearance, manner and spirit.

b As at the end of the previous scene, the focus is on the intense friendship between Antonio and Bassanio. But do you agree with what Portia says? Are close friends really like each other? Or do you choose your friends because they are *unlike* you? Write a paragraph outlining your thoughts and then swap it with your partner for comment and discussion.

1	in your presence	当着您的面
2	conceit	理解
3	bearing thus	用这种方式忍受
4	lover	挚友
5	customary bounty	寻常善举
6	waste	度过，打发（时间）
7	egal yoke	同等
8	lineaments	仪表，外貌
9	bosom lover	密友，挚交
10	bestowed	花费；给予
11	the semblance of my soul	与我灵魂（指博萨纽）类似的人（指安托纽）
12	husbandry and manage	管理，打理
13	contemplation	冥想

102

Act 3 Scene 4
Belmont   A room in Portia's house

Enter PORTIA, NERISSA, LORENZO, JESSICA, *and* BALTHAZAR
a man of Portia's

LORENZO	Madam, although I speak it in your presence[1],	
	You have a noble and a true conceit[2]	
	Of god-like amity, which appears most strongly	
	In bearing thus[3] the absence of your lord.	
	But if you knew to whom you show this honour,	5
	How true a gentleman you send relief,	
	How dear a lover[4] of my lord your husband,	
	I know you would be prouder of the work	
	Than customary bounty[5] can enforce you.	
PORTIA	I never did repent for doing good,	10
	Nor shall not now; for in companions	
	That do converse and waste[6] the time together,	
	Whose souls do bear an egal yoke[7] of love,	
	There must be needs a like proportion	
	Of lineaments[8], of manners, and of spirit;	15
	Which makes me think that this Antonio,	
	Being the bosom lover[9] of my lord,	
	Must needs be like my lord. If it be so,	
	How little is the cost I have bestowed[10]	
	In purchasing the semblance of my soul[11]	20
	From out the state of hellish cruelty!	
	This comes too near the praising of myself,	
	Therefore no more of it: hear other things.	
	Lorenzo, I commit into your hands	
	The husbandry and manage[12] of my house	25
	Until my lord's return; for mine own part	
	I have toward heaven breathed a secret vow	
	To live in prayer and contemplation[13],	
	Only attended by Nerissa here,	
	Until her husband and my lord's return.	30

Portia says she and Nerissa will stay at a convent. She sends her servant, Balthazar, to Padua to collect clothes and papers from Doctor Bellario.

 剧情简介：鲍霞说她和讷瑞莎会待在修道院。她命仆人巴尔特扎，去帕度亚帮她取回衣物和比拉瑞欧博士的信件。

1 Portia and Jessica (in pairs)

Brief though it is, Jessica eventually manages to speak a line to Portia.

- Work on lines 42–4, reading the words aloud in different ways. Use gestures and movements to illustrate their relationship (or lack of one). In one modern production, Portia forgot Jessica's name at line 44 and had to be reminded of it. Try that version in your own explorations. Then discuss what you think the script shows about the relationship between the two women.

1	monastery 修道院
2	abide 居住
3	imposition 职责
4	render 放到，递到
5	with imagined speed 以最快的速度
6	traject 泊船的地方，渡口
7	common 公共
8	trades to 开往，驶向

Themes 主题分析

Appearance and reality: what's Portia up to?

After formally committing the running of Belmont to Lorenzo and Jessica, Portia explains that she's going to live in a convent with Nerissa until the men return from Venice. Then, when Lorenzo and Jessica have left, she sends her servant Balthazar on a secret mission to her cousin, Doctor Bellario, and arranges to meet him at the boarding point for the ferry to Venice.

Again, the play is exploring the difference between what is true and what is false. At line 60, when Portia informs Nerissa that they will both adopt male disguises, we are reminded that we can't always trust what we see.

- Begin a new section in your Themes file, which will focus on Portia and Nerissa's disguises and how Shakespeare uses them in the unfolding drama of the final acts. Add evidence as it crops up (突然出现).

2 Ask Jessica (whole class)

Jessica will stand in for Portia as the mistress (女主人) of Belmont while Portia is absent. As a Jew, she is now in charge of a Christian household, and Portia has shown few signs of trusting her or respecting her views. She has just listened to her new husband praise Portia to the skies, yet she has received barely a word from him.

- What has she let herself in for? And how does she now feel about the decisions she's made in order to be with Lorenzo at Belmont? One person volunteers to be Jessica. The rest of the class put her in the 'hot-seat' and ask her questions to discover how she really feels about the way her life is shaping up.

There is a monastery[1] two miles off,
And there we will abide[2]. I do desire you
Not to deny this imposition[3],
The which my love and some necessity
Now lays upon you.

LORENZO   Madam, with all my heart   35
I shall obey you in all fair commands.

PORTIA   My people do already know my mind,
And will acknowledge you and Jessica
In place of Lord Bassanio and myself.
So fare you well till we shall meet again.   40

LORENZO   Fair thoughts and happy hours attend on you.

JESSICA   I wish your ladyship all heart's content.

PORTIA   I thank you for your wish, and am well pleased
To wish it back on you: fare you well, Jessica.

Exeunt [Jessica and Lorenzo]

Now, Balthazar –   45
As I have ever found thee honest-true,
So let me find thee still; take this same letter,
And use thou all th'endeavour of a man
In speed to Padua. See thou render[4] this
Into my cousin's hand, Doctor Bellario;   50
And look, what notes and garments he doth give thee
Bring them, I pray thee, with imagined speed[5]
Unto the traject[6], to the common[7] ferry
Which trades to[8] Venice. Waste no time in words
But get thee gone; I shall be there before thee.   55

BALTHAZAR   Madam, I go with all convenient speed.   [*Exit*]

PORTIA   Come on, Nerissa; I have work in hand
That you yet know not of. We'll see our husbands
Before they think of us.

NERISSA   Shall they see us?

Portia tells Nerissa of her plans. They will see their husbands again, but in disguise as men. In Scene 5, Lancelot fears that Jessica will be damned because she is a Jew's daughter.

 剧情简介：鲍霞把她的计划告诉了讷瑞莎。她们将再次见到各自的丈夫，不过是女扮男装。第五场，朗斯勒担心婕丝柯会下地狱，因为她是犹太人的女儿。

1 What men are like (in pairs)

In lines 65–76, as Portia shares her plans to adopt a male disguise with Nerissa, she gives a range of examples of what she considers typical male behaviour.

a Working in pairs, one of you chooses one of these 'examples' and works out how to mime it for your partner to identify.

b Swap roles, then work together on a single example that you will present to the rest of the class. Can the others recognise which image you chose?

c Make a list of five other habits or types of behaviour that the two women might adopt ('A thousand raw tricks … Which I will practise') if they are going to convince other people of their 'manhood'.

d Share your ideas with others in the class. Afterwards, try to rewrite your list in the same style and rhythm as lines 65–76 (see pp. 182–3 for help).

Characters 人物分析

Portia's attitude to men (in pairs)

a Having explored the kind of behaviour that Portia thinks is typical of men (Activity 1 above), use her lines 65–76 to write a short account of her attitude to the male sex. Focus on the language she uses and the tone that it creates. For example, do you think she is serious, or mocking and sarcastic? Show how her words add to your understanding of Portia's attitudes to men.

b On two occasions in the script opposite, Portia shows that she is fully aware of sexual language and behaviour. Lines 61–2, 'accomplished / With that we lack', mean 'equipped with male genitals'. Then, in response to Nerissa's question (lines 79–80), she deliberately misunderstands the words 'turn to', interpreting them as 'sexually entice (诱惑) or invite'. Talk together about whether this affects your previous understanding of how Portia's character is presented.

c Add your thoughts to the Character file you are keeping for Portia.

1 habit 装束，打扮
2 accomplishèd / With that we lack 拥有我们所缺少的（男性生殖器）
3 I'll hold thee any wager 我愿跟你打任何赌
4 accoutred 乔装打扮
5 speak … boy 假装用从大男孩变为成年人时变声的嗓音说话
6 a reed voice 尖锐的声音
7 mincing 婀娜细步
8 bragging 吹牛
9 quaint 精心编造的
10 I could not do withal 对此我束手无策
11 puny 无力；差劲
12 discontinued school / Above a twelvemonth 迈出校门一年多
13 raw tricks 幼稚把戏
14 bragging jacks 夸夸其谈的年轻人
15 turn to 变成，扮成（也有"挑逗，调情"之意）
16 lewd 猥琐，下流
17 device 计划
18 stays 等待
19 measure 赶（路）
20 plain 坦诚
21 agitation 担忧
22 bastard 野崽子；不正当

PORTIA	They shall, Nerissa, but in such a habit[1]	60
	That they shall think we are accomplishèd	
	With that we lack[2]. I'll hold thee any wager[3],	
	When we are both accoutred[4] like young men	
	I'll prove the prettier fellow of the two,	
	And wear my dagger with the braver grace,	65
	And speak between the change of man and boy[5]	
	With a reed voice[6], and turn two mincing[7] steps	
	Into a manly stride; and speak of 'frays	
	Like a fine bragging[8] youth; and tell quaint[9] lies	
	How honourable ladies sought my love,	70
	Which I denying, they fell sick and died –	
	I could not do withal[10]. Then I'll repent,	
	And wish for all that that I had not killed them;	
	And twenty of these puny[11] lies I'll tell,	
	That men shall swear I have discontinued school	75
	Above a twelvemonth[12]. I have within my mind	
	A thousand raw tricks[13] of these bragging jacks[14],	
	Which I will practise.	
NERISSA	Why, shall we turn to[15] men?	
PORTIA	Fie, what a question's that,	
	If thou wert near a lewd[16] interpreter!	80
	But come, I'll tell thee all my whole device[17]	
	When I am in my coach, which stays[18] for us	
	At the park gate; and therefore haste away,	
	For we must measure[19] twenty miles today.	

Exeunt

Act 3 Scene 5
Belmont   Portia's garden

Enter LANCELOT *the Clown and* JESSICA

LANCELOT Yes truly, for look you, the sins of the father are to be laid upon the children. Therefore I promise you I fear you. I was always plain[20] with you, and so now I speak my agitation[21] of the matter. Therefore be o'good cheer, for truly I think you are damned. There is but one hope in it that can do you any good, and that is but a kind of bastard[22] hope neither.

5

Jessica tells Lancelot that Lorenzo has converted her to Christianity. Lorenzo accuses Lancelot of making a black girl pregnant. Lancelot doesn't take it seriously.

剧情简介：婕丝柯告诉朗斯勒说劳仁佐已经说服她皈依了基督教。劳仁佐指控朗斯勒让一个黑人女孩怀孕了。朗斯勒并未将此事放在心上。

Stagecraft 导演技巧

Act out the scene (in threes)

a Scene 5 can be played in many different ways. Prepare your own performance or reading for the class, keeping in mind:

- how the conversation might have started before Lancelot's opening line
- what Lancelot and Jessica are doing in this particular place (are they working together, or is Lancelot waiting upon Jessica, or is there some other explanation?)
- what feelings Lancelot and Jessica might have for one another (see also Act 2 Scenes 3 and 5 for useful background information)
- how serious Lancelot is in his taunting of Jessica, especially the implication that Jews are 'damned'
- how Lorenzo makes his entrance and whether he really is jealous of Lancelot
- whether Lancelot is more intelligent than his customary 'clowning' suggests
- what specific feelings you want the audience to have towards these three characters at this moment.

You will find that the scene makes a fascinating human triangle. Use movement and gesture to enhance and increase the impact of your performance.

b Write up a commentary in your Director's Journal on your interpretation and the issues it raises.

1 **got you not** 没有生下你
2 **Scylla** 斯库拉（希腊神话中6头12脚的食人女怪，住在墨西拿 [Messina] 海峡的一侧，专吃穿过海峡的水手）
3 **fall into** （朗斯勒此话有明显的性暗示，含有"插入"的猥亵义）
4 **Charybdis** 卡律布迪斯（传说中墨西拿海峡另一侧的大漩涡，朗斯勒的困境可用一句英谚 **between Scylla and Charybdis** [或 **between the devil and the deep blue sea**] 来表达，意为"左右为难"）
5 **enow** = enough
6 **e'en** = even
7 **we … money** 马上我们连一片薄薄的熏肉都买不起啦
8 **out** 发生口角
9 **the commonwealth** 社会
10 **the getting … belly** 把那个黑人的肚子搞大了
11 **if … for** 如果她称不上良家妇女，那她确实大大超出我对她的看法
12 **discourse** 说话
13 **stomachs** 胃口

1 Thinking about mood (in small groups)

a In the light of your interpretation of this final scene in Act 3, prepare a short group presentation that focuses on the mood you think Shakespeare is trying to create at the close of Act 3. As preparation, make a list of all the 'serious' elements (for example, the possible anti-Semitic references, and the fact that Lancelot has made a black girl pregnant) and the more 'playful' ones (such as Lancelot's deliberate misinterpretations).

b Assess the 'balance' between 'serious' and 'playful', and explain your thinking as you present your ideas to other groups.

c Based on your enquiries about this scene, what do you think are the likely events Shakespeare is planning for Act 4?

JESSICA	And what hope is that, I pray thee?
LANCELOT	Marry, you may partly hope that your father got you not[1], that you are not the Jew's daughter.
JESSICA	That were a kind of bastard hope indeed; so the sins of my mother should be visited upon me.
LANCELOT	Truly, then, I fear you are damned both by father and mother; thus when I shun Scylla[2] your father, I fall into[3] Charybdis[4] your mother. Well, you are gone both ways.
JESSICA	I shall be saved by my husband; he hath made me a Christian.
LANCELOT	Truly, the more to blame he; we were Christians enow[5] before, e'en[6] as many as could well live one by another. This making of Christians will raise the price of hogs; if we grow all to be pork eaters, we shall not shortly have a rasher on the coals for money[7].

Enter LORENZO

JESSICA	I'll tell my husband, Lancelot, what you say: here he comes.
LORENZO	I shall grow jealous of you shortly, Lancelot, if you thus get my wife into corners.
JESSICA	Nay, you need not fear us, Lorenzo: Lancelot and I are out[8]. He tells me flatly there's no mercy for me in heaven, because I am a Jew's daughter; and he says you are no good member of the commonwealth[9], for in converting Jews to Christians you raise the price of pork.
LORENZO	I shall answer that better to the commonwealth than you can the getting up of the Negro's belly[10]: the Moor is with child by you, Lancelot.
LANCELOT	It is much that the Moor should be more than reason; but if she be less than an honest woman, she is indeed more than I took her for[11].
LORENZO	How every fool can play upon the word! I think the best grace of wit will shortly turn into silence, and discourse[12] grow commendable in none only but parrots. Go in, sirrah, bid them prepare for dinner.
LANCELOT	That is done, sir; they have all stomachs[13].

Lancelot deliberately misinterprets Lorenzo's words, but is sent off to arrange the serving of dinner. Jessica tells her husband how much she admires Portia. Lorenzo says he also has similar admirable qualities.

 剧情简介：朗斯勒故意曲解劳仁佐的话，但被打发去准备晚餐。婕丝柯告诉丈夫她如何钦佩鲍霞，劳仁佐说他自己同样有值得钦佩的品质。

Write about it 写作练习

Lancelot confesses all? (in pairs, then by yourself)

On the several occasions we have seen Lancelot, he has displayed a variety of moods and attitudes. He's been critical of his ex-master Shylock but supportive of Jessica; cruel in his treatment of his nearly blind father; and now news breaks that he's got a black girl pregnant. He seems to enjoy being 'centre stage' and twisting the meaning (sometimes accidentally!) of the language he uses.

- Imagine that after his exit (line 52) he writes a letter to his father, updating Old Gobbo on events since they separated (Act 2 Scene 2). With a partner, plan the content of his letter.
- By yourself, write the letter. Challenge yourself further by imitating Lancelot's playful use of language.

1 Jessica: Portia's biggest fan? (in pairs)

Notice that Lorenzo does not use Portia's name now that she is married to his friend. Jessica appears to be a huge admirer of 'Lord Bassanio's wife', and her speech is full of glowing compliments about Portia.

a Take it in turns to read lines 61–71. Then talk about whether Portia has earned Jessica's praise (and whether you think she deserves it).

b Identify examples of the language of religious adoration (崇拜) that Jessica uses, and write a comment on the impact of those words.

c Focus on the image created in lines 67–71, using the glossary to help you understand it, and draw your version of the image to show to other pairs.

2 But what does she think of Lorenzo? (in pairs)

As the two young lovers go in to dinner, Lorenzo comments that he is as admirable as Portia. Is he joking and affectionate? Or is he (as one production presented him) humourless, self-important and arrogant, treating his wife like a small child?

- Work through lines 71–8, trying both interpretations and any others that provide interesting dramatic possibilities.
- When you have settled on your favourite, run it through for others to watch, and freeze the action in a tableau that provides a striking finale to Act 3.

1 **witsnapper** 爱说俏皮话的人（莎士比亚自创词）
2 **cover** 摆饭（但朗斯勒后面有意将之理解为"戴上帽子"）
3 **quarrelling with occasion** 插科打诨，耍贫嘴
4 **humours and conceits** 感觉和想法；心血来潮
5 **discretion** 理智；判断力
6 **planted** 安插
7 **army of good words** 千军万马的好词
8 **A many** 很多
9 **Garnished** 配备好
10 **tricksy** 模棱两可
11 **Defy the matter** 罔顾事实
12 **meet** 适当
13 **merit** 配得上
14 **Pawned** 抵押，担保
15 **rude** 原始
16 **fellow** 同等，同样
17 **howsome'er** 无论怎么

THE MERCHANT OF VENICE ACT 3 SCENE 5
威尼斯商人

LORENZO Goodly Lord, what a witsnapper¹ are you! Then bid them prepare dinner.
LANCELOT That is done too, sir; only 'cover²' is the word.
LORENZO Will you cover then, sir?
LANCELOT Not so, sir, neither; I know my duty. 45
LORENZO Yet more quarrelling with occasion³! Wilt thou show the whole wealth of thy wit in an instant? I pray thee understand a plain man in his plain meaning: go to thy fellows, bid them cover the table, serve in the meat, and we will come in to dinner.
LANCELOT For the table, sir, it shall be served in; for the meat, sir, it 50 shall be covered; for your coming in to dinner, sir, why, let it be as humours and conceits⁴ shall govern. *Exit*
LORENZO   O dear discretion⁵, how his words are suited!
          The fool hath planted⁶ in his memory
          An army of good words⁷; and I do know 55
          A many⁸ fools that stand in better place,
          Garnished⁹ like him, that for a tricksy¹⁰ word
          Defy the matter¹¹. How cheer'st thou, Jessica?
          And now, good sweet, say thy opinion:
          How dost thou like the Lord Bassanio's wife? 60
JESSICA   Past all expressing. It is very meet¹²
          The Lord Bassanio live an upright life,
          For having such a blessing in his lady
          He finds the joys of heaven here on earth,
          And if on earth he do not merit¹³ it, 65
          In reason he should never come to heaven.
          Why, if two gods should play some heavenly match,
          And on the wager lay two earthly women,
          And Portia one, there must be something else
          Pawned¹⁴ with the other, for the poor rude¹⁵ world 70
          Hath not her fellow¹⁶.
LORENZO   Even such a husband
          Hast thou of me, as she is for a wife.
JESSICA   Nay, but ask my opinion too of that.
LORENZO   I will anon; first let us go to dinner.
JESSICA   Nay, let me praise you while I have a stomach. 75
LORENZO   No, pray thee, let it serve for table talk;
          Then howsome'er¹⁷ thou speak'st, 'mong other things
          I shall digest it.
JESSICA   Well, I'll set you forth. *Exeunt*

111

The Merchant of Venice
威尼斯商人

Looking back at Act 3 第3幕回顾
Activities for groups or individuals

1 Language: Shylock's lists and repetitions

In Act 3 Scene 1, Shylock often repeats certain words and phrases. He also uses lots of 'listing' (piling up item on item for dramatic effect – look, for example, at his lines 43–6).

- Write down the key words and phrases he repeats and any lists that he uses. Afterwards, write one paragraph exploring the kind of language that Shylock repeats. Then write another paragraph about what Shylock's use of lists adds to your understanding of his character.

2 Revenge: the defining moment?

'The villainy you teach me I will execute, and it shall go hard but I will better the instruction.' (Act 3 Scene 1, lines 56–7)

The director Sir Peter Hall described these lines as the most important in the play, because they show Shakespeare's understanding of why Shylock behaves so harshly.

- On page 76, you were asked to reflect on whether this is the moment when Shylock decides on revenge, and to consider alternative decisive moments through the rest of Act 3 Scene 1. In the light of your investigations, present your definitive judgement to your class. Be sure to justify your thinking using evidence from the script.

3 Why does Shylock hate Antonio?

'I oft delivered from his forfeitures / Many that have at times made moan to me' (Act 3 Scene 3, lines 22–3) is Antonio's explanation for Shylock's hatred of him. Shylock probably has other reasons for his hatred.

- Make a full list of Shylock's reasons for hating Antonio. Give a short quotation from the script as an example of each reason. Then consider how far you think Shakespeare has 'stereotyped' Shylock. Do his responses to Antonio seem understandable?

4 Venice and Belmont

What impressions of Belmont have you acquired so far? Using the template below, complete ten contrasting sentences for the two locations, Venice and Belmont: Belmont is _____ ; Venice is _____ .

5 The 'key' Shylock lines

Although Shylock's presence is very powerful in Act 3, Shakespeare gives him only 71 lines of script. (Note that many are prose, not verse lines.)

- Read quickly through them again and choose six key **sense units** (phrases or even single words that make sense on their own). Learn and perform them.
- On a second performance, film them (use your mobile phone if you wish) so that you can focus on action and gesture. Get your classmates to comment on your choice and interpretation of 'key' lines.

6 More of a voice

Tubal appears in only one scene (Act 3 Scene 1).

- Create a 'character profile' for him, exploring his Jewish background and his life in Venice. Then imagine that he meets another Jewish friend. Write a speech for him to deliver at that meeting, in which he describes his encounter with Shylock.

The jailer is one of Shakespeare's 'silent characters'.

- Look at the events he witnesses in Act 3 Scene 3 and write up his account in a formal report.

7 To cut or not to cut?

Some critics view Scene 5 primarily as a 'filler' scene to allow Portia and Nerissa time to change into male disguise ready for the trial scene that follows straight after. Others point to its considerable dramatic significance.

- In pairs, one argues for keeping the scene in a new production, the other against it. Give as many reasons as possible for your judgement.

Which moments in Act 3 do you think these two images capture? Which more powerfully conveys Shylock's vulnerability (脆弱)? Explain your thinking.

The Duke's court assembles to judge Shylock's case against Antonio. The Duke sympathises with Antonio, and tells Shylock that he expects him to show mercy at the last moment.

剧情简介：在公爵主持下，法庭开庭审判夏洛克告安托纽案。公爵同情安托纽，希望夏洛克最后一刻能表现出怜悯之心。

Stagecraft 导演技巧
Stage the entrances (in large groups)

In this scene, Shylock brings his case against Antonio to court.

a Use the stage direction to allocate parts, then work out how you would stage the Duke's entrance. Many modern productions give the Duke a throne at the back of the stage. Would you? Bear in mind that the magnificoes (high-ranking Venetians) are his fellow judges. Where would they sit?

b Consider Shylock's entrance, which in Shakespeare's time would have been from the left, the side associated with evil (the Latin word for 'on the left' is *sinister*). Shylock is often presented as a very isolated character in a court full of Christians. (You will find pictures of the trial scenes on pp. 143 and 196.)

c Annotate a sketch to show your ideas for staging the first 16 lines.

1 Ready 在（应答用语）
2 answer 应诉
3 stony 铁石心肠
4 adversary 对手
5 Uncapable 不会
6 void 完全缺乏
7 dram 一点儿
8 qualify 减轻，软化
9 obdùrate 顽固
10 envy 恶意，怨恨
11 tyranny 残暴
12 thou … act 你不到紧要关头不卸下这歹毒的样子
13 remorse 怜悯
14 strange 令人震惊
15 strange 不同寻常
16 exacts the penalty 要求处罚
17 loose 放弃
18 forfeiture 处罚
19 moiety 半数
20 Forgive … principal 减免一部分本金
21 huddled on 堆在……上

1 Are the odds stacked against Shylock? (in pairs)

First, the Duke (like all the Christians) takes away Shylock's identity in his lines 3–6, again denying him his name and labelling him an 'inhuman wretch'. His words are hardly those of a fair and impartial judge! Then Antonio is given a speech of great dignity and restraint (lines 6–13), which engages the audience's sympathy and respect. And this all happens before Shylock even enters the court.

- Talk together about the dramatic impact of the way Shakespeare chooses to begin the trial scene and how far things are already set against Shylock. Add your thoughts to a whole-class discussion.

Write about it 写作练习
Shylock: what's he thinking?

Shylock is 'ready at the door' (line 15). What do you think would be in his mind as he waits? He is about to enter a room full of enemies, but might be only minutes from gaining his much-desired revenge.

- Write a soliloquy for Shylock in modern English, expressing his inner thoughts and feelings at this dramatic moment in the play. Remember, Shylock doesn't always speak in verse in his most important speeches.

Act 4 Scene 1
The Duke's palace in Venice

Enter the DUKE, *the Magnificoes*, ANTONIO, BASSANIO, SALERIO, *and* GRATIANO, *with others*

DUKE	What, is Antonio here?
ANTONIO	Ready[1], so please your grace.
DUKE	I am sorry for thee. Thou art come to answer[2]
	A stony[3] adversary[4], an inhuman wretch,
	Uncapable[5] of pity, void[6] and empty 5
	From any dram[7] of mercy.
ANTONIO	I have heard
	Your grace hath tane great pains to qualify[8]
	His rigorous course; but since he stands obdùrate[9]
	And that no lawful means can carry me
	Out of his envy's[10] reach, I do oppose 10
	My patience to his fury, and am armed
	To suffer with a quietness of spirit
	The very tyranny[11] and rage of his.
DUKE	Go one and call the Jew into the court.
SALERIO	He is ready at the door; he comes, my lord. 15

Enter SHYLOCK

DUKE	Make room and let him stand before our face.
	Shylock, the world thinks, and I think so too,
	That thou but leadest this fashion of thy malice
	To the last hour of act[12], and then 'tis thought
	Thou'lt show thy mercy and remorse[13] more strange[14] 20
	Than is thy strange[15] apparent cruelty.
	And where thou now exacts the penalty[16],
	Which is a pound of this poor merchant's flesh,
	Thou wilt not only loose[17] the forfeiture[18]
	But, touched with human gentleness and love, 25
	Forgive a moiety[19] of the principal[20],
	Glancing an eye of pity on his losses
	That have of late so huddled on[21] his back,
	Enow to press a royal merchant down

115

The Duke asks Shylock to show pity. Shylock refuses to give his reasons for wishing to harm Antonio, except that it is his whim, and that he hates him.

 剧情简介：公爵要夏洛克表示怜悯。夏洛克拒绝说出他想伤害安托纽的理由，只说秉性使然，还说他就是憎恶安托纽。

1 The Duke's appeal to Shylock (in small groups)

This is the Duke's first major speech in the play. How do you think he should address his listeners?

- Read lines 16–34 aloud. Experiment with different styles (for example, powerful, remote, compassionate, reasonable, angry). Note the clues to the Duke's feelings for Antonio and his attitudes to non-Christians.
- Next, work together to summarise the key factual points he makes in this opening address.
- List all the potentially emotive or biased terms he uses.
- Individually, write a brief commentary on the impact these terms might have on: the court; Shylock; the audience.

Characters 人物分析

Focus on Shylock

a Shylock won't explain (in pairs)

Explore Shylock's lines 35–62. Earlier in the play (Act 1 Scene 3, lines 34–43), Shylock expressed his grievances against Antonio. Yet now, in the court, he refuses to discuss his feelings, except to confirm his hatred for Antonio (line 60).

- Talk together about the possible reasons for Shylock's behaviour and the dramatic effects that result from it at this vital point in his revenge plan. Be ready to pool your ideas with other pairs.

b Shylock's curse (by yourself)

Shylock is determined to use the Venetian code of law to press his case against Antonio. If the Duke will not enforce the law, then 'the danger' will result (lines 38–9).

- Write a paragraph to show what you imagine Shylock wishes might happen to 'your charter and your city's freedom' if the law is not followed.
- Write another paragraph exploring what this suggests about Shylock's character.

c Bizarre fears (in pairs)

In lines 44–52, Shylock lists things that some men find disturbing or unpleasant: 'a rat', 'a gaping pig', 'a cat' and the noise of bagpipes.

- Discuss why you think he uses such peculiar examples. Then talk about what those choices suggest about the kind of hatred he feels for Antonio.

---

1 **And pluck … flint** （意思是即使心肠最硬的人也会怜悯安托纽）
2 **Turks, and Tartars** 土耳其人和鞑靼人（基督徒认为土耳其人和鞑靼人跟犹太人一样都是异教徒）
3 **never … courtesy** 从未受过文明的熏陶
4 **gentle** 温和（与Gentile [非犹太人] 谐音）
5 **possessed** 告知，禀告
6 **Sabaoth** 安息日（犹太教徒把一周的第七天作为休息和拜神的日子）
7 **due and forfeit** 应得的处罚
8 **light / Upon** 落在
9 **charter** 特许权
10 **carrion flesh** 腐肉
11 **humour** 嗜好，禀性
12 **baned** 毒死
13 **sings i'the nose** 嗡嗡响
14 **affection / Masters of passion** 好恶，情感的主宰
15 **rendered** 给出
16 **woollen** 包着羊毛的（风笛多包着厚羊毛毡）
17 **but … offended** 忍不住得罪别人，因为自己被人得罪了
18 **lodged** 根深蒂固
19 **certain** 不可动摇，坚定不移
20 **losing** 无利可图
21 **current of thy cruelty** 你的身体里流淌的残忍

	And pluck commiseration of his state	30
	From brassy bosoms and rough hearts of flint[1],	
	From stubborn Turks, and Tartars[2] never trained	
	To offices of tender courtesy[3].	
	We all expect a gentle[4] answer, Jew.	
SHYLOCK	I have possessed[5] your grace of what I purpose,	35
	And by our holy Sabaoth[6] have I sworn	
	To have the due and forfeit[7] of my bond.	
	If you deny it, let the danger light	
	Upon[8] your charter[9] and your city's freedom!	
	You'll ask me why I rather choose to have	40
	A weight of carrion flesh[10] than to receive	
	Three thousand ducats. I'll not answer that –	
	But say it is my humour[11]: is it answered?	
	What if my house be troubled with a rat,	
	And I be pleased to give ten thousand ducats	45
	To have it baned[12]? What, are you answered yet?	
	Some men there are love not a gaping pig;	
	Some that are mad if they behold a cat;	
	And others when the bagpipe sings i'the nose[13]	
	Cannot contain their urine: for affection	50
	Masters of passion[14], sways it to the mood	
	Of what it likes or loathes. Now for your answer:	
	As there is no firm reason to be rendered[15]	
	Why he cannot abide a gaping pig,	
	Why he a harmless necessary cat,	55
	Why he a woollen[16] bagpipe, but of force	
	Must yield to such inevitable shame	
	As to offend, himself being offended[17]:	
	So can I give no reason, nor I will not,	
	More than a lodged[18] hate and a certain[19] loathing	60
	I bear Antonio, that I follow thus	
	A losing[20] suit against him. Are you answered?	
BASSANIO	This is no answer, thou unfeeling man,	
	To excuse the current of thy cruelty[21].	

Antonio says it's pointless to argue with the pitiless Shylock. Bassanio's offer of six thousand ducats is refused. Shylock demands the pound of flesh as his property, and due to him by law.

剧情简介：安托纽说和冷酷无情的夏洛克争论毫无意义。博萨纽提出愿意偿还六千块钱，但被夏洛克拒绝。夏洛克要求得到那一磅肉，因为那是根据法律规定属于他的财产。

Many modern productions choose to highlight Shylock's Jewishness in the trial scene (even if he is presented as fully assimilated into Venetian society in other scenes). How do you think he should be costumed for this scene?

1	Every … first	不是每一次冒犯一开始都出于仇恨
2	I … question	您为什么要跟（犹太人）争辩
3	main flood	大海
4	bate	降低
5	ewe bleat for the lamb	母羊为失去羔羊而咩咩哀啼
6	wag	摇摆
7	fretten	使烦恼，使忧虑
8	brief and plain conveniency	直截了当，简而言之
9	draw	接受，拿
10	abject	卑贱
11	slavish	下贱
12	parts	苦活儿
13	palates	腭，嘴巴
14	seasoned	增添风味
15	viands	食物
16	fie upon	让……见鬼去
17	decrees	法令，法律

Language in the play 剧中语言

Antonio's repetition

In lines 70–83, Antonio stresses how stubborn Shylock is. Reasoning with him is like trying to arrest nature itself. It is impossible to stop the waves on the beach or the wolf eating the lamb. Notice how he repeats the same phrase: 'You may as well' (used again in line 78).

- Look carefully at the dramatic impact of Antonio's repeated phrase. How effectively does it convey the utter hopelessness of Antonio's case? How much sympathy does it create for Antonio?
- Write a paragraph for your Language file in answer to the two questions above.

1 Give me judgement!

Lines 89–103 are Shylock's plea for his case to be heard. Just as the Venetians can do as they please with slaves they have purchased, he argues that he can do as he wishes with his 'dearly bought' bond.

a Try speaking aloud Shylock's speech in a variety of ways: defiantly (目中无人), angrily, calmly.

b Learn and rehearse your definitive version for performance in front of your peers, who each write up a short commentary on how it made them feel as they listened.

THE MERCHANT OF VENICE ACT 4 SCENE 1
威尼斯商人

SHYLOCK	I am not bound to please thee with my answers.	65
BASSANIO	Do all men kill the things they do not love?	
SHYLOCK	Hates any man the thing he would not kill?	
BASSANIO	Every offence is not a hate at first[1].	
SHYLOCK	What, wouldst thou have a serpent sting thee twice?	
ANTONIO	I pray you think you question[2] with the Jew.	70
	You may as well go stand upon the beach	
	And bid the main flood[3] bate[4] his usual height;	
	You may as well use question with the wolf	
	Why he hath made the ewe bleat for the lamb[5];	
	You may as well forbid the mountain pines	75
	To wag[6] their high tops and to make no noise	
	When they are fretten[7] with the gusts of heaven;	
	You may as well do anything most hard	
	As seek to soften that – than which what's harder? –	
	His Jewish heart. Therefore I do beseech you	80
	Make no moe offers, use no farther means,	
	But with all brief and plain conveniency[8]	
	Let me have judgement, and the Jew his will.	
BASSANIO	For thy three thousand ducats here is six.	
SHYLOCK	If every ducat in six thousand ducats	85
	Were in six parts, and every part a ducat,	
	I would not draw[9] them; I would have my bond.	
DUKE	How shalt thou hope for mercy, rendering none?	
SHYLOCK	What judgement shall I dread, doing no wrong?	
	You have among you many a purchased slave,	90
	Which, like your asses and your dogs and mules,	
	You use in abject[10] and in slavish[11] parts[12]	
	Because you bought them. Shall I say to you,	
	'Let them be free! Marry them to your heirs!	
	Why sweat they under burdens? Let their beds	95
	Be made as soft as yours, and let their palates[13]	
	Be seasoned[14] with such viands[15]'? You will answer,	
	'The slaves are ours.' So do I answer you.	
	The pound of flesh which I demand of him	
	Is dearly bought; 'tis mine, and I will have it.	100
	If you deny me, fie upon[16] your law:	
	There is no force in the decrees[17] of Venice.	
	I stand for judgement. Answer: shall I have it?	

Nerissa, disguised as a lawyer's clerk, arrives with letters from Bellario, a legal expert. Shylock sharpens his knife on the sole of his shoe, and Gratiano abuses him for his cruel nature.

 剧情简介：乔装成律师助理的讷瑞莎带着法律专家比拉瑞欧的信来到法庭。夏洛克在自己的鞋底上磨刀，格拉奇阿诺大骂夏洛克残忍无情。

Characters 人物分析

Antonio's self-pity? (in pairs)

Bassanio tries to cheer up Antonio (lines 111–13), and offers to take Antonio's place as Shylock pursues his forfeit. But Antonio insists (lines 114–18) that he must be the one to die, first referring to himself as a 'tainted wether' (sick ram), then as the 'weakest' fruit that drops from the tree because it does not grow vigorously enough.

- Talk together about whether you think Antonio is being selfless or selfish here.
- Draw up a table with two columns: one headed 'selfless', the other 'selfish'. Gather evidence about Antonio from the scene to fill each column, and explain why you placed each item in its column.

1 Gratiano attacks (in small groups)

Gratiano viciously abuses Shylock, saying that a dead wolf's soul entered his body whilst he was still in his mother's womb.

a One person, as Shylock, sits on a chair. The others experiment with different ways of speaking, shouting, sneering (嘲笑，冷笑) or whispering all his lines between 123 and 138 at him, changing over at each punctuation mark. Try moving around the seated Shylock or delivering your lines from different parts of the room. Take turns to be Shylock.

b In role as Shylock, talk to your group members about how defiant you felt as you experienced Gratiano's verbal onslaught (漫骂).

c Consider what these lines suggest about Gratiano, focusing on words and phrases that you find particularly striking or hostile. Add your responses to your notes on the characters.

1 determine 决定，解决
2 stays without 在外等候
3 New come 刚刚到达
4 tainted wether 生病的公羊
5 Meetest 最适合
6 employed 使从事于
7 still 继续
8 epitaph 墓志铭
9 whet 磨
10 sole / soul （夏洛克在他的鞋底上磨刀；格拉奇阿诺这里用了sole和soul的谐音双关）
11 keen 锋利；挽歌
12 wit 才智
13 inexecrable 无可救药，可恨至极
14 And ... accused! 你活在世上这么久，这是公道的耻辱！
15 waver in 动摇
16 To hold opinion with 赞同
17 Pythagoras 毕达哥拉斯（古希腊哲学家、数学家、灵魂轮回说的创立者，认为人的灵魂可进入兽的躯体，反之亦然）
18 infuse 充填，注入
19 trunks 躯体
20 currish 恶狗一般
21 gallows 绞刑架
22 did his fell soul fleet 凶恶的灵魂飞逃出来
23 unhallowed dam 污秽的母兽
24 ravenous 贪婪

DUKE	Upon my power I may dismiss this court,	
	Unless Bellario, a learned doctor	105
	Whom I have sent for to determine¹ this,	
	Come here today.	
SALERIO	My lord, here stays without²	
	A messenger with letters from the doctor,	
	New come³ from Padua.	
DUKE	Bring us the letters. Call the messenger.	110
BASSANIO	Good cheer, Antonio! What, man, courage yet!	
	The Jew shall have my flesh, blood, bones, and all,	
	Ere thou shalt lose for me one drop of blood.	
ANTONIO	I am a tainted wether⁴ of the flock,	
	Meetest⁵ for death; the weakest kind of fruit	115
	Drops earliest to the ground, and so let me.	
	You cannot better be employed⁶, Bassanio,	
	Than to live still⁷ and write mine epitaph⁸.	

Enter NERISSA [*disguised as a lawyer's clerk*]

DUKE	Came you from Padua, from Bellario?	
NERISSA	From both, my lord: [*Presenting letter*] Bellario greets your grace.	120
BASSANIO	Why dost thou whet⁹ thy knife so earnestly?	
SHYLOCK	To cut the forfeiture from that bankrupt there.	
GRATIANO	Not on thy sole¹⁰, but on thy soul¹⁰, harsh Jew,	
	Thou mak'st thy knife keen¹¹. But no metal can,	
	No, not the hangman's axe, bear half the keenness	125
	Of thy sharp envy. Can no prayers pierce thee?	
SHYLOCK	No, none that thou hast wit¹² enough to make.	
GRATIANO	O be thou damned, inexecrable¹³ dog,	
	And for thy life let justice be accused!¹⁴	
	Thou almost mak'st me waver in¹⁵ my faith,	130
	To hold opinion with¹⁶ Pythagoras¹⁷	
	That souls of animals infuse¹⁸ themselves	
	Into the trunks¹⁹ of men. Thy currish²⁰ spirit	
	Governed a wolf, who – hanged for human slaughter –	
	Even from the gallows²¹ did his fell soul fleet²²,	135
	And whilst thou layest in thy unhallowed dam²³	
	Infused itself in thee; for thy desires	
	Are wolfish, bloody, starved, and ravenous²⁴.	

Bellario's letter is read out. He is ill, but has sent Doctor Balthazar in his place. Portia enters in disguise as Balthazar and announces that she is fully informed of the case.

 剧情简介：公爵宣读比拉瑞欧的信。信中说，他因病委派巴尔特扎博士代他判案。鲍霞乔装成巴尔特扎上场，宣称她已完全了解案情。

1 Shylock will not budge

Shylock is immovable. His lines 139–142 show how unshakable is his belief that he is right, and that the law of Venice will uphold his cause.

- Try performing his lines in a way that matches his total conviction.
- Freeze your action at the end of line 142 in a still image that reflects his resolution and determination.

2 Bellario's letter
(in small groups)

The letter the Duke reads out is part of Portia's disguise. It pays 'Balthazar' (Portia) many compliments.

- Pick out the words and phrases about Balthazar that are intended to impress the court. Pool your suggestions about why Portia wants these to be heard before she enters the courtroom.

1	rail	辱骂
2	offend'st	伤害
3	hard by	附近
4	loving visitation	友好探望
5	cause in controversy	纠纷的原因，官司的性质
6	furnished	提供，给予
7	importunity	恳求
8	stead	代替
9	I … estimation	恳请殿下不要因他年轻而怠慢他
10	whose … commendation	这场考验会使他的声望大增
11	difference … question	双方争执的焦点

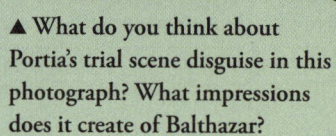

▲ What do you think about Portia's trial scene disguise in this photograph? What impressions does it create of Balthazar?

Stagecraft 导演技巧

Portia in disguise

Portia's entrance marks the beginning of the main phase of the trial scene. Her appearance is an example of dramatic irony: the audience is aware that Balthazar is really Portia in disguise, whereas of the characters, only Nerissa knows this. In Shakespeare's time, the convention was that all disguises (however basic) were impenetrable (无法识破). However, modern productions often try to make Portia's disguise fairly naturalistic and believable.

- What kind of disguise do you think Portia should adopt, bearing in mind that she is appearing in an all-male court? Sketch your costume ideas for a modern production and display them for other students to comment on.

The Merchant of Venice Act 4 Scene 1
威尼斯商人

SHYLOCK	Till thou canst rail¹ the seal from off my bond
	Thou but offend'st² thy lungs to speak so loud.
	Repair thy wit, good youth, or it will fall
	To cureless ruin. I stand here for law.
DUKE	This letter from Bellario doth commend
	A young and learned doctor to our court:
	Where is he?
NERISSA	He attendeth here hard by³
	To know your answer whether you'll admit him.
DUKE	With all my heart. Some three or four of you
	Go give him courteous conduct to this place.

[*Exeunt officials*]

Meantime the court shall hear Bellario's letter.
[*Reads*] 'Your grace shall understand, that at the receipt of your letter I am very sick; but in the instant that your messenger came, in loving visitation⁴ was with me a young doctor of Rome: his name is Balthazar⁵. I acquainted him with the cause in controversy⁵ between the Jew and Antonio the merchant. We turned o'er many books together; he is furnished⁶ with my opinion which, bettered with his own learning, the greatness whereof I cannot enough commend, comes with him at my importunity⁷, to fill up your grace's request in my stead⁸. I beseech you let his lack of years be no impediment to let him lack a reverend estimation⁹, for I never knew so young a body with so old a head. I leave him to your gracious acceptance, whose trial shall better publish his commendation¹⁰.'

Enter PORTIA [*disguised as Doctor Balthazar, followed by officials*]

	You hear the learn'd Bellario what he writes,
	And here I take it is the doctor come.
	Give me your hand. Come you from old Bellario?
PORTIA	I did, my lord.
DUKE	You are welcome; take your place.
	Are you acquainted with the difference
	That holds this present question¹¹ in the court?
PORTIA	I am informèd throughly of the cause.
	Which is the merchant here and which the Jew?

140

145

150

155

160

165

170

Portia appeals unsuccessfully to Shylock to show mercy. She explains that mercy can be neither forced nor diluted, and is greater than any monarch's power. Mercy and justice should go hand in hand, for mercy, not justice, will save us.

剧情简介：鲍霞请求夏洛克表现出仁慈之心，结果只是徒劳。她解释说，仁慈既不能强求也不能削弱，仁慈比任何君主的权力还要大。仁慈和正义应该携手并进，因为最终能拯救我们的是仁慈，而不是正义。

Stagecraft 导演技巧

Portia: taking control?

Portia's line 170 marks a turning point in the trial. Many productions make her tone quite scathing (严厉) in identifying Shylock ('which the Jew?')

- Study her words between her entrance (at line 162) and line 178. Then, in role as director, consider how she should deliver them to show that she quickly assumes control of proceedings in court. Think how her demeanour and position on stage could also be used to make an instant impact.
- Consider how to make the best use of the 'disguise' costume you created for her in the Stagecraft activity on page 122. Will she need any props (objects) to go with her disguise?
- Write all your ideas in your Director's Journal.

1 'The quality of mercy' (in small groups)

Portia's speech is world-famous. Try some of the following activities to help you understand its powerful appeal to women and men in all periods and cultures.

a Stand in a circle. Take turns to read aloud lines 180–93, handing over at each punctuation mark. Now read the lines again, but this time each reader adds a mime to illustrate the language. The whole group should repeat the reader's words and actions after each line.

b Work together to select from each of Portia's twenty-two lines just one word that you think is the most important in that line. Write your chosen words down. Keeping the words in their original order, present this new script in any ways that seem appropriate. Think about using choral speech, echoes, repetitions, sound effects or movements. Share your performance with the rest of the class.

c Look back to Shylock's speech (Act 3 Scene 1, lines 42–57) in which he declared not only his desire for revenge but also his common humanity with other men. Talk about the ways in which Portia's lines counterbalance (抵消) Shylock's declamation (雄辩). Then try intercutting the two speeches in any way that seems dramatically interesting. For example, you could alternate Shylock's lines with Portia's lines, and say some lines in chorus. Present the combined speeches to the rest of the class, and ask them to comment on the effects you have achieved.

1 impugn 反对；责难
2 proceed 做
3 within his danger 任他摆布
4 compulsion 义务
5 strained 强迫
6 becomes 适合
7 thronèd monarch 御座上的帝王（身份）
8 sceptre 御杖（王权的象征，通常由国王或王后携带）
9 temporal 俗世的
10 attribute to 属性，特征
11 Wherein … kings 那里就是帝王的威严
12 sceptred sway 君王的权威
13 enthronèd 高高坐在
14 likest 恰如
15 seasons 调和着
16 salvation 死后得救赎
17 render / The deeds of mercy 慈悲为怀
18 mitigate 减轻，缓和

The Merchant of Venice Act 4 Scene 1
威尼斯商人

DUKE	Antonio and old Shylock, both stand forth.
PORTIA	Is your name Shylock?
SHYLOCK	Shylock is my name.
PORTIA	Of a strange nature is the suit you follow,
	Yet in such rule that the Venetian law
	Cannot impugn[1] you as you do proceed[2].
	– You stand within his danger[3], do you not?
ANTONIO	Ay, so he says.
PORTIA	Do you confess the bond?
ANTONIO	I do.
PORTIA	Then must the Jew be merciful.
SHYLOCK	On what compulsion[4] must I? Tell me that.
PORTIA	The quality of mercy is not strained[5],
	It droppeth as the gentle rain from heaven
	Upon the place beneath. It is twice blest:
	It blesseth him that gives, and him that takes.
	'Tis mightiest in the mightiest, it becomes[6]
	The thronèd monarch[7] better than his crown.
	His sceptre[8] shows the force of temporal[9] power,
	The attribute to[10] awe and majesty,
	Wherein doth sit the dread and fear of kings[11];
	But mercy is above this sceptred sway[12].
	It is enthronèd[13] in the hearts of kings,
	It is an attribute to God himself,
	And earthly power doth then show likest[14] God's
	When mercy seasons[15] justice. Therefore, Jew,
	Though justice be thy plea, consider this:
	That in the course of justice, none of us
	Should see salvation[16]. We do pray for mercy,
	And that same prayer doth teach us all to render
	The deeds of mercy[17]. I have spoke thus much
	To mitigate[18] the justice of thy plea,
	Which if thou follow, this strict court of Venice
	Must needs give sentence 'gainst the merchant there.

Line numbers: 175, 180, 185, 190, 195, 200

> Bassanio asks Portia to bend the law to save Antonio, but she refuses, as other legal cases would be affected. Despite offers of trebled payment, Shylock implacably refuses to give way.
>
> 剧情简介：博萨纽请求鲍霞变通法律以拯救安托纽，但遭到拒绝，因为别的案子会受此影响。尽管有人提出以三倍的钱偿还欠款，夏洛克依然无动于衷。

Themes 主题分析

Appearance versus reality

a Doesn't her husband recognise her?

Portia and Bassanio have a conversation, yet he does not see through her disguise.

- In pairs, work together on their exchange and decide how Portia's appearance, tone of voice and movement can make Bassanio's lack of recognition seem credible.
- In your Director's Journal, write advice to the actors playing Portia and Bassanio about how to perform this episode.

b Shylock's misguided trust

The theme of false appearance masking true reality comes over strongly as Shylock increasingly believes that Portia/Balthazar supports him.

- Read lines 219–52, noting how Shylock praises Balthazar. Then prepare two tableaux. The first should focus on Shylock, showing his response to what he hears from Balthazar. The second should concentrate on Portia, revealing her true attitude to Shylock, not the outward impression she is presenting to him. Give each of your tableaux a motto (or a quotation from the script).

Write about it 写作练习

Antonio can't stand any more

Antonio is silent between lines 178 and 239. He has already confessed to the bond's validity and said that he is ready to die. Having listened to Portia trading lines with Shylock, he can no longer take the pressure and finally begs the court for judgement.

- Imagine that you are Antonio. After each other character's speech between lines 178 and 239, write one line of an aside for him in Shakespearean English. You should have fourteen 'new' lines in all, which lead up to Antonio's lines 239–40.
- Rehearse and present your new aside to the group.

---

1 My … head! 我为自己的行动负责！
2 crave 恳求
3 discharge 偿还
4 tender 偿付
5 malice bears down truth 邪恶战胜公理
6 Wrest … authority 运用您的权力变通法律一次
7 curb 制约
8 'Twill … state 这个恶例一开就会成为日后可以援用的先例，随之而来的弊端无以计数
9 Daniel 但以理（公元前6世纪希伯来预言家，以善断案著称；《旧约·但以理书》记载了他的事迹）
10 reverend 受尊敬
11 thrice 三倍
12 perjury 伪誓，伪证
13 tear 撕毁
14 tenour 借据上的条款
15 exposition 解释
16 sound 合理，滴水不漏

The Merchant of Venice Act 4 Scene 1
威尼斯商人

SHYLOCK	My deeds upon my head![1] I crave[2] the law,
	The penalty and forfeit of my bond.
PORTIA	Is he not able to discharge[3] the money?
BASSANIO	Yes, here I tender[4] it for him in the court, 205
	Yea, twice the sum; if that will not suffice,
	I will be bound to pay it ten times o'er
	On forfeit of my hands, my head, my heart.
	If this will not suffice, it must appear
	That malice bears down truth[5]. And I beseech you 210
	Wrest once the law to your authority[6];
	To do a great right, do a little wrong,
	And curb[7] this cruel devil of his will.
PORTIA	It must not be; there is no power in Venice
	Can alter a decree establishèd. 215
	'Twill be recorded for a precedent,
	And many an error by the same example
	Will rush into the state[8]: it cannot be.
SHYLOCK	A Daniel[9] come to judgement; yea a Daniel!
	O wise young judge, how I do honour thee! 220
PORTIA	I pray you let me look upon the bond.
SHYLOCK	Here 'tis, most reverend[10] doctor, here it is.
PORTIA	Shylock, there's thrice[11] thy money offered thee.
SHYLOCK	An oath, an oath. I have an oath in heaven!
	Shall I lay perjury[12] upon my soul? 225
	No, not for Venice.
PORTIA	Why, this bond is forfeit,
	And lawfully by this the Jew may claim
	A pound of flesh, to be by him cut off
	Nearest the merchant's heart. Be merciful:
	Take thrice thy money; bid me tear[13] the bond. 230
SHYLOCK	When it is paid, according to the tenour[14].
	It doth appear you are a worthy judge,
	You know the law, your exposition[15]
	Hath been most sound[16]. I charge you by the law,
	Whereof you are a well-deserving pillar, 235
	Proceed to judgement. By my soul I swear
	There is no power in the tongue of man
	To alter me. I stay here on my bond.
ANTONIO	Most heartily I do beseech the court
	To give the judgement.

Portia judges that Shylock must have his pound of flesh. Antonio is now prepared to die. He lovingly bids farewell to Bassanio, saying that he is glad to be spared a life of poverty.

 剧情简介：鲍霞做出判决，夏洛克必须得到属于他的那一磅肉。安托纽准备就死。他深情地向博萨纽告别，说他很高兴死后能免于贫困之苦。

1 A game of cat and mouse (in pairs)

As the trial scene gathers pace, Shakespeare makes the most of the opportunity to increase the tension, allowing Shylock and Portia to share lines and trade ideas quickly so that the tension mounts.

- Take parts and read lines 240–58. Practise ways of showing the gathering excitement.

Stagecraft 导演技巧

Add the stage directions (in fours)

There are no stage directions in the script opposite, but it is clear that a great deal is happening.

- Make a list (with line numbers) of movements and gestures you would direct actors to use in lines 240–60. How would you 'block' the actors (arrange where they stand and how they move)?
- Afterwards, one of you assumes the role of director; the others take parts (Portia, Shylock, Antonio). The director tests out the group's ideas by working through a performance of this episode.
- Revise your original ideas in the light of this experience.

Write about it 写作练习

Antonio's farewell: Portia's response

Invited to speak by Portia (line 259), Antonio launches into a moving farewell to Bassanio in which he expresses his intimate feelings for his friend. What does Portia make of what she hears and sees?

a Study Antonio's lines 260–7 and locate the emotional 'peaks' that might have a great impact on Portia. (You could plot these as a graph.) How would Portia react to these moments? Would she admire, or be troubled by, the way Antonio describes his 'love' for his friend Bassanio?

b Imagine that Portia later reflects on what she has heard in this exchange. Don't forget: she knows very little about Bassanio's life before he arrived at Belmont. Write up her thoughts in the form of a letter to Bassanio, and include a number of key questions that she would want her new husband to answer.

1 **intent and purpose** 意义和意图
2 **Hath full relation to** 完全赞同
3 **balance** 秤，天平
4 **Have by** 请……来这里（出席）
5 **on your charge** 由您出钱
6 **stop** 堵住
7 **nominated** 写明
8 **armed** 做好准备
9 **Fortune** 命运女神
10 **custom** 常规，惯例
11 **use** 习惯
12 **outlive** 活得比……长
13 **age** 老年，暮年
14 **penance** 折磨
15 **process of Antonio's end** 安托纽之死的情形
16 **speak me fair in death** 等我死后为我说些好话
17 **Repent but you** 您只要为……感到难过

THE MERCHANT OF VENICE ACT 4 SCENE 1
威尼斯商人

PORTIA	Why then, thus it is:	240
	You must prepare your bosom for his knife.	
SHYLOCK	O noble judge, O excellent young man!	
PORTIA	For the intent and purpose¹ of the law	
	Hath full relation to² the penalty	
	Which here appeareth due upon the bond.	245
SHYLOCK	'Tis very true. O wise and upright judge,	
	How much more elder art thou than thy looks!	
PORTIA	Therefore lay bare your bosom.	
SHYLOCK	Ay, his breast.	
	So says the bond, doth it not, noble judge?	
	'Nearest his heart': those are the very words.	250
PORTIA	It is so. Are there balance³ here to weigh	
	The flesh?	
SHYLOCK	I have them ready.	
PORTIA	Have by⁴ some surgeon, Shylock, on your charge⁵,	
	To stop⁶ his wounds, lest he do bleed to death.	
SHYLOCK	Is it so nominated⁷ in the bond?	255
PORTIA	It is not so expressed, but what of that?	
	'Twere good you do so much for charity.	
SHYLOCK	I cannot find it, 'tis not in the bond.	
PORTIA	You, merchant: have you anything to say?	
ANTONIO	But little; I am armed⁸ and well prepared.	260
	Give me your hand, Bassanio. Fare you well.	
	Grieve not that I am fall'n to this for you.	
	For herein Fortune⁹ shows herself more kind	
	Than is her custom¹⁰: it is still her use¹¹	
	To let the wretched man outlive¹² his wealth,	265
	To view with hollow eye and wrinkled brow	
	An age¹³ of poverty; from which ling'ring penance¹⁴	
	Of such misery doth she cut me off.	
	Commend me to your honourable wife.	
	Tell her the process of Antonio's end¹⁵,	270
	Say how I loved you, speak me fair in death¹⁶,	
	And when the tale is told, bid her be judge	
	Whether Bassanio had not once a love.	
	Repent but you¹⁷ that you shall lose your friend	
	And he repents not that he pays your debt.	275
	For if the Jew do cut but deep enough	
	I'll pay it instantly with all my heart.	

Portia gives judgement in Shylock's favour but, at the last moment, saves Antonio. Blood is not mentioned in the bond, so Shylock must break the law if he sheds Antonio's.

剧情简介：鲍霞做出有利于夏洛克的判决，但在最后一刻却救了安托纽。借契里没有提到流血，所以如果夏洛克让安托纽流血，就必然犯法。

Themes 主题分析

Appearance and reality: comic effect? (in pairs)

Both Bassanio (lines 278–83) and Gratiano (lines 286–8) would sacrifice their wives for Antonio. The audience knows (but the two men don't) that Portia and Nerissa are listening. In the middle of what looks like a tragic scene, Shakespeare lightens the mood.

- Talk about how Portia's and Nerissa's disguises are used to humorous effect. How should Portia and Nerissa respond to what they hear their husbands say? (For example, could they glance knowingly at the audience, making them co-conspirators?)
- Write up your ideas as a mini-essay, exploring the way this episode (lines 278–90) uses dramatic irony (see 'Portia in disguise', p. 122). Link your points to evidence from the script.

1 Are … life 在我的眼里都不如你的生命宝贵
2 deliver 挽救
3 by 附近，旁边
4 Entreat some power 恳求天神
5 else 否则
6 stock 家族
7 Barabbas 巴拉巴（《新约》中记载的一名强盗；人们以巴拉巴的后人指代囚犯或匪徒）
8 trifle 浪费
9 awards 把……判给
10 jot 滴
11 expressly 清楚地
12 confiscate / Unto 被收缴，充公
13 urgest 要求

1 'come, prepare' (in threes)

Line 300 contains the climactic moment of the trial scene. Antonio waits, his bare chest exposed, for Shylock to wield his knife (see picture below). Only after agonising (痛苦难熬) suspense does Portia break the silence – 'Tarry (wait) a little' – to deny Shylock's murderous intent. How near is Shylock to cutting Antonio when Portia stops him?

- Take parts as Shylock, Portia and Antonio, and experiment with different ways of presenting the drama that unfolds between lines 300 and 301. Share your versions with other groups.

THE MERCHANT OF VENICE ACT 4 SCENE 1
威尼斯商人

BASSANIO	Antonio, I am married to a wife
	Which is as dear to me as life itself;
	But life itself, my wife, and all the world,
	Are not with me esteemed above thy life[1].
	I would lose all, ay, sacrifice them all
	Here to this devil, to deliver[2] you.
PORTIA	Your wife would give you little thanks for that
	If she were by[3] to hear you make the offer.
GRATIANO	I have a wife who I protest I love;
	I would she were in heaven, so she could
	Entreat some power[4] to change this currish Jew.
NERISSA	'Tis well you offer it behind her back;
	The wish would make else[5] an unquiet house.
SHYLOCK	These be the Christian husbands! I have a daughter:
	Would any of the stock[6] of Barabbas[7]
	Had been her husband, rather than a Christian!
	We trifle[8] time; I pray thee pursue sentence.
PORTIA	A pound of that same merchant's flesh is thine,
	The court awards[9] it, and the law doth give it.
SHYLOCK	Most rightful judge!
PORTIA	And you must cut this flesh from off his breast;
	The law allows it, and the court awards it.
SHYLOCK	Most learned judge! A sentence: come, prepare.
PORTIA	Tarry a little, there is something else.
	This bond doth give thee here no jot[10] of blood.
	The words expressly[11] are 'a pound of flesh'.
	Take then thy bond, take thou thy pound of flesh,
	But in the cutting it, if thou dost shed
	One drop of Christian blood, thy lands and goods
	Are by the laws of Venice confiscate
	Unto[12] the state of Venice.
GRATIANO	O upright judge!
	Mark, Jew – O learned judge!
SHYLOCK	Is that the law?
PORTIA	Thyself shall see the Act.
	For as thou urgest[14] justice, be assured
	Thou shalt have justice more than thou desirest.

Line numbers: 280, 285, 290, 295, 300, 305, 310

Shylock is defeated, and Portia insists on justice. She will not allow him to be repaid any money, only to take the pound of flesh at his peril.

 剧情简介：夏洛克败诉，鲍霞坚持伸张正义。她不允许夏洛克得到任何金钱的偿还，只能得到那一磅肉，而且后果自负。

Characters 人物分析

Portia: always in control? (in fours)

a Do you think Portia knew all along about the loophole in Shylock's bond (that Shylock will break the law if he sheds a drop of Antonio's blood)? Or did the idea suddenly come to her in the courtroom? Justify your thinking with evidence from the script.

b Sensing that victory is slipping away, Shylock agrees to accept a financial settlement of his bond. But Portia insists that 'justice' must prevail and that Shylock must exact the penalty. She shows that she is more than equal to the men of Venice (see 'Characters', p. 177, on modern and feminist attitudes to Portia).

- Together, work out what gestures she could use to accompany each statement she makes opposite.
- Then, individually, choose three quotations to show that Portia is in charge of events. Explain to your group how you think each one shows Portia's assertiveness.

1 Peripeteia (剧情反转): a reversal of fortune

A few moments earlier, Shylock seemed triumphant, but now Portia has turned the tables on him. This is an example of **peripeteia** (a reversal of fortune), a term that originates in ancient Greek tragedy. Portia is determined to punish Shylock for his treatment of Antonio.

- Read Shylock's lines 294–342, and trace his gradual loss of dignity. Present the stages of his decline visually, using a type of graph.

Language in the play 剧中语言

Gratiano: the piling up of insults (in pairs)

In typically offensive fashion, Gratiano hurls (大声骂出) racist language at Shylock (line 288), calling him a 'currish (dog-like) Jew'. In this scene, Shylock has been denied his name many times and defined only by the term 'Jew'. Now Gratiano is pleased to use Shylock's own words against him (lines 319, 329 and 336).

- Find Shylock's original expressions in this scene. Line 330 also echoes an earlier expression of Shylock's (in Act 1 Scene 3).
- Then write a paragraph about what these very personal insults suggest about Gratiano's character.

1 **penalty** 处罚，赔偿（契约上说的那磅肉）
2 **just** 精确
3 **As … scruple** 哪怕是不足或超过一丁点儿（scruple是古罗马的衡量单位，相当于20粒麦粒的重量；substance意思是"分量，重量"）
4 **But … hair** 仅毫发之差
5 **on the hip** 处于不利地位（参见夏洛克在第1幕第3场第38行说的话）
6 **principal** 本金（3000达克金币）
7 **merely** 仅仅
8 **barely** 甚至，仅仅
9 **the devil … it** 让魔鬼给他好运吧
10 **I'll … question** 这场官司我不打了

GRATIANO	O learned judge! Mark, Jew: a learned judge.
SHYLOCK	I take this offer then. Pay the bond thrice
	And let the Christian go.
BASSANIO	Here is the money.
PORTIA	Soft.
	The Jew shall have all justice; soft, no haste;
	He shall have nothing but the penalty¹.
GRATIANO	O Jew, an upright judge, a learned judge!
PORTIA	Therefore prepare thee to cut off the flesh.
	Shed thou no blood, nor cut thou less nor more
	But just a pound of flesh. If thou tak'st more
	Or less than a just² pound, be it but so much
	As makes it light or heavy in the substance
	Or the division of the twentieth part
	Of one poor scruple³ – nay, if the scale do turn
	But in the estimation of a hair⁴,
	Thou diest, and all thy goods are confiscate.
GRATIANO	A second Daniel; a Daniel, Jew!
	Now, infidel, I have you on the hip⁵.
PORTIA	Why doth the Jew pause? Take thy forfeiture.
SHYLOCK	Give me my principal⁶, and let me go.
BASSANIO	I have it ready for thee; here it is.
PORTIA	He hath refused it in the open court.
	He shall have merely⁷ justice and his bond.
GRATIANO	A Daniel, still say I, a second Daniel!
	I thank thee, Jew, for teaching me that word.
SHYLOCK	Shall I not have barely⁸ my principal?
PORTIA	Thou shalt have nothing but the forfeiture,
	To be so taken at thy peril, Jew.
SHYLOCK	Why then, the devil give him good of it⁹!
	I'll stay no longer question¹⁰.

Portia reveals another trap for Shylock. If a foreigner plots to kill a Venetian, the punishment by law should be confiscation of all their wealth, and their possible execution.

剧情简介：鲍霞透露夏洛克面临的另一个陷阱。如果外国人图谋杀害威尼斯公民，依据法律，要没收谋害者全部财产，并可能判处死刑。

1 The laws of Venice

Portia's words in lines 342–59 sound almost as if she is reading from the laws of Venice.

a Rewrite her speech in modern English, as if you are explaining to a friend how Shylock has broken the law and how he might be punished. Ask another student to listen to your version and check its accuracy.

b Write a paragraph explaining what you think about the terms and conditions imposed on Shylock by the laws of Venice.

1 hold　追究
2 enacted　规定
3 alien　外国人
4 The party … contrive　被图谋的一方
5 privy coffer　大公的银库
6 'gainst all other voice　他人概不得过问
7 predicament　困境
8 by manifest proceeding　显然
9 danger formerly by me rehearsed　我刚才所列的罪名
10 Down　跪下
11 leave　允许
12 Thou … cord　你连绳子也买不起了
13 charge　花费
14 spirit　本性，性格
15 drive unto　转化为，变为
16 You … house　你们拿走了支撑房屋的柱子，就是拆毁了我的房子
17 halter gratis　免费的吊绳

Identify the two characters on either side of Shylock in this photograph.

Write about it 写作练习

Shylock's suffering (in groups of four or five)

In addition to the punishment of the law, Shylock suffers two further personal affronts (公开侮辱). First, Portia orders him to kneel to the Duke and plead for mercy. Then Gratiano again abuses Shylock, this time going as far as urging him to go and hang himself. When Shylock speaks (lines 370–3), it is to express his devastation at the loss of his wealth.

- In role as Shylock, write an interior monologue exploring your thoughts about the dizzying way in which events have unfolded and your feelings about the way you are being treated.
- Then read quickly through to Shylock's exit at line 396 and add a final section to your monologue, covering your last moments in court.

PORTIA	Tarry, Jew:
	The law hath yet another hold[1] on you.
	It is enacted[2] in the laws of Venice,
	If it be proved against an alien[3] 345
	That by direct or indirect attempts
	He seek the life of any citizen,
	The party 'gainst the which he doth contrive[4]
	Shall seize one half his goods, the other half
	Comes to the privy coffer[5] of the state, 350
	And the offender's life lies in the mercy
	Of the Duke only, 'gainst all other voice[6].
	In which predicament[7] I say thou stand'st;
	For it appears by manifest proceeding[8]
	That indirectly, and directly too, 355
	Thou hast contrived against the very life
	Of the defendant, and thou hast incurred
	The danger formerly by me rehearsed[9].
	Down[10], therefore, and beg mercy of the Duke.
GRATIANO	Beg that thou mayst have leave[11] to hang thyself – 360
	And yet, thy wealth being forfeit to the state,
	Thou hast not left the value of a cord[12];
	Therefore thou must be hanged at the state's charge[13].
DUKE	That thou shalt see the difference of our spirit[14],
	I pardon thee thy life before thou ask it. 365
	For half thy wealth, it is Antonio's;
	The other half comes to the general state,
	Which humbleness may drive unto[15] a fine.
PORTIA	Ay, for the state, not for Antonio.
SHYLOCK	Nay, take my life and all, pardon not that: 370
	You take my house when you do take the prop
	That doth sustain my house[16]; you take my life
	When you do take the means whereby I live.
PORTIA	What mercy can you render him, Antonio?
GRATIANO	A halter gratis[17] – nothing else, for God's sake. 375

Antonio requests – and is granted – partial mercy for Shylock: he can keep half his wealth; Antonio will invest the rest. Unwittingly, Bassanio tries to reward Portia with her own money.

 剧情简介：安托纽请求并得到准许给予夏洛克一些慈悲：可让他保留一半财产，另一半由安托纽用于投资。还蒙在鼓里的博萨纽试图用鲍霞自己的钱来酬谢她。

1 Antonio: a merciful Christian? (in small groups)

Has Antonio given up his earlier vicious (充满仇恨) prejudice towards Shylock? Or are his suggested reduced punishments (lines 376–86) still calculated to inflict humiliation on his adversary? For example, the demand that Shylock becomes a Christian would be deeply offensive because Shylock's religion specifically prohibits such conversion (see 'History and the Jews', pp. 186–8, for more on the religious context of the play).

- In your groups, come up with between five and ten questions that you would want to ask Antonio. Then put Antonio (played by your teacher) in the hot-seat and ask your questions.

Write about it 写作练习
The Duke's court report

Imagine that, after the trial, the Duke sits down to write his official record of what has taken place in court. Will he strive to be factually accurate and unbiased in his account? Do you think the way he has conducted the trial suggests that he can be objective and fair?

- Using appropriately formal language, write the Duke's record of the trial, to be placed in the legal archives (案卷) of the Venetian court.
- Compare your report with those written by other students. Identify similarities and differences in your accounts, and come up with possible reasons for the differences.

Stagecraft 导演技巧
Shylock: the final curtain (落幕) (in pairs)

A director said that Shylock should speak his last lines 'with all the ruefulness (懊悔，悲伤) of a man who realises he's made a very silly mistake … to take on the establishment and play it at its own game'. The actor playing Shylock must decide how to leave the stage. Sometimes he exits with great dignity, sometimes as a broken man. When Laurence Olivier played Shylock, he made his exit in a dignified manner but a long, agonised scream was heard after he'd left.

- Try reading Shylock's last lines in a variety of ways.
- Then, in role as director and the actor playing Shylock, discuss how he should leave the stage.

1 So … quit 要是公爵殿下和法庭愿意免除
2 so 只要
3 have … use 让我用另一半财产
4 record a gift 立下赠予的契据
5 of all he dies possessed 他死后的全部财产
6 recant 撤回
7 late 最近
8 deed of gift 财产赠予契据
9 christening 受洗礼的时候
10 godfathers 教父
11 Had I … more 要是我做法官，我要再给你请10个教父（英国法庭的裁决员一般为12个）
12 To bring … font 送你上绞架而不是领你去受洗（font指洗礼时用的圣水盘）
13 entreat 邀请
14 meet 必要
15 leisure 空暇
16 gratify 感谢，酬谢
17 bound 多亏了
18 acquitted 摆脱
19 grievous 骇人的，夺命的
20 in lieu whereof 取代，代替
21 We … withal 我们奉送给您，报答您的辛苦

ANTONIO	So please my lord the Duke and all the court	
	To quit¹ the fine for one half of his goods,	
	I am content, so² he will let me have	
	The other half in use³, to render it	
	Upon his death unto the gentleman	380
	That lately stole his daughter.	
	Two things provided more: that for this favour	
	He presently become a Christian;	
	The other, that he do record a gift⁴,	
	Here in the court, of all he dies possessed⁵	385
	Unto his son Lorenzo and his daughter.	
DUKE	He shall do this, or else I do recant⁶	
	The pardon that I late⁷ pronouncèd here.	
PORTIA	Art thou contented, Jew? What dost thou say?	
SHYLOCK	I am content.	
PORTIA	Clerk, draw a deed of gift⁸.	390
SHYLOCK	I pray you give me leave to go from hence;	
	I am not well. Send the deed after me	
	And I will sign it.	
DUKE	Get thee gone, but do it.	
GRATIANO	In christening⁹ shalt thou have two godfathers¹⁰:	
	Had I been judge, thou shouldst have had ten more¹¹,	395
	To bring thee to the gallows, not to the font¹².	

Exit [Shylock]

DUKE	Sir, I entreat¹³ you home with me to dinner.	
PORTIA	I humbly do desire your grace of pardon.	
	I must away this night toward Padua,	
	And it is meet¹⁴ I presently set forth.	400
DUKE	I am sorry that your leisure¹⁵ serves you not.	
	Antonio, gratify¹⁶ this gentleman,	
	For in my mind you are much bound¹⁷ to him.	

Exit Duke and his train

BASSANIO	Most worthy gentleman, I and my friend	
	Have by your wisdom been this day acquitted¹⁸	405
	Of grievous¹⁹ penalties, in lieu whereof²⁰	
	Three thousand ducats due unto the Jew	
	We freely cope your courteous pains withal²¹.	
ANTONIO	And stand indebted over and above	
	In love and service to you evermore.	410

Portia refuses money, but asks insistently for Bassanio's ring: the very one she gave him in Act 3, saying then that its loss would mark the end of his love for her. Bassanio cannot part with it, and Portia mocks him.

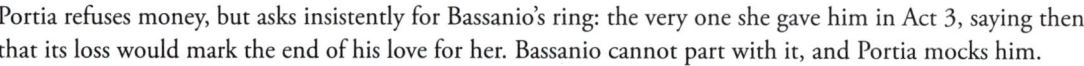剧情简介：鲍霞婉拒酬金，但执意要博萨纽的戒指（在第三幕，她将该戒指交于博萨纽，并说戒指失爱情亡）。博萨纽无法答应，遭到鲍霞的嘲笑。

Stagecraft 导演技巧

Nerissa: a nod to the audience (in threes)

Once again Shakespeare uses dramatic irony to add a further twist to the plot (this time for comic effect). Unlike Bassanio and Antonio, Nerissa and the audience know Portia's true identity.

a   Two people read aloud the whole of the script opposite. The third stops them at lines or phrases that might bring a smile to Nerissa's lips, to explain exactly why Nerissa might be amused.

b   After your reading, talk together about the comic possibilities that Portia's comments give the actors on stage. Write in your Director's Journal your ideas about how Nerissa should react to what she hears, and how she should convey this to the audience.

1 Light or darkness?

After Shylock and the Duke exit, the mood of the scene changes again.

- Read quickly through to the end of Scene 1 and draw up a mood graph for the whole scene. Number the left axis (轴) from +10 ('lighter moments') to -10 ('darker moments'). Then plot a timeline for the whole scene, placing key incidents in the appropriate positions on your graph.
- Pair up to examine each other's graphs and discuss the balance of moods in Act 4 Scene 1. Think of possible reasons to explain why Shakespeare decided to structure it in this way.

Characters 人物分析

Portia – revealing a streak of cruelty? (in pairs)

Portia insists on having the ring (line 428). She knows its importance and the anguish its loss will cause Bassanio. Why does she deal with her husband with the same ruthlessness as she has shown to Shylock?

a   Talk together about whether she is cruel or wise in setting this test for Bassanio. Why does she insist on having the ring? For example, is her decision prompted by the way her husband has behaved with Antonio? Jot down possible reasons, and compare them with those listed by other pairs.

b   Portia and Nerissa leave at line 444. Script their conversation about the dramatic events in the courtroom.

1 My … mercenary 我心里从没想过别的报答（我不在乎钱；mercenary 指钱财）
2 know 认识或发生性关系（为了讽瑞莎而说的双关语）
3 of … further 我一定要再向您提出一个请求
4 remembrance 纪念品
5 You press me far 您如此坚持
6 a trifle 不值钱的小玩意儿
7 I have … it 我很想要它
8 proclamation 公开征求
9 liberal 慷慨
10 scuse = excuse（借口）
11 save 守住
12 hold out enemy 与您争吵不休（生博萨纽的气）

THE MERCHANT OF VENICE ACT 4 SCENE 1

威尼斯商人

PORTIA	He is well paid that is well satisfied;
	And I delivering you am satisfied
	And therein do account myself well paid;
	My mind was never yet more mercenary[1].
	I pray you know[2] me when we meet again. 415
	I wish you well, and so I take my leave.
BASSANIO	Dear sir, of force I must attempt you further[3].
	Take some remembrance[4] of us as a tribute,
	Not as a fee. Grant me two things, I pray you:
	Not to deny me, and to pardon me. 420
PORTIA	You press me far[5], and therefore I will yield.
	Give me your gloves, I'll wear them for your sake;
	And for your love I'll take this ring from you.
	Do not draw back your hand; I'll take no more,
	And you in love shall not deny me this. 425
BASSANIO	This ring, good sir? Alas, it is a trifle[6];
	I will not shame myself to give you this.
PORTIA	I will have nothing else but only this;
	And now methinks I have a mind to it[7].
BASSANIO	There's more depends on this than on the value. 430
	The dearest ring in Venice will I give you,
	And find it out by proclamation[8].
	Only for this I pray you pardon me.
PORTIA	I see, sir, you are liberal[9] in offers.
	You taught me first to beg, and now methinks 435
	You teach me how a beggar should be answered.
BASSANIO	Good sir, this ring was given me by my wife,
	And when she put it on, she made me vow
	That I should neither sell, nor give, nor lose it.
PORTIA	That scuse[10] serves many men to save[11] their gifts; 440
	And if your wife be not a mad woman,
	And know how well I have deserved this ring,
	She would not hold out enemy[12] for ever
	For giving it to me. Well, peace be with you.

Exeunt [*Portia and Nerissa*]

Antonio persuades Bassanio to part with the ring. Gratiano brings it to Portia. Nerissa plans to set the same test for her husband by making him give her his ring too.

 剧情简介：安托纽劝博萨纽让出戒指，格拉奇阿诺将戒指交给鲍霞。讷瑞莎也打算用同样的方式考验丈夫，让他把戒指送给自己。

Write about it 写作练习

At Shylock's house (in pairs)

Nerissa is sent to Shylock's house (lines 1 and 11) for him to sign the deed of gift, naming Jessica and Lorenzo as his heirs.

- One of you steps into role as Nerissa. Write your own account of the visit – what mood will you be in after the trial, and the trick you and Portia have just played on your new husbands? How does Shylock receive you? How will you respond to him?
- The other should also write an account of Nerissa's visit, but this time from Shylock's perspective. What might he be feeling?
- When your writing is completed, sit back-to-back and each read your accounts aloud, with other students acting as your audience. Ask them to comment on the impressions you have created.

Themes 主题分析

Appearance and reality: a third 'trial' ahead

First there was the 'trial' of the caskets, where 'all that glisters' was 'not gold'. Next the 'trial' of Shylock, where he was defeated by a woman dressed as a man who spotted a hidden loophole in the bond. Now, as Portia anticipates that she and Nerissa will be able to force grovelling (奴颜婢膝) confessions from their husbands when they meet up again, Shakespeare sets a third 'trial' plot in motion (the rings). This is also deeply rooted in trickery and deception.

- Look back at all the deceptions the two women have practised in Act 4 Scene 1. Write a paragraph giving your response to what they have done and what they intend to do.

Stagecraft 导演技巧

A weak ending? (in pairs)

The lengthy and exciting trial is followed by the brief interlude (插曲) of Scene 2. Again, this is a scene that could easily detract from the drama and end Act 4 in an anti-climactic (反高潮；高潮突降) way.

- Imagine you are two directors with opposing views about the dramatic value of this scene. In a 'Meet the directors' TV discussion, argue about whether to retain or cut Scene 2.

1 Let … commandement 他的功劳加上我跟您的情分，与您夫人的命令相比，您掂量掂量哪个重（withal意思是"加在一起"）
2 thither presently 马上到那里去
3 Enquire the Jew's house out 打听这个犹太人住在哪里
4 deed 字据，契约
5 Fair … o'ertane 好先生，很庆幸我追上（overtake）您了
6 Thou mayst 你能的
7 I warrant 我确定
8 old 老一套
9 outface them 比他们更一本正经
10 outswear them 比他们更能诅咒

The Merchant of Venice Act 4 Scene 2
威尼斯商人

ANTONIO	My lord Bassanio, let him have the ring.	445
	Let his deservings and my love withal	
	Be valued 'gainst your wife's commandement¹.	
BASSANIO	Go, Gratiano, run and overtake him;	
	Give him the ring, and bring him if thou canst	
	Unto Antonio's house. Away, make haste.	450

Exit Gratiano

Come, you and I will thither presently²,
And in the morning early will we both
Fly toward Belmont. Come, Antonio.

Exeunt

Act 4 Scene 2
Venice   A street

Enter PORTIA *and* NERISSA

PORTIA	Enquire the Jew's house out³, give him this deed⁴,	
	And let him sign it. We'll away tonight	
	And be a day before our husbands home.	
	This deed will be well welcome to Lorenzo.	

Enter GRATIANO

GRATIANO	Fair sir, you are well o'ertane⁵.	5
	My lord Bassanio upon more advice	
	Hath sent you here this ring, and doth entreat	
	Your company at dinner.	
PORTIA	That cannot be.	
	His ring I do accept most thankfully,	
	And so I pray you tell him. Furthermore,	10
	I pray you show my youth old Shylock's house.	
GRATIANO	That will I do.	
NERISSA	[*To Portia*] Sir, I would speak with you.	
	[*Aside*] I'll see if I can get my husband's ring	
	Which I did make him swear to keep for ever.	
PORTIA	Thou mayst⁶, I warrant⁷. We shall have old⁸ swearing	15
	That they did give the rings away to men;	
	But we'll outface them⁹, and outswear them¹⁰ too.	
	– Away, make haste, thou know'st where I will tarry.	
NERISSA	Come, good sir, will you show me to this house? [*Exeunt*]	

141

The Merchant of Venice
威尼斯商人

Looking back at Act 4 第4幕回顾
Activities for groups or individuals

1 The trial

a Storyboard the action!
Imagine that you are going to produce a ten-frame photo-strip of the action in this scene.

- Draw your storyboard and sketch in your selected shots. Include notes for each photo that clearly identify what you intend it to show. Then write a caption for each one, using your own words and a quotation from the script. Having done this, try shooting your version, using your classmates as the actors.

b Justice versus mercy
The trial scene displays the struggle between justice and mercy (see 'Perspectives and themes', p. 169). Write a paragraph exploring the balance between justice and mercy in:

- the major characters' contributions to the scene
- the final outcome of the trial.

c Does Shylock receive a fair trial?
Consider this from the point of view of:

- the State of Venice
- Shylock
- Shakespeare's audience
- yourself.

Give reasons to justify your findings.

2 Focus on Shylock

a The knife and the scales
Design your ideal versions of Shylock's knife and set of scales for a modern production. Ensure that both items appear to be genuinely owned by Shylock. Then annotate your drawings for the 'props manager', explaining what kind of objects you have in mind.

b 'Give me some lines!'
In defeat, Shylock – normally a man of many words – says little. Dustin Hoffman, who played Shylock, said, 'Halfway through the trial Portia takes over and Shakespeare doesn't give me anything to say … if he was still alive, I'd be saying "Give me some lines!"'

- Have a go at writing one extra speech for Shylock, using modern English (or Shakespearean English if you want to challenge yourself). Explore your feelings about the way you are viewed by the Christians, and how you are treated. At what point would you include this speech?

c How do you respond to Shylock?
Shylock's exit at the end of the trial scene marks his final appearance. Over the centuries, there have been questions about the way Shakespeare presents him.

- In pairs, review all that Shylock says and does, and what other characters say about him. One of you should write a critical essay exploring how you respond to Shylock, and the other an essay on how Shakespeare intended an Elizabethan audience to respond to him. Then compare your two essays and discuss how closely they match.

3 The end of the trial – the end of the play?

Some critics have argued that the play would retain its dramatic integrity if it finished with the end of the trial scene in Act 4, with Shylock defeated and Antonio saved. But Shakespeare clearly has other dramatic intentions in mind as he sets up the 'rings' episode at the end of Act 4.

- In a small group, discuss these issues. Try to come up with three reasons why you might a) agree and b) disagree with critics who favour Act 4 Scene 1 becoming the end of the play. Be prepared to share your reasons in a whole-class debate.

142

Compare the dramatic effectiveness of these two modern stagings of the trial scene. What do you think each director had in mind?

Lorenzo and Jessica are reminded by the moonlit night of famous lovers from classical mythology. They speak, somewhat ambiguously, of their love for each other.

剧情简介： 月夜让劳仁佐和婕丝柯联想到经典神话中的著名恋人，他们转弯抹角地倾诉相互的爱慕。

Compare Jessica pictured here (in Belmont) and pictured with her father (page 48). Identify differences in her appearance and demeanour. What do you think the director was trying to suggest?

Language in the play 剧中语言

'The moon shines bright' (in pairs)

- Take parts and read the script opposite aloud. Concentrate on the patterning of the verse ('In such a night' is repeated eight times) and how the shared lines and balanced phrases suggest a mood of harmony and romance.
- On a second reading, pause to allow time for your classmates to mime the actions that the two lovers' words describe. They should try to make their mimes suitably dream-like and as atmospheric as possible.

1 Classical lovers (in groups of three or four)

In this perfect setting, Jessica and Lorenzo recall the deeds of famous (but unfortunate) lovers. On 'such a night':

- Troilus climbed the walls of Troy to be with his lover Cressida. She later betrayed him.
- Thisbe met her lover Pyramus secretly and against her father's wishes. Their love pact ended in suicide.
- Dido, queen of Carthage, stayed on the shore trying to entice her lover, Aeneas, back to her. But he had deserted her.
- Medea gathered enchanted (被施魔法的) herbs to refresh Aeson, the father of her lover Jason, whom she had helped to win the Golden Fleece. She was later deserted by Jason.

Make a written table showing how these tales of tragedy, betrayal and loss are reflected by events in *The Merchant of Venice*. Display your work.

---

1 **Troilus** 特洛伊罗斯（特洛伊王子，当恋人克蕾希达 [Cressida] 被作为人质送到希腊并变心后，他痛不欲生，杀死许多希腊人后阵亡）
2 **Troyan** 特洛伊的
3 **Cressid** 克蕾希达（特洛伊罗斯与克蕾希达原为恋人，后因交换俘虏，克蕾希达被送到希腊人营地，与特洛伊罗斯分离）
4 **Thisbe** 提兹碧（提兹碧和丕若莫 [Pyramus] 是古罗马诗人奥维德的神话诗《变形记》里的一对恋人，在私奔的路上双双自杀身亡）
5 **o'ertrip** 踩着
6 **Dido** 荻朵（迦太基 [Carthage] 女王）
7 **waft** 召唤
8 **Medea** 美荻亚（希腊神话中科尔喀斯国的公主，伊阿宋的妻子。伊阿宋取得金羊毛后对她变心，她愤而杀死自己和伊阿宋的两个孩子）
9 **renew** 返老还童
10 **Aeson** 埃宋（伊阿宋的父亲，美荻亚用草药使他恢复青春）
11 **unthrift** 慷慨；大手大脚
12 **shrew** 悍妇（本义是鼩鼱，一种如鼠的小动物，转指坏脾气的女人，如莎剧《悍妇降服记》[*The Taming of the Shrew*] 所述）
13 **Slander** 诋毁
14 **outnight** 在讲夜晚典故上胜过
15 **did nobody come** 倘若没人来
16 **hark** = listen
17 **footing** 脚步声

Act 5 Scene 1
Belmont   Portia's garden

Enter LORENZO *and* JESSICA

LORENZO	The moon shines bright. In such a night as this,
	When the sweet wind did gently kiss the trees,
	And they did make no noise, in such a night
	Troilus[1] methinks mounted the Troyan[2] walls
	And sighed his soul toward the Grecian tents, 5
	Where Cressid[3] lay that night.
JESSICA	In such a night
	Did Thisbe[4] fearfully o'ertrip[5] the dew,
	And saw the lion's shadow ere himself,
	And ran dismayed away.
LORENZO	In such a night
	Stood Dido[6] with a willow in her hand 10
	Upon the wild sea banks, and waft[7] her love
	To come again to Carthage.
JESSICA	In such a night
	Medea[8] gathered the enchanted herbs
	That did renew[9] old Aeson[10].
LORENZO	In such a night
	Did Jessica steal from the wealthy Jew 15
	And with an unthrift[11] love did run from Venice
	As far as Belmont.
JESSICA	In such a night
	Did young Lorenzo swear he loved her well,
	Stealing her soul with many vows of faith,
	And ne'er a true one.
LORENZO	In such a night 20
	Did pretty Jessica (like a little shrew[12])
	Slander[13] her love, and he forgave it her.
JESSICA	I would outnight[14] you, did nobody come[15]:
	But hark[16], I hear the footing[17] of a man.

Stephano brings news of Portia's imminent return to Belmont. Lancelot informs Lorenzo that Bassanio is also on his way home. Lorenzo proposes to welcome them with music.

 剧情简介：斯迪法诺带来消息说鲍霞即将回到贝尔蒙。朗斯勒告诉劳仁佐，博萨纽也在归途中。劳仁佐提出奏乐迎接他们。

1 Lorenzo and Jessica

Many stage productions have Lorenzo and Jessica speaking lovingly and playfully together at the start of the scene. But it's also possible to suggest the uncertainty of their relationship and foreshadow later problems for the couple. For example, Lorenzo (lines 14–17) adds Jessica to the list of unfortunate lovers and uses words like 'steal' and 'run' to describe her actions. In reply, she accuses her husband of false vows (婚誓) of love. He then labels her a 'shrew'. (In Elizabethan times, the word 'shrew' meant a bad-tempered woman as well as an endearing little animal!)

- In pairs, read aloud lines 14–23 first in a loving way, then in an irritable manner. Decide which portrayal is more effective.
- In role as director, write advice for the two actors about how you think they should deliver the lines and what this style of delivery would suggest about their relationship.

1 stray about 走了弯路
2 wedlock hours 婚姻
3 ceremoniously 隆重地
4 Sola, sola! Wo ha, ho! （打猎时的呼喊）
5 Leave = Stop
6 with his horn full of 带着充满……的丰饶角（这里的 horn 指 cornucopia，哺乳小宙斯的羊角，后来人们用它象征丰收和幸运）
7 expect 等待着

How closely does the depiction of Jessica and Lorenzo's relationship in this picture match your findings in Activity 1 above? Explain your thinking.

Stagecraft 导演技巧

Establishing mood (in small groups)

We learn that, on her way back from Venice, Portia stopped to pray that she would have a good marriage. She was (apparently) accompanied by a holy hermit (隐士). Then Lancelot embarks on some comic buffoonery (插科打诨) as he tries to locate Lorenzo in the darkness.

- Work together to produce a spider diagram of the different moods created by Shakespeare in the opening 53 lines of Act 5 Scene 1. Link each idea to a key bit of evidence from the script.

Enter [STEPHANO,] *a messenger*

LORENZO Who comes so fast in silence of the night?
STEPHANO A friend.
LORENZO A friend? What friend? Your name, I pray you, friend?
STEPHANO Stephano is my name, and I bring word
My mistress will before the break of day
Be here at Belmont. She doth stray about[1]
By holy crosses where she kneels and prays
For happy wedlock hours[2].
LORENZO   Who comes with her?
STEPHANO None but a holy hermit and her maid.
I pray you, is my master yet returned?
LORENZO He is not, nor we have not heard from him.
But go we in, I pray thee, Jessica,
And ceremoniously[3] let us prepare
Some welcome for the mistress of the house.

Enter [LANCELOT,] *the Clown*

LANCELOT Sola, sola! Wo ha, ho![4] Sola, sola!
LORENZO Who calls?
LANCELOT Sola! Did you see Master Lorenzo? Master Lorenzo, sola, sola!
LORENZO Leave[5] holloaing, man! Here!
LANCELOT Sola! Where, where?
LORENZO Here!
LANCELOT Tell him there's a post come from my master, with his horn full of[6] good news: my master will be here ere morning, sweet soul.
LORENZO Let's in and there expect[7] their coming.
And yet no matter: why should we go in?
My friend Stephano, signify I pray you,
Within the house, your mistress is at hand,
And bring your music forth into the air.

[*Exit Stephano*]

Lorenzo tells Jessica of the harmony of the heavens. As the musicians play, he describes the healing powers of music.

剧情简介：劳仁佐跟婕丝柯说起天上的和谐景象。音乐响起，他描述音乐的治愈效力。

1 The music of the spheres (in small groups)

Lorenzo's lines 54–68 describe 'the music of the spheres': the ancient belief that moving stars and planets revolved on crystal spheres and made heavenly music as they orbited.

a Read the lines aloud, each person taking a short, meaningful unit of the script. First emphasise all the words connected with the senses; on a second reading, those connected with religion. Try other ways of reading to bring out the melodious, dreamlike and romantic mood of the verse. Record your favourite version to play back to the class, and give a short commentary on the effects you set out to achieve.

b One of you slowly reads Lorenzo's lines 70–88, pausing regularly to give the others time to draw what they hear Lorenzo describe.

c Put all the drawings together and use them (and the glossary opposite) to help you write a modern English translation of these lines. Do you agree with the points Lorenzo is making?

2 Jessica's legacy? (in pairs)

Lorenzo is saddened that humans, who are imperfect, cannot hear the heavenly music (lines 64–5). Jessica admits that music does not cheer her, even though Lorenzo assures her of its healing powers.

- Look back to Shylock's lines 27–35 in Act 2 Scene 5, in which he described the music of Christian masques as 'shallow foppery'. Talk about how Lorenzo's lines 70–88 implicitly criticise Shylock's values. Is Jessica's line 'I am never merry when I hear sweet music' supposed to reflect her upbringing with her father? Why else might Lorenzo and Jessica feel so differently?

Stagecraft 导演技巧

What kind of music?

At the end of line 88, Lorenzo urges Jessica to 'Mark (listen to) the music'. What kind of music should accompany this episode?

- Do some research, and make a list of five possibilities ranging from traditional to modern. See if you can get recordings to play to your classmates. Explain why you've chosen these pieces of music, and have a class vote to find the favourite.

1 Become 适合
2 inlaid 镶嵌
3 patens （基督教圣餐礼用的）小圆盘
4 orb 天体，星星
5 thou behold'st 你看
6 But … sings 在运行时像天使歌唱那般动听
7 Still choiring 永远在歌唱
8 cherubins 小天使
9 muddy vesture of decay 这易朽的泥土之躯（人体）
10 close it in 套在它（灵魂）之上
11 merry 快活
12 wanton 放荡不羁
13 race … colts 一群朝气蓬勃、未被驯服的小马
14 Fetching mad bounds 狂奔乱跳
15 hot 热烈，奔放
16 perchance 碰巧
17 air 曲调
18 mutual stand 一齐站立不动
19 the poet （指奥维德）
20 feign 编造出
21 Orpheus 俄耳甫斯（希腊神话中的音乐和诗歌之神）
22 drew 吸引
23 Since … nature 因为不管多么愚蠢、粗粝、野蛮的东西，音乐都能暂时改变它们的禀性
24 stratagems 阴谋
25 spoils 掠夺
26 Erebus 希腊神话中从阳间到阴间的黑暗地带
27 Mark 听

How sweet the moonlight sleeps upon this bank!
Here will we sit, and let the sounds of music 55
Creep in our ears; soft stillness and the night
Become[1] the touches of sweet harmony.
Sit, Jessica. Look how the floor of heaven
Is thick inlaid[2] with patens[3] of bright gold.
There's not the smallest orb[4] which thou behold'st[5] 60
But in his motion like an angel sings[6],
Still choiring[7] to the young-eyed cherubins[8].
Such harmony is in immortal souls,
But whilst this muddy vesture of decay[9]
Doth grossly close it in[10], we cannot hear it. 65

[*Enter* STEPHANO *with musicians*]

Come, ho! and wake Diana with a hymn.
With sweetest touches pierce your mistress' ear,
And draw her home with music.
Music plays

JESSICA I am never merry[11] when I hear sweet music.
LORENZO The reason is your spirits are attentive. 70
For do but note a wild and wanton[12] herd
Or race of youthful and unhandled colts[13]
Fetching mad bounds[14], bellowing and neighing loud –
Which is the hot[15] condition of their blood –
If they but hear perchance[16] a trumpet sound, 75
Or any air[17] of music touch their ears,
You shall perceive them make a mutual stand[18],
Their savage eyes turned to a modest gaze
By the sweet power of music. Therefore the poet[19]
Did feign[20] that Orpheus[21] drew[22] trees, stones, and floods; 80
Since naught so stockish, hard, and full of rage,
But music for the time doth change his nature[23].
The man that hath no music in himself,
Nor is not moved with concord of sweet sounds,
Is fit for treasons, stratagems[24], and spoils[25]; 85
The motions of his spirit are dull as night
And his affections dark as Erebus[26].
Let no such man be trusted. Mark[27] the music.

Portia and Nerissa return, unnoticed at first, and comment on the light and the music. They discover that their husbands have not yet arrived in Belmont, and plan to keep quiet about their own absence.

剧情简介：鲍霞和讷瑞莎毫不声张地先回来了，边走边评论着灯光和音乐。她们发现自己的丈夫还没回到贝尔蒙，她们决定隐瞒自己外出过这件事。

Characters 人物分析

'So shines a good deed in a naughty world' (in small groups)

Portia's lines 89–91 echo words spoken by Jesus in St Matthew's Gospel (Matthew 5:14–16), which include the phrase 'Let your light so shine before men'. She seems to be associating herself with 'light' (shining from her hall) in a symbolic way. Is the 'good deed' she speaks of (line 91) the saving of Antonio? Remember, too, that Lorenzo has already informed us that she 'doth stray about / By holy crosses where she kneels and prays'.

- Discuss the possible importance of these details in shaping your impression of Portia, especially as they appear in Act 5. Add your conclusions to your Character file.

1 his = its
2 naughty 邪恶
3 by 在附近
4 main of waters 大海
5 respect 比较，陪衬
6 neither is attended 没有对方陪伴
7 cackling 嘎嘎叫
8 wren 鹪鹩
9 season 时节
10 seasoned 使更有趣味
11 Endymion 恩底弥翁（希腊神话中的俊美青年，月亮女神荻阿娜的情郎；或许鲍霞说这句话时指着酣睡中的劳仁佐和婕丝柯）
12 speed 顺畅
13 take … hence 别提我俩出过远门

1 Relative values (in pairs)

In her speeches from line 93 to line 110, Portia insists that only comparisons can reveal the true worth of anything. Her comparisons include measuring the relative values of a substitute against a real king, and an inland river against the sea.

- Take turns to read her lines. Then discuss whether you agree that 'Nothing is good … without respect (comparison)'. Give reasons, supported with examples from your own experience.

Stagecraft 导演技巧

A secret entrance? (in threes)

- Take parts and read the script opposite.
- Then consider how Portia and Nerissa should enter and position themselves for lines 89–110. How would you arrange them and the characters already on stage (the non-speaking Lorenzo, Jessica, Stephano and the musicians)? What would they be doing? Decide upon the most dramatically effective way for Portia and Nerissa to enter and appear to the other characters.
- Write up all your ideas, including a diagram of the stage which shows all the characters' positions and movements as the episode unfolds.

Enter PORTIA *and* NERISSA

PORTIA | That light we see is burning in my hall.
| How far that little candle throws his¹ beams! | 90
| So shines a good deed in a naughty² world.
NERISSA | When the moon shone we did not see the candle.
PORTIA | So doth the greater glory dim the less:
| A substitute shines brightly as a king
| Until a king be by³, and then his state | 95
| Empties itself, as doth an inland brook
| Into the main of waters⁴. Music, hark!
NERISSA | It is your music, madam, of the house.
PORTIA | Nothing is good, I see, without respect⁵;
| Methinks it sounds much sweeter than by day. | 100
NERISSA | Silence bestows that virtue on it, madam.
PORTIA | The crow doth sing as sweetly as the lark
| When neither is attended⁶; and I think
| The nightingale, if she should sing by day
| When every goose is cackling⁷, would be thought | 105
| No better a musician than the wren⁸.
| How many things by season⁹ seasoned¹⁰ are
| To their right praise and true perfection.
| Peace, ho! The moon sleeps with Endymion¹¹
| And would not be awaked!

[*Music ceases*]

LORENZO | That is the voice, | 110
| Or I am much deceived, of Portia!
PORTIA | He knows me as the blind man knows the cuckoo
| By the bad voice.
LORENZO | Dear lady, welcome home!
PORTIA | We have been praying for our husbands' welfare,
| Which speed¹² we hope the better for our words. | 115
| Are they returned?
LORENZO | Madam, they are not yet.
| But there is come a messenger before
| To signify their coming.
PORTIA | Go in, Nerissa:
| Give order to my servants that they take
| No note at all of our being absent hence¹³ – | 120
| Nor you Lorenzo, Jessica nor you.

Bassanio returns with Antonio and Gratiano. Nerissa challenges Gratiano. He has given away her ring, which he swore to wear as long as he lived!

 剧情简介： 博萨纽跟安托纽和格拉奇阿诺一起回来了。讷瑞莎逼格拉奇阿诺拿出戒指，但格拉奇阿诺已经把戒指送给别人了，而他曾发誓只要他活着就会戴着那枚戒指。

Themes 主题分析

Appearance and reality

Portia and Nerissa arrive in Belmont before their husbands. Portia orders her household to keep quiet about their absence. She does not wish the men to know of the part she and Nerissa played in the trial.

- Begin a chart tracking the final revelations of the play, the dénouement (the unravelling) of all the intricate loose ends of the plot. One strand will focus, for example, on the explanations Gratiano and Bassanio give about what happened to their rings – before the truth finally emerges.
- When you get to the end of the play, compare your chart with those of other students, and discuss any variations you find.

Write about it 写作练习

Antonio: first impressions of Belmont

This is Antonio's only visit to Belmont. The traumatic (痛苦，不幸) experience of his trial is still very recent. What do you think will be in his mind as he arrives? He gives only a brief insight into his thoughts at line 138.

- Use your own ideas to write a short monologue for Antonio (in modern English), which explores his initial response to arriving at Bassanio's new home.

1 Husbands versus wives

Portia can't help teasing Bassanio. When she uses the word 'light' in line 130, she puns on its meaning as 'unfaithful'. Another pun on 'bound' in line 136 darkly echoes Antonio's imprisonment and Bassanio's debt to him.

a In groups, talk about Portia's wordplay in the script opposite. Is it comic, serious, barbed or something else? How does it fit with your assessment of her character in lines 89–121? When you have decided what this exchange suggests about Portia's character, add notes to your Character file.

A quarrel breaks out at line 142 between Nerissa and Gratiano. She accuses him, saying that despite all his vows he has given his ring to 'a judge's clerk'. But how did Nerissa 'notice' that Gratiano had lost the ring?

b In pairs, improvise the way Nerissa and Gratiano's conversation begins, developing it as far as 'By yonder moon … wrong!' (line 142).

1 the Antipodes 地球对面；住在地球对面的人
2 light 轻浮
3 heavy 沉闷，心情沉重
4 sort 安排
5 acquitted of 原谅；解脱
6 scant 减少
7 this breathing courtesy 这些客套话
8 gelt 阉割
9 paltry 不值钱
10 poesy 格言
11 cutler's poetry 低劣的诗
　（如刀匠刻在刀把上的话）
12 vehement 发自肺腑
13 You should have been respective 您应该爱惜
14 The … it = The clerk that had it will never wear hair on his face
　（脸上不长胡子，是个女的）

THE MERCHANT OF VENICE ACT 5 SCENE 1
威尼斯商人

                         [A tucket sounds]

LORENZO	Your husband is at hand, I hear his trumpet.
	We are no telltales, madam; fear you not.
PORTIA	This night methinks is but the daylight sick,
	It looks a little paler; 'tis a day 125
	Such as the day is when the sun is hid.

        Enter BASSANIO, ANTONIO, GRATIANO, *and their followers*

BASSANIO	We should hold day with the Antipodes[1],
	If you would walk in absence of the sun.
PORTIA	Let me give light, but let me not be light[2],
	For a light wife doth make a heavy[3] husband, 130
	And never be Bassanio so for me –
	But God sort[4] all! You are welcome home, my lord.
BASSANIO	I thank you, madam. Give welcome to my friend.
	This is the man, this is Antonio,
	To whom I am so infinitely bound. 135
PORTIA	You should in all sense be much bound to him,
	For as I hear he was much bound for you.
ANTONIO	No more than I am well acquitted of[5].
PORTIA	Sir, you are very welcome to our house.
	It must appear in other ways than words: 140
	Therefore I scant[6] this breathing courtesy[7].
GRATIANO	[*To Nerissa*] By yonder moon I swear you do me wrong!
	In faith, I gave it to the judge's clerk,
	Would he were gelt[8] that had it, for my part,
	Since you do take it, love, so much at heart. 145
PORTIA	A quarrel ho, already! What's the matter?
GRATIANO	About a hoop of gold, a paltry[9] ring
	That she did give me, whose poesy[10] was
	For all the world like cutler's poetry[11]
	Upon a knife: 'Love me, and leave me not.' 150
NERISSA	What talk you of the poesy or the value?
	You swore to me when I did give it you.
	That you would wear it till your hour of death,
	And that it should lie with you in your grave.
	Though not for me, yet for your vehement[12] oaths 155
	You should have been respective[13] and have kept it.
	Gave it a judge's clerk! No, God's my judge
	The clerk will ne'er wear hair on's face that had it[14].

153

Gratiano insists that he gave the ring to the judge's clerk. Portia reproaches him, saying that Bassanio would never have parted with her ring. Gratiano tells Portia that's exactly what Bassanio has done.

  剧情简介：格拉奇阿诺坚持说，他把戒指给了法官的书记员。鲍霞指责他说，博萨纽永远不会把她的戒指送人。格拉奇阿诺告诉鲍霞，博萨纽的戒指确实也送人了。

1 Bassanio and Gratiano: feeling uneasy (in threes)

Portia and Nerissa are in a 'conspiracy' with the audience. Portia's lines 166–76 sound very serious to the two husbands, but are very amusing to the audience. She already has the ring in her possession, and she wants to make Bassanio squirm (坐卧不宁)! Bassanio must be feeling very guilty because Gratiano is being reprimanded (遭责难) for the same misdeed that he has committed. His agitation comes to the surface in his aside (lines 177–8), and continues as Gratiano reveals that he's given away Portia's ring.

a Take parts as Portia, Bassanio and Gratiano, and read lines 161–91. As one person speaks, the other two react appropriately, especially showing the expressions on the men's faces. Practise different readings and reactions, and decide which are most effective. Use pauses and timing to increase the comic impact of the sequence. Share your favourite version with the whole class.

b If this were a cartoon strip (连环漫画), what would Bassanio be thinking while he was listening to Gratiano giving him away to Portia? Write his 'thought bubbles' together.

1 scrubbèd　(身材) 矮小 (像矮灌木丛)
2 prating　话多，喋喋不休
3 slightly　粗心大意
4 riveted　铆在
5 the wealth … masters　世间所有财富
6 unkind　不仁义
7 And 'twere to me　若是我的话
8 of me　从我这里
9 void … truth　虚情假意

Characters 人物分析

Bassanio's honesty – has he changed? (in pairs)

When Bassanio is forced to admit that he no longer has the ring (lines 186–8) he does so without excuses. But is this the same Bassanio you've seen in Acts 1, 2, 3 and 4?

a On page 8, you were asked to make your first assessment of Bassanio's character. Work together to review his subsequent appearances in the play. Alongside each one, give him a 'sincerity' rating (that is, how frank and truthful his words and actions suggest he is). Use a scale from 0 (utterly untrustworthy) to 10 (completely honest). Do you find this rating changes depending on the character he's interacting with or the situation he's in? Display your findings as a flow chart or line graph.

b Talk together about how much you think his character seems to change permanently as a result of all that happens to him in the course of the play. What is your final judgement of Bassanio? Write up your response, remembering to link your observations clearly to evidence in the script.

THE MERCHANT OF VENICE ACT 5 SCENE 1
威尼斯商人

GRATIANO	He will, and if he live to be a man.	
NERISSA	Ay, if a woman live to be a man.	160
GRATIANO	Now by this hand, I gave it to a youth,	
	A kind of boy, a little scrubbèd¹ boy	
	No higher than thyself, the judge's clerk,	
	A prating² boy that begged it as a fee;	
	I could not for my heart deny it him.	165
PORTIA	You were to blame, I must be plain with you,	
	To part so slightly³ with your wife's first gift,	
	A thing stuck on with oaths upon your finger	
	And so riveted⁴ with faith unto your flesh.	
	I gave my love a ring, and made him swear	170
	Never to part with it, and here he stands.	
	I dare be sworn for him he would not leave it	
	Nor pluck it from his finger for the wealth	
	That the world masters⁵. Now in faith, Gratiano,	
	You give your wife too unkind⁶ a cause of grief;	175
	And 'twere to me⁷, I should be mad at it.	
BASSANIO	[*Aside*] Why, I were best to cut my left hand off	
	And swear I lost the ring defending it.	
GRATIANO	My lord Bassanio gave his ring away	
	Unto the judge that begged it, and indeed	180
	Deserved it too; and then the boy his clerk	
	That took some pains in writing, he begged mine,	
	And neither man nor master would take aught	
	But the two rings.	
PORTIA	What ring gave you, my lord?	
	Not that, I hope, which you received of me⁸?	185
BASSANIO	If I could add a lie unto a fault,	
	I would deny it; but you see my finger	
	Hath not the ring upon it, it is gone.	
PORTIA	Even so void is your false heart of truth⁹.	
	By heaven, I will ne'er come in your bed	190
	Until I see the ring.	
NERISSA	Nor I in yours	
	Till I again see mine.	

Portia and Bassanio spar over the missing ring. Bassanio insists that he gave it to the lawyer who saved Antonio's life. Portia declares that her revenge will be to deny this lawyer nothing.

 剧情简介：鲍霞和博萨纽为失去的戒指争论不休。博萨纽坚持说他把戒指给了拯救了安托纽性命的法官。鲍霞宣称她的报复是她要对那个法官有求必应。

Language in the play 剧中语言

A war of words (in pairs)

The first sequence of an elaborate verbal battle between Portia and Bassanio occurs in lines 192–208.

a Read the lines, concentrating not on fierce argument but on skirmishing with words. Emphasise any repetitions, patterns or echoes (the repeated rhythms of the lines are very strong).

b Read the lines again, focusing on the repeated word 'ring'. Try to make each usage sound different. Then talk about the effects you have created, and explain your intentions to another pair.

c Although the humorous interplay is usually entertaining, it has occasionally been played with a degree of spite or torment, reinforcing the victory that Portia has so obviously won (see p. 177, for more on Elizabethan gender roles). Try playing it using a spiteful tone, then talk about this way of delivering the lines and whether the dramatic effects created are more or less striking than in other versions.

Characters 人物分析

Portia – still in control and utterly determined?

Portia referred to Bassanio as her 'lord' in Act 3, but in the trial scene she acts as a woman of fierce independence and authority. Who has the upper hand now: Bassanio or Portia? Does it make any difference that Portia uses the word 'ring' the same number of times as Bassanio, or that she has the last word?

a Write a paragraph comparing Portia's attitude to Bassanio in Act 3 Scene 2 and in Act 5 Scene 1. Identify and explain any similarities and differences in the way she treats her husband at these times.

The 'rings' episode has strange echoes of the trial scene. Portia has trapped Bassanio by exploiting his inability to fulfil the terms of a bond. Like Shylock, she is utterly determined on her course of action.

b Make a list of similarities and differences between Portia and Shylock. Which do you think are more important: their similarities or their differences? Add to your list as you work through to the end of the play.

1 left 放弃
2 abate 减少，减弱
3 virtue 魔力
4 contain 拥有
5 unreasonable 不讲理
6 terms of zeal 激烈的言辞
7 urge 强求
8 What ... ceremony? 只要您满怀感情解释这枚戒指的意义，哪个不讲理的人会硬要把这爱情的信物拿走？
9 civil doctor 律师
10 suffered ... away 看着他快快而去
11 held up 守护
12 enforced 迫不得已
13 beset with 被……情感困扰
14 besmear 玷污
15 candles 繁星
16 Know 认识或发生性关系（双关语，同第4幕第1场第415行）

THE MERCHANT OF VENICE ACT 5 SCENE 1
威尼斯商人

BASSANIO   Sweet Portia,
          If you did know to whom I gave the ring,
          If you did know for whom I gave the ring,
          And would conceive for what I gave the ring,   195
          And how unwillingly I left[1] the ring,
          When naught would be accepted but the ring,
          You would abate[2] the strength of your displeasure.
PORTIA   If you had known the virtue[3] of the ring,
          Or half her worthiness that gave the ring,   200
          Or your own honour to contain[4] the ring,
          You would not then have parted with the ring.
          What man is there so much unreasonable[5],
          If you had pleased to have defended it
          With any terms of zeal[6], wanted the modesty   205
          To urge[7] the thing held as a ceremony?[8]
          Nerissa teaches me what to believe:
          I'll die for't, but some woman had the ring!
BASSANIO No by my honour, madam, by my soul
          No woman had it, but a civil doctor[9],   210
          Which did refuse three thousand ducats of me,
          And begged the ring, the which I did deny him,
          And suffered him to go displeased away[10],
          Even he that had held up[11] the very life
          Of my dear friend. What should I say, sweet lady?   215
          I was enforced[12] to send it after him;
          I was beset with[13] shame and courtesy;
          My honour would not let ingratitude
          So much besmear[14] it. Pardon me, good lady,
          For by these blessèd candles[15] of the night,   220
          Had you been there I think you would have begged
          The ring of me to give the worthy doctor.
PORTIA   Let not that doctor e'er come near my house.
          Since he hath got the jewel that I loved
          And that which you did swear to keep for me,   225
          I will become as liberal as you;
          I'll not deny him anything I have,
          No, not my body, nor my husband's bed:
          Know[16] him I shall, I am well sure of it.

Bassanio begs forgiveness, swearing always to be faithful. Portia mocks him; Antonio tries to help him. The rings are returned, but the teasing of Bassanio and Gratiano continues.

 剧情简介：博萨纽请求鲍霞宽恕，发誓永远对她忠贞不渝。鲍霞讥笑博萨纽，安托纽想帮他说话。戒指物归原主，但大家还在拿博萨纽和格拉奇阿诺取乐。

Write about it 写作练习

Bassanio: what does he make of Antonio's offer?

In contrast to what happens at the trial, here it is Antonio who speaks up for Bassanio (lines 249–53), swearing that his friend will always remain true to his word in future ('nevermore break faith advisedly'). Antonio pledges his soul as collateral (抵押品). Bassanio does not have time to reply before the rings plot moves towards its climax (高潮). But what does he think about his friend's new offer to be 'bound' on his behalf?

- As Bassanio, write a short aside for the audience in which you express your feelings about Antonio's selfless gesture. Take your turn to read your speech aloud, while the rest of the class makes an assembly of Bassanios.

Themes 主题分析

Appearance and reality: 'Swear by your double self' (in fives)

The speeches opposite alternate between those that are completely honest and truthful (for example, Antonio's: 'I am th'unhappy subject of these quarrels') and those that are layered with irony or hidden meaning. For instance, Portia says 'For by this ring the doctor lay with me' after handing Bassanio's ring back. Her husband's relief at acquiring his ring is therefore immediately undercut by Portia's assertion that she gained it from the lawyer in return for sleeping with him. Nerissa informs Gratiano that he too has been made a 'cuckold'.

a Take parts as Portia, Nerissa, Gratiano, Antonio and Bassanio and read aloud lines 230–65. After each speech, in role as your character, voice your unspoken thoughts about what you have just said publicly.

b Make a quick sketch of the characters with their key lines in speech bubbles and their motives in thought bubbles.

c Talk together about the balance of comedy and seriousness that underpins this episode. Consider what might justify the two women taking their baiting of their husbands to such extremes. Write up your thoughts about the mood that Shakespeare creates here.

1 **Argus** 阿尔戈斯（希腊神话中的百眼怪物）
2 **be well advised** 留心
3 **mar the young clerk's pen** 毁掉那年轻书记员的那根笔（把他阉掉）
4 **unhappy subject** 不幸的缘由
5 **double** 假的
6 **of credit** 可信（讽刺的说法）
7 **advisedly** 故意
8 **surety** 担保人
9 **lay** 同床共枕
10 **In lieu of** 作为回报
11 **mending … enough** 夏天路况好，无须修路（喻指新婚女子无须找情人）
12 **cuckolds** 戴绿帽的人

	Lie not a night from home. Watch me like Argus[1].	230
	If you do not, if I be left alone,	
	Now by mine honour which is yet mine own,	
	I'll have that doctor for my bedfellow.	
NERISSA	And I his clerk; therefore be well advised[2]	
	How you do leave me to mine own protection.	235
GRATIANO	Well, do you so. Let not me take him then,	
	For if I do, I'll mar the young clerk's pen[3].	
ANTONIO	I am th'unhappy subject[4] of these quarrels.	
PORTIA	Sir, grieve not you; you are welcome notwithstanding.	
BASSANIO	Portia, forgive me this enforcèd wrong;	240
	And in the hearing of these many friends	
	I swear to thee, even by thine own fair eyes	
	Wherein I see myself –	
PORTIA	Mark you but that?	
	In both my eyes he doubly sees himself:	
	In each eye one. Swear by your double[5] self,	245
	And there's an oath of credit[6]!	
BASSANIO	Nay, but hear me.	
	Pardon this fault, and by my soul I swear	
	I nevermore will break an oath with thee.	
ANTONIO	I once did lend my body for his wealth,	
	Which but for him that had your husband's ring	250
	Had quite miscarried. I dare be bound again,	
	My soul upon the forfeit, that your lord	
	Will nevermore break faith advisedly[7].	
PORTIA	Then you shall be his surety[8]. Give him this,	
	And bid him keep it better than the other.	255
ANTONIO	Here, Lord Bassanio, swear to keep this ring.	
BASSANIO	By heaven, it is the same I gave the doctor!	
PORTIA	I had it of him; pardon me, Bassanio,	
	For by this ring the doctor lay[9] with me.	
NERISSA	And pardon me, my gentle Gratiano,	260
	For that same scrubbèd boy the doctor's clerk,	
	In lieu of[10] this, last night did lie with me.	
GRATIANO	Why, this is like the mending of highways	
	In Summer where the ways are fair enough[11]!	
	What, are we cuckolds[12] ere we have deserved it?	265

Portia reveals the truth about her deceptions and tells Antonio that three of his ships have been saved. Lorenzo and Jessica learn that Shylock will leave all his possessions to them.

 剧情简介：鲍霞说破了她冒名顶替的秘密，然后告诉安托纽他的三艘商船已经获救。劳仁佐和婕丝柯得知夏洛克将把其所有财产留给他们。

1 All is revealed (in pairs)

These unravellings of complex plots, when final disclosures are made, are a feature of many of Shakespeare's plays. One person should read Portia's lines 266–79. The other can react as each character in turn: Lorenzo and Antonio.

1 **amazed** 困惑
2 **as soon as** 和……同时
3 **And even but now returned** 刚刚回到家
4 **suddenly** 出乎意料
5 **living** 生存的办法，活路
6 **of all … of** 他死后全部遗产
7 **manna** 吗哪（《旧约·出埃及记》里提到的上帝赐给逃出埃及的以色列人的食物）
8 **And … full** 我知道你们还想了解这些事情的更多细节
9 **charge us there upon inter'gatories** 命我们如实招来（像在庭审时发誓讲真话那样）

▲ Identify as many characters as you can in this photograph. Then write a paragraph about how effectively you think this production stages the closing episode of the play.

Write about it 写作练习

Shylock's legacy

Nerissa's final words tell us that Shylock has committed himself by 'deed of gift' to leave all his wealth to Lorenzo and Jessica when he dies. Once again, he is un-named, referred to only as 'the rich Jew'.

- Reproduce the actual document that Nerissa hands to Lorenzo. Think about the kind of formal language that would be appropriate for such a document, and use it in your writing.

THE MERCHANT OF VENICE ACT 5 SCENE 1
威尼斯商人

PORTIA	Speak not so grossly; you are all amazed[1].
	Here is a letter, read it at your leisure;
	It comes from Padua, from Bellario.
	There you shall find that Portia was the doctor,
	Nerissa there her clerk. Lorenzo here
	Shall witness I set forth as soon as[2] you,
	And even but now returned[3]; I have not yet
	Entered my house. Antonio, you are welcome;
	And I have better news in store for you
	Than you expect. Unseal this letter soon;
	There you shall find three of your argosies
	Are richly come to harbour suddenly[4].
	You shall not know by what strange accident
	I chancèd on this letter.
ANTONIO	I am dumb.
BASSANIO	Were you the doctor and I knew you not?
GRATIANO	Were you the clerk that is to make me cuckold?
NERISSA	Ay, but the clerk that never means to do it,
	Unless he live until he be a man.
BASSANIO	Sweet doctor, you shall be my bedfellow;
	When I am absent, then lie with my wife.
ANTONIO	Sweet lady, you have given me life and living[5];
	For here I read for certain that my ships
	Are safely come to road.
PORTIA	How now, Lorenzo?
	My clerk hath some good comforts too for you.
NERISSA	Ay, and I'll give them him without a fee.
	There do I give to you and Jessica
	From the rich Jew, a special deed of gift
	After his death of all he dies possessed of[6].
LORENZO	Fair ladies, you drop manna[7] in the way
	Of starvèd people.
PORTIA	It is almost morning;
	And yet I am sure you are not satisfied
	Of these events at full[8]. Let us go in,
	And charge us there upon inter'gatories[9],
	And we will answer all things faithfully.

Line numbers: 270, 275, 280, 285, 290, 295

It is almost dawn as the characters go into Portia's house. Gratiano looks forward to going to bed with Nerissa, determined never again to relinquish her ring!

 剧情简介：众人来到鲍霞家时，已经接近黎明时分。格拉奇阿诺盼望着和讷瑞莎同床共枕，决心不再把她的戒指送人。

1 Final questions (in small groups)

As the characters prepare to leave the stage, Portia uses the language of the courtroom and promises to 'answer all things faithfully'.

- By yourself, make up a question that each character in the play wishes to ask her about what has been going on.
- Pool your questions with other group members and together pick out the two strongest ones that can then be put to a student (or your teacher) in role as Portia.

2 Last words (in pairs)

a Gratiano's final line not only puns on the word 'ring' (which had the double meaning of 'female genitals' for the Elizabethans) but also reminds the audience of the need to protect and value love tokens. Discuss your thoughts about ending the play in this way, and come up with two possible reasons why Shakespeare might have given the final lines to Gratiano.

b Read again what each character says in their final lines. Do you think the speeches reveal something important about each character?

c Jessica is silent. What is she thinking? Write a short internal monologue for her. What does she think about the events she has witnessed at Belmont? And how do you think she feels about what has happened to her father?

d Imagine that Shylock comes across the photograph on page 160 (Jessica is in the middle). Write his thoughts as he looks at it.

1 inter'gatory 问题
2 couching 上床，睡觉
3 sore 厉害
4 ring （本剧最后一个双关，在莎士比亚时代ring也指女性的生殖器）

Stagecraft 导演技巧

Curtain! Lights fade (in groups)

Although Shylock does not appear in Act 5, many productions try to keep him in the audience's minds. The 2004 film ended with Shylock excluded from a Jewish ceremony and cut to Jessica standing alone by a lake, sadly turning over on her finger Shylock's 'turquoise' ring. One stage production ended with Shylock at prayer. Another had Jessica left alone and desolate (冷落) on stage as all the Christians had gone off, ignoring her.

- What final impression would you wish to create? Present a tableau of the final moment of your own production.

THE MERCHANT OF VENICE ACT 5 SCENE 1
威尼斯商人

GRATIANO Let it be so. The first inter'gatory¹   300
That my Nerissa shall be sworn on is:
Whether till the next night she had rather stay,
Or go to bed now, being two hours to day.
But were the day come, I should wish it dark,
Till I were couching² with the doctor's clerk.   305
Well, while I live I'll fear no other thing
So sore³ as keeping safe Nerissa's ring⁴.

Exeunt

FINIS

The Merchant of Venice 威尼斯商人

Looking back at the play 本剧回顾
Activities for groups or individuals

1 Morning has broken
- Look back through the single scene that comprises Act 5. Pick out words and phrases that show day gradually breaking. Display these extracts visually in a way that charts how the act begins in moonlight and darkness and ends with daylight.
- Write a couple of paragraphs on why you think Shakespeare designed the act in this way.
- Afterwards, work in groups to produce a lighting design for Act 5 for a modern stage version of the play. Link your lighting ideas to the evidence you have identified in the script.
- As an extension activity, you could produce your own lighting design for a film version of the final act of your stage production.

2 Tensions and contrasts
- Head up three columns with the oppositional themes 'Appearance versus reality'; 'Justice versus mercy'; 'Love versus hate'. Record all the examples of each theme that you can find in Act 5.
- Then write a short essay comparing the different dramatic effects created in Acts 4 and 5 by these three thematic oppositions.

3 To cut or not to cut?
Now that you have studied Act 5, revisit Activity 3 on page 142, which asked you to think about whether the play should end after the trial scene in Act 4.
- Review all that happens in Act 5 and consider the act's dramatic value.
- Then discuss with a partner whether you would retain Act 5 or cut it altogether. One of you argues for its retention (保留), the other that it should be cut, each giving as many supporting reasons as possible.

4 Antonio's sadness
Just as Antonio's sadness haunts the opening of the play, many productions tend to focus on his loneliness at the end of the play (see image on p. xii, bottom). Although his life has been saved and his finances have been restored, his sadness seems unresolved. Imagine that he visits a therapist (心理医生，治疗师) to help him deal with this very personal issue.
- Either write the script of their discussion or, as a pair, role play the first meeting between Antonio and his counsellor.

5 Ten years later
Act 5 focuses on three married couples: Portia and Bassanio; Nerissa and Gratiano; and Jessica and Lorenzo.
- Working in a team of three, imagine that you have been commissioned to research a 'Where are they now?' television programme which focuses on the marriages of these rich and famous Venetian couples. Each of you manages to track down one of the pairs of characters listed above. Write notes on what you discover the characters are now doing and the state of their relationship. You could include brief interviews with key characters.
- Put together the feature, ready for filming; then go ahead and shoot your report. Your introductory voiceover (画外音) could give a brief summary of the characters' roles in the play.

6 An interview with Shylock
Shylock does not appear in Act 5. There is only news that he has willed his remaining wealth to Jessica and Lorenzo.
- Imagine that you are a researcher for a magazine. You have been asked to interview Shylock ten years after the play ends, and find out how his life has changed. Conduct the interview, then write up your article. Remember to give it an appropriate headline and to think carefully about your target audience.

Compare the way these two images present the relationship between Bassanio and Portia. In what historical periods are they set?

The Merchant of Venice
威尼斯商人

Perspectives and themes 视角与主题

What is the play about?

The Merchant of Venice has fascinated and intrigued audiences and critics ever since Shakespeare wrote it in around 1597. Although it brilliantly fuses a host of dramatic elements and at least four separate narrative strands, the play has become best known for the character Shylock and the relentless pursuit of his bond. Shylock appears in only five of the twenty scenes, but his presence dominates the play.

One way of answering the question 'What is *The Merchant of Venice* about?' is to think of it as the dramatic weaving together of four stories:

- the bond: Shylock and the pound of flesh
- the caskets: the winning of Portia
- the elopement: Jessica and Lorenzo
- the rings: a love test.

None of these strands was Shakespeare's own invention. The 'bond' and 'rings' narratives were probably based on a contemporary Italian short story, the tale of Gianetto of Venice and the lady of Belmont. The collection of short stories from which it was taken was called *Il Pecorone* (*The Idiot*). Shakespeare drew on this source but made it more dramatic. In the original, it is the hero's godfather who is to be punished by losing a pound of flesh. Shakespeare also makes the device of the rings more comic by adding the parallel story of Gratiano and Nerissa. The 'caskets' and 'elopement' narratives were drawn from well-known traditional stories that were part of the popular culture of Shakespeare's time. Again, he gave them new dramatic life; for example, in the play's version of the 'caskets' story, not only is Portia restricted by her dead father's will, but she also receives three different suitors, rather than the same one three times as in the original tale.

- ◆ Use the Internet or the library to find a detailed synopsis (梗概) of *Il Pecorone*. Working in a group, trace all the changes that Shakespeare makes to his original source material. What do you think he had in mind? Prepare a mini-presentation based on your thoughts.

- ◆ Look back at the play and place the four strands (bond, caskets, elopement, rings) in ascending order of importance. Write your rank order on a sticky note to display, then compare it with other students'. Finally, write a paragraph about each strand, saying what the play would lose or gain if it were omitted.

To help you deepen your understanding of the plot, try one or more of the following activities.

The bare bones of the script

- ◆ Have a go at retelling the story of the play in just one sentence, or rewrite the play as a mini-saga (微型传奇故事) (exactly fifty words).

- ◆ Imagine you are a newspaper sub-editor. Decide what type of paper you work for ('serious' or 'popular'). Your job is to write brief, memorable headlines for each of the five acts in the play. Of course, they may include puns or clever wordplay to gain attention and interest, but they must also be accurate.

Longer versions

- ◆ In a group of five, each take responsibility for retelling the story of an individual act, then put the narrative together to form a wall chart. Display your version on the classroom wall and compare it with those of other groups. Have they included anything that you have missed out? Argue the case for your omissions.

- ◆ Try writing a sentence about Act 1 Scene 1, then pass your paper to another student who can pick up the narrative. Keep working around the group, adding a sentence about each scene, until you reach the end of the play.

- Review the photo gallery at the start of this edition, which tells a version of the play in pictures and captions. What events have been missed out? Suggest three other images you would include, giving reasons for your choices.

- Stage a TV production meeting at which your task is to cut the narrative of the play to two hours, ready for filming. Decide which episodes to keep, then storyboard your version.

Fifteen-minute theatre

- Divide into five groups, with each group taking one act of the play. Produce a three-minute version of your act, using only the words from the script. Then put the five acts together to create a fifteen-minute version of the whole play.

Sculpture park

- Divide the class into two groups. As one group looks away, the other half of the class (working in pairs) freezes into 'sculptures' representing some of the key moments of the play. When the first group of students turns round, they see various statues depicting moments from the play set out before them. Their task is to identify as many of the sculptures as possible.

Whose story is it?

Tom Scutt, designer of the Royal Shakespeare Company (RSC) 2011 production, said:

> Another good thing is to look at whose story it is. It's a completely different play if you take it as Jessica's story, Portia's story, Bassanio's story. Antonio, the 'merchant of Venice' of the title, is often sidelined (设为副线). The play carries his name and yet he tends to get pushed to the side. The poor guy sets the world in motion and then does nothing. It would be interesting to focus on his journey.

- Try re-telling the story of *The Merchant of Venice* from the perspective of one of the four characters mentioned above, as a monologue.

Themes: tensions and oppositions in *The Merchant of Venice*

Another way of looking at the play is to consider its themes. Themes are ideas or issues or topics that recur throughout the play, suggesting that Shakespeare was preoccupied (心事重重) by particular ideas as he wrote, and explored them through drama that would entertain his audiences – and make them think. Oppositions and contrasts abound in *The Merchant of Venice*.

Love versus hate

On the one hand, the play is full of love and friendship. Bassanio's courtship of Portia is romantic and passionate. Portia is a woman in love, desperate to give herself to the man she desires. She speaks of 'ecstasy' and 'joy'. Bassanio praises Portia as a 'demi-god' with 'sugar breath'. Gratiano and Nerissa fall in love at first sight. 'Lorenzo and his amorous Jessica' are two young lovers who elope romantically. Antonio and Bassanio seem to share a deep, homoerotic closeness. Solanio says of Antonio: 'I think he only loves the world for him [Bassanio]'. It is, at the very least, a 'true friendship' that prompts Antonio to great self-sacrifice.

On the other hand, bitterness and hatred are constantly evident. Portia is overtly racist in dismissing her suitors ('Let all of his complexion choose me so'). Virtually all characters express racist attitudes at some point in the play. Lancelot and Gratiano openly insult Shylock, Lancelot comparing Shylock's Jewishness with 'the devil'. Hatred is expressed through verbal insults directed against Shylock, many of which take his name away from him (see pp. 62 and 74). Shylock turns his hatred of Christians ('I hate him [Antonio] for he is a Christian') into revenge on his Christian tormentors (折磨人的人). Jessica, Shylock's only child, hates the restrictions of home and smears (抹黑) his name as well as plundering his possessions.

The Merchant of Venice
威尼斯商人

- Working in a group, look back to the 'Language' boxes on pages 28, 40, 74, which focus on the language of hate. Expand your study to find as many other 'hate' expressions as you can. In each case, identify the context: who is speaking, where and when? Then comment on the impact of the images, particularly at that point in the play. Repeat the process, this time focusing on expressions of love (see the 'Language' boxes on pp. 86 and 144 to get you started). Finally, in the centre of a large sheet of paper, stick or draw an image that is typically associated with 'hate'. Do the same with a 'love' image on another sheet. Then display all your language extracts in a striking, visual way.

- In pairs, study the photo gallery at the start of this edition. From the selection, choose two pictures that you think express love and three that convey hate in a particularly powerful or effective way. In each case, explain the reasoning behind your choice to your partner.

- Use the oppositions outlined in the paragraphs on page 167 as the basis for an extended piece of writing. In it, explore how *The Merchant of Venice* dramatises the conflicts between love and hate. You might begin by heading up a piece of paper with two columns, 'Love' and 'Hate', and gathering evidence from the action of the play to fill out those columns. You should look not only at the incidents but also at the dramatic effects created.

Appearance versus reality: 'All that glisters is not gold'

The Merchant of Venice shows the danger of valuing only what can be seen on the surface. When Antonio calls Shylock 'a villain with a smiling cheek', he hints at the dark intentions that lie behind Shylock's apparent kindness. Prosperous Venice contains prejudice at all levels. Behind Portia's 'fair' exterior and politeness there lurks (暗藏) nasty racism. The caskets of gold and silver disguise secrets that contradict their outward appearance.

Gratiano must hide his naturally loud and raucous behaviour in order to accompany Bassanio to Belmont. Lancelot cruelly deceives his father, and Jessica deceives hers, but with more devastating effect. She also disguises her womanhood in male garments to escape Shylock's control. Similarly, Portia and Nerissa adopt male disguises to challenge the men in the courtroom.

The device of the rings explores the issue of betrayal, as well as adding to the confusion of identities. Characters frequently mislead or deceive each other.

- There are twelve 'Themes' boxes focusing on this idea of appearance versus reality (on pp. 6, 24, 44, 56, 60, 84, 104, 126, 130, 140, 152 and 158). Remind yourself of the content of each one. Then use the material from these boxes to help you produce a short presentation for your class on how Shakespeare uses the theme to create a range of dramatic effects in the play.

- Create a sequence of photographs (or freeze-frames) that, act by act, highlight the contrast between appearance and reality. In each case, try to find a suitable extract from the script to use as a caption. Be prepared to explain your intentions to other students as they view your images.

- Working in a small group, list the main characters. Alongside each name, write the various deceptions they practise. Rate the scale of their deceptions on a range between 1 and 10 and display these findings as a bar graph. Compare your graph with those of other groups.

Venice versus Belmont

To Shakespeare's contemporaries, Venice was a legendary city of prosperity, sophistication (现代，先进) and culture. It was renowned as a city built on extensive trading links with Europe and beyond. Antonio's ships have sailed 'From Tripolis, from Mexico and England, / From Lisbon, Barbary, and India', as did English traders. Venice was opulent (富裕) – a world-famous centre for banking and trade. The city promoted the ventures and interests of its powerful merchants, whilst still protecting the established social privileges of its aristocracy (贵族阶级).

Shakespeare gives Venice many of the qualities of England in the 1590s. The merchants in Act 1 Scene 1 behave just like their English counterparts. They are strongly aware of class (Salarino speaks of 'signors' [gentlemen] and 'rich burghers' [important citizens]). They seem to have plenty of time for leisure and relaxation; they are not seen at business.

▲ What does this image suggest about the lifestyle and values of the Venetian Christians?

Venice was also renowned for its acceptance of foreigners, founded upon a legal system that protected the rights of all individuals, not only its own citizens. It was known for its tolerance of outsiders and had a reputation as a melting-pot of different cultures and minorities, especially entrepreneurs. However, it confined its Jewish inhabitants to their own neighbourhood – the ghetto (贫民区，犹太人居住区).

Shylock, as a typical Jewish merchant of the time, practises usury: lending money and charging interest on its repayment. To him, making money from money is legitimate business and an art at which he is skilled. 'I make it breed as fast', Shylock proudly boasts to Antonio, comparing his own generation of profit with the ingenuity of the biblical figure Jacob. Since Shylock earns his living from lending money, he is critical of Christians who 'lend out money gratis' (without charging interest).

But Christianity forbade the charging of interest and Antonio scornfully challenges Shylock's practice: 'I neither lend nor borrow / By taking nor by giving of excess'. The Christians condemn usurers but, hypocritically, depend on the money of the Jews to underwrite (提供经济担保) their own economic projects. Bassanio has frittered (挥霍) away his wealth but is quite prepared to use Shylock's lending service to support his courtship of Portia, seeing it as a business venture.

Belmont (literally 'fair mountain') does not exist. It is Shakespeare's imaginative creation, based on an idea he took from his source material. Belmont seems to reflect the Elizabethan ideal of the country estate, resonating with artistic, musical and cultural assurance. It is a place of beauty and elegance, presided over by an intelligent and gracious mistress. But is it so different from Venice? Despite its charm, it is riddled with patriarchal control and intolerance of foreigners.

◆ Choose a scene from the play that you think typically represents Venetian values and principles. Do the same for Belmont. Write an analysis of the similarities and differences in the two settings used by Shakespeare.

Justice versus mercy

One of the central preoccupations of the play is justice: the right, proper and fair treatment of individuals according to what they deserve. The conflict between justice and mercy is most dramatically explored in the trial scene, where the trial of Antonio turns into the trial of Shylock. Although he is constantly asked to show mercy to the accused Antonio, Shylock refuses. Portia's moving declaration in her speech beginning 'The quality of mercy is not strained' summarises the argument that justice is most appropriately done when mercy tempers it. At the end of the trial, both the Duke and Antonio boast of their merciful attitude. Shylock receives judgement, but does he receive justice?

◆ In a group, talk together about the trial scene. Which characters display mercy, and how?

The Merchant of Venice
威尼斯商人

Happiness versus suffering

The first published version of the play appeared in 1600. Its title page described it as 'The Comical History of the Merchant of Venice'. In keeping with that description, the play seems to end on a happy note, with the resolution of the test of the rings and the celebration of three marriages. The action shifts to Belmont, and symbolically Shakespeare makes the final act track the movement from night to dawn. The trial scene, the bond and Shylock himself are features of the past.

The play certainly cannot be described as a 'tragedy' (for example, there are no deaths). However, from the start it was felt to have powerfully tragic undertones (隐含意). The English dramatist and poet Nicholas Rowe commented in 1709: 'I cannot but think it was design'd Tragically by the author. There appears in it such a deadly Spirit of Revenge'.

In many productions, dark and troubling aspects cast shadows over any bright and hopeful ending. For example, Shylock leaves the court a broken man, crushed by the instruction that he must convert to Christianity. Antonio often stands alone among the pairs of married couples at the end of the play, his sadness unresolved. In some productions, Jessica is shunned and ignored in Belmont. Lancelot's cruel treatment of his blind father leaves a sour taste. And it is impossible to forget Shylock's suffering: he has been constantly baited (以侮辱性言语激怒) and humiliated by Christian characters (who are sometimes seen spitting on him). They delight in his misfortune and mock his losses, creating a really unpleasant atmosphere.

◆ Working in a group of five, each take an act of the play. Draw a timeline for your act.

◆ Go through your allocated act. For each scene within it, identify all the features that might fit 'happiness'. Write these above your line. Do the same for 'suffering', which you should display below the line. Give them a rating, then incorporate (整合) your findings into a flow diagram.

◆ Reconvene (重新整合) and put all five acts together. What do you notice about the pattern created? Choose from within your flow chart two moments or episodes: one that appears to hit a peak of happiness, the other a trough of sadness. Work on two group tableaux of your two chosen moments. Photograph them and add them to your timeline display.

◆ Use your timeline as the basis for a five-minute presentation discussing how you would direct the play to bring out its happy and sad aspects.

Fathers versus daughters

Both Portia and Jessica struggle to come to terms with their fathers' demands. Shakespeare gives little information about Portia's father, but he controls her destiny from beyond the grave ('so is the will of a living daughter curbed by the will of a dead father'), insisting that her choice of husband is dictated by the lottery of the caskets. Jessica is uncomfortable at home ('Our house is hell') and speaks of being 'ashamed' to be Shylock's daughter (see images on pp. viii, 48, 52, 73). She is clearly unhappy with the tediousness of her domestic life and plans to elope with the Christian Lorenzo as a way of escaping to a more fulfilling life.

◆ Although Portia's father was a Christian and lived in Belmont and Shylock is Jewish and lives in Venice, do they share any common attitudes towards fatherhood and to their daughters? Talk about this with a partner and then give a short presentation to the class on your observations.

Characters 人物分析

In earlier centuries, people writing about characters tended to do so as if they were living human beings with real personalities. More recently, critics have argued that playwrights such as Shakespeare were not concerned with creating psychologically consistent 'people' but rather with dramatic 'constructs', embodying certain dramatic functions and set in a social and political world with particular values, attitudes and beliefs. What is especially noticeable about all the characters in this play is the way Shakespeare presents them: they are all complex, ambiguous and riddled with contradictions and paradoxes (悖论). Keep all these considerations in mind as you explore Shakespeare's characterisation.

Shylock

There has always been controversy about Shylock. To some, he is a miserly money-lender who delights in the prospect of cutting a pound of flesh from the noble merchant who has exposed his corrupt ways. He is a bloodthirsty fiend armed with scales and a knife, who cares more for his money than for his runaway daughter. Such a view sees him as a comic or unpleasant villain who gets what he deserves in the end.

A quite different perspective sees him as the victim of the society around him. Here he is a godly, respectable family man who merely wishes to conduct his business without interference. He becomes a man driven to revenge by mindless persecution (迫害) and the cruel 'theft' of his only child. This view casts him as a naive, misguided soul who tries to get even within the law of those who hate him, only to be cruelly tricked and humiliated yet again.

There's no simple answer to the question 'villain or victim?', but the fact that Shylock has fascinated audiences for 400 years is evidence that he is one of Shakespeare's most intriguing (吸引人) and compelling (引人注目) characters. What follows will help you to form your own view of Shylock, although you will detect a strongly anti-racist stance in what we, the editors of this edition, have written. No one can be neutral about *The Merchant of Venice*.

▼ When thinking about how Shylock is presented in the play, start by studying the two images below. Which gets closer to how *you* see Shylock, and why?

The Merchant of Venice
威尼斯商人

Consider the comments below that come from actors, directors and performance critics:

The age-old dilemma about Shylock is this: is he tragic or is he comic? And, of course, he's both. He's one of the most complex human beings Shakespeare wrote.
Sir Peter Hall, theatre director

He becomes that which he most abhors. He's torn to shreds emotionally by the society around him. He becomes the very thing that's reduced him ... that's taken his humanity away.
Dustin Hoffman, actor

I would interpret Shylock as an outsider, not who happens to be a Jew, but because [he is] a Jew. The Jewish element is unavoidably very important. He's only actually called by his name Shylock six times, [he is called] Jew twenty-two.
David Suchet, actor

He's an alien in a world where he's forced to put up with insults and intolerance just to do his job.
Ian Bartholomew, actor

I found [the] darkness in him fascinating ... The challenge for an audience, since the Holocaust (大屠杀), is to deal with a villain who is a Jew, and that isn't easy. Shylock should really be a small part – he's in only five scenes – but he breaks the confines of the play.
Angus Wright, actor

He's a widower; his daughter steals from him and marries a gentile; and he's left with this void, which he fills with the most negative of emotions, revenge. It didn't make him any more pleasant a man, but a very human man, subject to all the fallibilities (易误性) that humans are prey to.
Paul Rider, actor

Shylock is ... an embittered (愤恨) father in search of revenge for his daughter's ruin.
2004 film review

[Shylock is] slight, pale and acutely intelligent. His cold, searching eyes and tight movements suggest a man accustomed to insults and hardened in grief.
Sarah Hemming, performance critic

He is so naked in his religiosity (宗教狂热), in his hatreds, in his money-dealings, in his grief, in his vengeance ... He is awesome and embarrassing.
Alastair Macauley, performance critic

Shylock is cultivated, quiet and reasonable, with ... resentment waiting to blaze up.
Martin Hoyle, performance critic

I had a very large, bushy beard and a lot of long, dirty, tangly hair. I wore a shabby, dirty, broken-down frock coat, because I think the most important thing for Shylock in the play is money, possessions and finance.
Patrick Stewart, actor

◆ **In pairs, discuss which of these statements you think most accurately sums up the essence of Shylock's character, and why. When you have identified the one that you think gets closest to the truth, join up with other students and have a wider discussion about the statements.**

How Shylock responds to prejudice

It could be argued that Shylock's bloodthirsty campaign against Antonio is morally indefensible (站不住脚). He rejects the simple purity of his normal life and degrades himself in his animal-like quest to win a pound of the Christian's flesh. His behaviour is wrong, but it is understandable. Shylock is a foreigner in his own city. He may have lived all his life in Venice, but he is treated as an alien.

Like his fellow Jews, he tries to rise above such prejudice. He seeks security and success in money-lending, which he calls 'well won thrift'; Antonio disparagingly (轻蔑地, 鄙夷地) calls it 'interest'. Antonio and the Christians won't allow themselves to lend money for profit, but to support their extravagant lifestyles they still need loans from the Jews they persecute. Shylock has been waiting to strike back at Antonio, one of Venice's principal anti-Semites (反犹太分子), and sees his chance when the merchant is compelled to come to him for credit.

Significantly, Shylock tries to attack his enemy within the law of Venice. He is often at pains to point out the

CHARACTERS

legality of his actions, and after the loss of Antonio's ships he repeatedly refers to his 'bond'. In the trial, he openly questions the validity of Venetian justice if it is not to be enforced on his behalf. He demands that his case is dealt with according to the letter of the law, and this is turned harshly against him when it is revealed that he himself has behaved illegally.

◆ Collect Shylock's references to his legal agreement with Antonio and other comments he makes about the law. Use your findings to write several paragraphs about why it is so important to Shylock to be able to use the law of Venice against Antonio.

Shylock despises Antonio from the start of the play. His hatred is intensified by the loss of Jessica, which is perhaps the key to his emotional reactions from then on. In his clash with Salarino and Solanio just after Jessica's elopement (Act 3 Scene 1), he claims that his suffering and anger are caused by the Christians. He blames his villainy on them, arguing that it is simply imitation of their own prejudice and cruelty.

◆ Read lines 42–57 of Act 3 Scene 1. How convinced are you by Shylock's justification for his actions? Think of actual examples in history or modern times which show that racism provokes similar cruelty in its victims.

The Merchant of Venice
威尼斯商人

How should Shylock be portrayed?

Shylock was probably played in Elizabethan times as a stereotypical (模式化，刻板化) comic villain, in a grotesque (奇异) orange beard and wig. Subsequently, the more evil and menacing aspects of his character were given prominence. Then, in the nineteenth and twentieth centuries, he was increasingly portrayed in a more positive and sympathetic light. Today, he usually makes a more complex impression – as a man looking to catch Antonio just 'once upon the hip' but also as a man preaching (劝诫) the common humanity of both Christian and Jew.

◆ Your task is to explore the challenges posed by the depiction of Shylock and to resolve potential difficulties. Work your way systematically through the numbered questions below. Find evidence from the play script to support your investigation, and write a paragraph in response to each question.

1. How would you deal with Shylock's profession of usury? Do you share the Christian Antonio's disapproving attitude towards it (even though he is quite happy to do business with Shylock)?

2. How deep and long-standing is Shylock's trouble with the Christians and the 'ancient grudge' which he bears? How unacceptable is Antonio's racist bullying (Act 1 Scene 3) and other Christian hostility directed at Shylock throughout the play?

3. Do the bond negotiations genuinely begin as a 'merry sport' or something more sinister (阴险)? How important is it that Antonio willingly enters into the agreement, knowing full well its terms and conditions and its legal status?

4. Is Shylock's attitude to Christian celebrations (Act 2 Scene 5) unattractive?

5. How do Jessica and Lancelot add to our sympathy for (or disapproval of) Shylock, especially in the domestic scenes?

6. How do you view Shylock's attitude to the runaway Jessica and her 'betrayal' of him? How sympathetic are you towards Jessica?

7. How far do the Christians conspire against Shylock (inviting him to dinner, then 'stealing' his daughter and money)?

8. How can (or should) you try to justify Shylock's insistence on having his pound of flesh? How much is Antonio to blame for his own involvement in the deadly affair?

9. How far do you feel Portia plans her action against Shylock? In the trial, she waits until the very moment he is going to cut Antonio's flesh to reveal the loophole she has discovered in the bond between them. Before that, she repeatedly gives Shylock the chance to back down, so adding to the humiliation she clearly wishes to inflict on him in her hour of victory. When Shylock is defeated, he is shown little of the mercy that was so earnestly recommended to him earlier by Portia. Half his wealth is confiscated and – far worse – he must lose his faith and convert to Christianity. How far do you sympathise with Shylock at this point?

10. Is it to his credit that Shylock, having lived all his life in Venice, looks to gain revenge through its laws, trying to claim what is legally his?

11. How valid is it that Shylock blames his own villainy on the Christians, claiming to be only imitating their prejudice and cruelty?

12. How dangerous is Shylock? Do you ever feel that Antonio is in mortal danger? Or does the mood and tone of the play suggest that all will turn out well for him in the end?

Characters

Was Shakespeare anti-Semitic in his depiction of Shylock?

Shakespeare's characters, notably in *The Merchant of Venice*, often express racist views, but whether Shakespeare himself was a racist is open to debate. It is clear that he understood the suffering and the behaviour that can result from racial prejudice. Shylock's key speech in Act 3 Scene 1 is a supremely eloquent plea to acknowledge our common humanity. However, Shakespeare's handling of Shylock is deeply ambiguous. Shylock is intensely and movingly human, yet at the end he receives the same treatment as a stage villain. He leaves the court in Act 4 with hardly a word, apparently completely defeated. He doesn't appear in Act 5 and is barely mentioned there. If Shakespeare wanted the audience to view this central character as a victim, surely he would have given him something to say or do in the final act?

- ◆ Your school or college drama group wishes to stage *The Merchant of Venice*, but the Principal fears that the play might offend minority groups in the school and the local community, and calls a meeting of those involved. Decide who would be present and improvise this difficult encounter in front of the rest of the class. Everyone, including observers, has the right to stop the action to ask questions, to express opinions, and to ask for (or offer) advice.

The Merchant of Venice
威尼斯商人

Portia

◆ Just as you did with Shylock, consider each of the following comments about Portia from actors, designers and performance critics. In pairs, talk together about which comment you think is most important in defining the essence of Portia's character, and why. When you have identified the one that you think gets closest to the truth, join up with other students and have a wider discussion.

I finally worked out that the great problem for the actress playing Portia is to reconcile the girl at home in Belmont early in the play with the one who plays a Daniel come to judgement in the Venetian court. I couldn't understand why Shakespeare makes her so unsympathetic in those early scenes: the spoilt little rich girl dismissing suitor after suitor in a very derisory (嘲弄的) fashion. The girl who does that, I thought, is not the woman to deliver the 'quality of mercy' speech.

Sinead Cusack, actor

We are so used to seeing Portia depicted as a wise figure, full of self awareness and dry wit … what's brilliant is that Portia's naivety in our production allows her to talk directly from her heart. The 'quality of mercy' speech therefore comes from a place of complete innocence and connection with God, pure Christian thought.

Tom Scutt, designer

Portia was unambiguously wholesome and a touch matronly (主妇一样稳重) although she managed to convey the impression there was a depth of passion in her nature.

Andrew Wilson / John Barber, performance critics

This Portia was ruled by her spontaneous (自发，自然) passions rather than by a duty to her father.

1984 production review

She takes control of every scene and gives us Portia as melancholy damsel (少女) and mischievous (机敏) wit, as great lady and canny (精明) hero.

Alastair Macauley, performance critic

A confident and knowing woman: a keen-witted social voyeur (偷窥狂).

2004 film review

Portia as herself (far right) and in disguise as Balthazar (left).

CHARACTERS

Portia: a victim of patriarchy (男权制)?

In Shakespeare's England, husbands and fathers strictly controlled the lives of wives and daughters. Under the 'tyranny of patriarchy' (rule by men), female rights were heavily restricted, legally, socially and economically. Shakespeare's Venice is ruled entirely by men. Women have no role at all in trade, politics or law. It seems that they cannot even own property. As soon as Portia enters Venetian society by becoming engaged to Bassanio, she gives him all her wealth as well as her own freedom:

> This house, these servants, and this same myself
> Are yours, my lord's.
>
> Act 3 Scene 2, lines 170–1

Patriarchy rules in Belmont as well as Venice. Portia might be head of the household at first, but her father still controls her destiny, even from the grave. When she escapes from her father's will, she subjects herself immediately to her husband's authority. From now on she will be known as 'Lord Bassanio's wife' rather than Portia. And when she enters the male domain of the courtroom she must do so in disguise, as the male Doctor Balthazar.

◆ In pairs, talk together about this aspect of the presentation of Portia. List all the ways in which she seems to be subservient (屈从) to males and male attitudes and values.

Portia: reconciling paradoxes?

Most criticism points to the inconsistencies in Portia's presentation. She has many seemingly paradoxical identities.

◆ In groups of six, each person takes one of the 'cards' and researches the play to find evidence in support of the stance it takes. Then, as a group, argue the merits of each 'reading'.

Card A Portia is the dutiful daughter who acknowledges the importance of her dead father's will, even though it places restrictions upon her freedom.

Card B Portia is a sexually inexperienced and naive young woman ('unlessoned … unschooled, unpractised') who submits herself willingly to her husband's authority.

Card C Portia is a wealthy and independent woman who knows more about men and male behaviour than she likes to let on to other people.

Card D Portia is the 'mortal-breathing saint' who possesses 'god-like amity (友好)' and who is the advocate of Christian mercy.

Card E Portia is the hard-headed, calculating lawyer who is totally familiar with the tricks of the legal trade and ruthlessly destroys Shylock.

Card F Portia is the racist mocker of the suitors she finds unappealing, and the cruel teaser and tormentor of her husband in the 'rings' test.

Portia: modern perspectives

Some modern criticism highlights Portia's willingness to embrace racist attitudes, rejecting her as an innocent, virtuous 'Victorian' heroine. Instead, she is seen as a devious (不正直) manipulator (操控者), who subverts (颠覆) the meaning of what she says. She is fundamental to the preservation of the values and beliefs of the male world of Venice (and Belmont). But some feminist criticism argues that she stands for female resistance in a male world, showing that she is able to take on, and defeat, men at their own game (winning in the law court and using the 'rings' test to establish control over her husband). But the play poses an unanswered question at the end: will being subservient to a man like Bassanio suit Portia?

The Merchant of Venice
威尼斯商人

◆ Study the two pictures (of Portia and 'Balthazar') on page 176. Write a paragraph advising the actor playing Portia on how to make these two distinct 'roles' convincing in performance.

Barrie Rutter, director of the 2004 Northern Broadsides production of *The Merchant of Venice*, played down the frequent centralisation (集中) of Shylock: 'He's only in five scenes … It's Portia's play'.

◆ You are directing a new, modern version of the play and you agree wholeheartedly with Rutter. Prepare detailed notes, ready for a presentation to your cast (your classmates). Explore the importance of Portia's role, scene by scene, and explain how you plan to bring her character to the fore. Use your notes to write a detailed casting brief, explaining the qualities you are looking for in your Portia.

Jessica and Nerissa

Portia, Jessica and Nerissa, the three women in the play, have very different personalities. Nonetheless, they all marry friends of Antonio at roughly the same time and are all involved in the defeat of Shylock. All adopt disguises as men in order to carry out that defeat. Both Portia and Jessica are victims of their fathers' patriarchal authority and control. Portia cannot marry freely. Jessica, perhaps frustrated by her father's over-protectiveness, decides to convert to Christianity.

◆ Study the pen portraits of Jessica and Nerissa that follow. Check how far you agree with each, then write a short essay of your own (using quotations to back up your points) on each of the two women, or attempt the activity that follows each portrait.

Jessica

Jessica is ashamed to be Shylock's daughter and views her life at home as 'hell'. Only the joking of Lancelot relieves the domestic gloom. She is perhaps frustrated by her father's over-protectiveness and killjoy attitude. She willingly becomes involved in a Christian plot and schemes against her father behind his back. She steals from him much of his money and jewels, including a turquoise ring of great sentimental value, which she is later alleged to have squandered (挥霍). In order to elope with Lorenzo, she adopts a male disguise. On arriving at Belmont, she is apparently cold-shouldered by the Christians whose religion she will soon embrace.

Questions that arise when considering Jessica include: does she willingly condemn her father's pursuit of revenge in Act 3 Scene 2, or is she seeking to ingratiate (使迎合) herself with her Christian hosts? Is she really a huge admirer of Portia (as she claims in Act 3 Scene 5, lines 63–71), or does she have little reason to like or respect her? How will she get on being married to Lorenzo, whom she teasingly accuses of 'Stealing her soul with many vows of faith, / And ne'er a true one'?

◆ You are a women's magazine journalist and it is ten years after the play ends. You decide to interview Jessica for a 'Where Are They Now?' feature. Write your article, describing how Jessica feels about the events of the decade before, and how her life has changed since.

Nerissa

Nerissa is more than a servant to Portia; she appears to be both a lady-in-waiting and a confidante (知己，密友). Portia trusts her completely, and Nerissa takes orders from Portia without question. Nerissa has a sensible approach to life, displaying humour and worldly wisdom in her attitude to Portia's suitors and to men in general.

Characters

In view of the fact that she has no illusions about men, why does she fall for Gratiano? She can tell that Bassanio 'was the best deserving a fair lady' but apparently ignores the fact that her own husband is a show-off and a racist bully. After watching the lengthy, ritualistic courtship of Portia, why does she agree to marry Gratiano after knowing him such a short time? How will she cope with such a husband?

◆ Nerissa (below, right) volunteers to be interviewed for a local radio feature on 'Life at Belmont'. Script her contribution, making clear her attitudes to her life with Portia and her new husband.

The Christians

Venice is almost completely characterised by friendships between men. The Christians are 'friends' but are largely a band of merchants and traders bound together by a group identity. They oppose the Jews and the Jewish practice of usury. They profit from trade. The Venetians are competitive and commercially driven, conscious of status and hierarchy (等级制度), although they seem to have many idle hours to spend together.

Antonio

Antonio is the merchant of the play's title (although an eighteenth-century version of the play renamed it *The Jew of Venice*). Traditionally, he has been seen as an affluent (富裕) gentleman, at ease within refined social and economic circles, very much associated with the values and attitudes represented by Venice.

Antonio is generous to Bassanio but loathes Shylock. The reason for his sadness at the start of the play is left unresolved, although in many modern productions his loneliness and sadness have been attributed to homoerotic feelings for Bassanio. He is quite willing to die under Shylock's knife as long as he can see Bassanio one last time. Some productions ensure that he is left isolated at the end of the play as the married couples celebrate.

Bassanio

Like the other male Christian characters, Bassanio belongs to a wealthy, privileged class in Venice, but as a result of his reckless spending he is impoverished (贫穷) as the play opens. He conforms to the Elizabethan model of a gentleman as 'a scholar and a soldier'. He might love and desire Portia, but he also views marriage to her as a business opportunity and he quickly assumes his role as head of Belmont. His friendship for Antonio is strong (Antonio is 'The dearest friend to me, the kindest man' and a 'true friend'), powerful enough to postpone his marriage to Portia as Antonio nears his trial. But Bassanio is passionately attracted to Portia, whom he describes in heightened, romantic terms as: 'fair, and – fairer than that word – / Of wondrous virtues' and a 'demi-god'.

Gratiano, Solanio and Salarino

These three men are united not only by their friendship but also by their violent hostility (敌意) towards Shylock. Gratiano's withering attacks peak during the trial scene. Solanio and Salarino gloat (幸灾乐祸) over Shylock's loss of his daughter and his jewels, then taunt him publicly and excruciatingly (极度) about Jessica's elopement.

◆ Use the pen portraits above, and the information on 'Venice versus Belmont' on pages 168–9, to prepare a short presentation on how you think the Venetian Christians should be presented in the play. Include drawings and illustrations showing how they should appear physically.

THE MERCHANT OF VENICE
威尼斯商人

The language of *The Merchant of Venice*
《威尼斯商人》的语言

Imagery

The Merchant of Venice is rich in **imagery**: vivid words and phrases that help create the atmosphere of the play as they conjure up emotionally charged pictures or associations in the mind. When Portia describes the concept of 'mercy', she declares that 'It droppeth as the gentle rain from heaven', showering heaven's blessing on both the giver and receiver. Similarly, Antonio voices his mistrust of Shylock (and his motives in agreeing to the 'bond') by calling him 'a villain with a smiling cheek', outwardly innocent and appealing but inwardly corrupt.

Images enrich particular moments in strikingly dramatic ways. They provide insight into character, and intensify meaning and emotional force. When Shylock strengthens his determination to seek revenge on the Christians who have persecuted him, he twists one of the insults used against him back on his tormentors: 'Thou call'dst me dog before thou hadst a cause, / But since I am a dog, beware my fangs.'

◆ Imagery repeatedly illuminates the themes of the play, such as appearance versus reality. Below is a series of quotations, each linked to that theme. In pairs, identify where each reference comes from (speaker, act, scene and lines). Then write a brief comment on how it explores the theme and why its use of language is thought-provoking.

'Let me play the Fool'
'How like a fawning publican he looks'
'A goodly apple rotten at the heart'
'But love is blind, and lovers cannot see / The pretty follies that themselves commit'
'All that glisters is not gold'
'So may the outward shows be least themselves'
'The world is still deceived with ornament'
'A stage where every man must play a part'
'There be fools alive iwis / Silvered o'er, and so was this'

◆ Now read the section on 'Appearance versus reality' on page 168. Use the information there to help guide you towards other images in the play that explore the same theme. Taking each image in turn, comment on how it works and how it helps convey the theme.

In *The Merchant of Venice*, the imagery is sometimes so highly embroidered (润色；渲染) and extravagant that it seems full of **hyperbole** (an exaggeration not meant to be taken literally). Bassanio's praise of Portia's picture, which he finds in the lead casket, is often judged as showy, perhaps reflecting his posturing and insincerity:

> Here are severed lips
> Parted with sugar breath; so sweet a bar
> Should sunder such sweet friends. Here in her hairs
> The painter plays the spider, and hath woven
> A golden mesh t'entrap the hearts of men
>
> Act 3 Scene 2, lines 118–22

◆ Turn to this speech of Bassanio's. Try reading it aloud, first in a showy and over-elaborate fashion and then in a way that emphasises its sincerity and intense adoration (崇拜；爱慕). How do the two readings differ in their dramatic impact?

Shakespeare's imagery uses metaphor, simile and personification. All are comparisons, which substitute one thing (the image) for another (the thing described).

A **simile** compares one thing to another, using 'like' or 'as'. In the opening scene, Salarino describes Antonio's merchant ships as being 'Like signors (gentlemen) and rich burghers (important citizens) on the flood', quickly establishing the link between trade and status or class. Later, Arragon (Act 2 Scene 9), ironically, declares that the fool who chooses by outward show is 'like the martlet (swift)' building its nest on an exposed outer wall, vulnerable to danger and misfortune.

The language of The Merchant of Venice

A **metaphor** is also a comparison, suggesting that two dissimilar things are actually the same. When Arragon leaves, Portia judges: 'Thus hath the candle singed the moth.' Arragon ('the moth') has been emotionally wounded ('singed') in his unsuccessful attempt to win Portia and her wealth, signified by the silver casket ('the candle'), which has so attracted him.

Personification turns all kinds of things into persons, giving them human feelings or attributes. Lorenzo personifies the attractive qualities of the night: 'How sweet the moonlight sleeps upon this bank!' Portia acknowledges the radiant power of light: 'How far that little candle throws his beams!' Jessica insists that 'love is blind'.

◆ Check your understanding of metaphors, similes and personification. Identify each language device and how it works in the following lines:

- 'laugh like parrots at a bagpiper'
- 'for a wilderness of monkeys'
- 'The portrait of a blinking idiot'
- 'We are the Jasons, we have won the fleece'
- 'Here are severed lips / Parted with sugar breath'
- 'if he lose he makes a swan-like end'
- 'There's not the smallest orb which thou behold'st / But in his motion like an angel sings'
- 'Here in her hairs / The painter plays the spider'
- 'But since I am a dog, beware my fangs'

Image clusters

Classical mythology

Bassanio's pursuit of Portia is compared to Jason's seeking the Golden Fleece at 'Colchos' strand'. Gratiano relates his and Bassanio's success at Belmont to that of the great heroic adventurer: 'We are the Jasons, we have won the fleece'. Portia is a worthy prize, likened to 'Cato's daughter, Brutus' Portia'. Portia's reputation is further strengthened when Shakespeare compares her to the revered prophetess (女先知) Sibylla and to the goddess of chastity, Diana. Portia sees Bassanio as the heroic warrior Hercules, who rescued Hesione (a sacrificial virgin) from a threatening sea monster. In the final act, Shakespeare draws on a list of doomed romantic partnerships to create an ominous mood: Troilus and Cressida, Thisbe and Pyramus, Dido and Aeneas, Medea and Jason.

◆ Use the library or Internet to research the classical stories outlined above. Then prepare a wall display or collage, and use words, drawings and pictures to re-tell the famous myths.

◆ After your research, write a short essay exploring how some of these classical images work. Include your thoughts on how the play benefits from having these classical references threaded through it.

Love and hate

Images of different types of love abound (see also page 167 on the theme of 'Love versus hate'). Portia, anxious that Bassanio might choose incorrectly, predicts 'my eye shall be the stream / And watery deathbed for him'. But when he chooses the lead casket, she declares 'In measure rain thy joy'. To Bassanio, Portia is a 'demi-god' whose hair 'hath woven / A golden mesh t'entrap the hearts of men'. Morocco describes her as 'this shrine, this mortal breathing saint'. Lorenzo finds Jessica to be 'sweet, / Even in the lovely garnish of a boy'. Shakespeare also uses images to define character. Gratiano's expressions of love are, typically, coarsely (粗俗) sexual, as when he includes the phrase 'stake down' (with a limp penis) as he bets with Bassanio on who will have the first son.

Images of hatred are frequent too. Lancelot compares Shylock's Jewishness with 'the devil'. Verbal insults directed against Shylock include 'cut-throat dog', 'stranger cur', 'dog Jew' and 'wolf (see p. 188). Jessica hates her home: 'Our house is hell'. Shylock detests Christian entertainment: 'fools with varnished faces'. He turns his hatred back on his Christian tormentors: 'If I can catch him once upon the hip, / I will feed fat the ancient grudge I bear him.'

◆ Identify a dozen striking and powerful love and hate images in the play. Draw them in a bold, visual way that explores the comparison at the heart of each one.

The Merchant of Venice
威尼斯商人

Antithesis (对偶)

Antithesis is the opposition of words or phrases against each other, as in Portia's command to Antonio in the trial scene: 'You must prepare your bosom for his knife'. This setting of word against word ('your bosom' stands in vulnerable contrast to the menace of 'his knife') is one of Shakespeare's favourite language devices.

In *The Merchant of Venice*, conflict occurs in many forms: Christian versus Jew, mercy versus justice, father versus daughter, appearance versus reality (see pp. 167–70). Antithesis intensifies that sense of conflict.

In Lancelot's first appearance, his **soliloquy** shows him struggling to weigh the arguments of 'fiend' versus 'conscience': should he run away from Shylock's service, or stay? '"Budge!" says the fiend. "Budge not!" says my conscience' (Act 2 Scene 2, lines 14–15).

Antonio's description of Shylock (Act 1 Scene 3, lines 90–4) bristles with (充斥着) antitheses. As he questions Shylock's integrity, he sets 'devil' against 'Scripture' (《圣经》), 'evil soul' against 'holy witness', and so on. The same theme of false appearance is explored in a long series of antitheses as Bassanio contemplates making his choice of caskets (Act 3 Scene 2, lines 73–107). He considers in turn law, religion, cowardice, courage and beauty, showing how vice can be hidden beneath a mask of virtue:

> *There is no vice so simple but assumes*
> *Some mark of virtue on his outward parts.*
> Act 3 Scene 2, lines 81–2

In Act 3 Scene 1, where Shylock makes his plea for common humanity and considers his revenge, the differences between Christian and Jew are powerfully expressed: 'amen' and 'prayer' pivot against (以……为中轴点) 'devil' (line 17). Shylock antithetically sets all he holds dear against Antonio's reaction: 'laughed' against 'losses'; 'mocked' against 'gains'; 'scorned' against 'nation'; 'cooled my friends' against 'heated mine enemies' (lines 43–5).

◆ Work through the play collecting about twenty examples of antithesis. Use them in an extended essay, showing how antithesis helps create a sense of conflict in *The Merchant of Venice*.

Verse and prose

About eighty per cent of the play is in verse, and twenty per cent is in prose. How did Shakespeare decide whether to write in verse or prose? One answer is that he followed theatrical convention. Prose was traditionally used by comic and low-status characters. High-status characters spoke verse. Comic scenes were written in prose (as were letters, like Bellario's), but audiences expected verse in serious scenes. The poetic style was thought to be particularly suitable for moments of high dramatic or emotional intensity, and for tragic themes.

Many of the Christians in the play are wealthy and educated, so they speak mainly in verse. Just as their clothes are richly elaborate, their language is similarly extravagant or high-flown. Salarino's ships would 'Enrobe the roaring waters with my silks'.

Lancelot (low-status) uses prose consistently. He and Old Gobbo, his father, represent the poor and uneducated in the play. Lancelot's language is usually comic and fast-moving. Old Gobbo refers constantly to his Christian faith – much more so than his social superiors. With these characters, Shakespeare sticks rigidly to the language rules for social class.

But both Portia (very high-status) and Nerissa speak all of Act 1 Scene 2 in prose, perhaps because Shakespeare considered it a comic scene. Similarly, Lorenzo (high-status) speaks prose in his dialogue with Lancelot in Act 3 Scene 5, as does Jessica (but they revert to verse when speaking to each other). Shylock, as a Jew, has low status in Venice, and many of his speeches are in prose. The fact that his 'Hath not a Jew eyes?' speech is in prose demonstrates that Shakespeare can use prose just as effectively as verse to express the deepest feelings and the most profound thoughts. Nonetheless, in the trial scene Shylock consistently uses verse, perhaps because the scene is serious, and he is in the company of high-status characters.

The verse of *The Merchant of Venice* is mainly **blank verse** (无韵诗；素体诗): unrhymed verse written in **iambic pentameter** (抑扬五音步). It usually has ten syllables per

The language of The Merchant of Venice

line, and each line has five beats or 'stresses'. This line of Portia's is marked to show the stressed (/) and unstressed (×) syllables:

> × / × / × / × / × /
> *Behold, there stand the caskets, noble prince.*

- In pairs, read the line aloud in unison, but pronounce each syllable very clearly, almost as if each one were a separate word. As you read, beat out the five-stress rhythm (e.g. clap hands or tap the desk).

- Now turn to lines 33–7 in Act 1 Scene 3 and repeat what you have just done. Can you find the rhythm? When you have found it, try the exercise again with verse spoken by another character. Choose any verse lines you like.

- Choose another verse speech and learn it, ready to deliver in a way that emphasises the metre (five beats). Then read it as you feel it should be delivered on stage.

By the time Shakespeare wrote *The Merchant of Venice*, he was becoming more flexible and experimental in his use of iambic pentameter. End-stopped lines (尾断行) are less frequent, and there is more use of **enjambement** (跨行), where one line flows into the next, seemingly with little or no pause, giving a greater sense of natural fluency. You will find examples of both end-stopping and enjambement in Shylock's speech, Act 1 Scene 3, lines 33–7.

- Explore the rest of this speech by Shylock. Write a paragraph on the dramatic effects created by the rhythmic variety.

Language and gender

The language of the characters is determined not only by their social class but also partly by their gender. An important question to consider is whether there is a male way of speaking which is different from a female way. Most of the men in the play are preoccupied with matters of finance and the law. The women, though conscious of the importance of wealth, are trapped into hatching (孵化; 策划) love plots on the fringes of male activities. Portia has an interest in the law, but has to resort to dressing up as a man before she can act on behalf of her husband's best friend.

- Working in pairs, one of you reads through the entirely male Act 1 Scene 1, collecting examples of what you think are stereotypical 'male' words. (As a starting point, you may want to focus on words connected with business and commerce.)

- The other reads through Act 1 Scene 2 to discover the main topic of the women's conversation.

- Then join together to explore any important differences between the language of the two scenes. Keep your roles and work through the rest of the play, analysing other scenes in which there is a strong male or female 'voice'.

- Individually, write an essay setting out your views, with examples, on whether or not you think there is distinctive 'men's language' and 'women's language' in *The Merchant of Venice*.

The Merchant of Venice
威尼斯商人

Shylock's language

Repetition Different forms of linguistic repetition run through the play, contributing to its atmosphere, creation of character and dramatic impact. Three of the most frequently repeated words are 'Jew' and 'Jews' (used nearly seventy times), 'bond' (around forty times) and 'ring' (thirty-seven times). Their repetition is a clear indication of major preoccupations (关注点) of the play.

Repetition is a distinctive feature of Shylock's speech. His first four speeches in the play (Act 1 Scene 3) reveal his careful, calculating mind: 'Three thousand ducats, well'; 'For three months, well'; 'Antonio shall become bound, well'; 'Three thousand ducats for three months, and Antonio bound'.

The actor can use those lines to convey how much Shylock enjoys his power in this situation, as he deliberately keeps Bassanio waiting. The repetitions can also be used by the actor either to convey an impression of Shylock's playful good humour or his sinister coldness.

Other repetitions reveal different aspects of his personality: his implacable (不饶人) insistence that 'I'll have my bond' (repeated five times in thirteen lines), his anguish at his losses ('My daughter! O my ducats!') and his enthusiastic praise of Portia in the trial scene when he thinks she will award him his bond ('O wise young judge'). There are at least ten versions of this praise.

Shylock's famous 'Hath not a Jew eyes?' speech also has distinctive repetitions of words, phrases and rhythms which are used to affirm his passionate argument for the common humanity of Jew and Christian.

The language of The Merchant of Venice

◆ Find other examples of Shylock's repetitions. Write a few paragraphs about how they increase the dramatic effect of the scenes in which he appears and how they are used to reveal something about his character.

Shylock and religion Shylock is an outsider and cannot therefore be categorised with either the wealthy or the poor Christians. The content of his language is also markedly different from theirs. He disapproves of the Christians' prodigal and extravagant behaviour, preferring a quiet and simple life in keeping with his strict religious faith. These characteristics are reflected in his language, and his adherence to his faith is intensified through the misfortunes and grief that he experiences.

While the Christians refer to the lurid (可怕) stories of classical mythology, Shylock speaks of Old Testament morality tales. These frequent references to the Bible would have been familiar to a great many of the Elizabethan audience members who, by law, had to attend church regularly.

◆ Collect examples of Shylock's references to the Bible. Consider their likely effect on a) an Elizabethan and b) a modern audience's reaction to his character.

Creating atmosphere

Shakespeare often creates atmosphere through his use of language. Remember, for example, that his plays were originally staged in broad daylight so the words had to establish the setting and atmosphere (see pp. 189–90). A good example of his atmospheric (营造氛围的) technique is the opening to Act 5 Scene 1, where the language has to suggest that the moon is shining brightly and the sweet wind kisses the trees.

◆ In a small group, choose your own favourite scene (or focus on Act 5 Scene 1). Talk together about its atmosphere (tense, fearful, joking, boisterous [热闹], romantic, and so on). Compile a 'language list' of phrases or lines from your chosen scene that create the atmosphere. Use your list to make up a scene or your own (or a short play) with your own plot and characters. Create as powerful an atmosphere as you can by using Shakespeare's words.

Creating character

Most of Shakespeare's characters have a distinctive way of speaking, but their style can change from one situation to another. For example, Bassanio seems to adjust the way he speaks depending on the situation in which he finds himself. His elaborate, showy (炫耀) and hyperbole-filled courtship of Portia (Act 3 Scene 2) is replaced by a more direct and frank way of speaking ('When I told you / My state was nothing, I should then have told you / That I was worse than nothing) once he has 'won' her hand in marriage. It is perhaps only in the final scene (see p. 154) that he speaks plainly, sincerely and without excuses.

◆ Why do you think Shakespeare adapts Bassanio's language in this way throughout the course of the play?

◆ Choose a character, follow them through the play and compile a list of their 'typical' language in different situations. Afterwards, write a short commentary exploring what their different language styles tell you about them as characters and how they interact with other characters.

The Merchant of Venice
威尼斯商人

History and the Jews 历史和犹太人

Who are the Jews?

Two thousand years ago, the Jews were known as Hebrews or Israelites and lived in the part of the world now known as Israel. At that time, their land was occupied by the Romans, who at first allowed them religious freedom but later tried to crush the Jewish faith and culture. Such persecution led many Jews to seek new lives in other countries.

At the time when Shakespeare wrote *The Merchant of Venice* there were still some Jews left in England, although they may have been reluctant to display their faith too obviously for fear of retribution (惩罚). Their presence in England dated back to the time of William the Conqueror, who encouraged them to settle there after the Norman Conquest.

In the twelfth century, they were granted the right to govern their own community according to their own laws and they were publicly recognised by King John. There were occasional waves of anti-Jewish feeling (largely focused on unfounded accusations that they attacked Christian children). Nonetheless Jews were largely tolerated during the reign of King Henry II, although they were still excluded from joining the growing town guilds (行会) and from owning land.

The main reason for the toleration of the Jews was their contribution to England's financial well-being. The Christian Church was firmly set against the idea of money-lending and forbade the charging of interest on loans. In addition, there was no facility for the lending of money commercially within society. A group of comparatively wealthy Jews therefore established themselves as money-lenders, providing a valuable service to society. The service they offered ranged from the individual issuing of loans to providing a safety net for the rich and powerful landed gentry (乡绅) who were faced with cashflow problems as they struggled to collect taxes from poverty-stricken tenants.

Why were the Jews persecuted?

Once their financial success became so marked, wealthy Jews developed into increasingly attractive targets. (Having accumulated huge fortunes, several Jews became powerful and prestigious bankers.) They were taxed heavily, had their assets seized when they died, and had to pay taxes to the Christian Church (even though they were still denied many of the basic rights of Christians). Nonetheless, although Jews made up a tiny minority of the population, they had a considerable influence on the financial state of the nation. For example, it was their money that was primarily used to fund King Richard I's crusades (十字军).

Yet by the end of the thirteenth century, the Jews had largely been expelled from England. In 1290, in the reign of Edward I, they were officially exiled and thousands left. The rise of other banking houses, such as the Italian

History and the Jews

Lombards (放债者，钱庄主), had marginalised (边缘化) Jewish money-lenders as English suspicion and bigotry (偏执) grew against them. By the thirteenth century, they were being forced to wear a humiliating yellow badge that labelled them as Jews. To the medieval and Tudor English, the word 'Jew' was also a label, signifying the stereotype of a shifty (诡诈) profiteer who was not to be trusted.

By Shakespeare's time, the Jews who remained in England probably still adhered to the Jewish faith even though they publicly professed to be Christian converts. Scholars have tried hard to identify any individuals who might have provided the original model for Shylock; but no one has been able to do so. However, in 1594, two or three years before the first performance of *The Merchant of Venice*, there was a high-profile trial and execution of a Jewish doctor to Queen Elizabeth, Roderigo Lopez. He was accused of attempting to poison the queen. There was great public interest in the case, and considerable speculation about his plotting (阴谋) within the court. The trial and the gossip, in turn, sparked a hasty revival of a contemporary work, Christopher Marlowe's *The Jew of Malta*, which was staged in the days after Lopez's hanging.

All kinds of malicious (恶毒) myths and legends grew up around the concept of Jewishness, many of them suggesting that Jews spread the Black Death by poisoning the water; that they were ritual murderers and child sacrificers. A tradition had developed in medieval morality plays of stereotyping Jews and emphasising their villainous (罪恶的) wickedness (邪恶) by making them grotesque and evil, dressed in black cloaks, horned hats and carrying the badge of European Jewry (the yellow circle) on their costume.

In spite of this, Jews resolutely (坚决；执意) kept up their customs and their religion. They formed tight-knit communities and became known for their intelligence, hard work and business acumen (精明). These qualities often led to their being mistrusted and resented. This was especially the case in Christian countries, where anti-Jewish feeling (anti-Semitism) can still be very strong. The history of the Jews is still marked by terrible hardship and atrocities (残暴) (known as pogroms [大屠杀]). You will find that most European countries have past records of crimes against Jews.

The greatest Jewish suffering was endured during the Nazi domination of Europe before and during the Second World War (1939–45). Under the leadership of Adolf Hitler, the Nazis took control of Germany in 1933. They persuaded many Germans that the Jews were responsible for their country's problems. With widespread popular support, the Nazi government conducted a programme of persecution and mass extermination (消灭) of Jewish men, women and children in Germany and the other European countries it occupied. Six million Jews lost their lives during this terrible time: the period of history known as the Holocaust. This appalling cruelty began with the casual everyday racism that Shylock has to endure from the Christians of Venice.

▼ This photograph was taken in Munich in 1933 at the start of the Nazi domination of Germany. Dr Siegel was a Jewish lawyer who asked the police for protection against the Nazis. The placard they forced him to wear reads: 'I'll never again make any complaints to the police'. What similarities are there between Shylock and Dr Siegel?

◆ Research the history of the Jewish community in your own country, or your own town or district. Use your findings as part of an assignment on the social background of the play.

The Merchant of Venice
威尼斯商人

How Shylock is persecuted

Shylock's treatment at the hands of his fellow Venetians is typical of the intolerance suffered by Jews over the centuries. Throughout the play he endures constant verbal abuse.

- Work in groups of four or five. One person sits, and the others surround them, calling out insults from the list below. If the person in role as Shylock closes their eyes or dares wear a blindfold (眼罩), the intensity of this experience is heightened. Only use volunteers for the Shylock role and for no longer than thirty seconds. Afterwards, talk about how you felt in role as either Shylock or one of his accusers. Then consider the effect of such habitual abuse on Shylock.

- BEG THAT THOU MAYST HAVE LEAVE TO HANG THYSELF
- WOLFISH, BLOODY, STARVED AND RAVENOUS
- O BE THOU DAMNED, INEXECRABLE DOG
- DEVIL
- GOODLY APPLE ROTTEN AT THE HEART
- CRUEL DEVIL
- VILLAIN WITH A SMILING CHEEK
- CURRISH SPIRIT
- CUT-THROAT DOG
- INHUMAN WRETCH
- BLOODY CREDITOR
- HARSH JEW
- FAITHLESS JEW
- DOG JEW
- MISBELIEVER
- UNFEELING MAN
- STRANGER CUR
- EVIL SOUL

The Merchant of Venice in performance
《威尼斯商人》的演出

On Shakespeare's stage

The Merchant of Venice seems to have been a popular play right from the time it was first performed in 1596 or 1597, although very little is known about productions in Shakespeare's time. Audiences who watched it probably had in their minds Christopher Marlowe's hugely successful *The Jew of Malta* and the trial and execution of Dr Lopez (see p. 187), the Jewish doctor who allegedly (据称) tried to poison Queen Elizabeth.

Many of Shakespeare's plays were performed at the Globe Theatre in London, one of many specially built outdoor playhouses that appeared at the end of the sixteenth century.

Because women were banned from acting in public in Shakespeare's day, Portia, Jessica and Nerissa were played by boys, which made the 'women' dressing up as men doubly amusing! Shylock was probably played as a comic stereotype with a flaming red beard.

Although a modern audience cannot be neutral about the presentation of Shylock, it seems likely that he was received in an atmosphere of contempt and scorn by an Elizabethan audience.

Hatred of Jews was embedded (嵌入) in the social conventions of the time and Shylock would have been played without sympathy or compassion. He was presented as a malicious, ridiculous and extremely provocative (挑衅的) figure.

There were no elaborate sets on the bare stage of the Globe Theatre. Scenery was sparse but the actors wore attractive and expensive costumes – usually the fashionable dress of the time.

The stage of the original Globe Theatre was probably quite large (about 40 feet wide and 25 feet deep). The wealthier people watched from seats in the galleries while the 'groundlings' (站票观众) stood in the yard, closely packed around the three edges of the stage, just a few feet away from the actors. Very wealthy members of the audience could pay to sit on a stool on the stage itself in order to see and, no doubt, be seen.

There was an entrance door on either side of the back wall, plus a larger central door that opened into a 'discovery space' or interior area. The balconies above could be used by the actors for certain scenes and also to house the musicians.

The Merchant of Venice
威尼斯商人

Indoor Elizabethan theatres, such as the Blackfriars, were lit by candles and torches, but performances at the open-air Globe took place mostly in summer and were always in broad daylight. As there were no special lighting effects, Shakespeare had to use language to establish the time, setting and atmosphere. This is particularly noticeable in Act 5 of *The Merchant of Venice*, which begins in darkness and ends with daylight. In addition, Shakespeare often used the words of the script to suggest how the actors should move and behave. For example, the Duke welcomes Shylock to court with: 'Make room and let him stand before our face (in front of me)'.

On stage, just a few props were used (swords, chairs, and so on). As you look through *The Merchant of Venice*, you will notice that some basic props become very important to the action of the play. These include:

- the bond
- masks and torches
- the caskets
- Portia's and Nerissa's rings
- Bellario's letter
- Shylock's knife
- Shylock's scales.

◆ Choose one or more of the items listed above. Then produce two sets of designs for the props you have selected: one for a period Elizabethan production and one for a very modern version.

Only basic sound effects and 'noises off' were possible, but there would probably have been a lot of background noise, especially from the groundlings in the yard. These people were often restless and enjoyed some lively interaction with the performers. In order to ensure that the audience fully engaged with key ideas, Shakespeare uses a good deal of repetition in his language. You will notice this is a feature of the writing in every scene!

The Globe has now been rebuilt on London's Bankside, close to its original site. Each year, at least one production is staged as Elizabethan audiences probably saw it.

The rebuilt Globe has an international reputation and sometimes invites visiting companies from overseas to perform there. For its 1998 production, the Globe invited the leading German actor Norbert Kentrup (opposite, top right) to play the part of Shylock.

◆ In small groups, discuss how you would stage *The Merchant of Venice* in an open-air theatre such as the rebuilt Globe. How would you quickly establish the change of location from Venice to Belmont and how would you give Belmont its own specific identity?

◆ How would you use the Globe stage to present Shylock's home (Act 2 Scene 5)?

◆ How would you stage the trial scene (Act 4 Scene 1)? What kind of courtroom arena would you seek to create?

◆ Actors at Shakespeare's Globe often comment on how effectively its stage layout can be made to work dramatically, and especially on the close rapport (亲近关系) with the audience that it encourages. What parts of *The Merchant of Venice* do you think would work well on this stage, with the audience so close to the actors, and why? What parts do you think it would be difficult to stage convincingly, and why?

◆ How would you stage the gradual movement from night to day in Act 5? Bearing in mind that lighting effects are extremely limited in daylight productions, in what ways could your actors convincingly suggest to the audience that dawn is slowly breaking?

◆ A professional theatre designer would produce a three-dimensional model of the set with its key features reproduced in miniature. Try creating such a model for yourselves, perhaps by using a shoe box as the basic structure.

◆ Compare your set designs with those of other students. How different do you think the audience's response will be to the different sets?

▲▼ Identify the possible scenes from which these images were taken. Explain your thinking.

The Merchant of Venice
威尼斯商人

The Merchant of Venice in performance

Performance after Shakespeare

It seems likely that King James saw the play twice in 1605. But *The Merchant of Venice* was virtually neglected throughout the seventeenth century until George Granville reworked the script in 1701 as *The Jew of Venice*. Granville rewrote the play, removing Lancelot, Old Gobbo, Morocco, Arragon, Tubal and some other characters and promoting Shylock to the title role. He cut and rearranged scenes, adding his own lines and a banquet scene, in which Shylock was entertained by Antonio and Bassanio and an impressive masque was performed. In the trial scene, Bassanio drew his sword in an attempt to prevent a verdict (裁决).

Granville's version thrived for forty years until Shakespeare's own play returned to the stage in 1741. The new version was heavily cut but Charles Macklin's Shylock became a terrifying villain, brooding (阴郁；险恶) and malicious, determined on revenge. This concept of Shylock became the norm until 1814, when Edmund Kean transformed the role.

Kean's Shylock was a sympathetic portrayal, acknowledging the complexity of his character and highlighting his intelligence, vulnerability and dignity.

It set the benchmark for future productions. Although elaborate scenery and costumes were added in an attempt to capture the authentic atmosphere of Venice and Belmont, it was Shylock who continued to dominate the play. Some productions cut Act 5 completely, ending the play with Shylock's defeat. At the end of the nineteenth century, Henry Irving won acclaim for his tragic portrayal of Shylock, which showed his inherent humanity and nobility.

In the twentieth century, theatrical attempts to realise the full complexity of Shakespeare's play were accelerated by the appalling treatment Hitler and the Nazis meted out to (使受苦) the Jews. The Nazis even used Shakespeare as part of their propaganda (宣传). In 1943, Baldur von Schirach, the Nazi governor of Vienna, ordered the local theatre to mount a production of *The Merchant of Venice*. The actor Werner Krauf played Shylock as 'loathsome, strange and amazingly horrible, crawling across the stage'. Of course, there is no justification in Shakespeare's script for such a gross distortion, but the terrible crimes that the Nazis committed against the Jews have made it impossible for any serious stage version after 1945 to perform *The Merchant of Venice* without taking full account of the Holocaust.

Particularly in the closing decades of the twentieth century, and in the twenty-first, producers have been alert to the problematic nature of the play. Productions have tended to move away from very romantic portrayals of Belmont, choosing instead to emphasise the unpleasant social aspects of the play, particularly the brutal intolerance of anti-Semitic Venice. In a number of productions, Shylock is spat upon by the Christians and reviled or assaulted in other ways. In one production he was constantly ridiculed, jostled (推搡) and beaten. The audience saw street urchins (顽童) hound and pelt (扔，砸) him with stones. And the victorious Christians wrestled him to the floor at the end of the trial scene.

Some portrayals have stressed Shylock's Jewishness and the importance of his faith and kinship with his race. Others have shown him as fully assimilated into a world of traders and bankers. The complexity of his relationship with Jessica has been highlighted, variously showing how he loves her overwhelmingly and is sharply angered by her betrayal.

The Merchant of Venice
威尼斯商人

Modern productions – distinctive interpretations

Most directors, set designers and production teams work in harmony to create a particular 'vision' for their staging of the play. However, many comment that one of the challenges of producing *The Merchant of Venice* is that it's one of Shakespeare's 'problem plays' – neither a comedy, nor a romance, nor a tragedy. RSC designer Tom Scutt has said: 'It's very easy to be cynical (怀疑) about the play and about the characters within it. It's very hard to love any of them … to find out whose story it is you're meant to be identifying with.'

So how does each production address these challenging issues and make *The Merchant of Venice* engaging and interesting? In the 'Stagecraft' boxes in the main part of this edition, you've been encouraged to consider and try out ideas for lifting the script off the page.

Five 'script boxes' follow, which focus on key elements of the play:

1 Venice and the Venetians
2 The world of Belmont
3 The trial scene
4 Shylock
5 Interesting stagecraft

Inside each of the boxes you'll find information about how particular productions have approached specific aspects of the play and attempted to make them distinctive or unusual.

- In pairs, select one of the numbered boxes and work through the ideas described in it, discussing each one in turn. Which do you find the most interesting and why? In your discussion, consider what the director might have had in mind when approaching the play in this way.

- Talk together about how any of these ideas for staging have helped further your understanding of *The Merchant of Venice*. Add your evaluative comments to the Director's Journal that you began on page 2.

1 Venice and the Venetians

a The Venetians were a 'spoiled, boorish (粗野) bunch, much given to throwing bread-rolls … and other types of horseplay' (恶作剧).

b Set in the eighteenth century, this Venice was dominated by dark colours and rich velvets.

c Crumbling (摇摇欲坠) palaces and dim lighting showed an 'old and jaded civilisation'. A large wall denoted the entrance to the Jewish ghetto, with inscriptions of harsh decrees imposed on Jews.

d A Star of David (大卫之星，六角形，犹太人标记) was daubed (涂抹) like graffiti (涂鸦) on a wall as the backdrop to this production.

e Venice was a male-dominated 1980s office of 'steel stairs, walkways and vast slanted tubes'.

f Brooding mists, oppressive black walls and spitting Christian racists defined Venice.

g Located in late-Victorian times, this set was a wall of huge burnished-gold (金光闪闪) doors.

h Venice became 1930s Germany, a riot of colour. The play opened in a nightclub, with champagne, music and cabaret (卡巴莱歌舞表演) girls.

2 The world of Belmont

a An outline of branches behind the backcloth (背景幕) suggested Belmont was a 'fairy land'.

b To show Belmont, a central fountain revolved a few feet to the left. Net curtains added femininity, while acknowledging that the same peeling walls and prejudices were part of both worlds.

c Belmont was a world of 'rainbow-hued' backdrops (背景幕).

d Belmont had a 'gilded portal (大门) and a silver castle'.

e Belmont had fresh-coloured frescoes (湿壁画), which made it look like a Renaissance painting.

f Portia was the prize in the Belmont TV game show *Destiny*.

3 The trial scene

a The opening of the trial was played in a mood of calmness and polite restraint. The Duke served Shylock coffee.

b Humiliated but not destroyed, Shylock accepted his punishment with 'wry, rueful resignation'.

c At the close of the trial, 'pride and a bleak fatalism stiffen [Shylock] as, head erect, he walks unhurried from the court'.

d Shylock left behind his 'pointed yellow hat' after his enforced conversion to Christianity.

e Shylock chanted in Hebrew and had a black attendant with him.

f When ordered to hand over his wealth, this Shylock wrote a couple of cheques, confirmed the date on his watch and left unperturbed (平静).

g Shylock was further humiliated by his slipping on a 'carpet of gold coins flung down for him'.

h This Shylock carried a flick-knife (弹簧折刀) with which he was about to cut out Antonio's heart.

i Tubal was at the trial. When Shylock insisted on his pound of flesh, Tubal stared at him, then left the court. When Shylock had to convert to Christianity, he placed his yarmulke (犹太男子戴的圆顶小帽) on the scales that he had brought with him.

4 Shylock

a Shylock 'was grubby (肮脏), shabbily dressed …, smoked hand-rolled cigarettes down to stubs which he saved in a little metal can, and swiped change left for tips on café tables'. He slapped Jessica hard across the face in Act 2.

b Cigar-smoking and black-coated, Shylock was 'every inch an orthodox businessman'. He expressed tender feelings towards Jessica and could not come to terms with her desertion.

c Shylock's moment of greatest despair came with the loss of his wife's ring, symbolic of a wife and mother absent from the play.

d Shylock's racial traits were exaggerated: a heavy accent, a shuffling gait (曳行步态), a beard, long hair and exotic clothes.

e Shylock was played as an assimilated banker; a laptop and a Bible on either side of his desk.

f Shylock's Jewish identity became visible during the course of the play. In the trial scene he wore the Jewish yarmulke and the prayer shawl (披巾).

5 Interesting stagecraft

a Set in LA, the Venice (Venice Beach) stage had TV cables draped (悬挂) in front of seascapes (海景画). Affluent Bel Air's leafy gardens and mock-classical buildings signified Belmont. African-Americans played the Jewish characters, Latin-Americans Venetian Christians. Belmont characters were Asian-American.

b The order of light and dark was reversed, with Venice in bright light and Belmont in autumnal shadows.

c Staged in contemporary dress, this production's main stage was a 9800-litre pool of water, covered or revealed as needed.

d This production was set in a Las Vegas casino. Lancelot was an Elvis Presley lookalike who frequently burst into Presley-type songs.

e The three caskets were laptops linked to screens displaying their digital contents.

f The set was square, white and divided in two, joined by bridges. Portia's flame-red outfits contrasted with the men's grey suits. She had a regional accent and entered holding a mug of tea.

THE MERCHANT OF VENICE
威尼斯商人

Staging the trial scene (法庭场景)

You are about to direct a production of *The Merchant of Venice* and want especially to focus on how to stage the trial scene (Act 4 Scene 1).

Write some pre-rehearsal introductory briefing notes to pass on to members of your team, both the production supervisors (set design [布景设计], costume people, lighting engineers, sound/music effects team, etc.) and the actors themselves. Explain your overall concept for this scene and add your notes to your Director's Journal.

Choose one section of Act 4 Scene 1 to work on (for example, the opening section before Shylock's entrance) and write detailed notes on how that episode would work within your design framework.

Read the following 'prompts' to get you started:

- In what specific era or period is your version to be set? Clearly, any historical setting, particularly one that is post-Holocaust, will have significant resonances. Or will it be a 'timeless' setting, or a mixture of periods?
- How will your setting affect the costuming of the characters? (Remember that Portia and Nerissa are disguised as men.)
- What will your courtroom look like?
- What music and sound effects will accompany the scene (e.g. the heckling [起哄] of Shylock)?
- How will your actors move and speak? Where will they be arranged? How will you manage their entrances and exits? (Two crucial entrances are those of Shylock and the disguised Portia.)
- How will the scene (or sections within it) be lit? Will you spotlight key characters at key moments (specific line numbers?) or use 'mood' lighting to create effects?
- How will you present the Duke (on his first appearance)? Will you introduce extra characters? Will you have a public gallery in the court?
- How will you address the struggle between Christian and Jew? Will you, like many productions, highlight Shylock's Jewish faith by having him chant in Hebrew or include elements of Hebraic (希伯来人的) ritual in his behaviour?

◆ The trial scene has inspired many striking sets such as the two below. Use these photographs (and others on pp. x and 143) to help identify the staging that offers the most interesting dramatic possibilities. Write an essay comparing the dramatic possibilities in that particular production with your own design.

The Merchant of Venice in performance

The Merchant of Venice on film

Director Michael Radford's 2004 film version of *The Merchant of Venice* was shot on location in Venice itself. Set in the sixteenth century, it showed Shylock in his opening scene 'chopping a lump of meat out of a dead goat as if he was carving a diamond. He carefully wraps up his bloody purchase in a piece of sackcloth and then turns around, blanks the camera, and strikes his chilling bargain with Antonio.'

The use of the grand architecture of Venice suggests the financial motivations that lie beneath the surface of all behaviour, including Bassanio's pursuit of Portia. Shylock is seen wandering the misty, dark streets in pouring rain, calling out Jessica's name and stumbling into a brothel (妓院) where he is greeted by Christian taunts and jeers.

When a stage play is transferred to the medium of film, it offers the director considerable artistic freedom. In addition to a variety of camera angles (panning shots [摇摄], close-ups [特写镜头], etc.), special effects and the addition of a soundtrack, the action can be presented in a more naturalistic way. Editing techniques and multiple 'takes' can also ensure that what you see is a 'perfect' interpretation of the director's intentions.

◆ Make a list of some of the qualities and effects of a good stage production that could be lost in a film version.

◆ Choose one scene, or part of a scene, that you think lends itself to being filmed. Write a design brief, showing clearly how this would work.

Plan a movie pitch (电影推介)

◆ Imagine that you are making a film pitch to a group of media moguls (传媒大亨). These people have the money to finance a new movie version of the play – if you can convince them of the merits of your concept. Part of your pitch will be based on your original ideas for the setting and location of your version.

◆ Write an account of how you think the play could be filmed to maximise its dramatic effect. You will need to persuade your audience that your ideas are fresh, striking and well-matched to the medium of film. Describe how you would set the play and how you think different sections of it could be played. Add further ideas about how lighting, costume and music could contribute to the overall effect. Use images from magazines to give a visual aspect to the pitch.

◆ Pick your ideal cast (you can choose any actors you think would suit the roles of Shylock, Portia, etc.), then identify several speeches you think are particularly important and write instructions on how they should be delivered. Remember that your production can have a big budget!

197

The Merchant of Venice
威尼斯商人

Writing about Shakespeare 笔论莎士比亚

The play as text

Shakespeare's plays have always been studied as literary works – as words on a page that need clarification, appreciation and discussion. When you write about the plays, you will be asked to compose short pieces and also longer, more reflective pieces like controlled assessments, examination scripts and coursework – often in the form of essays on themes and/or imagery, character studies, analyses of the structure of the play and on stagecraft. Imagery, stagecraft and character are dealt with elsewhere in this edition. Here, we concentrate on themes and structure. You might find it helpful to look at the 'Write about it' boxes on the left-hand pages throughout the play.

Themes

It is often tempting to say that the theme of a play is a single idea, like 'death' in *Hamlet*, or 'the supernatural' in *Macbeth*, or 'love' in *Romeo and Juliet*. The problem with such a simple approach is that you will miss the complexity of the plays. In *Romeo and Juliet*, for example, the play is about the relationship between love, family loyalty and constraint; it is also about the relationship of youth to age and experience; and the relationship between Romeo and Juliet is also played out against a background of enmity between two families. Between each of these ideas or concepts there are tensions. The tensions are the main focus of attention for Shakespeare and the audience; this is also how the best drama operates – by the presentation of and resolution of tension.

Look back at the 'Themes' boxes throughout the play to see if any of the activities there have given rise to information that you could use as a starting point for further writing about the themes of the specific play you are studying.

Structure

Most Shakespeare plays are in five acts, divided into scenes. These acts were not in the original scripts, but have been included in later editions to make the action more manageable, clearer and more like 'classical' structures. One way to get a sense of the structure of the whole play is to take a printed version (not this one!) and cut it up into scenes and acts, then display each scene and act, in sequence, on a wall, like this:

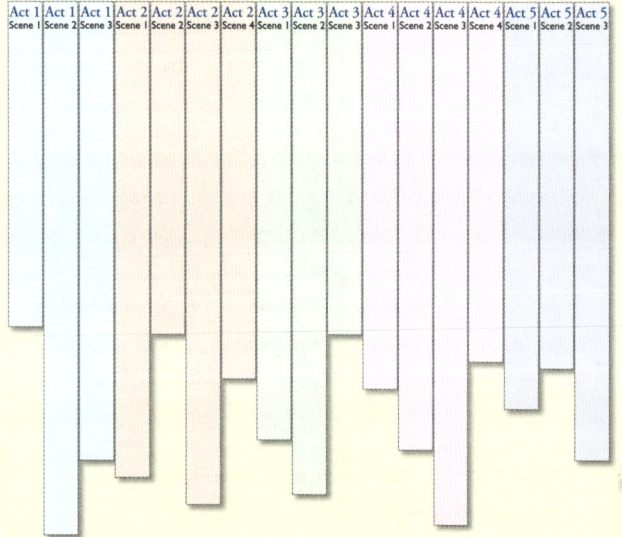

As you set out the whole play, you will be able to see the 'shape' of each act, the relative length of the scenes, and how the acts relate to each other (such as whether one act is shorter, and why that might be). You can annotate the text with comments, observations and questions. You can use a highlighter pen to mark the recurrence of certain words, images or metaphors to see at a glance where and how frequently they appear. You can also follow a particular character's progress through the play.

Such an overview of the play gives you critical perspective: you will be able to see how the parts fit together, to stand back from the play and assess its shape, and to focus on particular parts within the context of the whole. Your writing will reflect a greater awareness of the overall context as a result.

The play as script

There are different, but related, categories when we think of the play as a script for performance. These include *stagecraft* (discussed elsewhere in this edition and throughout the left-hand pages), *lighting*, *focus* (who are we looking at? Where is the attention of the audience?), *music and sound*, *props and costumes*, *casting*, *make-up*, *pace and rhythm*, and other *spatial relationships* (e.g. how actors move around the stage in relation to each other). If you are writing about stagecraft or performance, use the notes you have made as a result of the Stagecraft activities throughout this edition of the play, as well as any information you can find about the plays in performance.

What are the key points of dispute?

Shakespeare is brilliant at capturing a number of key points of dispute in each of his plays. These are the dramatic moments where he concentrates the focus of the audience on difficult (sometimes universal) problems that the characters are facing or embodying.

First, identify these key points in the play you are studying. You can do this as a class by brainstorming what you consider to be the key points in small groups, then debating the long-list as a whole class, and then coming up with a short-list of what the class thinks are the most significant. (This is a good opportunity for speaking and listening work.) They are likely to be places in the play where the action or reflection is at its most intense, and which capture the complexity of themes, character, structure and performance.

Second, drill down at one of the points of contention and tension. In other words, investigate the complexity of the problem that Shakespeare has presented. What is at stake? Why is it important? Is it a problem that can be resolved, or is it an insoluble one?

Key skills in writing about Shakespeare

Here are some suggestions to help you organise your notes and develop advanced writing skills when working on Shakespeare:

- Compose the title of your writing carefully to maximise your opportunities to be creative and critical about the play. Explore the key words in your title carefully. Decide which aspect of the play – or which combination of aspects – you are focusing on.
- Create a mind map of your ideas, making connections between them.
- If appropriate, arrange your ideas into a hierarchy that shows how some themes or features of the play are 'higher' than others and can incorporate other ideas.
- Sequence your ideas so that you have a plan for writing an essay, review, story – whichever genre you are using. You might like to think about whether to put your strongest points first, in the middle, or later.
- Collect key quotations (it might help to compile this list with a partner), which you can use as evidence to support your argument.
- Compose your first draft, embedding quotations in your text as you go along.
- Revise your draft in the light of your own critical reflections and/or those of others.

The following pages focus on writing about *The Merchant of Venice* in particular.

THE MERCHANT OF VENICE
威尼斯商人

Writing about *The Merchant of Venice*
笔论《威尼斯商人》

The purpose of this section is to help you to write about *The Merchant of Venice* in an informed, coherent and convincing fashion. Before you begin to write down your ideas, do keep two key considerations in mind:

1. *The Merchant of Venice* is a play, so you should always appreciate its form and genre. In Shylock's first scene (Act 1 Scene 3), for example, there is a huge amount of 'stagecraft' built in to the writing (entrances, exits, 'stage business', action and so on). It's all about what the audience sees, hears and experiences.

   ◆ Look at the script on page 21 of this edition. Try writing about how the language might be brought to life on stage. Speculate about different ways of playing this short episode.

2. *The Merchant of Venice* is not about 'real' people and 'real' situations, so don't treat it as such. When Shakespeare pays close attention to the presentation of Shylock's home life in the play it's as much about making a dramatic point (when Jessica and Lancelot desert him, he is left alone and vulnerable, even in the sanctity [神圣] of his own home) as trying to make it all credible and naturalistic. The play is a dramatic construct and often characters, for example, are vehicles for ideas about themes and structure. Remember the Duke? Shakespeare presents him very sketchily as a figure (and he's been played on stage in a variety of ways), but he has a crucial role in the drama.

How many different kinds of writing might you tackle? You could write about:

- an extract (a key speech, such as Shylock's 'To bait fish withal … ', or a longer passage of dialogue, such as the exchange between Bassanio and Portia which precedes the casket choice in Act 3 Scene 2).
- a key scene (such as the setting up of the bond in Act 1 Scene 3)
- a character (Antonio), or group of characters (the Venetian Christians in the play)
- a core theme (the conflict of love and hate)
- an element of the text re-creatively (that is, rewriting it in another genre or from another perspective or in the persona of one of the characters).

◆ Individually, consider each of these 'types' of writing in turn. See if you can come up with three additional focuses or frameworks for questions besides the ones that are mentioned in brackets above. Then pass your ideas to a partner for consideration. Together, settle on two questions for each category that you think would generate interesting written responses. Keep these in mind as you work through the next section.

Writing about an extract or a key scene: the whole of Act 3 Scene 1

1. Locate the extract in the play, and contextualise it. What has just happened? (Jessica's elopement with Lorenzo) What is about to come? (Shylock begins to fasten onto the idea of revenge, perhaps spurred on by what he hears from Tubal).

2. Concentrate on exploring the specific mood or atmosphere of the extract. (Solanio and Salarino bemoan Antonio's lost ship, then savagely taunt Shylock about Jessica. Shylock's response is a plea for understanding but the final episode is dominated by his anguish and desire for revenge.)

3. How might the lines be spoken – tone, emphasis, pace, pauses, etc. What are key words and images (of insult, of common humanity, of revenge)?

200

Writing about The Merchant of Venice

4. Think about Shakespeare's stagecraft – how he assembles and groups characters (the two men at the start of the scene), the interplay between them and Shylock, the use of entrances/exits and blocking on stage, and the enigmatic (谜一般) character of Tubal.

5. Link the details of the extract to key themes or issues in the play (the persecution of Shylock, his attitude to Jessica, the shaping of his revenge).

6. Show how the extract links to the dramatic construction of the play (a turning point, and a prelude to the pursuit of Shylock's revenge through the trial of Antonio).

◆ Working in a group of six, take one numbered section each of the above essay framework. Plan your answer by researching your specific area of focus. Then divide up a large sheet of sugar paper into six sections. Take turns to fill in the notes you have compiled. Use this large sheet as a resource to help you produce an essay plan of no more than one side, which you could include in a revision booklet to be given to students for examination preparation.

Writing about character

Planning an essay on the character of Bassanio

1. Summarise what Bassanio does in each act: his interactions with other characters, his decisive actions.

2. Explore how Bassanio relates to other characters and note down the different ways he treats them. How do they speak to him and about him?

3. Focus on the type of language that Bassanio uses – the imagery he employs, the tone he strikes, his typical way of speaking. Identify quotations that will back up your points. Link Bassanio's role to key themes and aspects of the drama.

4. Finally, think about the ways in which Shakespeare shows the development and change within his character over the course of the play.

Writing creatively

Many assessments offer you the opportunity to write about *The Merchant of Venice* creatively as well as critically. There are a number of such activities that you have been encouraged to try, act by act. You can be as imaginative and original within the framework of such responses as you choose to be: *The Merchant of Venice* is a complex, rich and intriguing text which offers lots of opportunities for creative approaches.

Summing up

Keep in mind the focus on *The Merchant of Venice* as a dramatic script. What features of the play as a theatrical performance enhance the impact of key issues? Remember that there is no single, right interpretation – both from you as a critic, but also from a director. How might an audience respond – in Shakespeare's time, and now? How do you respond? What are your own personal responses to the question and how can you justify them?

Possible questions

Below you'll find questions on character, theme, extracts and re-creative tasks. Have a go at one of each, or invent your own.

1. 'All of the characters in the play are flawed and unlikeable.' Do you agree or disagree, and why?

2. *The Merchant of Venice* is a strange mixture of happiness and sadness. Discuss.

3. Discuss the presentation and development of the theme of revenge in the play.

4. Explore the dramatic construction of Act 4 Scene 1.

5. Explore the contrasts between love and hate.

6. In role as one of the characters, write about a key incident in the play from your point of view.

7. Portia's character is full of irreconcilable (相互矛盾的) differences. Explore the presentation of Portia in the light of this comment.

8. Argue the case for retaining Act 5 in a production of the play.

9. Write an additional speech for a character, or script a section of dialogue between a character who appears in the play and one who doesn't.

THE MERCHANT OF VENICE
威尼斯商人

William Shakespeare 莎翁年表
1564–1616

1564	Born Stratford-upon-Avon, eldest son of John and Mary Shakespeare.
1582	Marries Anne Hathaway of Shottery, near Stratford.
1583	Daughter Susanna born.
1585	Twins, son and daughter Hamnet and Judith, born.
1592	First mention of Shakespeare in London. Robert Greene, another playwright, described Shakespeare as 'an upstart crow beautified with our feathers'. Greene seems to have been jealous of Shakespeare. He mocked Shakespeare's name, calling him 'the only Shake-scene in a country' (presumably because Shakespeare was writing successful plays).
1595	Becomes a shareholder in The Lord Chamberlain's Men, an acting company that became extremely popular.
1596	Son, Hamnet, dies aged eleven. Father, John, granted arms (acknowledged as a gentleman).
1597	Buys New Place, the grandest house in Stratford.
1598	Acts in Ben Jonson's *Every Man in His Humour*.
1599	Globe Theatre opens on Bankside. Performances in the open air.
1601	Father, John, dies.
1603	James I grants Shakespeare's company a royal patent: The Lord Chamberlain's Men become The King's Men and play about twelve performances each year at court.
1607	Daughter Susanna marries Dr John Hall.
1608	Mother, Mary, dies.
1609	The King's Men begin performing indoors at Blackfriars Theatre.
1610	Probably returns from London to live in Stratford.
1616	Daughter Judith marries Thomas Quiney. Dies. Buried in Holy Trinity Church, Stratford-upon-Avon.

The plays and poems

(no one knows exactly when he wrote each play)

1589–95	*The Two Gentlemen of Verona, The Taming of the Shrew, First, Second and Third Parts of King Henry VI, Titus Andronicus, King Richard III, The Comedy of Errors, Love's Labour's Lost, A Midsummer Night's Dream, Romeo and Juliet, King Richard II* (and the long poems *Venus and Adonis* and *The Rape of Lucrece*).
1596–99	*King John,* **The Merchant of Venice,** *First* and *Second Parts* of *King Henry IV, The Merry Wives of Windsor, Much Ado About Nothing, King Henry V, Julius Caesar* (and probably the *Sonnets*).
1600–05	*As You Like It, Hamlet, Twelfth Night, Troilus and Cressida, Measure for Measure, Othello, All's Well That Ends Well, Timon of Athens, King Lear.*
1606–11	*Macbeth, Antony and Cleopatra, Pericles, Coriolanus, The Winter's Tale, Cymbeline, The Tempest.*
1613	*King Henry VIII, The Two Noble Kinsmen* (both probably with John Fletcher).
1623	Shakespeare's plays published as a collection (now called the First Folio).

Acknowledgements 鸣谢

Cambridge University Press would like to acknowledge the contributions made to this work by Rex Gibson and Jonathan Morris.

Picture Credits

Thanks are due to the following for permission to reproduce illustrations:

p. iii: Michael Radford film 2004, © Sony Pictures Classics/The Kobal Collection/Steve Braun/Photostage; p. v top: RSC, Stratford-upon-Avon 2011, © Geraint Lewis; p. v bottom: RSC, Stratford-upon-Avon 1987, © Donald Cooper/Photostage; p. vi: Northern Broadsides, Halifax 2004, © Donald Cooper/Photostage; p. vii top: RSC/The Barbican Theatre, London 2001, © Colin Willoughby/ArenaPAL/Topfoto; p. vii bottom: RSC, Stratford-upon-Avon 1997, © Geraint Lewis; p. viii: National Theatre, London 1999, © Donald Cooper/Photostage; p. ix top: RSC/Aldwych Theatre, London 1981, © Donald Cooper/Photostage; p. ix bottom: Chichester Festival Theatre, West Sussex 2003, © Marilyn Kingwill/ArenaPAL/Topfoto; p. x top: RSC/Swan Theatre, Stratford-upon-Avon 2007, © Donald Cooper/Photostage; p. x bottom: Propeller & Watermill Theatre Newbury & Liverpool Everyman and Playhouse co-production, Liverpool Playhouse 2009, © Donald Cooper/Photostage; p. xi: Shakespeare's Globe, London 1998, © Donald Cooper/Photostage; p. xii top: RSC/Courtyard Theatre, Stratford-upon-Avon 2008, © Donald Cooper/Photostage; p. xii bottom: Goodman Theatre Chicago/The Barbican Theatre, London 1994, © Donald Cooper/Photostage; p. 2: Michael Radford film 2004 © KPA/Topfoto; p. 8: Chichester Festival Theatre, West Sussex 1984, © Donald Cooper/Photostage; p. 18: RSC, Stratford-upon-Avon 2011, © Geraint Lewis; p. 22: © The Granger Collection/Topfoto; p. 28: Shakespeare's Globe, London 2007, © Donald Cooper/Photostage; p. 31 top: Arcola Theatre, London 2007, © Donald Cooper/Photostage; p. 31 bottom: RSC/Swan Theatre, Stratford-upon-Avon 2007, © National Pictures/Topfoto; p. 32: The National Theatre, London 1999, © Donald Cooper/Photostage; p. 36: RSC, Stratford-upon-Avon 2008, © Nigel Norrington/ArenaPAL; p. 44: RSC/Swan Theatre, Stratford-upon-Avon 2007, © Donald Cooper/Photostage; p. 48: RSC, Aldwych Theatre, London 1981, © Donald Cooper/Photostage; p. 52: RSC, Stratford-upon-Avon 1997 © Donald Cooper/Photostage; p. 56: Royal Shakespeare Company/Aldwych Theatre, London 1981 © Donald Cooper/Photostage; p. 60: RSC/The Barbican Theatre, London 1988, © Donald Cooper/Photostage; p. 68: RSC/The Barbican Theatre, London 1988, © Donald Cooper/Photostage; p. 73 top: RSC/Swan Theatre, Stratford-upon-Avon 2007, © Geraint Lewis; p. 73 bottom: National Theatre, London 1999, © Nigel Norrington/ArenaPAL/Topfoto; p. 78: Northern Broadsides, Halifax 2004, © Donald Cooper/Photostage; p. 84: RSC/Aldwych Theatre, London 1981, © Donald Cooper/Photostage; p. 86: Northern Broadsides, Halifax 2004, © Donald Cooper/Photostage; p. 88: Shakespeare's Globe, London 2007, © Donald Cooper/Photostage; p. 90: Shakespeare's Globe, London 1998, © Donald Cooper/Photostage; p. 98: Propeller & Watermill Theatre Newbury & Liverpool Everyman and Playhouse co-production, Liverpool Playhouse 2009, © Donald Cooper/Photostage; p. 113 top: RSC, Stratford-upon-Avon 1997, © Donald Cooper/Photostage; p. 113 bottom: Michael Radford film 2004, © Sony Pictures Classics/The Kobal Collection/Steve Braun/Photostage; p. 118: Chichester Festival Theatre, West Sussex 1984, © Donald Cooper/Photostage; p. 120: Northern Broadsides, Halifax 2004, © Donald Cooper/Photostage; p. 122: Goodman Theatre Chicago/The Barbican Theatre, London 1994, © Donald Cooper/Photostage; p. 130: Phoenix Theatre, London 1989, © Donald Cooper/Photostage; p. 134: RSC/The Barbican Theatre, London 1988, © Donald Cooper/Photostage; p. 143 left: RSC/Swan Theatre, Stratford-upon-Avon 2007, © Donald Cooper/Photostage; p. 143 right: Goodman Theatre Chicago/The Barbican Theatre, London 1994, © Donald Cooper/Photostage; p. 144: RSC/Aldwych Theatre, London 1981, © Donald Cooper/Photostage; p. 146: RSC/Courtyard Theatre, Stratford-upon-Avon, 2008, © Nigel Norrington/ArenaPAL/Topfoto; p. 160: RSC/Aldwych Theatre, London 1981, © Donald Cooper/Photostage; p. 165 top: RSC/The Pit/Barbican Centre, London 2001 © Donald Cooper/Photostage; p. 165 bottom: National

The Merchant of Venice
威尼斯商人

Theatre, London 1999 © Donald Cooper/Photostage; p. 169: National Theatre, London 1999, © Colin Willoughby/ArenaPAL/Topfoto; p. 171 top: RSC, Stratford-upon-Avon, 2011, © Donald Cooper/Photostage; p. 171 bottom: RSC/Barbican Centre, London 2001 © Donald Cooper/Photostage; p. 173: RSC/Donmar Theatre London 1979, © Donald Cooper/Photostage; p. 175 top right: Propeller & Watermill Theatre Newbury & Liverpool Everyman and Playhouse co-production, Liverpool Playhouse 2009, © Donald Cooper/Photostage; p. 175 bottom right: RSC/The Barbican Theatre, London 1994, © Donald Cooper/Photostage; p. 175 left: RSC, Stratford-upon-Avon 1997 © Donald Cooper/Photostage; p. 176 left: Chichester Festival Theatre, West Sussex 1984, © Donald Cooper/Photostage; p. 176 right: Chichester Festival Theatre, West Sussex 1984, © Donald Cooper/Photostage; p. 178: RSC/Courtyard Theatre, Stratford-upon-Avon, 2008, © Nigel Norrington/ArenaPAL/Topfoto; p. 179: Michael Radford film 2004, © KPA/Topfoto; p. 183: Michael Radford film 2004, © KPA/Topfoto; p. 184: Chichester Festival Theatre, East Sussex 2003, © Donald Cooper/Photostage; p. 186: Shakespeare's Globe, London 2007, © Nigel Norrington/ArenaPAL/Topfoto; p. 187: Bundesarchiv, Bild 183-R99542/Heinrich Sanden; p. 188: RSC, Stratford-upon-Avon 1997, © Donald Cooper/Photostage; p. 189: © The Granger Collection/Topfoto; p. 191 top left: Shakespeare's Globe, London 2007, © Donald Cooper/Photostage; p. 191 top right: Shakespeare's Globe, London 1998, © Donald Cooper/Photostage; p. 191 bottom: Shakespeare's Globe, London 1998, © Donald Cooper/Photostage; p. 192: RSC/The Barbican Theatre, London 1988, © Donald Cooper/Photostage; p. 196 left: Goodman Theatre Chicago/The Barbican Theatre, London 1994, © Donald Cooper/Photostage; p. 196 right: Propeller & Watermill Theatre Newbury & Liverpool Everyman and Playhouse co-production, Liverpool Playhouse 2009, © Donald Cooper/Photostage; p. 197: Michael Radford film 2004, © KPA/Topfoto.

Produced for Cambridge University Press by White-Thomson Publishing
+44 (0)843 208 7460
www.wtpub.co.uk

Managing editor: Sonya Newland
Project editor: Kelly Davis
Designer: Clare Nicholas
Concept design: Jackie Hill